Carl Weber's Kingpins:

Queens 3,

King of Kings

Carl Weber's Kingpins:

Queens 3, King of Kings

Erick S. Gray

www.urbanbooks.net

Urban Books, LLC
300 Farmingdale Road, N.Y.-Route 109
Farmingdale, NY 11735

Carl Weber's Kingpins: Queens 3, King of Kings
Copyright © 2024 Erick S. Gray

ISBN 13: 978-1-64556-656-4
EBOOK ISBN: 978-1-64556-657-1

First Trade Paperback Printing October 2024
Printed in the United States of America

10 9 8 7 6 5 4 3 2 1

This is a work of fiction. Any references or similarities to actual events, real people, living or dead, or to real locales are intended to give the novel a sense of reality. Any similarity in other names, characters, places, and incidents is entirely coincidental.

Distributed by Kensington Publishing Corp.
Submit orders to:
Customer Service
400 Hahn Road
Westminster, MD 21157-4627
Phone: 1-800-733-3000
Fax: 1-800-659-2436

Carl Weber's Kingpins:

Queens 3,

King of Kings

Erick S. Gray

Prologue

Spring 2005

A yellow cab arrived at Old Springfield Cemetery in Queens, New York. The rear door opened, and Nasir climbed out of the cab's back seat. He clutched a single rose and stared at the sprawling cemetery. It had been one year since her death, and Nasir wanted to show his respect. He was risking his life by showing his face back in Queens. He had several high-paying contracts out on him, shoot to kill on-site, no questions asked. And the men out to kill him meant business. Nasir knew he was living on borrowed time, but he needed this closure. He'd been tormented for too long by her death, always considering the what-ifs. What if he'd never connected with Denise that night? What if they'd left the city sooner rather than later? Would she still be alive? What if they'd killed him that night instead of her? He was haunted by regrets and heartrending thoughts. Nasir wished he could make things right with Sincere, but it was too late. A man that he had once considered his brother wanted him dead.

Although his love affair with Denise was transitory, he'd loved her, and she'd meant everything to him. It wasn't supposed to end this way. They were supposed to head west and begin a new life there. They'd talked about settling down in Arizona, New Mexico, or Nevada, places thousands of miles away from New York, isolated desert locations where no one knew their names or their past. However, Nasir lived in hiding, where he always had to look over his shoulder.

"Keep it idling. I'll be a few minutes," Nasir told the cabdriver.

He handed the driver a fifty-dollar bill for good measure. The driver nodded sure. Nasir strutted toward the cemetery underneath the threatening dark clouds indicating heavy rain was about to come. The gloomy and ominous atmosphere didn't bother Nasir. *Let it rain*. The downpour might wash away his sins and guilt.

Nasir entered the cemetery and removed a poorly drawn map of the place. He stared at the X, which marked the spot. Denise's grave was nearby. Nasir sighed heavily and headed in the direction of her grave.

This was going to be rough for him.

Sincere had made some connections to help pay for her funeral. He'd called in some favors and arranged his sister's burial while in prison. He didn't want his sister buried in the potter's field on Hart Island. The place was a paupers' graveyard for the city's unknown, unclaimed, and indigent people. He wasn't going to allow that for his little sister. Denise deserved more than to be buried unclaimed, with her remains rotting away on a small island just off the Bronx.

It took several minutes for Nasir to find her grave, an embedded small headstone with her name, her sunrise and sunset, and the saying LOVE YOU ALWAYS, BABY SIS. MISS YOU. Nasir stood over her grave with a sorrowful gaze. He'd watched her grow up, intimately connected with her, loved her, and now she was gone. Nasir placed the single rose against her grave and faintly uttered, "I'm sorry."

There was no one left. Lou was dead. Denise was dead. Sincere was incarcerated, and they were at odds, and his daughter and her mother didn't want anything to do with him. Nasir was alone, becoming a man without a country. Though he grew up in Queens, it felt like he was now behind enemy lines.

Nasir stared at the sky, which was completely covered in dark clouds, with zero breaks in between. Then, brimming with contrition, he stared at Denise's grave in silence and with trickling tears. Finally, he clenched his fists, becoming angry with himself. What he wanted was revenge. But Zulu was incarcerated, so he would be hard to get to. Zodiac had become the new power on the streets. Getting close to him would be difficult, but it wasn't impossible.

He missed Denise.

After her death, Nasir had fled to the Midwest, to Kansas City, and reunited with an old flame there, Sunday. Sunday was a stunning woman with ebony skin, hazel eyes, and long, flowing dreadlocks. But although strikingly beautiful, she was deadly. She'd taken Nasir in; it'd been his home for nearly a year.

While in Kansas, Nasir tried to get a job and live a straight life away from trouble. Still, he became the epitome of the saying "You can take the lion out of the jungle, but you can't take the jungle out of the lion." Working a nine-to-five wasn't his forte. He was used to the streets, to hustling and making money. Nasir was a leopard that couldn't change its spots. And Sunday became his enabler so that he could continue his life of crime. They rekindled their sexual affair, and she introduced him to her crew. They called themselves the Mob Squad Killers, or MSK. Recut, Sheek, Diane, Sunday, and Havoc were the members. They were from North Blue Ridge, one of the worst neighborhoods in Kansas City. The crew was into everything illegal: burglaries, violent home invasions, selling drugs, extortion, and even murder for the right price.

Knowing Sunday, Nasir fell right into place with the crew, and they went on a crime spree throughout the Midwest, robbing banks, pawnshops, and jewelry stores in small towns. Sunday was the ringleader; she was smart, ruthless, calculating, and ambitious. She was about her money and business, and anyone that got in the way of that was expendable.

The Mob Squad Killers' reign of crime began in Kansas City and continued in Oklahoma, Texas, New Mexico, and Arizona. It was in Arizona where it went left, bad! They tried to rob a jewelry store. Their routine was to scope out the place for a week, single out the security system, and stalk the managers of the business. They wanted to hit two birds with one stone—rob the manager's home and the pawnshop simultaneously. It always worked as planned, and the score was always lucrative. The night before a robbery, the crew would hit the owner's or manager's home. They would duct-tape the family and threaten the kids and wife, leaving the patriarch to comply with their demands. Then, early the following day, they would hit the locations before opening, holding the proprietor hostage at gunpoint and not worrying about customers or the police, because if anything went wrong, they would kill everyone.

But one robbery didn't go as planned. Recut, Sheek, and Diane held the family hostage. At the same time, Sunday, Nasir, and Havoc took the father to the jewelry store to clean him out before he opened. Unfortunately, they ran into two issues: the father had an attractive nineteen-year-old daughter, and Sheek decided to rape her repeatedly in her bedroom. And at the store, they didn't anticipate that the father, the owner of the store, had a brother who was a cop and was a partial business owner. The cop had keys to the store, and when he entered the store early that morning, he received the surprise of his life. They were being robbed. The cop drew his gun, but Sunday shot him twice in the back, killing him. They had to kill his brother too. And when Sunday found out what Sheek had done to the daughter, they had no choice but to execute the entire family.

Five people were killed that morning, and though it happened in an Arizona small town, it made national news because one of the victims was a cop.

Sunday was furious with Sheek, and she reprimanded him with a pistol-whipping.

"You stupid, muthafucka! You couldn't keep your dick in your fuckin' pants, Sheek? When you raped that bitch, you're leaving behind DNA, cuz I know you didn't use a fuckin' condom!" she screamed.

"I'm sorry, Sunday. I don't know what came over me," he uttered with shame.

"If you weren't my fuckin' brother, I would've killed you for being so fuckin' stupid," Sunday hollered.

They'd killed a cop. Sunday and Nasir knew they needed to keep a low profile, fall back from committing any more robberies, and leave the Midwest until everything calmed down. So Nasir decided it was time to head back east to New York.

Nasir stared at Denise's grave, filled with guilt. He sighed forcefully. Though he was nostalgic and grieving, Nasir quickly noticed a man wearing a black trench coat enter the cemetery. Immediately, something felt off about him, and Nasir became alert. He coolly reached for the 9mm Beretta tucked in his waistband. He didn't want to take any chances. No one knew he was back in town, so it might be a coincidence, but he didn't believe in coincidences.

"Fuck," Nasir muttered.

With it being the anniversary of Denise's death, he deduced that today would be the perfect time to catch him slipping. So Sincere most likely had sent this man, knowing Nasir would return to pay his respects someday. He had guessed right.

Nasir kept his eyes on the man, who pretended to be looking for a certain grave, but he knew differently. The figure in the trench coat coolly made his way toward Nasir. Nasir slowly but calmly removed the 9mm from his waistband, anticipating a hit on him. And he frowned; this was the one moment he got to spend with Denise and show his respect, and it was about to be ruined.

Immediately, the man's walk became deliberate as he headed toward Nasir. He hurriedly removed something from inside his trench coat, and that something was a submachine gun. He aimed it at Nasir. Nasir's eyes widened with fear.

"Shit!" Nasir exclaimed.

Before Nasir could react, the man fired his way.

Ratatatatat. Ratatatatat. Ratatatatat.

Nasir immediately took cover, hauling himself behind a towering tombstone as bullets slammed into the thick granite. The gunfire echoed deafeningly throughout the sprawling cemetery. Nasir clutched his pistol, waiting for the right moment to react. He was outgunned by the submachine gun, but he was grateful there was only one of them. He was determined not to die today—not now! He had unfinished business to attend to.

The gunman continued to fire at the tombstone Nasir was hiding behind, chipping away at the granite. He loomed closer to Nasir's position. The moment there was a break in the gunfire, Nasir leaped to his feet, rapidly returned fire, and then took cover behind another tombstone, this one shorter.

"Fuck me!" he cursed.

Finally, the dark clouds above ruptured, and heavy rain fell toward the earth. It was the type of rain that could create floods. However, the torrential downpour didn't discourage the gunman; he was determined to end Nasir's life in the cemetery. Nasir couldn't hide behind headstones forever. He had to make his move right now. He tightly gripped the gun and quickly glimpsed from behind the tombstone to see this man in the long trench coat coming at him like he was the Terminator. Nasir yelled to himself, *Fuck it! Now!*

Nasir sprinted from his hiding spot, cutting loose with gunfire, and emptied the gun toward his attacker. Then he hit the ground again hard, landing on his side, and scrambled behind a tree this time.

Shockingly, his rapid reaction was a success. Nasir peeked from behind the tree to see the gunman clutching his neck, then staggering and falling back. Clearly, it wasn't that easy. But it was. Finally, the killer collapsed on his back. Nasir slowly removed himself from behind the tree and approached with caution.

"Who fuckin' sent you?" Nasir exclaimed.

The killer gurgled his defiance.

"I said, who fuckin' sent you to kill me?" Nasir aimed his gun at the man's head, but it was useless. He was already dead. No breath, nothing.

Nasir huffed. The heavy rain cascaded down on him as he stood there in shock and awe. He looked into the distance, searching for the cab, but it was gone. Obviously, the cabbie had sped off when the gunfire erupted. Nasir kept the 9mm by his side and seethed. He'd returned to

New York for two things: to have closure with Denise and to seize what he had wanted for years. And that was the crown. He wanted to become the king of New York. He was a different person now, one with nothing to lose, and he came with reinforcements. And if Sincere wanted him dead, then two could play that game.

One

You can close your eyes to reality but not to memories.

Sincere sat on his cot, staring at the most recent picture of his son, Tyriq. He was eleven years old and looked like his father. It was painful not being in his son's life or all his kids' life, matter-of-fact. But this was one of the consequences of a choice he had made—placing revenge before family. His three kids were growing up without him. Monica had remarried and was pregnant with her third child, and Asuka and his daughter Akar were still in Japan. Sincere had no idea what was happening with Akar in Japan. He'd lost all contact with them. But Monica had decided to write him, and she'd sent him two recent pictures of his son and his daughter Ashley. Ashley was five years old and a cutie, with a bright smile for her father.

Sincere stared at his daughter, and tears trickled down his face. He quickly wiped away his tears of regret and nostalgia and sighed. It was hurtful to see his children only in photos, unable to hug them or physically be with them. What hurt more was that Monica had changed their last names to that of her present husband, Concord. This man had the family that Sincere had always wanted. It haunted Sincere that he'd fucked up with Monica and that she hadn't wanted anything to do with him ever since the beginning of his prison bid. So, it was surprising that he'd received a letter from her with pictures of his kids.

Monica had written to tell him that she had forgiven him and had found Christ in her life with the help of her husband. And though he was incarcerated, she wanted their kids to know their father. It was a lengthy two-page letter, and Sincere read it several times and became transfixed by his kids' pictures. He wanted to stare at their photos all day and smile.

"We do make some beautiful children," Sincere said aloud to himself, smiling.

Despite his condition and how he felt, Sincere was grateful they were happy, safe, and living a good life outside New York. And he was thankful Monica had had a change of heart. However, sadness and remorse suddenly overcame him when he thought about Denise, his little sister. She was dead, and he had failed at protecting her. Sincere would have given his own life for hers in a heartbeat. But since he knew Nasir was responsible for her death, there was no forgiving that muthafucka. How could Nasir have dragged his sister into that life, knowing she was the only family he had left? Sincere had placed a hit on his former friend, and his mind was not changing.

Withdrawn in his prison cell, Sincere remained trapped in his thoughts; he thought about an alternate life, one where he was a husband to Monica and a father to his children. What if he had become a cop and Marcus and Denise were still alive? It was a fleeting thought. His memories were like shadows; they followed him everywhere.

Sincere had built a somewhat quality life inside the prison, with his high status as a shot caller. In six years, he'd built a name throughout the system and earned the respect of everyone around him. He had no problem putting in work, but he also pushed inmates to try to better themselves. Sincere encouraged inmates to take advantage of programs and classes to help them stay out of prison once released. But he also remained that muthafucka who carried his weight and was the one involved in life-and-death decisions, which happened every day in the penitentiary system. If someone had to be taken care of, he made it happen.

"Yo, you got company," Row suddenly uttered from the threshold of his cell.

Sincere perked up. He immediately placed his kids' pictures into a magazine and focused on the tier. A young white correctional officer came into view and stepped into his cell. Sincere eyed her stoically. She immediately reached into her uniform and removed several cellophane wrappers and tightly packaged drugs from her person. She tossed the contraband items onto Sincere's cot.

"Any issues?" Sincere asked her.

She smiled and replied, "No."

Sincere nodded. He stood up and approached her. Melody had been a guard for two years, and she was a resident of the county. She secretly ferried drugs, mobile phones, and weapons into the state prison and provided information for him. Melody had fallen in love with Sincere and was willing to do anything for him, risking her employment and freedom.

"Row, keep a lookout, a'ight?" said Sincere.

Row nodded. "I got you." He stood guard outside Sincere's cell, with his attention on a swivel.

"We good? You in a rush?" Sincere asked Melody.

Melody smiled. "No. We got time."

Sincere grinned. He wanted to take his mind off Monica and his kids, and Melody was the perfect remedy. Soon after she started smuggling drugs and contraband into the prison for him, the two began a clandestine sexual affair. With Row keeping an eye out for any unwanted company, Sincere roughly grabbed Melody and unfastened her pants. He then dropped his own pants, curved the correctional officer over the desk, and thrust himself into her from behind. He drove his hard dick repeatedly into her wet pink folds. He began pounding her like a jackhammer, and she loved every minute of it. The correctional officer's cries were primal, and she kept yelling, "Fuck me!" The words echoed in the cell, and he had hushed her.

Their sexual tryst was quick: five minutes inside her and Sincere came. He grabbed the back of her neck and shuddered and panted. Quickly he pulled out of her, and the wet, frothy juices on his dick told him that she had loved every moment of it. Though things had gotten hot and heavy between them, their reality was still guard and inmate, and they had to be careful.

Melody began to get decent. She grinned warmly at Sincere and uttered, "I needed that."

Sincere ignored her statement; instead, he decided to ask about business. "Are we okay for next week?"

Melody nodded. "Yes, I'm on it. I have it worked out with the guard at the front gate. He wants an extra three hundred."

Sincere frowned. "He's becoming a greedy mutha-fucka."

"He's our nucleus, baby. What you're asking him to do costs," said Melody.

Sincere sighed and replied, "Make it happen."

"I will."

The two were decent again when Row uttered, "Yo, we got company."

Melody looked at Sincere and huffed. The last thing she needed was to be caught fucking an inmate. She immediately exited the cell to find two male correctional officers approaching, one black and one white. Both men were known abusers and mean as fuck.

Melody nervously smiled their way and said, "Hey. Everything okay?"

The two guards snubbed her and marched into Sincere's cell with authority. Their personas screamed nothing nice.

Sincere stared at them with caution and asked, "What's up? Everything okay, fellows?"

"We need you to come with us, Sincere," uttered Conner, the white guard.

"For what?" Sincere replied.

"We ain't here to answer your fuckin' questions. Just come with us," the black guard, Manny, said, chiming in.

Sincere looked past them and at Melody and Row. They both stood on the tier, looking helpless. They were no help to him now, but something was going down. Sincere had yet to learn what. The guards' demeanor was off-putting, but Sincere smirked and kept his cool. He ran this prison, but there were always hiccups. This was one of those hiccups. Before departing with the guards, Sincere quickly and smoothly slipped a small shank onto his person for protection. The last thing he wanted was to be naked during an attack. But he was a soldier and was always ready for war.

"Whatever!" uttered Sincere.

He did as he was instructed and left with the two guards flanking him.

"Where are y'all taking him?" asked Melody.

They ignored her question and kept walking. Melody decided to go with them, but Manny turned to her with a steely glare and said, "What? Are you worried we might do something to your boyfriend?"

Melody gasped, shocked that they knew.

Manny smirked and added, "You gonna fuck me like you love fucking him?"

Melody was at a loss for words.

"I figure not," said Manny.

Manny chuckled, and he and Conner proceeded to escort Sincere to some unknown destination. Sincere went without questioning them, but he knew something was wrong. He didn't recognize this part of the prison. The guards continued to flank him while they walked down a concrete corridor. It was the three of them at first. Sincere remained alert and ready. He wondered where they were taking him. Both men remained stone faced and silent; it felt like they were following orders from someone. Suddenly two inmates appeared farther down the corridor. They were coming his way and glaring at Sincere. Sincere knew he was walking into a setup. *But by who?* Who would be stupid enough to try to kill him, knowing he ran this prison?

Sincere knew he had to act first. While the two inmates menacingly approached, Sincere speedily slammed his shoulder into the guard on his right, Conner, knocking him against the wall. Sincere then punched Manny in the face. Knowing they no longer had the element of surprise, the two inmates began charging toward Sincere, ready to kill him. Sincere was prepared for them. This was his element, fighting battles in a war.

One of the inmates came at Sincere wildly and recklessly, with his shank going for Sincere's stomach and chest. Sincere sidestepped the danger and countered the attack with several swift punches to the man's face. His knuckles snapped against bare flesh. The second inmate thrust himself at Sincere with a mixture of untrained punches, and his attack was fruitless. Sincere counterattacked the second attacker with a fast jab to his face, catching him off-guard. Then he slammed his blade several times into one of the attackers' chest and stomach, killing him immediately.

"Y'all comin' for me! Fuck y'all niggas! C'mon then. C'mon!" Sincere heatedly shouted.

Manny and Conner charged at him, followed by the second inmate. Together, they began attacking Sincere, and a violent tussle ensued. Sincere decided he wasn't going out without a fight, and he became a brute. He violently headbutted and slammed Manny onto the floor like a pro wrestler. But suddenly, Conner grabbed Sincere into a tight chokehold from behind. Sincere struggled to breathe; however, he was able to jab the shank into Conner's left side. Conner screamed and released Sincere from his chokehold. The second inmate was on top of Sincere now, pummeling him with punches until Sincere slammed his fist into the man's rib cage twice. The inmate cringed and hunched over in pain. So it had begun with four against one, with Sincere being vastly outnumbered, but with one inmate dead and Conner injured, the odds had changed.

However, Manny and the second inmate kept coming for Sincere. And though he was hurt and winded, Sincere readied himself for another attack.

"C'mon, muthafuckas! I'm gonna kill every last one of y'all!" shouted Sincere.

They tried to jump him, and Sincere went on the defensive. He wrestled with Conner and the inmate. He struck Conner with a left hook, but abruptly, it felt like an hot iron poker had been shoved through his gut repeatedly. The shock was almost instant, and Sincere lost his footing as he grabbed his side and abdomen. He had been stabbed by the inmate. The pain was blinding, and he began having trouble breathing.

Sincere collapsed right there, knowing he was going to die. But before they could finish him off, Melody and several other guards intervened. Melody was shocked to see Sincere on the floor. Blood was everywhere, and an inmate was dead. Immediately, Melody got on her horn and called in the incident. However, she didn't know if Sincere would live or die.

Two

The seven-by-twelve-foot cell had become Zulu's permanent home at ADX Florence, a federal prison near Florence, Colorado. He was locked inside there twenty-three hours a day and received his meals through a slot in the cell door. His only glimpse of the outside world was through a thin slit of a window aimed at an empty sky. His cell was decorated with an immovable bed, desk, and stool. And there was a shower on a timer. Zulu also had a TV set for good behavior. ADX was a facility with reinforced concrete to deter self-harm, and its inmates were under twenty-four-hour supervision. It had been over a year since Zulu's arrival at ADX, a place deliberately designed to strip people or criminals of their humanity.

The facility was built to house the most dangerous people in America, and on that list was Zulu—a drug kingpin who had once controlled the streets of New York and had placed a contract hit on a NYPD detective. ADX housed foreign and domestic terrorists, such as Zacarias Moussaoui, Abu Hamza al-Masri, Dzhokhar Tsarnaev, and notorious crime figures, such as Luis Felipe, O. G. Mack, Joaquín "El Chapo" Guzmán, and Peter "Pistol Pete" Rollock. Zulu was among the elite of criminals, and his name remained notorious. But he had accepted his fate and refused to snitch; he would stay a gangster and his reputation would be intact until the day he died. And a life sentence in federal prison wasn't going to break him.

However, Zulu sat on his bed and thought about the old glory days with Mob Allah and Zodiac. They'd created a brotherhood, and at one time, they'd been a triple threat in Queens and a powerhouse on the streets. They'd been respected and feared and known for their greed and the murders they committed. Now those days were long gone, and Zulu was alone. He knew that with Cynthia gone, he would never see his kids again.

To pass the time, he exercised until he became exhausted, doing push-ups, sit-ups, and dips. Zulu also did a lot of reading and some writing. But it was depressing being locked down for twenty-three hours a the day. Zulu had no actual personal contact with anyone inside ADX aside from whatever communication with a guard he had. Inmates rarely saw one another, and when Zulu was out of his cell, he had to wear leg irons, handcuffs, and chains. When Zulu came across another inmate during his one hour of recreation, they would exchange a finger handshake through the fence that separated their recreation space. Since contact between inmates was highly restricted, it was one of the few things that reminded Zulu and the other inmates they weren't alone.

Zulu couldn't help but become jealous of Zodiac. While he was rotting in a supermax prison, Zodiac was free and living his best life. Zulu frowned at his friend's betrayal. It was Zodiac's turn to wear the crown, and Zulu wondered how long it would last. But it was the game; unfortunately, every drug kingpin had an expiration date.

Zulu's only comfort was knowing Detective Acosta had taken his own life. He hated the cop passionately and had smiled when he heard the news. The cop had constantly harassed him. Zulu wished he had witnessed the act. But Zulu was uncomfortable knowing Cook Gamble was still alive somewhere. He wanted the snitch dead, but it seemed impossible with him in the supermax and Zodiac focused on other things. Zulu wondered where they were keeping him.

Zulu paced around the small cell, trying to keep from going crazy. He could do only so much reading, writing, and TV watching. It was a privilege to have those three luxuries, and an inmate would be fortunate to receive a letter from a loved one twice a year. Unfortunately, it took nearly three months for inmates' letters to be mailed out and just as long for inmates to receive mail. Suffering from a mental disorder or PTSD was common in the supermax. Spending the rest of your life in the supermax was considered hell on earth, and each inmate had their own coping skills.

Zulu glanced out the small cell window to see if it was a clear day. Several guards came to his door to alert him that it was his time for an hour of recreation. It was something he was looking forward to. They shackled him with leg irons, handcuffs, and chains and escorted him to the recreation area. Zulu was placed into a metal cage four paces wide and eight paces long. It was about twice the size of his cell. There was an old basketball hoop and a deflated basketball to keep him busy. In a similar cage next to him was a notorious leader of the Aryan Brotherhood. His neck, face, and arms were with hateful insignias, including a swastika. Zulu locked eyes with this inmate. The only things these two men had in common were serving a life sentence in supermax and having a notorious reputation. Their racial difference made them sworn enemies, but if they wanted to kill each other, they couldn't.

Zulu kicked away the deflated basketball and began walking in circles around the cage. He wanted to savor the fresh air and think. The Aryan inmate decided to sit on the ground Indian style to meditate. For the duration of their recreation, they ignored each other.

Then, suddenly, out of nowhere, the Aryan inmate uttered to Zulu, "Our time is coming, nigger."

Zulu was caught off-guard by the statement. What the fuck was he talking about? Did he threaten me? Zulu thought. He stopped pacing in circles and glared at the Aryan inmate.

"What the fuck did you just say?" Zulu exclaimed. "And I'm not your fuckin' nigger!"

The Aryan inmate locked eyes with Zulu and smirked. "Of course not."

Zulu glared at him for a moment and then walked away. The guards were watching their every movement, but they weren't worried. The steel fence between them made the guards' jobs easier. Zulu picked up the deflated basketball and held it. He didn't bounce it or attempt to shoot the ball into the hoop. He had a half hour of recreation time left before they escorted him back to his jail cell. The fresh air was welcome, but it did little to ease the restrictions of his confinement. His hour of recreation was over quickly, and it was time to be escorted back to his jail cell.

ADX was designed to keep inmate movement to a minimum and to allow guards to have as much control as possible. Once he was back in his tiny cell, Zulu was unshackled and unchained. He stood massaging his wrists because of the tight handcuffs and sighed. An eerie quiet engulfed him, because his enclosure was soundproof. This was hell on earth. Zulu walked to the small window. From his vantage point, there was nothing to see—not even the mountains surrounding the facility were visible. It had been thirteen months since his arrival, and Zulu feared his mental health might be in jeopardy.

"Zulu, your lawyer's here," the guard informed him.

Zulu was taken aback by the news. It was unexpected and a shock. He had last spoken to his lawyer a few

months ago. Why would his lawyer visit him now? Zulu
went through the meticulous process of being shackled,
handcuffed, and chained once more, and then he was
escorted from his cell to the visiting room. Usually,
prisoners met with visitors through a glass window, and
the two parties used telephones on either side to commu-
nicate. The staff would monitor all activities, including
meetings with family. However, when an attorney visited,
the inmate received the privilege of an unmonitored chat
with their legal team.

Two guards ushered Zulu into a bland, windowless
concrete room where the only decoration was a metal
table and two chairs. This would be something other
than an ordinary attorney-client visit, not a chat on a
telephone in front of a glass window. Once again, Zulu
was shocked to see his supposed lawyer, a beautiful,
leggy woman in business attire and heels, waiting for his
arrival. She wore a dark skirt with a button-down shirt,
her hair was styled in a French bun, and her visiting pass
was hooked to her skirt. Her briefcase was on the table.

She stared at the two guards and said, "You can un-
shackle him and leave us. I'll be fine."

The guards did what they were told, and Zulu was
impressed. Immediately he understood this bitch had
juice and some kind of authority. The guards had broken
protocol for her by unchaining him.

Once Zulu was released from his restraints, the guards
left him alone with the woman. Zulu stared at her, un-
smiling, and asked, "Who the fuck are you?"

She smiled. "My name is Cashmere."

"Cashmere? Are you even a fuckin' lawyer?" Zulu uttered.

"I am indeed an attorney and am adept at the law," she
replied.

Cashmere walked over to her briefcase and removed a pack of Newports. "Do you care for a smoke?"

Zulu looked hesitant for a moment. Having a cigarette in the supermax was equivalent to enjoying a culinary delicacy: it was something pleasing but luxuriously rare. He nodded. She removed a cigarette from the pack, lit it, and handed it to him. Zulu took a needed drag. But he knew nothing came for free; she wanted something from him.

Zulu took a few more drags from the Newport and then asked, "Who the fuck sent you? And what do you want from me?"

Cashmere grinned. She replied, "First, I want to inform you that your children are in good hands and are being well taken care of."

Zulu frowned when she mentioned his kids. "How the fuck do you know about my kids and their well-being?"

He wanted to wrap his hands around her neck but knew it would be a mistake.

"Our authority, resources, and reach are infinite. As easy as it is for me to visit you alone in this room in the supermax and smoke a cigarette, it's just as easy to track down your children," she replied.

Zulu was on edge. Something about her was intimidating.

"Do you believe in miracles, Zulu?" she asked him.

Zulu chuckled. "What the fuck are you now? Santa Claus?"

"What if I told you there's a chance of you being released from here?" she added.

"Unless you're the fuckin' president of the United States with a fuckin' pardon, then I find that impossible," Zulu retorted.

"*Impossible* is a formidable word to you but a small task for my client," she said.

"And who hired you? Who is your client?"

"Unfortunately, I cannot divulge that information," she replied. "However, during your sovereignty of the drug trade in New York, you accumulated quite an impressive wealth portfolio, Zulu . . . over forty-five million dollars. A quarter of it is in offshore bank accounts, quite the cash reserve. Money that you can't legally claim right now."

"So that's it. You want fuckin' money, huh?" Zulu chided.

"We're here to help."

"By stealing from me?"

"What is it that you desire more, Zulu? To be finally free from this place or to continue to protect assets while serving a life sentence? My client will move mountains to make sure you're no longer suffering in this place. And we can give you monthly updates about your children," said Cashmere.

Her hand disappeared inside her briefcase, and she removed a few documents for him to sign. "All that is needed is your signatures," she told him.

Zulu groaned. What was their endgame?

"Freedom from this place is costly. You sign some papers, we'll liquidate a few properties and assets the government didn't seize or was unaware of, and the nightmare for you will be over," she proclaimed.

"And how soon?"

Cashmere grinned. "You've been tortured by this place long enough."

Zulu thought about it. Was she for real? He was trapped in a corner or a small box and had no leverage over this stranger. She was beautiful, but could he trust her? He didn't have a choice.

"You're a smart businessman, Zulu. And what you accomplished in five years was impressive. But it doesn't have to end here in this place. So, I'm giving you a second chance at redemption," said Cashmere coolly.

Zulu huffed and groaned. "Fuck it!"

He signed the necessary papers, and Cashmere grinned again. "It's a pleasure doing business with you."

Zulu scowled and muttered, "Don't fuck with me, bitch! I want out of here now."

"I assure you, my client always keeps his promises. You'll be free from this place soon," Cashmere replied.

She placed the signed documents in her briefcase and alerted the guards that she was ready to leave. Zulu was placed in his restraints and ushered from the room, a bit baffled. Though there was something off-putting about Cashmere, he went with the risk.

A week later Zulu still hadn't heard anything about his release from the supermax prison. He began having his doubts. He'd signed away a third of his hidden fortune, tucked in several offshore accounts, to leave ADX. If Cashmere had lied and manipulated him, Zulu could not strike back.

Fuck! he muttered to himself.

The guard approached his door with his evening meal. The slot in the steel door opened, and a tray of food was pushed inside the cell. Zulu took it, and the opening closed immediately. Zulu sat on his bed with the tray of food. It wasn't anything special, just the same slop they served every evening. Adhering to his routine, Zulu began to eat, devouring bread, chicken, beans, and a piece of fresh fruit. Minutes later, something was wrong. Zulu's stomach began to violently churn, and then he began to choke, unable to breathe. Zulu collapsed on the floor in severe pain, squirming and clutching his throat gasping for air. He deduced that he'd been poisoned. He tried to call out for the guard, but it would have been fruitless; the prison cell was soundproof. His only hope was the guard monitoring the CCTV camera saw him choking and dying.

Ironically, Cashmere kept her promise to free Zulu from the supermax prison, though it wouldn't be physically but via death. Finally, several guards rushed into Zulu's prison cell to aid him, but it was too late. Zulu was dead.

Three

Ghana was a beautiful country, blessed with some of the world's most untouched beaches and lush forests. It was considered one of the more stable countries in West Africa, and it had a vibrant and rich history. The stretch of sandy shoreline was known for its warm tropical waters and swaying palms.

Zodiac stood on the cliff and watched the waves crawling gently to the shore. He could see a length of white sand, a gash of zephyr-haunted cliffs, and a wide expanse of the bay. It was a watery nirvana, and the beach was saturated in a light-gold dawn haze. The sprawling and glistening sea was so blue, staring at it felt hypnotic. Zodiac took in the ocean momentarily and then pivoted to stare at an iconic structure in the heart of the town. Cape Coast Castle. It was one of about forty commercial forts, or "slave castles," built on the Gold Coast of West Africa by European traders in timber, gold, and slaves. The sprawling fortification was impressive, with its soaring whitewashed walls, underground dungeons, and multiple cannons aimed at the deep blue sea. This castle was once a place of horror in an African paradise: it held enslaved Africans before their endless journey across the Atlantic Ocean.

"It's impressive, eh?" a man named Joc uttered to Zodiac.

"It is," Zodiac replied.

"It has what they call the Door of No Return, the last place our ancestors walked before being forced to board a ship and cross the Atlantic Ocean," said Joc. "Imagine it, men, women, and children crammed into the dungeons belowdecks, a space of terror, death, and darkness, not knowing their fate . . . not knowing if they'll ever see their family again."

"I can only imagine it," said Zodiac.

"We came a long way, eh? Our people no longer need to worry about slave traders, but now we have other demons," said Joc. "Modern civilization comes with a cost for so many of us."

"I guess it does," Zodiac replied indifferently.

Joc grinned and added, "Ghana's history is complicated but captivating. But we're not here to talk about my country's history, are we?"

"I'm here for business, Joc . . . Taking in your country's beauty is a plus for me," Zodiac replied.

"Enjoy it. There are beautiful women, beaches, great food, and many places to indulge in. We fought hard for our independence from the British," said Joc proudly.

Joc was a well-put-together man, wearing black slacks and a collared shirt that hugged his physically fit body. He was handsome, with ebony skin and a gleaming bald head. His cool image, sharp dressing, and gangster charm had catapulted him to the top of the food chain in the criminal world. Joc was born in Ghana, lived in Nigeria in his late teens, and received his education in the States and in Kenya. On paper, he was an educated scholar, but behind the scenes, he was one of the top drug suppliers in Africa.

After Zulu's incarceration, Zodiac took over the empire, and he was growing it fast. He'd become one of the top drug distributors in New York City and most of the Tristate area. And what Mob Allah had started six years ago, Zodiac was now steering to perfection, running a major real estate firm with his girlfriend, Trina, while still maintaining his position as a drug kingpin. He lived like a king in plain sight and felt he had more money than Fort Knox. There were extravagant trips to the Caribbean, Europe, and Africa, mansions on the East and West Coasts, luxury cars, and shopping sprees. His trip to Ghana was about business first, but he wanted to make it pleasurable too.

The two men continued to tour Cape Coast Castle. They seemed alone, but Joc had his security nearby, hiding in plain sight. Zodiac had his number one bodyguard, Mighty Mouse, slightly trailing behind him. Mighty Mouse was a powerhouse-looking man who stood six-one, had an imposing physique, and was trained in mixed martial arts. An ex-Navy Seal, he was loyal to Zodiac and willing to kill anyone to protect his employer.

"I've done my homework on you, Zodiac, and I'm impressed. You've built quite the empire for yourself, eh?" said Joc.

"I'm a businessman, Joc, a serious one at that. You can rely on me when moving your product in the States. I need a reliable connect, someone like yourself. I've established an elaborate network of routes, couriers, territories, and loyalty. I'm maintaining a stranglehold on the Tristate area. But I want the entire eastern district," Zodiac responded.

Joc laughed. "You're ambitious. Someone with too much ambition cannot sleep in peace."

"Who wants to sleep? And making money gives me peace."

Joc chuckled. "I like you, Zodiac. But liking someone and trusting someone are two different things. Can I trust you to move two to three hundred kilos weekly, twelve hundred kilos monthly through your organization?"

Zodiac didn't hesitate to answer. "Yes! I wouldn't have come to you if I couldn't move tons instead of kilos."

"If you weren't on my radar, you wouldn't have come this close to meet me," Joc replied.

Zodiac and Joc entered the castle and blended in with the other tourists. While the two men walked side by side, they continued to talk. It was Zodiac's first time in Africa, and it was a site to see gold weights and measuring scales, paintings, guns, and stone implements for hunting. Next, they moved through the courtyard and came across an entrance with a sign above it that read MALE SLAVE DUNGEON. It was a dreadful thing to see. Zodiac rubbed his hand against the old stone walls and imagined the horrors that took place there and the screams of the captives.

Some of the dungeons were made of brick and were cramped, with little ventilation and no windows. Zodiac was saddened by what he was seeing. He was a notorious drug kingpin with some sentiment about the past.

"The British called the dungeons 'slave holds.' They say around twelve million slaves were sent from Africa, millions of whom died in the process. Europeans and Americans have been buying our people for centuries," Joc proclaimed.

"If these walls could talk," Zodiac uttered.

Joc chuckled. "But they don't. And I didn't invite you to my country to bore you with history. So tonight come to my nightclub, and we'll talk more business, drink, dance, and laugh. The past is the past, and the present and the future will change by us becoming rich men."

Zodiac nodded. He had seen enough. He and Joc exited the dungeon and stepped into the courtyard. It was a bright and sunny day, a day that was still young. Trina had decided to stay behind at the hotel. She didn't care to tour a slave castle or mingle with tourists. She and Zodiac were in Ghana for one reason: to establish stable distribution to the States with Joc, an international drug trafficker. Joc had established an elaborate drug network for drug trafficking. He was also a warlord, with thousands of men under him, and was involved in nearly 30 percent of global cocaine and heroin sales.

"I hope to see you tonight, Zodiac, to continue our conversation," said Joc.

"You will. I'm looking forward to it," said Zodiac.

"Bring your lady too. You're my guest, and we treat our guests with the best here. You'll see."

Zodiac nodded.

The two men pivoted away from each other and went their separate ways. Zodiac and Mighty Mouse climbed into the back seat of a Mercedes-Benz S55 AMG sedan and drove away. Zodiac was returning to the hotel to meet up with Trina. The Benz traveled through the streets of Cape Coast, Ghana. It was a beautiful city, complete with a lively fishing port, festivals, markets with many stalls, and a rich history.

The Mercedes-Benz arrived at Coconut Grove Beach Resort, a three-star hotel on one of the sandy beaches of the historic town of Elmina. Zodiac and Mighty Mouse climbed out of the back seat and entered the hotel. Mighty Mouse followed Zodiac to his hotel room on the second floor, and then he went to his own room.

Zodiac wanted to unwind inside his plush hotel room, equipped with air-conditioning, a terrace with a sea view, a flat-screen TV, a deep sunken bathtub, and the latest amenities.

"Trina, where are you?" he called out.

"I'm out on the terrace," she replied.

Zodiac joined her on the terrace, immediately wrapped her in his arms from behind, and warmly embraced her. Together, they took in the beautiful, glistening blue ocean.

"It's beautiful, isn't it?" said Trina.

"It is," Zodiac said.

"How did things go with Joc?"

"Good, really good," said Zodiac. "He sees the big picture in dealing with me. I can make him so much money not even God will fuck with him."

Trina giggled. She turned around in his arms to face him. She was a transexual, but she was beautiful. She was glowing in a bathrobe, her long, sensuous black hair flowing down her shoulders. Trina had transitioned into a woman three years ago by taking hormones to suppress the physical characteristics of her assigned gender. The hormone supplements had promoted breast growth, changed her voice, and contributed to a more traditionally feminine appearance. She had also undergone gender confirmation surgery.

Zodiac stared at Trina and proclaimed wholeheartedly, "You're beautiful."

She smiled. The two then passionately kissed on the terrace. Zodiac undressed her and stared at her figure— she might have been born a man, but to him, she was all woman. They fucked on the terrace that afternoon and prepared to conclude their business with Joc that night.

Four

Accra's raw and unfiltered streets were crowded with vehicles, mopeds, and people. It was a beautiful, warm night, with a full moon above, and the night sky was aglow with bright city lights. The sleek black Mercedes-Benz traveled down Oxford Street, passing banks, foreign exchange bureaus, and curio shops, and soon arrived at a nightclub. The place, called Tigress, was a vibrant, popular, and spacious nightclub in Accra, one of many owned by Joc.

Their driver opened the rear door of the Benz, and Zodiac and Trina climbed out of the vehicle, looking like royalty. Trina wore a seamless black minidress highlighting her curves and exposing her long legs in heels. Zodiac wore stylish jeans with a casual button-down shirt and loafers without socks. They walked arm in arm and were immediately escorted into the nightclub by one of Joc's security men. They were Joc's personal guests and considered VIPs. They were hit with some calypso music when they entered the nightclub. The revelers were packed on the dance floor, gyrating to the explosive beat.

Trina smiled because she wanted to dance right away. This was her thing, Caribbean and reggae, and she wanted to have a good time tonight. However, Zodiac wanted to conclude some business with Joc first. The two made it to the lavish VIP area and greeted Joc. He was a man of power, style, and charisma. Joc wore black slacks and a fashionable open-collar polo shirt underneath a dark blue blazer. A diamond Rolex and a diamond bracelet peeked from underneath the blazer. Joc found Trina beautiful and remarkable. He greeted her with a kiss on her cheek, and she blushed.

"You're beautiful," he complimented.

"Thank you," Trina replied.

"Zodiac, I'm glad you were able to bring her. I want the two of you to have a good time tonight at my expense," said Joc.

"Your place is amazing," Trina said to him.

Joc smiled. "I'm glad you like it. We have a good time tonight, eh? You don't have to worry about anything."

Trina grinned.

Joc had no idea she was born a man, and Zodiac wanted to keep it that way. He had no idea how Joc felt about transexuals. They were in a foreign country, meeting with a powerful international drug lord. Though Zodiac didn't consider himself gay, he didn't know how Joc would feel if he found out about Trina. He was there for business and not to discuss his love life.

The couple took a seat in the VIP area with Joc. Joc immediately snapped his fingers, and a curvy bottle girl quickly approached their area. Joc smiled at her and uttered, "Bring me three bottles of Dom Pérignon and Moët."

The bottle girl nodded and smiled. Then she pivoted and hurriedly marched away to fill the don's order. Naturally, Joc wanted to impress his guests, and Zodiac and Trina were impressed.

"This is one of a dozen nightclubs I own in Ghana, Nigeria, Miami, Jamaica, and France," Joc boasted.

"Impressive," Trina replied.

"I like music, nightclubs, bringing people together for enjoyment and a good time. It's like charity to me, eh. What's the point of being rich and powerful if I can't have fun with the money?" Joc proclaimed.

Zodiac nodded in agreement.

A few minutes later two bottle girls arrived with the top-notch chilled champagne and placed the bottles in ice buckets. Joc became excited. "Finally, we drink, mingle, and enjoy the night, eh . . ." he exclaimed.

"Let's enjoy the night . . . and finish discussing our business from earlier," Zodiac reminded him.

Joc grinned. "That we will do too."

Joc stood up, grabbed a bottle of Dom Pérignon from one of the ice buckets, and popped the cork. The popping of the champagne cork was like an explosion of joy. It was the bang to get the party started, the sound of success. He filled Zodiac's and Trina's glasses and then his own.

Joc raised his champagne glass in the air for a toast, and Zodiac, Trina, and a few others followed suit.

"A toast to the good life, good friends, money, and longevity. And anyone that tries to take that away from us, let 'em burn in hell, because that's where I'm gon' send them for messing with anything I love," Joc proclaimed.

Everyone toasted and downed their champagne.

Trina was ready to join the revelers on the dance floor and dance, but Zodiac wanted to sit and talk to Joc. So he told Trina to go ahead and enjoy herself. She was ready to unwind, grind, and paint the town red. So, she gladly made her way toward the dance floor to gyrate her hips to some Beenie Man. While Trina was swaying and bopping on the dance floor, Zodiac and Joc sat alone in the VIP area to talk.

"You're a lucky man to have her," said Joc.

Zodiac nodded and smiled. "I know," he replied. "Listen, I want us to work together, Joc. I respect everything you've built here. It is impressive . . . like a modern-day Rome. Never seen anything like it."

Joc chuckled slightly. It was flattery at its finest. He downed some more champagne, sat back, and draped his arms across the back of the velvet lounge couch. He stared at Zodiac. It was business now, and it showed in his eyes.

Zodiac continued. "And I guarantee you I can move your product in the States without any hiccups, and we can make each other a ton of money. But your prices a key are a bit steep . . ."

"My prices are my prices, Zodiac. Do you expect me to compromise my value for your benefit?"

"No. But I want our relationship to be reasonable," Zodiac countered. "Understand when I say this. It's a new era, and things are changing. The game is changing. Bribing the proper authorities is becoming more expensive. Coke and dope compete against meth, other synthetic drugs, ecstasy, and opioids. It's like a vending machine on the streets to get high. And with your rivalries opening the borders and the rapid flow of product, cocaine and dope are losing their value. And I'm facing the pressure to stay competitive," Zodiac proclaimed.

Joc waited to reply. Instead of talking, he downed some more champagne and stared at Zodiac indifferently. This was a man who had an army at his beck and call. He was known to be a brutal tyrant in Africa and a shrewd businessman too. It was known he had committed multiple murders in various countries and hadn't lost a night's sleep over it. Joc's name and reputation were undisputed and preceded him. Therefore, Zodiac knew he needed to tread wisely during their negotiations. The last thing he wanted to do was upset or offend this man.

"Like I said to you earlier, Zodiac, I like you, but can I trust you?" said Joc.

"I want to build trust with you, Joc. And that can only happen if we come to a mutual understanding and work together . . . build trust between us brick by brick," Zodiac replied wholeheartedly.

Joc grinned. It was the correct answer. Joc hated it when men assured him that he could trust them when he hardly knew them.

"A solution to both our problems, then . . . eh?" Joc began. "I'm against lowering my prices, but I want to build a relationship and trust with you, eh. So, if you can guarantee that you'll be able to move two thousand kilos a month, I'll drop the price by a thousand per kilo. So, what is it, Zodiac? Can you guarantee me this?"

Moving two thousand kilos a month was nothing to sneeze at. But Zodiac was confident he could move two thousand kilos monthly because he had the manpower, the connections, and the resources. His domain was New York City and the Tristate area, but Zodiac was expanding into other cities.

He locked eyes with Joc and proclaimed unequivocally, "It's a deal. Let's start trusting each other."

Joc nodded. The two men lifted their champagne glasses and clinked them together to signify unity. Trina returned to the VIP area, and the look on her man's face indicated that everything had been finalized.

"Come dance with me, baby," said Trina, reaching for her man.

Zodiac was hesitant. But Joc uttered, "We talked business. Now you must go and dance with this beautiful woman. So enjoy my club, my friend. It's a good night."

Zodiac relented, and he got off the couch and allowed Trina to pull him toward the dance floor. Zodiac was not much of a dancer, but he tried his best with his two steps and hip movement. Trina was full of life and excitement. She was happy and wanted to make Zodiac happy when they returned to their hotel suite.

The night wound down, and it was getting late. Zodiac felt it was time to leave. Trina was tipsy but functional. Zodiac signaled to Mighty Mouse and a second man on his security detail that they were ready to go. Joc had shown them a wonderful time tonight, but now it was time to return to their hotel suite, where they could continue their private celebration.

Trina and Zodiac were all smiles and laughter when they exited the nightclub and climbed into the back seat of the sleek black Benz. The streets of Accra were still bustling and buzzing with activity.

"Ghanaians love to party," Trina laughed.

"They do," said Zodiac.

The driver started the engine, coolly drove away from the nightclub, and merged onto crowded Oxford Street. Trina snuggled against Zodiac, feeling safe and happy. She closed her eyes and felt Zodiac wrap his arm around her. While the Benz carefully moved through the traffic, Zodiac's cell phone rang, and it was an unknown number.

"Who is it?" asked Trina.

"I don't know," Zodiac replied.

He reluctantly answered the call and immediately heard a woman's voice on the other end. She said, "Zulu's dead, and you're next."

"Who the fuck is this?" Zodiac cursed.

Her man angrily shouting into the phone alarmed Trina. "Who is it, Zodiac? Who are you talking to?"

He ignored her, and the phone call ended abruptly. Zodiac knew something was really wrong and went on high alert. The Benz stopped at an intersection, near a crowd of people. Suddenly, a black SUV came to a screeching stop parallel to their Benz. Zodiac knew what was coming next. Everything happened simultaneously: two armed men dressed in black burst from the SUV, gripping assault rifles, and two more armed men in black emerged from the crowd nearby.

"It's a hit!" Zodiac shouted.

Trina and Zodiac quickly ducked for cover in the back seat as heavy gunfire erupted.

Ratatatatatatatatatatatat . . .
Bratatatatatatatatatatatat . . .

Unbeknownst to the shooters, the Mercedes-Benz was bulletproof, with thick shatterproof windows and ballistic armor. The gunfire spiderwebbed the windows but didn't penetrate the glass. Nevertheless, the driver immediately popped the vehicle into reverse, stomping on the gas hard. The Benz screamed back through the tight spaces of the street and then quickly turned to face forward. Gunfire sprayed the vehicle as the driver thrust the Benz into drive and sailed through the constricted, busy street of Accra to safety.

When they were blocks away, Zodiac huffed and asked Trina if she was okay. Fortunately, everyone in the vehicle was unscathed by the incident. Zodiac became angry. He looked at Trina and uttered, "Zulu's dead."

Trina was taken aback by the news. "What . . . ? How?"

He had no idea how or why it had happened, but Zodiac knew for sure that Zulu's death and the sudden attempt on their lives weren't coincidences.

When they reached the hotel, Mighty Mouse retrieved a Heckler & Koch MP7A1 from the trunk and hurriedly ushered Zodiac and Trina into the building. Trina was a bit shaken up from the attack. If their Mercedes-Benz wasn't bulletproof, they would be dead.

"What is going on, Zodiac? Who tried to kill us?" Trina exclaimed once they were alone inside their hotel suite.

"I don't know!" Zodiac shouted. "But I'm gonna find out. So pack your things. We're leaving this place right now."

Zodiac began making phone calls. The news that Zulu was dead had hit him hard. Though they'd become estranged, Zulu had been his brother for life. Mob Allah, Zulu, and Zodiac had once been considered the Three Musketeers of the ghetto—becoming untouchable and running things on the mean streets of Jamaica, Queens. Now he was the last man standing.

But for how long?

Who was after him?

Five

It was a beautiful spring morning. The sky was blue, the trees were blossoming, the birds were chirping, and the flowers were pushing up through the earth. Spring represented rebirth and awakening. The weather was turning warmer, and things were coming to life. But Nasir wasn't in the mood to celebrate or enjoy the glorious weather. Instead, he had a lot on his mind. He stood in the backyard of the rental property in Newark, New Jersey. He had almost been killed while trying to visit Denise's grave site. He believed the hit had come from Sincere, inside the prison, and was thinking about payback.

A 9mm tucked into his waistband, Nasir stared at the towering trees in the backyard, observing how they gently swayed from the spring breeze. Nasir had no idea why he was staring at trees this morning; he was just doing so, looking hypnotized and thinking.

Sunday decided to join Nasir in the backyard. She was becoming worried. Her long dreadlocks flowed down to her shoulders, and her pretty hazel eyes zeroed in on Nasir. Sunday was a beauty and a beast rolled into a beautiful woman. She was a dangerous and seductive woman, a femme fatale with a modern tough-girl edge, an icy bitch motivated by ambition, power, and bloodlust.

She loved money, sex, and violence, all of which made her pussy wet.

"Why are you out here alone?" Sunday asked him.

"I need to go see him," Nasir told her.

"See who . . . ? Sincere?" Sunday replied. "Oh, *him*. You believe he tried to have you killed. So why would you go see that fool?"

"I wanna look him in the eyes and find out for myself."

"What is there to find out, Nasir? You know it was him. He blames you for his sister's death, right? That's what you told me."

"He's not wrong. If Denise had never met me, then she would be alive today."

"You don't know that, Nasir," Sunday chided.

"She's dead because of me! And I need to make it right," Nasir exclaimed.

Sunday sighed and groaned.

Guilt was eating Nasir alive. Denise had been his everything, and he had been in love with her. Sunday had begun to feel some kind of way; it was jealousy. She stared at Nasir and asked, "When you fuck me, do you think about her?"

Nasir stared at her impassively; his eyes were cold and black. He wasn't the same person he'd been years ago. But he didn't have anything to lose now. Lou was gone, Denise was gone, Sincere had become his foe, and his baby mother and daughter weren't in his life, so now he wanted it all. The only thing Nasir had to gain was the streets and the title of drug kingpin in New York. He wanted the respect he felt he had always deserved.

Nasir refused to answer her; he didn't want to tell her the truth.

"Don't forget, Nasir, we're here for a reason. You have a bunch of hungry wolves inside that crib, ready to make anything happen and get this money. We can't go back to Kansas City or anywhere in the Midwest. So this is our time to shine, Nasir. Don't forget it," Sunday proclaimed wholeheartedly.

"I didn't forget anything," replied Nasir. "We're here for a reason, right? I want this fuckin' city by any means necessary."

Sunday smiled. "That's my nigga."

They kissed passionately in the backyard. Then Sunday took Nasir by the hand, pulled him back into the house, and headed to the bedroom. Many guns were displayed on the kitchen counter, including handguns, assault rifles, and machine guns. It looked like they were ready for a war. The goons, the Mob Squad Killers Recut, Sheek, Havoc, and Diane, sat inside the living room. They were smoking weed, drinking alcohol, and playing *Call of Duty* on a PlayStation. It was a den of iniquity. Every person inside that room, including Diane, had committed some kind of unspeakable crime or appalling act, from robbery, extortion, and rape to cold-blooded murder. The group had become a violent brotherhood, and they didn't give a fuck. They wanted it all: sex, money, and power. And Sunday and Nasir had become the de facto leaders of MSK.

Sunday and Nasir trekked through the living room, which was clouded by weed smoke and filled with cursing. Quickly, all eyes became fixed on them. Sheek joked, "Don't get her pregnant."

"Fuck you," Sunday responded.

"Sunday, when we gon' make fuckin' moves?" Recut asked. "A nigga becoming antsy stayin' in this bitch."

"Soon," Sunday uttered.

She and Nasir went up the stairs and disappeared into the bedroom. They continued to kiss passionately and removed their clothing. Nasir stared at Sunday for a moment; her body was amazing, top-notch, mind-blowing. She could be a top model.

Damn!

"I want you to fuck me, baby," Sunday said.

Nasir felt the softness of her lips as their tongues danced together. Then, with her butt naked, he pushed her against the bed. Sunday spread her legs and arched her back. Her pussy lips spread, and her exposed clit was an invitation. Nasir buried his face between her luscious full ass cheeks before him. Immediately his tongue darted out to lick her holes, and he could smell and taste her juices. Next, he pushed her legs back and began to feast on her wetness. Sunday's juices were flowing freely. She grabbed her legs and held them back, giving Nasir access to her most private places. Nasir lapped gently, licking her clit, softly sucking on her pussy lips, and slid his fingers inside her tight spot, making Sunday create sounds from deep in her throat that could only mean she was enveloped by absolute pleasure.

"Aah," she moaned. "It feels good. Please, don't stop."

The more Nasir licked and fingered her, the more her juices flowed. She was on the edge, deeply aroused and horny, and begging for more.

"Fuck me, nigga!" Sunday cried out with a glazed look in her eyes.

Nasir squeezed her breasts together and played with and pinched her hard nipples. Sunday was out of her mind with lust. He positioned himself between her legs. Sunday grabbed his hard dick and placed the head at the entrance to her pussy. Lights danced behind their eyes, and then Nasir was deep inside her.

"*Ooh*, shit," Nasir moaned, feeling the sensation of her wet pussy surrounding him.

His heart was racing, and waves of pleasure consumed him. Nasir was in his zone. He closed his eyes as he thrust into Sunday's pleasure box. He didn't want to think about her, but it was inevitable. Visions of Denise rushed to his mind while he was inside Sunday. He could see Denise clearly, her smile, could hear her laughter, and yearned for her touch.

With Sunday's legs wrapped around him, he fucked her deep and slow and hard. But he saw Denise.

Sunday's eyes began to roll back in her head. "Shit, nigga . . . more. Fuck, more!"

And Nasir gave her more because it was Denise he was now seeing—and fucking. He was hallucinating. But it didn't matter. Nasir built up his pace, fucking Sunday faster and harder, making her howl. He could feel her pussy grabbing him and began throbbing. Nasir wanted nothing more but to drive his dick inside Sunday until his thick cream coated her insides.

"I'm coming!" Sunday announced.

In a flash, Nasir flipped her over, placing Sunday on her knees, and he pulled that glorious ass up. Then, with a precision aim, he was inside her again from the back, fucking her like a wild animal. There was nothing to hold him back. This was fucking like it was meant to be—hot, sweaty, juicy sex, complete with panting and heavy breathing—and it left Sunday screaming into the pillow as Nasir grabbed her hips while they exploded together.

"Damn, that dick is good," Sunday praised, trying to collect herself.

Nasir grinned.

They always had great, mind-blowing sex. However, Sunday wasn't the cuddling and pillow-talking type of bitch. The minute she got her nut, that was it. She didn't linger in bed. Now she got up from the bed and said to Nasir, "We got work to do, nigga. Let's do this."

Nasir agreed.

Nasir, Sunday, Recut, and Diane sat in a Ford Explorer parked across the street from a high-end jewelry store in Jackson Heights, Queens. They observed the place like a soaring hawk stalking its prey. The site was on a busy street, with lots of traffic and storefronts. Sunday was fixed on the jewelry store.

"Why this place?" asked Diane. "Why not hit some shit up in the city, like in the Diamond District, get more for the risk? Or go after drug dealers? You know they ain't gonna call the cops."

"Because this place is perfect," Sunday responded. "I did my homework on this place, and there's no less than two, maybe three million dollars' worth of valuables at a time here. It's high-end. Jay-Z, Jennifer Lopez, and Puffy be comin' here to get their shit. So we hit 'em hard and fast."

"The same MO?" Recut asked.

"Yeah, I already have a bead on his family. He has a nice house, kids, a pretty wife, and a dog. He has much to lose if he doesn't wanna play ball. We hit this place, and we'll be set to meet with this connect," Sunday proclaimed.

"When you tryin' to do this?" Nasir asked her.

"Tomorrow. We get this money, pay this connect, and do us. It's our time," Sunday said excitedly.

Recut grinned and uttered, "No doubt!"

The group continued to watch the jewelry store and observed a clean-cut middle-aged white male exit the place. He was the owner and was nicely dressed, and he climbed into a luxury Lexus and left.

"Yeah, this gonna be our come-up! We do this right, no fuckups, and we gonna own this city," Sunday declared proudly.

The following evening Adyen Rockford exited his place of business, Rockford & Hales Jewelry, and climbed into his dark blue Lexus ES. Adyen was forty-nine years old and was considered a success. He was winning in life. He owned three lucrative jewelry stores, was invested in real estate, and had a beautiful, loving family. Life was good, but the sharks were circling in the waters, unbeknownst to him.

Adyen was casually dressed and was smiling when he got into his Lexus, on his way home. He owned a five-bedroom house with a three-car garage in an affluent neighborhood of Queens. It was a warm and pretty spring evening, and Adien was ready to have dinner with his family and spend quality time with his wife. He arrived home and parked in the garage, as was his routine. His wife's Benz was parked in the garage too, and everything seemed normal when he climbed out of the Lexus and walked into the kitchen via the garage. Adyen lived on a quiet tree-lined street, and nearly all his neighbors had spacious front and back yards, decorated driveways, and luxury vehicles parked in the driveway or on the street. It was the kind of neighborhood that was in sync with everyone's current lifestyle, one that catered to their specific needs. It was so safe that parents could let their children walk alone to the nearest park and a woman could walk alone at night.

When Adyen entered the kitchen, he saw that the lights and the TV were on and his wife had begun making dinner. He called out to his family, "Hey, I'm home. Where's everyone?"

He didn't receive an answer. It was a big house, so he figured no one had heard him come home. He moved through the house and continued to call out to his family. There was no reply, only the TV blaring. Adyen went upstairs, wondering where everyone was. He would soon find out. When he entered the bedroom, Adyen immediately froze in horror. He found his entire family in the master bedroom, but they weren't alone. Sunday and her crew were holding everyone hostage at gunpoint. She was wearing a mask. Adyen's wife and his seventeen-year-old daughter were bound to a chair, butt naked and gagging from the duct tape over their mouths. His younger kids, Peter and Larry, who were ten and eleven years old, were lying face down on the floor. Havoc stood over them with a shotgun.

"Wh-what is this? Wh-what's going on?" Adyen stammered. He began to panic.

Sunday aimed her Glock 19 at his head and muttered, "Just chill, muthafucka, and things won't get messy."

"What do you want? Just take it and leave, please," Adyen pleaded.

"What we want will come in the morning," Nasir uttered.

Adyen saw that Havoc, a young thuggish white boy, and Recut wore delivery service uniforms. That was how they could enter the house, by posing as clean-cut deliverymen.

"I can give you money, anything. But please, don't hurt my family," Adyen begged with teary eyes.

"No one will get hurt as long as you do precisely what we say. You don't, then shit gonna get messy in here," said Sunday.

Adyen couldn't believe this was happening. It had to be a nightmare. He wanted to close his eyes, reopen them, and see things return to normal. But they weren't. He looked at his wife and daughter bound to the chair and saw absolute terror written on their faces. And why were they naked?

"Why are my wife and daughter naked?" he asked.

"They'll be fine as long as you come through for us," Nasir replied.

Sunday and Nasir informed Adyen that they were there to rob his jewelry store early tomorrow morning. In the meantime, they would make themselves at home. Throughout the night, the crew took turns holding the family at gunpoint. At the same time, everyone else went rummaging through their things, finding money, jewelry, fur coats, and other valuables to sell or pawn, and raided their fridge.

It was 7:00 a.m. when Sunday told Adyen it was time to implement their plan. They had complete control of the situation. They made Adyen change clothes, and Sunday, Nasir, and Recut went with Adyen to the jewelry store. At the same time, Sheek, Havoc, and Diane stayed behind to watch the family. The trio with Adyen climbed into his Lexus once he was in the back seat and made the forty-minute drive to his store.

Sunday, Recut, and Nasir watched as Adyen deactivated the alarm system at the jewelry store, and then, duffel bags in hand, they followed Adyen through the unlocked glass door. Nasir quickly took out the security cameras, and Recut zip-tied Adyen by his wrists. Next, they went for high-end watches, gold rings, necklaces, and other sparkly jewelry. They began packing everything into the duffel bags. They also hit the safe in the back room. Adyen reluctantly gave them the combination to the safe, where he stored priceless diamonds and nearly a hundred thousand dollars in cash.

"Please, you took everything from me. Now can you release my family and leave us alone?" Adyen begged. He was on his knees, with his wrists zip-tied behind him.

Sunday glared at him through her mask and pressed the Glock 19 to his forehead. Adyen cowered and cringed.

"Please, don't kill me. I won't go to the police," he pleaded.

"Sure you will. Why wouldn't you? We took everything from you, right?" Sunday replied chillingly.

Without hesitation, she fired the gun and shot Adyen in the head. Sunday and Recut weren't shocked. They both knew it was coming. All that mattered to them was that they had two duffel bags filled with valuables and cash, more than they had expected.

"Let's go," said Nasir.

Meanwhile, back at Adyen's house, his wife and daughter remained tied to the chair in the master bedroom. Havoc had locked the boys in the closet. However, Sheek was lustfully eyeing the blond-haired and blue-eyed daughter. She was pretty, and he had urges that he couldn't control. He tucked the gun into his waistband and approached the daughter.

"C'mere! Get the fuck up, bitch!" Sheek cursed, roughly pulling the girl from the chair.

The mother wanted to cry out and protect her daughter, but the duct tape covering her mouth made her mute and the rope binding her rendered her powerless.

"Sheek, what the fuck? Really, nigga?" Diane griped.

"Shut the fuck up. I got this! Mind ya fuckin' business!" Sheek scolded.

Diane knew there wasn't anything she could do. Once Sheek had that lustful gleam in his eye, it was over with. Sheek began dragging the daughter out of the room, with her kicking and screaming. The mother angrily squirmed in the chair and began to cry, knowing what would happen to her daughter.

Before Sheek dragged the daughter out of the master bedroom, he glared at the mother and his cohorts and said, "Yo, tie that bitch face down to the bed. She could get it too."

Sheek forced the daughter into the second bedroom and removed the duct tape from her mouth. He kept the bedroom door open and removed the tape because he wanted her mother to hear her daughter's horror. Sheek began to assault the naked girl by punching her in the face; then he roughly subdued her on the bed doggy style and forced himself into the girl. It didn't matter what hole he was in; he was determined to fuck her in all three of them. For fifteen minutes, Sheek brutally raped and assaulted the girl, and her mother heard every sound of it. When he was done with her, he strangled her.

Sheek walked into the master bedroom, shirtless, sweaty, and slightly disheveled. The mother was beside herself with grief. He grinned, nearly satisfied with his horrendous actions.

"Yo, I thought I told y'all to tie that bitch to the bed," Sheek griped.

"Fuck you, nigga. You don't run us. You wanna rape her, you do that shit on your own," Havoc retorted.

Sheek was a monster. His sexual appetite was strong and not quickly curbed. The mother became his second victim. He approached the mother and began to pistol-whip her. And when she was bleeding and barely conscious, Sheek untied her, forced her to the floor, and brutally raped her while Havoc and Diane watched.

"You're a sick muthafucka, Sheek," Diane uttered. "What is wrong with you?"

"I love fuckin' a bitch when they're scared," Sheek replied.

Diane shook her head in disgust.

When he was done, he climbed off the mother and stood over her proudly, admiring his twisted handwork. Sheek looked like he had had a full-course meal. To make matters worse, Sheek decided to urinate on her for fun. The mother remained on the floor, whimpering, bleeding, and despondent. They'd taken everything from her. While Sheek was urinating on the mother, Havoc's cell phone rang. It was Sunday calling.

"What's up?" answered Havoc.

"We good. Clean it up and meet us you know where," said Sunday, speaking in code.

Havoc nodded. "Okay."

Havoc looked at Diane and Sheek and said, "It's time to go."

Sheek smiled. He stared at the mother and mockingly uttered, "It's been fun." Then, he shot his gun at her twice, killing her instantly.

"What about the two boys in the closet?" asked Sheek.

Sheek and Diane looked at Havoc, pushing him to do the dirty work.

"Go ahead, white boy. Earn your stripes today," said Sheek.

Havoc sighed. Killing kids was hard and off-limits, but he was under pressure. And Havoc wanted to prove to this crew that he was capable and built to kill like they were. So reluctantly, Havoc gripped the .45 and slowly made his way to the closet. He opened the door and stared at the two boys tied on the floor. They stared back at him with worry and panic in their eyes. Havoc wanted to get it over with. So he aimed the gun and fired rapidly inside the closet, instantly killing both children. He knew he was going to hell for this.

Sheek grinned. "You a real nigga, Havoc."

The three gathered the valuables they'd collected throughout the house and climbed into the wife's Benz, parked in the garage. It was still early morning when they exited the garage and hurried away from the house, leaving behind a tragedy. Everyone believed they'd hit the jackpot by hitting the jewelry store and the mansion-style home.

Six

The trip to upstate New York was quiet and nerve-racking for many inmates on the prison bus headed to Elmira Correctional Facility, also known as "the Hill." It was a maximum-security state prison in Chemung County, New York. Nearly a dozen prisoners were being transferred to the state prison via the prison bus, a highly protected vehicle with bars and wire mesh over the windows, bulletproof glass, segregated prisoner compartments, and additional seating for escorting officers. The prisoners remained quiet, and the only sound was the large diesel engine humming loudly as the bus traveled slowly through the mountains toward the correctional facility. They would soon arrive at their new home. For some, the state prison would become a permanent residence.

One prisoner on the bus was Rondell. He sat shackled and handcuffed and stared out the window with a deadpan gaze, eyeing the rural scenery of upstate New York. Some inmates were new and nervous, and would be fresh meat for some seasoned inmates. Others were trying to act like they were hard. Rondell was the real deal: a dangerous man with high-end connections everywhere. This wasn't Rondell's first rodeo inside a state prison. He stood six-two and had a slim but intimidating physique, a thick goatee, and a little Afro. And nearly 90 percent of his body was covered with gang tattoos and war scars. At the age of twenty-nine, Rondell was the epitome of a gangster.

The bus arrived at Elmira Correctional Facility, and one by one, the guards escorted the shackled and handcuffed inmates off the bus. The facility was like a castle on a hill, one that looked impenetrable. Rondell moved with the other arriving inmates into the giant prison and entered the receiving and discharge section. The new arrivals were going to be cataloged and inventoried. They were coldly greeted by the prison captain, Markest Wagstaff, a towering black man, and his lieutenant, Sydnor Freemon, surprisingly another black man with authority in the rural prison. Their attitude condescending, both men in charge scowled as they stood in front of the inmates.

"Welcome to your worst nightmare, gentlemen, a maximum state prison. You all are here because you don't know how to behave in society. You are all fuckups, degenerates, and lowlifes in my book. And some of y'all may be considered dangerous men. Well, guess what? In this facility, in my home, if you act up, misbehave, or fuck up, there will be consequences for your fucking actions," Captain Wagstaff proclaimed sternly.

He slowly and menacingly walked by each inmate, glaring at them, including at Rondell, who stood and stared deadpan at nothing in particular.

"I am responsible for every inmate and staff member's safety and security. First, you make my job hard, then I make things hard for you. Do you understand me?"

A few prisoners nodded.

"This is one of my trusted lieutenants in this place, Lieutenant Freemon. He's here to handle the day-to-day decision-making, and you do not want to get on his or my bad side. And while you're in my home, you will refer to him and me as 'sir' and will answer, 'Sir,' 'Yes, sir,' or 'No, sir.' Do you understand me?"

They did.

Captain Wagstaff continued to give them his uninspiring welcome speech while Rondell remained deadpan. The inmates stood still and quiet, like they were in a military boot camp and the correctional officers were the drill sergeants.

"And here comes the fun part, gentlemen. We get you cleaned up and ready for your new home," said Captain Wagstaff mockingly.

Every man stripped off his clothing until he was completely naked. All the men were then thoroughly searched for any contraband. The inmates stood before several correctional officers, who ran fingers through their hair, made them open their mouths, and then had them squat and cough. Also, their blood was drawn, they showered, and their hair was sprayed with white vinegar, which supposedly killed lice. Next, they were given official state jumpers and cheap sneakers.

Being processed and entering incarceration became a reality. At this point, the inmates realized there was no turning back and no chance of an alternative to imprisonment. No one wanted their concern to show, since looking scared was a sign of weakness. Elmira Correctional Facility was big, loud, busy, and intimidating. It housed some of the worst of the worst, and you either became a predator or prey.

After receiving their bedrolls and other items, the new arrivals entered the housing units, or general population, joining over two thousand inmates.

"Oh shit. We got some fresh fuckin' meat!" an inmate shouted at the new arrivals.

"Yo, c'mere, sweet cheeks. You lookin' pretty in that color," shouted another inmate to a particular newbie.

"Oh, yeah! Oh, yeah, don't get scared now."

"It's on tonight!"

Some inmates shouted out their gangs and affilia-tions. It seemed like organized chaos as the newbies walked through the central part of the prison. Heavy metal gates clank open and shut while they shuffled in single-file lines, guided by a few guards. The chatter, shouts, and crackling of radios echoed. Not every new ar-rival was shaking with anxiety and nervousness. Rondell walked with the others with a deadpan gaze. He was new to Elmira, but this wasn't his first rodeo behind bars. Rondell had done time in Clinton and Sing Sing, and he knew how to integrate into prison life. Oddly, a few in-mates recognized Rondell, but they kept quiet about it.

Each newbie was assigned a prison cell on a three-tiers.

"Rondell, welcome to your new home," said the guard.

Rondell coolly entered the seven-by-fourteen-foot cell, which featured only a metal toilet and sink and a bunkbed. Another inmate occupied the bottom bunk. The cell door closed behind Rondell, and he stood there quietly, eyeing the man on the bottom bunk.

"Listen clearly, nigga. I'm gonna need that bottom bunk," Rondell said to his new cellmate.

The man on the bunk stood up; he was tall and phys-ically strong, with tattoos indicating his gang affiliation. He glared at Rondell and retorted, "What the fuck you say?"

"You know who the fuck I am, nigga?" Rondell shot back.

The man clenched his fists and scowled at Rondell. He wasn't about to be punked by his new cellmate, but Rondell had made it clear he wasn't going to back down. Rondell's eyes were black, cold, and menacing. He was ready to snap his cellmate's neck right where he stood if needed.

Suddenly, it registered to the cellmate who Rondell was. *Fuck!* he thought. The man nervously uttered, "My bad. The bottom bunk is all yours."

Rondell smirked. "What's your name, nigga?" he asked. "Joe-Joe," his cellmate replied.

"We ain't gonna have any problems, right?"

"Nah, we good," Joe-Joe replied.

Rondell began to settle in on the bottom bunk. This place would be his home for nearly two decades, and he would make the best of things. Rondell had been hit with a twenty-year prison sentence for second-degree murder, manslaughter, and conspiracy. Following his uncle's advice, Rondell decided to take a plea deal. It would be best for the family, his uncle had suggested. Besides, they had unfinished business to take care of.

"Joe-Joe, let me ask you a question," said Rondell.

"What is it?"

"Who the fuck is Sincere? I heard he the nigga running things in here," said Rondell.

Sincere winced from the pain he felt when he woke up in the local hospital. He was shocked to still be alive, but he was. He had been transferred to the local hospital, where doctors had had to perform emergency surgery to save his life. He was in critical condition, but so far he had beaten the odds. Sincere opened his eyes and saw that he was handcuffed to the bed and that a guard was posted outside his room. Initially, it all felt like a blur, but then he remembered everything that had happened. They'd tried to kill him.

"You're lucky to be alive," said the nurse as she entered his room to check his vitals.

"Am I?" Sincere responded.

"They're discharging you tomorrow and sending you back to the prison," she said.

"I can't wait," Sincere replied sarcastically.

The nurse chuckled. She was black, short, and cute. She'd been one of the primary nurses who attended to his care. She did find him attractive, but he was a convict. Sincere had spent two weeks recovering in the hospital. Now that he was awake and recuperating, he'd been evaluated by the medical staff. They had determined Sincere was medically stable and was ready to be discharged.

"You're one lucky son of a bitch. You should be dead," said the guard watching him.

"It's gonna take much more than two inmates and two corrupt guards to finish me off," Sincere replied haughtily.

"You just need to watch your back, Sincere," said the guard.

Sincere knew the guard was right, but the million-dollar question was, who'd put the hit out on his head? The first person that came to his mind was Nasir. They were now estranged, and Nasir had his reasons, but Sincere knew Nasir didn't have the kind of muscle and influence to attack him inside the prison. The last he'd heard, Nasir had left New York after Denise was killed, and he hadn't been heard from since.

Sincere had made a lot of enemies over the years, and there was a list of people that probably wanted him dead. He'd become a shot caller inside the prison, so the hit could have also come from a jealous inmate looking to make a name for himself. Sincere knew he needed to find out what the fuck was going on. They'd come at him hard and fast, and if he hadn't reacted in a timely fashion, he would be dead.

The following morning Sincere was released from the local hospital and transferred to the prison infirmary for a few more days of recuperation and observation. While in the local hospital, Sincere had faced some discrimination from the hospital staff and other patients. Security had been assigned to his room to ensure everyone's safety. And he'd been under constant supervision. It was known that he was a cold-blooded killer, a big deal, and a distraction. People were afraid of him. His actions had made the news a few years ago, and his name rang bells.

In everyone's eyes, he was considered one of the most dangerous men in America.

For the return to the facility, he was handcuffed, shackled, and escorted onto the prison bus. Though he still needed to heal, Sincere felt in good shape. He'd beaten the odds. He rode quietly back to the state prison. There was a lot to think about.

After finally arriving at Elmira Correctional Facility, he had to undergo a thorough strip search, including a body cavity search, though he was still recovering from the attempt on his life. Word quickly spread through the prison that Sincere was back, and everyone figured there was going to be hell to pay for those who had tried to take his life.

Seven

Life is short, and death is forever! And death doesn't discriminate.

It was almost evening when Detective Chris Emmerson and his new partner, Shelly Mack, arrived at the mansion-style home in an affluent neighborhood in Queens. The day had been warm, the sun was setting behind the horizon, and death was forever! The property was already a circus of police, media, and shocked neighbors, who outside the crime scene, which was meant to be a home with a family. When the detectives received the call, they both knew it would be bad, and so they gave this investigation priority status. But they had no idea what they were about to walk into.

Detective Emmerson sat behind the steering wheel, looking a bit hesitant. Finally, Detective Mack looked at him and asked, "Are you okay, partner?"

"Yeah. I'm fine. Give me a moment, will you? I'll be right behind you," he responded.

Detective Mack nodded. Clad in a dark gray pantsuit, she climbed out of the black Crown Vic and coolly approached the home. Shelly Mack was a pretty black woman with curves and ass but a hard exterior. She was from Brownsville, Brooklyn, had grown up rough and poor, and had become a cop after high school because she wanted to make a difference in her community. She did three years in the NYPD's Gang Division before transferring to become a homicide detective.

Emmerson stared at her for a moment and sighed. They'd been partners for a few months now. And at first, he'd been against it. But Shelly Mack was becoming a female Michael Accosta. She was sharp, witty, and demanding. And she was on her way to becoming a top-notch detective.

Detective Emmerson continued to be haunted by his partner's suicide. Things weren't the same without Accosta around—the job wasn't the same. Accosta was a good cop and one helluva detective. He was able to see things with a third eye. He was a celebrated and respected officer with many merits. His suicide didn't make sense to Detective Emmerson. He had gone through a lot in the past year or so. There'd been therapy, grief, doubt, and guilt. He'd been torn apart, wishing he could rewind time and prevent the suicide from happening. Every day Emmerson questioned himself. What could he have done differently? What had he missed? Why had Accosta done it? During one stretch of time, Emmerson felt angry at his old partner, believing he was selfish by eating his gun and taking his own life. No one had seen it coming, but should they have?

Cops killed themselves every year. The same year Detective Accosta killed himself, eight other officers committed suicide. It was becoming an epidemic. And the crisis had led the department to create a new confidential suicide prevention program. But it was too late for Emmerson's partner. It was absolute heartbreak, and Emmerson had to fight from falling into a deep depression. It was bad enough that he saw the worst of humanity up close and personal every day. But it was frightening to experience a personal tragedy this close to home, and it was frustrating that he had not known that his partner—his friend and a brother—was thinking about taking his own life.

After Detective Michael Acosta's funeral, Emmerson's captain told him to take some time off to be with his family—and to heal personally. It was mandatory. The last thing the department needed was another burnt-out detective grieving over his partner's death. So, he took his family to Disney World for a few days. The trip was expensive, but it was worth it. It took the edge off to be surrounded by adorable Disney characters, phenomenal attractions, thrilling theme park rides, sunshine and warm weather, and his wife and kids. And Emmerson was able to smile and laugh. He needed the trip, and it might have saved his life.

But a few weeks later, it was back to his reality and back to the real world, a dramatic contrast to Disney World. In Emmerson's world, Mickey Mouse was holding a smoking .45, standing over the bodies of Goofy and Donald Duck, who owed him drug money. Minnie Mouse was a prostitute turning tricks a block away from the castle, Pluto was a vicious pit bull, and Disney World was a dangerous criminal empire.

Finally, Emmerson climbed out of the Crown Vic and began walking toward the house. It was a quiet community, and the place looked too lovely to believe something horrific could have occurred there. But being a seasoned detective, Emmerson knew evil didn't discriminate. And the dark and foreboding atmosphere of the crime scene began to make him uneasy. When he entered the home, it screamed to him that it was family oriented. The place's décor was high-end, and there were pictures of the family everywhere—a loving husband, his beautiful wife, and their doting kids. And now some kind of monster had entered their perfect lives and ended them.

"The nightmare is upstairs," said a cop on guard.

Detective Emmerson joined his partner inside the master bedroom and saw the body of a naked and battered woman on the floor. Shelly Mack was crouched near the body, gloved up and examining the scene with soft eyes. Then he saw the bodies of two young boys in the closet, who had been shot execution-style, and the scene became even more horrendous.

"What are they? Nine, maybe ten years old?" said Emmerson.

"There's a naked teenage girl in the second bedroom. She appears to have been raped," said Detective Mack.

Detective Emmerson entered the second bedroom to find a pretty teenage girl lying on her back on a beautiful queen-size bed. She was naked and had been badly beaten and raped. Her eyes were still open and were protruding slightly from her face. He could sense the fear she'd felt. Emmerson immediately noticed the marks around her neck and knew she'd been violently strangled. He sighed heavily. "Damn, she suffered," he uttered.

The crime scene photographer rapidly snapped pictures of the body while Emmerson examined the bedroom. It was a teenage girl's bedroom, pink and purple, with teddy bears and pop star and rap artist posters lining her walls. It was full of youthfulness, colors, and her life. It reminded him of his own daughter's bedroom.

"Take a few pictures of the room too," he told the photographer.

She nodded and began doing so. The bedrooms where the murders had occurred were surprisingly pristine, despite the fact that they were the site of so much violence.

Detective Emmerson rejoined his partner in the main bedroom, and together they tried to deduce what had happened. The police had gone through the entire house and had seen that it had been ransacked. The medical examiner had determined that the victims' time of death was twenty-four hours ago, based on the victims' stage of rigor mortis, which usually lasted from one to four days. But the chaotic state of the crime scene made it somewhat challenging to determine what exactly had happened throughout the carnage and *why*.

"Home invasion gone wrong?" Mack uttered.

"Where's the husband?" Emmerson wondered aloud.

It was a good question. A neighbor had called in the tip. She'd felt something was afoul when the mother didn't take her kids to school on time this morning. The neighbor, Mrs. Simmons, had told the cops that Mrs. Rockford was a creature of habit. She would take the kids to school, meet her for their daily exercise, and walk at the gym. So when Mrs. Rockford didn't show up, and the kids were absent from school, the neighbor knew something was wrong. And when she found their front door unlocked and both of their cars missing from the garage, she was beyond convinced.

The detectives planned to have DNA collected from the woman and the girl. If they'd raped, hopefully, their attacker(s) hadn't used a condom, and maybe his or their information was in the system. Detective Emmerson knew how imperative it was to solve this case; it was quickly becoming a high-profile case.

"So, where's the husband?" Mack questioned.

Suddenly, Detective Emmerson's cell phone rang, and recognizing the number, he answered it. He received the news about the husband being killed at his place of business in Jackson Heights, and hearing that changed everything. Emmerson ended the call and looked at his partner.

"They found the husband shot dead at his jewelry store in Jackson Heights," said Emmerson.

Detective Mack was stunned by the news. "Shit. This was planned and organized. This crew knew what they were doing. This wasn't their first rodeo. They stalked this family and waited for the right time."

Detective Emmerson agreed. What were they dealing with? And how many were involved? These were burning questions, and he and wanted to get answers to them as soon as possible. The crime scene was chaotic, but the detectives tried to gather as much evidence as possible. The two of them were determined to find these killers. They'd two young boys, a teenage girl, and the children's parents, totally destroying a family. And Emmerson and Mack feared this was only the beginning. Whoever this crew was, the detectives were certain they were going to strike again.

Eight

The Gulfstream private jet quickly descended toward the runway. It landed at a Long Island airport on a clear and sunny day. The private plane taxied toward the nearest terminal. And when the door opened and the stairs came down, customs agents were already waiting for Zodiac's arrival from Africa. He was on their radar, and several agents were waiting to board his plane and check the passengers' documentation. Zodiac was a patient man and had expected this. Minutes later the agents boarded the aircraft and collected passports and certain documents from the passengers. Then they conducted a quick inspection. Zodiac wasn't concerned about the agents inspecting his aircraft. He was clean. However, he needed clarification about what had taken place in Ghana. He was frustrated.

The moment he disembarked from the private jet, his cell phone rang. It was Joc calling him. Zodiac answered immediately.

"I heard about the attempt on your life, Zodiac, and I assure you I had nothing to do with it," said Joc.

"My woman was with me, and if it wasn't for the car being bulletproof, they would have succeeded," Zodiac exclaimed.

"I promise you, I'll find out what happened here. And if it was any of my people, they will be dealt with, eh. You have my word, Zodiac," said Joc wholeheartedly.

"I know. And thanks," Zodiac replied half-heartedly before they ended the call.

Zodiac didn't know what or whom to believe. But it wouldn't have made sense for Joc to try to have him killed. They were in business together, and Zodiac had an extensive network in the States that would benefit Joc. And the attempt on his life had come right after Zulu's death. So Zodiac knew it wasn't a coincidence. He didn't believe in coincidence; nothing happened by chance. This was an organized and strategic hit implemented in a foreign place. And someone had a reason to come after Zulu and him, and unfortunately, they had succeeded with Zulu. But why and who?

"What did he say?" Trina asked him.

"It wasn't him."

"Do you believe him?"

"Why would he attack us after everything went so well?" said Zodiac.

"I wouldn't trust anyone, Zodiac. Whoever attacked us knew exactly where to find us, and they came at us with everything they had. They wanted us dead in Africa, Zodiac," Trina replied.

He found being attacked suddenly in Africa while on business, Zulu being killed, and not knowing who your enemy was daunting. Was the perpetrator a foe pretending to be a friend?

Customs finished their routine search of the plane and disembarked. Zodiac stared at them deadpan, but he was really annoyed. He had a lot on his mind, and the last thing he wanted to deal with was the authorities. Zodiac and Trina deplaned and then made their way toward the idling black luxury Escalade waiting for their arrival. Idling behind their black Escalade was a black Tahoe filled with armed goons for their protection. Zodiac wasn't taking any chances with his life or Trina's. They were at war, but the scary thing about it was they had no idea with whom.

Once Zodiac and Trina were seated inside the Escalade, the vehicles drove off. Zodiac sat back, with Trina in his arms. It was good to be back home. Spending time in Africa had benefited their business, but to them, there was no place like America, the land of the free. Thinking about the word *free*, Zodiac chuckled slightly.

"What's so funny?" asked Trina.

"Nah, nothing. I was just thinking about something."

"I'm glad to see you can find humor in something when we were nearly killed in Africa," said Trina agitatedly.

"I'm going to find out who tried to come at us. And when I do, God help 'em, because I'm gonna get biblical with their asses," Zodiac replied animatedly.

Trina smiled. "I know you will, baby."

They arrived at their luxurious Manhattan penthouse late that afternoon. The driver steered the armored black Escalade to the front of the towering building. And when the security unit was confident everything was safe, the two climbed out of the SUV and hurried into the building. Zodiac was greeted by Frank, the man who was head of their security team.

"Everything's clear," Frank said to Zodiac. "My team swept the entire place, top to bottom. And we updated the system and cameras while you were in Africa. So you have no worries, Mr. Joseph. Your safety is in great hands. We'll protect you and your woman better than the president. We're good at what we do."

Zodiac nodded. He wanted to be untouchable and impervious to any attacks. He was not only a drug kingpin, but he'd also become a prominent businessman by learning from the best. He wore two faces and had two lives—the streets and the world of a venture capitalist. He had a net worth north of sixty million dollars and was linked to well-known hedge funds and investment banking. Yet he wasn't taking any chances with his life. A new threat out there wanted him dead. So far, it was unseen. Although Zodiac had his street goons and killers on standby to combat his rivals, Zodiac had called in a mini army to watch over him and Trina. This team included eight personal bodyguards on twenty-four-hour watch and a twenty-man security group. A few of his private security guards were former intelligence agents and ex-marines. Zodiac had spent an outrageous amount on revamping his entire security team. The cost was in the ballpark of four million dollars.

Zodiac and Trina entered their penthouse apartment, and it was a place to marvel over. The penthouse's wraparound terrace featured a magnificent unobstructed view of Central Park and an unparalleled skyline view of New York City. The impeccable four-bedroom and three-and-a-half-bathroom corner unit featured eleven-foot ceilings and floor-to-ceiling windows, which flooded the rooms with natural light. It was luxury at its finest.

The first thing Zodiac did when he arrived home was head to his bar and pour himself a needed drink. He downed that and poured himself another one. He had a lot on his mind. Then Trina approached him and threw her arms around him to comfort him. She didn't want to worry him, but she was worried.

"Are you hungry?" she asked him.

"I can't eat right now. I need to think," he replied.

"You sure? I can make you something, or we can—"

"I said I'm fine, Trina," Zodiac barked, interrupting her.

"You know I'm always here for you whenever you need me."

"I know. I just wanna be alone. Okay?"

Trina huffed and left him alone. She decided to get more comfortable in their bedroom while Zodiac poured himself another glass of liquor.

Zodiac stepped out onto the wraparound terrace and stared at the sweeping view of Central Park, his liquor glass in hand. It was a view to die for . . . breathtaking. This was something he'd always dreamed about, having lots of money and being able to do what the fuck he wanted without any restrictions. It was about power and having control of your own destiny. Zodiac had hated being poor. He'd come a long way from the streets of Jamaica, Queens. And now he was becoming one of the most influential figures in the city. He was wealthy, powerful, and becoming significant. But he thought about Zulu and Mob Allah, and it bothered him that he was the last man standing. They'd grown up together, become brothers from another mother, and always had each other's back. In the late eighties, they'd started the Supreme Nation gang to emulate the notorious Supreme team. He, Mob Allah, and Zulu had been ambitious young teens and had yearned to have the same respect their elders, like Supreme, Fat Cat, and Prince, had in the streets.

Mob Allah was older by three years. And he was the top dog, the man in charge, and the one to follow. He was charismatic, intelligent, motivated, and ruthless. Mob Allah had taken Zodiac and Zulu under his wings and taught them how to live on the streets—and how to hustle. He'd become a mentor to them, and it was a painful for Zodiac when they had to kill their mentor, Mob Allah. But Zulu assured him it needed doing for their survival. Mob Allah had changed, and he'd become sloppy. Sincere had made them look weak, and their lawyer had made them vulnerable. For a few days, Zodiac was beside himself with guilt and anguish, but he understood it was business, nothing personal.

Zulu had promised that they wouldn't make the same mistakes Mob Allah did. Instead, they would become more prominent, better, wiser, and more prosperous. Zulu had kept his promise. They'd insulated themselves from the streets and the daily activities of their drug empire. And they'd laundered so much drug money through cash businesses, corporations, investments, fundraisers, real estate, and so on. Zodiac was sitting on a fortune now. On paper, he looked like Warren Buffet. He had more money than he could spend, and he wielded more than enough power and influence to assassinate anyone, from local hood niggas to politicians and rival drug kingpins.

But who was out to kill him?

Zodiac lingered on the terrace and watched the sunset. His eyes became fixed on the glorious colors of the sky above Central Park. It was a perfect conclusion to his day. *What's going to be my fate?* Zodiac thought to himself.

He and Zulu had killed Mob Allah; then Zulu had gone to federal prison for life, and now someone had killed him. Zodiac couldn't help but think about his own fate. He was doing everything he could to avoid ending up like his two former friends. This criminal life, this wearing two masks out in public, sometimes Zodiac felt it came more with downs than ups. He wanted to become legit and leave this life behind, but he was in too deep. He'd spent nearly twenty years in the game, putting in the needed work in the streets for his gang to advance and become notorious. He'd caught his first body when he was seventeen years old. He'd looked up to Mob Allah and Zulu and wanted to make an impression on them.

Now he was on his own, the HNIC (Head Nigga In Charge), and there was no one else for him to impress. Everyone wanted to make an impression on him. *Heavy's the head that wears the crown*, he thought. And a man in his position might seem popular, but Zodiac knew king-pin criminal charges were real, with severe consequences.

The last thing he wanted was to end up like his former brothers in crime with a series of harsh charges and the potential of spending decades in prison.

Zodiac huffed. First, he needed to uncover the threat against him. He placed his glass on the ledge and made a phone call. He knew having information was imperative to stay alive and ahead of your enemies. The more you knew, the stronger you became.

The phone rang, and someone answered, "Yeah?"

"We need to meet. I have a job for you," said Zodiac.

"When and where?"

"Tomorrow night, Chelsea Piers," Zodiac said.

"I'll be there."

Zodiac ended the call and remained on the terrace, looking pensive. He wasn't going to end up like Mob Allah and Zulu. And he was willing to do everything possible to prevent that fate.

Nine

Miami was a vibrant city, a coastal metropolis with a distinctly tropical vibe, beautiful beaches, and year-round sunshine. And it had a nonstop nightlife, an unparalleled party scene, first-class hotels, pristine beaches, and second-to-none dining. Why would anyone want to leave the city?

It was a beautiful night, with a glowing full moon, and South Beach's nightlife was bustling. A white Range Rover crossed over the MacArthur Causeway and arrived at a popular club in South Beach named Studio 69. It was a vibrant and fashionable two-story club with an open courtyard. The Range Rover stopped right in front of Studio 69. A line outside the place wrapped around the corner. Security outside and inside was top-notch, the people were attractive, and the music was bumping. Finally, the rear door to the Range Rover opened, and Cashmere climbed out of the SUV, clad in a provocative bright red cocktail midi dress that highlighted her curves and stylish stilettos. Her hair was no longer styled in a French bun but fell to her shoulders, and her neck and wrists were bedecked with diamonds. Cashmere was a tall African American beauty. She was ripped, as if steel cables moved under her smooth dark skin. Out of the Range Rover also climbed two beefy men dressed in black.

All eyes were on Cashmere and the two goons in black as she was met at the entrance by security, who quickly recognized her and allowed her to effortlessly slide by them. Techno music blared throughout the large-scale club. Its driving beat, synthesized melody, and heavy bass drum sound energized the revelers underneath the dancing disco lights. It was a packed place. Her goons parting the crowd for her like the Red Sea, Cashmere easily moved through the club. She made her way to a set of stairs guarded by well-dressed security. They, too, recognized her, and she was allowed to pass. As she went up the stairs, her two goons stood below patiently.

Cashmere walked down a short, narrow hallway and entered a private office that was attractively decorated with pricey artwork, leather sofas, and several flat-screen TVs, which were monitoring every inch of the night-club. Immediately, she smiled at a man named Ezekial Montoya. He was seated behind his desk in a high-back leather chair, watching the security monitors. And on the other side of the office was a large, plain glass wall overlooking the dance floor and bar below.

"It's done," Cashmere declared proudly. "Down to the last nickel has been wired into one of your offshore accounts, and whatever properties Zulu had left were liquidated. And like I promised him, he's been released from maximum security."

Ezekial smiled. "It's why I love you, Cashmere. You never fail me."

Cashmere nodded and smiled. "It's what I do."

"I should have put you in charge of that other thing too," said Ezekial. "It would have been handled appropriately."

"I assume it didn't go as planned."

Ezekial frowned. He then stood up from his high-back leather chair and walked toward the plain glass wall. Cashmere joined him and stood by his side. Perched in the private office, the two peered down at the many revelers on the dance floor. They were jumping up and down to the techno music and having a good time. They looked like they didn't have a care in the world. And the five bartenders behind the long full bar were hard at work fulfilling drink orders. Studio 69 was one of Ezekial's many cash cows. The ten-thousand-square-foot space boasted state-of-the-art technology, large LCD flat-screens, a full bar, and multiple VIP suites.

"Look at them, a medley of characters and personalities crammed together in my nightclub to forget about their troubles out there. A real buzz of energy has infused the revelry and enjoyment. It's why I love Miami," Ezekial stated out of the blue.

"People like to have a good time," Cashmere replied.

"Indeed. All of 'em out there are nothing but sheep in a lion's den," said Ezekial.

Ezekial was a towering man—he stood six-one—with an intimidating physique. He wore a dark gray three-piece suit and had a gleaming bald head and a beard so thick he could conceal a weapon in it. A transnational drug trafficking kingpin, the leader of an illicit multi-national operation, he was an incredibly wealthy and powerful man. Ezekial, a man in his early fifties, was so feared and connected that he was considered a threat to national security. He was intelligent, brutal, handsome, calculating, and untouchable.

Ezekial shifted his attention to Cashmere. She was a raging beauty, an African filly who quickly had men swooning and eating out of her hands. She was educated and smart, with many awards and several degrees from high-ranking schools. She'd graduated top of her class from Columbia Law School. Thanks to Ezekial's influence, Cashmere was on her way to becoming a senior partner at one of New York's infamous law firms. She was deeply in love with Ezekial, who was twice her age. And she was known to be ruthless.

Ezekial had taken Cashmere from the sewers and gutters of society and shaped her into the woman she was today. Cashmere had grown up in extreme poverty. She was from the South Bronx; she had never known her father, and her mother had been a crack whore. Her grandmother had tried to raise her right, but Cashmere had been a wildcat, and she had taken no shit from anyone. During her youth, she'd done nearly every crime, from shoplifting and selling drugs to committing assault and attempted murder when she was fifteen years old. Cashmere had tried to kill one of Ezekial's street lieutenants, a young goon named Zero. Zero had disrespected Cashmere by calling her out of her name and groping her. And she countered by plunging a knife into his stomach twice. Zero was a violent thug and was feared, yet Cashmere reacted to him like he was an annoying fly. Ezekial was impressed by her fearlessness and her actions. So he bailed her out of jail, made sure the charges were dropped, and took Cashmere under his wing.

Nearly twenty years later, Cashmere's feelings for Ezekial remained the same. Cashmere stared at Ezekial now with admiration. She would do whatever he needed her to do without hesitation, even if he needed her to murder someone. She loved him and felt she owed him everything, including her life.

"You do look beautiful tonight," Ezekial said, complimenting her.

Cashmere beamed. A compliment coming from Ezekial was significant. He stared at her with something more— something enduring. Long ago, their friendship and her apprenticeship with him had become carnal. Ezekial's power, influence, and animalistic mannerisms were such a turn-on to Cashmere that the slightest touch from him made her pussy wet. Cashmere was utterly submissive in the face of Ezekial's dominance. But if anyone else tried to dominate her, she would cut off their balls and hang them around her neck.

They stood closer to each other near the plain glass wall overlooking the dance floor, the partygoers below raging on to the techno beat. Ezekial placed his hand between Cashmere's thick thighs and coolly glided it upward, noticing she had on no panties, and cupped her pussy. Cashmere moaned slightly, feeling his fingers move inside her. While he fingered her, she began massaging his crotch, creating an erection inside his pants. Next, she casually unzipped his pants, pulled out his big black dick, and began stroking him nice and slow. Then she lowered herself before Ezekial, ready to take his hard dick in her mouth. The only thing on Cashmere's mind was pleasing him. And she began doing so, placing his hard, big dick in her mouth and taking him all the way in. Her head bobbed up and down while she cupped his balls. Ezekial thrust into her mouth. He looked down at her as she stared up at him.

"I want you inside me," Cashmere uttered. Her voice oozed sex, and her eyes flared with hungry lust.

She rose from her position, her arms sliding up Ezekial's back as she stood. His dick was still hard, and he was ready to fuck her on his desk. Cashmere lifted her cocktail midi dress, exposing her ample butt cheeks. Ezekial was ready to curve her over his desk and fuck her doggy style. Unfortunately, a sudden knock at the office door disrupted their sexual tryst.

Ezekial glanced at the security monitor and saw it was one of his lieutenants, Moses, outside the office door.

"We're going to have to continue this next time," said Ezekial.

Cashmere frowned and huffed. When he opened the door to allow Moses in, Cashmere scowled at him so hard he almost turned into stone.

"Boss, we're ready," said Moses.

Ezekial nodded and replied, "We'll be out in a few minutes."

"Are we going somewhere?" asked Cashmere.

"I have to address a problem," said Ezekial.

Ezekial and Cashmere left the office, hurriedly moved through the place, exited the nightclub through the back door, and climbed into an idling luxury black Escalade. At the same time, several goons made it their business to protect them by any means necessary. Everyone treated Ezekial and Cashmere like royalty, like the president and the First Lady.

The ride to their destination, on the other side of Miami, was quiet. Ezekial seemed deep in thought about something. They soon arrived at a remote warehouse a few miles from the Everglades. Ezekial and Cashmere climbed out of the Escalade and entered the building. Right away, they were greeted by a man named Doc, a haunted, odd individual with a penchant for violence, torture, and bloodshed. Doc was a thin, dark man with a buzz cut fade, scars, and burns, and he wore round bifocals.

"We could have done it my way, Ezekial. They fucked it up. I should be the one to deal with them," Doc griped.

"Not now, Doc. Next time you'll get the glory. I promise you. But this . . . I want it to be messy and ugly," Ezekial replied. "They failed me."

Doc nodded.

Cashmere followed behind Ezekial as they marched farther into the warehouse and entered a drab room with cinder-block walls and no windows. The faint smell of cleaning chemicals lingered in the air. Over a dozen men were in the room, awaiting Ezekial's arrival. Standing in a back corner were two of Ezekial's dog handlers, each clutching a long chain with a large and muscular pit bull at the end of it. The dogs were barking loudly and were ready for some action. Something was brewing, and it wasn't going to be pretty.

Ezekial walked, unafraid, toward the two pit bulls and crouched down to greet them like they were his sons.

"Look at my two bitches. Y'all excited, huh? Yeah, I know y'all are. But I want y'all to put in some work for me, let these fools know I don't like failure," Ezekial uttered, stroking the dogs' heads.

The dogs' teeth had been filed down to make them as sharp as possible in order to inflict maximum damage, their eyes appeared bloodshot, and their upper-body strength was menacing. With their ferocious appearance, the dogs looked like two hellhounds—creatures straight from the pits of hell. No one other than Ezekial dared to get too close to these creatures and pet them like they were two tiny puppies. Ezekial glanced at the two men handling the pit bulls on their chain leashes and nodded. The men were as eager as the pit bulls to see some action.

"Bring them fools out here now," Ezekial ordered his men.

Two white men were forced into the center of the room a few seconds later, and it was clear that they were captive to their fears. Finally, Ezekial stood up and approached them with a deadpan gaze. His approach was casual, like they were about to discuss business at a café. But they weren't inside a café, having drinks. Both men were absolutely horrified when they noticed the barking and snarling dogs. One man fell to his knees, already begging for mercy.

"Please! Not like this! I have a family," he cried out.

"Ezekial, it wasn't our fault," the second man quickly exclaimed.

"Shut the fuck up!" Ezekial snapped at them.

Ezekial moved aggressively closer to them and glared at them for a moment. His silence was daunting. The room was quiet, besides the dogs barking. Everyone knew what was coming, and it wouldn't be pretty.

Finally, Ezekial spoke. He proclaimed, "Being weak is a choice. So is being strong. And when I paid the two of you an exorbitant amount of money to get something done, I expected the two of you not to make me look weak! You promised it would get done. But it didn't. And not only one, but all three are still alive today! How the fuck does that happen? The two of you made me look fuckin' weak!"

"We hired the best, Ezekial—"

Ezekial immediately grabbed the man by his throat to shut him up and began to squeeze. His strength was remarkable, and the man's eyes began to bulge as he struggled to breathe and pleaded to live with his eyes.

"I don't pay for a fuckin' service. I paid to get results," Ezekial ranted.

Ezekial's fingers continued to dig into the man's neck, and a look of panic and confusion took over the man's face. And when it felt like the man was about to die, Ezekial finally released his stranglehold from the man's neck and stepped back. The man coughed and clutched his throat, breathing again. But he wasn't out of the frying pan yet.

"I'll tell you what. I try to be a fair man. If the two of you survive this, you're forgiven for your failures, and you'll never hear from me again. You have my word," said Ezekial coolly.

Ezekial nodded to his dog handlers, and they moved into the center of the room, the "ring," with their canines. How would the men survive being attacked and mauled by two canines that looked like they could take down King Kong? One of the men tried to escape from the room, but two of Ezekial's men drew guns on him and forced him to stay put.

"Ezekial, please! Don't do this!" the other shouted hysterically.

Ezekial looked at him and coldly replied, "I'll give the two of you ten minutes to survive this. The clock starts now."

Their pleas for mercy fell on deaf ears. Everyone was about to witness some gruesome entertainment. Finally, Ezekial nodded to both dog handlers, and there was no hesitation in releasing the vicious hellhounds. When their chains were unhooked from their collars, both beasts began to charge ferociously at their targets. Immediately, one of the men tried to run, but there was no way out. The second man completely surrendered to his fear and cowardice and quickly fell victim to one of the animals. The beast grabbed the man's right leg, violently brought him to the floor, and then went berserk on his flesh, his jaws like a chain saw. The second canine immediately went in for the kill and lunged for the second man's face and throat.

The second man tried to stand firm and fight the canine off, but it was fruitless. He was easily ripped apart by a pair of sharp teeth. The men's screams were loud and terrifying. The dogs' aggressiveness in the ring was nearly demonic. Pieces of the men began to fly everywhere, and a bloody ear struck Cashmere. She laughed while wiping off the blood on her dress. The men's screaming was loud but fading fast, and it soon came to a sudden stop. The dogs had brutally killed them. They began devouring them savagely, their mouths thickly coated with their blood. The only sound in the room now was the grunting of the dogs as they feasted on their victims. It was a bloodbath.

Cashmere had stood by Ezekial's side and watched the entire thing unfold without cringing or squirming. Seeing

men being ripped apart by two pit bulls was entertainment for her. She even smiled at the viciousness, and it
turned her on. In fact, while she watched it, her hand
gradually moved up her dress, and she began touching
and pleasing herself. A sensual moan escaped from her
lips, and Ezekial noticed her naughty action, and he
grinned. She was a beast herself and borderline psychotic. It was why he loved her. While some of his men
had flinched and cringed at the bloodshed, Cashmere
had become fixated on it.

"We need to do this more often," Ezekial joked.

Cashmere grinned. She wanted Ezekial to fuck her
right there, but they had to wait.

Ezekial huffed. He stepped into the ring while the
canines continued gnawing on the bodies. He released
a loud whistle, and the pit bulls stopped on command.
They sat in the blood of their victims and remained
obedient to their master. As Ezekial stood in the center of
the room, he had everyone's undivided attention. What
they had witnessed was something diabolical. And Doc
and Cashmere were proud to have seen it.

"My sons are dead, while their killers are still alive.
That is unacceptable. And if you fail me, this will be your
fate too!" Ezekial shouted.

Every man in the room heard him loud and clear.
The mutilated bodies of the two white men in the ring
were the motivation they needed not to fail him. Ezekial
wanted war and bloodshed for the deaths of Drip-Drip
and Rafe. And Sincere, Nasir, and Zodiac were all on
his hit list. He wanted them dead, and he wished to tear
down everything they'd built brick by brick. They'd taken
something special from him; now he wanted them to
suffer and die.

Ezekial looked at one of his men and said, "Prepare my
jet. We're leaving for New York in the morning."

He then looked at Cashmere and uttered, "When you make an example of someone, ensure everyone knows the lesson. Punish one, teach a hundred. So now everyone knows not to fail me again."

Cashmere nodded and smiled.

Ten

"It's good to see you back, my nigga," Row said to Sincere. He gave his prison buddy a proud dap and a brotherly hug.

"It's good to be back," Sincere replied.

"You're Superman, Sincere!" Row joked. "They came at you wit' everything, and they still couldn't take you out. You a fuckin' beast, nigga! Real talk, my nigga!"

Sincere was flattered somewhat by his friend's words, but now wasn't the time to praise him for his survival. Although he felt 100 percent again, he had some vital concerns. First, he'd been down for nearly three weeks, and that long absence meant a lifetime in prison.

The two men reconnected in Sincere's jail cell. It was home sweet home again, with barred windows, iron bars, a metal toilet and sink, a thin mattress, a metal desk, and a chair. But things were different now. Pictures of his kids and his books had been taken from his cell, and they'd rummaged through his things. Sincere knew it was the guards who had done this.

Sincere frowned and angrily exclaimed, "They do me like this!"

"Fuck 'em! I got you, my nigga," Row uttered whole-heartedly. "But listen, we need to talk."

"Where's Melody?" Sincere asked him.

Row stared at him, and it was clear that he had some upsetting news to deliver. "She's gone."

"What the fuck you mean, she's gone?" Sincere griped.

"They found out she was in your pocket and that you was fuckin' her, and the warden got rid of her," Row said.

Sincere moaned. "Fuck!"

"Shit has gone bad since they tried to take you out. It's what we need to talk about."

"What the fuck? Talk to me, Row. I need to be in the fuckin' loop," said Sincere. "What the fuck is going on?"

Row was about to talk and pull Sincere's coat to what was happening, but they were interrupted by a passing guard. He stopped at the foot of the cell and frowned at the two men.

"What the fuck y'all talking about?" the guard exclaimed.

"We just hangin', boss," Row replied smugly.

"Well, you need to go hang somewhere else," the guard replied. "Leave, nigga."

Row chuckled, then frowned but relented. "Whatever!"

Sincere frowned at the new guard. Row gave Sincere dap again and exited the cell, scowling at the new guard as he passed him. The guard was tall, black, physically fit, with a military cut—and with a huge chip on his shoulder, for some reason.

"What's your name?" Sincere asked him.

The guard ignored the question and glared at Sincere. He stood at the cell's threshold, eyeballing Sincere, sizing him up.

"You have a fuckin' problem with me?" Sincere griped.

"Yeah, I fuckin' do," the guard retorted.

"You know me?"

The guard smirked and then walked away, leaving Sincere puzzled. What the fuck was that about? Sincere wondered. He knew this new guard might be a problem, not a duck—a gullible or corrupt prison officer who could easily be bribed.

Sincere huffed. He lay down on his cot to get some needed rest. He closed his eyes and began to think about his family. He imagined Monica lying beside him as they snuggled, their kids lying at the foot of their bed. She kissed him and wholeheartedly proclaimed, "I love you." Sincere smiled. He was no longer in hell but at home, enjoying his family, becoming intimate with his woman. Maybe she would become his wife—and maybe she would become pregnant a third time.

Sincere had always wanted a big family, four, maybe five kids—like Cosby or Cliff Huxtable. He had grown up watching *The Cosby Show*. It had been one of his favorite shows. He'd envied the kids on *The Cosby Show*. They not only had both parents in their lives, but also their parents, a doctor and a lawyer, were rich and successful. Living in a Brooklyn brownstone and having many siblings, loving grandparents, a doting mother, a providing father, and a bright future . . . How much better could it get?

Sincere remembered watching *The Cosby Show* at night, while his mother would be sucking dick or doing crack in the adjacent bedroom. Sometimes she would become belligerent toward her children, especially Sincere. And when she went on her crack binges, he and his siblings resorted to self-preservation mode. As he became older, Sincere began to doubt whether *The Cosby Show* reflected real life. *Do black people actually live like that?* He was sure that none in his neighborhood lived that kind of lifestyle. He began to despise niggas like Theo Huxtable—soft muthafucka! Sincere would curse at the TV, knowing a nigga like Theo wouldn't survive one minute in his hood. Subsequently, Sincere became proud of his turbulent upbringing, because it had made him stronger and respected.

But as Sincere rested on his prison cot in his small, dingy cell, consumed with his thoughts, a few tears began trickling down his face. Because he had just had the realization that he wanted to become Theo Huxtable. Most likely, Theo would've married and enjoyed the company of a beautiful wife and his kids. He would have been successful at something and acquired a lovely home a nice car, and a few pets and relished summer vacations. In addition, Theo Huxtable would not have served a lengthy sentence at Emira Correctional Facility.

The bright sun sat high over the high stone walls and the prison yard. The prison yard was full of life, activity, and hazardous tension between the inmates. It was a polarizing place. The prison was a stressful environment, and the yard was where most of the inmates' frustrations were released. A few inmates were busy exercising: doing squats, push-ups, and pull-ups, playing basketball, lifting weights, or spinning the yard.

Sincere entered the yard with an air of power about him and began searching for Row and other associates. All eyes were on him as if he was some kind of magnetic force. Some inmates were happy to see him back, while others were sorry he had survived. Finally, the guards became alert, knowing Sincere's presence was polarizing and threatening to some. Immediately, Row approached Sincere, and they gave each other dap and began to spin the yard.

"Let's talk," said Row.

Sincere and Row were like hamsters in a cage, and spinning the yard felt like walking through an inner-city neighborhood. Although there were no bodegas, bars, or project buildings, the numerous inmates posted every-where made it feel like they were in the ghetto. There were a few inmates who greeted Sincere with a "What's up?" or "One up, my nigga!" followed by a fist bump. However, the two kept walking, deep in conversation.

"Something big is brewing," said Row.

"Like what?"

"I don't know. Shit don't feel right since they tried to take you out, my nigga. Three guards in the pocket, including Melody, are gone, transferred out for no reason. Somebody's moving in, trying to pull strings and rank," said Row.

Sincere huffed. It was bad news, and it was disrupting their money and their way of life. Having a duck in prison, a gullible or corrupt prison officer who could easily be bribed, was imperative, as this person served as a life source.

"So, what's the grape?"

"I think ya being x-ed out," said Row.

"By who, nigga?"

"You know a nigga named Rondell?"

"Nah, never heard of him," Sincere replied.

"Me too. This nigga's been quietly asking around about you. I've been watching this fool and the way he moves. I don't know, Sincere . . . something 'bout him ain't right. I don't like it, and I don't trust this nigga. He's quiet but respected somehow. He came in a week after you got hit, with no noise, no trouble, but with questions."

"You think he's connected, an OG?" asked Sincere.

"He might be. I don't doubt it," Row replied. "The fact that he moves like a wolf but is quiet about it . . ."

"Listen, keep ya ears up and alert. The last thing we need right now is a heat wave in this bitch. I got eyes on me, and muthafuckas lookin' to crucify me, Row. But get this nigga's jacket and see what he's about," said Sincere.

Row nodded. "I'm on it, my nigga. I got you."

Before Row could give Sincere Dap and walk away, Rondell came into their view as he stepped into the yard.

"Speak of the devil. That's the nigga right there." Row pointed him out.

Sincere shot his stern gaze Rondell's way and kept his eyes fixed on the new inmate's movement. Sincere had never seen him before. With his gang tattoos and his imposing build, Rondell screamed gang ties and trouble. Sincere wondered why a nigga like him hadn't made any noise immediately. And why was he asking about him? Who was he? Rondell came to a stop by the entrance and aimed his matching stern gaze at Sincere. Then he smirked and turned his gaze elsewhere. About a minute later two inmates with known gang ties to the Bloods approached Rondell and greeted him respectfully.

Row gave Sincere dap and walked away. Sincere stood on the other side of the yard, observing Rondell's actions, trying to deduce things. He believed it wasn't a coincidence that this new inmate had arrived at Elmira Correctional Facility around the same time an attempt had been made on his life. Sincere diverted his attention from Rondell to another problem that was brewing: the new guard, who was already giving him trouble. He was an asshole, and Sincere despised him. Once again, he thought that it was strange that the three guards he had in his pocket were gone, and now this new guard, their replacement, was giving him problems.

Sincere huffed. Row was right. Something big was brewing, and Sincere knew he would soon get the short end of the stick. He wasn't about to let that happen.

Eleven

Hip-Hop music blared throughout the packed strip club in Brooklyn. Sweet Dreams was a popular underground strip club, with two floors of debauchery and entertainment. The best of the best and the worst frequented the club because of the beautiful women who danced there. The owner of the place made sure he handpicked ladies to work at his club who were the cream of the crop, nothing short of a ten. This was why everyone from hood celebrities to drug kingpins attended the establishment, looking to have a good time, to partake of top-shelf liquor, and to enjoy some extracurricular activities.

A voluptuous, big-booty stripper named Bubbles became the center of attention on the stage. She was thick, curvy, and pretty, a man's wet dream. Butt naked, Bubbles twirled around the pole like she was into gymnastics. She had Sheek's undivided attention. He smiled like a fat kid in a bakery, ready to stuff his face with every cake, cookie, and cupcake. He clutched a fist full of money and was prepared to make it rain on the big-booty stripper.

"Damn, you got my dick hard right now," Sheek shouted. "I want a private dance with you, shorty."

She smiled and moved closer to Sheek, who'd become her number one tipper for the night. He flooded the stage with money and downed expensive champagne. He made it evident to everyone inside the place that he was thirsty for pussy and attention and that he had money to burn. Sheek was sporting a diamond-encrusted pit bull pendant with a matching bracelet and pinkie ring, which he'd recently purchased. He wore new Jordans and designer clothes. His attire was gaudy, and his demeanor was the same.

Bubbles began busting it wide open for Sheek onstage; her energy was vibrant, and Sheek couldn't control himself.

"Yo, I wanna fuck you right now, shorty. I don't give a fuck how much it's gonna cost me. I got it," he proclaimed loudly.

Bubbles grinned and replied, "You think I'm that kind of girl?"

"Name your price and become any kind of bitch I want you to be," he replied brashly and fanned nothing but hundred-dollar bills in front of her and everyone else.

Sheek had nearly five thousand dollars on him, and he was willing to blow through the money on pussy tonight. Besides, he knew there was plenty more where that came from. So he became more aggressive with Bubbles. He groped her ass, squeezed her tits like he owned them, and attempted to push his fingers into her pussy. But Bubbles quickly moved his hand away and frowned.

"Don't do that," she griped.

"Don't do what, bitch?" Sheek uttered.

"I don't know where ya fuckin' hand have been. Don't fuckin' touch me like that," Bubble countered irately.

Sheek downed champagne and shot back, "I know where I want my dick to be. I wanna fuck you right now. What's up, bitch!"

He laughed while massaging his crotch.

Sheek was ready to unzip his jeans, pull out his hard dick, and fuck her on the stage. He didn't give a fuck. He was a brute, a crass and horny one. And he was becoming drunk. He was also beginning to attract unwanted attention his way.

Nasir, Sunday, and Recut noticed the disturbance happening by the stage. They were quietly discussing their next move at a table. Sunday had a connect she wanted Nasir to meet. This would be their step into the drug trade—they planned to buy three kilos from this connect and move it for a healthy profit. Sunday wanted to become a boss bitch. She wanted to wear the crown in New York, especially in Brooklyn, where she'd grown up. She idolized women like Griselda Blanco, Thelma Wright, Enedina Arellano Félix, and Stephanie St. Clair. It was her time, and she planned to move in by force. The problem was finding the right territory to move into. However, Sunday was confident she had a powerhouse of killers and hustlers to back her, because MSK would grow into a machine, and they would be feared like no other.

"You need to get Sheek," said Recut, tipping his head in the direction of the stage.

Sunday frowned. *This fuckin' fool*, she thought. It was always something with him. The last thing they needed was for a fight to break out and the cops to be called. When Sheek became drunk, he became a completely different person, much worse than he was ordinarily. Sheek was dangerous and violent, and Sunday knew he was a few seconds away from assaulting the stripper and everyone around him.

Quickly, Sunday and Nasir intervened, hurrying over to the stage. This was the kind of club where they didn't want any trouble. The owner was connected and hated ignorance and trouble inside his establishment. Sheek was already in Bubbles's face, his fists clenched. He was cursing at her and was ready to strike. But Nasir hurriedly came between the two of them and roughly grabbed Sheek to prevent him from attacking Bubbles.

"Yo, get ya fuckin' hands off me, nigga!" Sheek growled at Nasir.

"You need to chill," Nasir shouted.

"Don't fuckin' tell me what to do, muthafucka! That bitch is being disrespectful. Fuck that bitch! I'ma show her who she fuckin' with."

"You're drunk, nigga!" Nasir hollered.

"I don't give a fuck! That bitch think she better than me!" Sheek hollered.

By now the disturbance by the stage had also grabbed the attention of security, and three men hurried in their direction, their main agenda to protect the dancers from unruly patrons. Sunday frowned. Sheek was creating a scene, and she wanted it to stop. Besides, they'd left their guns in the truck parked outside. So, before security could intervene and interrupt their way of doing things, Sunday stepped toward Sheek and smacked him so hard that the sound echoed through the club. Sheek was stunned, but Sunday wasn't playing games with him, *her little brother*.

"Are you serious, nigga? You're fuckin' embarrassing us, muthafucka!" Sunday heatedly exclaimed. "We're fuckin' leaving! Now!"

All eyes were on them now. Although Sheek towered over Sunday by four inches, it was clear who the dominant authority was. Everyone was taken aback by how Sunday had quickly handled the situation. The strippers and the security personnel were in awe. The last thing Sunday wanted to see was security manhandling and roughing up her little brother. Because if that had happened, she would have gone to the truck, retrieved her pistol, and shot every last one of the security guys dead. Sheek was the only family Sunday had left, and she wanted to protect him, though he was a monster.

Sunday continued to scold Sheek while he marched toward the door. And to smooth things over with security and the club's owner, Sunday handed one of the men a stack, a thousand dollars, and uttered, "I apologize for everything. This should cover the inconvenience."

Even when they were outside the strip club, Sunday did not stop reprimanding her brother. She shouted, "You can be so fuckin' stupid, Sheek! What the fuck is wrong with you?"

Sheek scowled and muttered, "Yo, Sunday, you ain't had to do me like that."

"Look at you, nigga! You're drunk and about to get us fucked up over some bitch . . . some pussy! Get in the fuckin' truck."

"I'm sorry," Sheek said.

"Yeah, you're fuckin' sorry. You need to control your fuckin' drinking and your hormones, nigga. I'm sick of this shit."

Sheek huffed and retreated into the back seat of the Durango. Recut climbed into the truck, too, to keep his friend company. But Nasir and Sunday remained outside for a moment. Nasir stared at Sunday, with something on his mind, and immediately, Sunday picked up on his peculiar gaze.

"What, Nasir? What the fuck is on your mind?" she exclaimed.

"Is he gonna be a problem?" asked Nasir.

"He's my little brother."

"I know that. But he's becoming a problem, Sunday. The drinking, the girls . . . raping them, killing them . . . That ain't us. I don't get down like that."

She chuckled at the statement. "Really? It's a little too fuckin' late for that, right?" Sunday griped. "Don't worry about him. I got this. I got it under control. So don't worry about us."

Nasir huffed. He wanted to believe her, but he knew men like Sheek only became worse with time and would always be a problem.

"Besides, we got to meet with this connect soon. And when that happens, we're gonna be on our way. No more setups and robberies. I want this, Nasir. I wanna be somebody . . . more than some just hood bitch with a crazy little brother. I want the respect. I deserve it." Sunday stared hard at him. "And I want you by my side when it happens," she added.

Nasir smiled slightly. "I'm with you, bae, no doubt."

Sunday smiled back. It was ironic. Sunday had the brightest and nicest smile, but behind that golden sunshine of a smile and those hazel eyes was a ruthless bitch—a killer with a chip on her shoulder. Sunday wanted to become rich and powerful. She wanted to shine by any means necessary.

Sunday placed her arms around Nasir and proclaimed, "I love you, and I can't do this without you."

The two kissed passionately. It was clear she was completely in love with Nasir. They were going to ride or die for each other. She imagined the two of them becoming the twenty-first-century Bonnie and Clyde: feared, rich, and powerful. Sunday suffered from megalomania. She was obsessed with having power and domination over others. And MSK and the drug trade would be the avenue to that power.

"How do I look?" Sunday asked Nasir.

Nasir smiled and replied, "You look phenomenal."

Sunday grinned. That meant a lot coming from Nasir. She stared at him and tried to catch her breath, because her man was taking her breath away. They both were dressed for a night out on the town. Sunday wore a basic seamless black cami dress that accentuated her lovely curves, and her long dreadlocks flowed down her shoulders. Nasir wore a stylish button-down with black dress slacks and had a fresh haircut. Sunday looked beautiful, and Nasir couldn't help but beam with pride.

The two wanted to have a good time tonight. They wanted to take a time-out from the crew and the streets to spend quality time with each other. It was needed. Though Sunday and Nasir were gangsters, they were still human beings with needs and wants. And Sunday wanted to look fabulous tonight, go clubbing, down a few drinks, dance, and enjoy her man's company.

Nasir and Sunday climbed out of the Durango and headed toward the front door of a nightclub in the city called the Shadow. It was an old club located on the west side of Midtown Manhattan. It was an upbeat and warm night in town, and a long line had formed outside the nightclub. However, Sunday and Nasir decided to bypass the end of the line and made a beeline to the front entrance. Immediately, Sunday was recognized by one of the three gorilla-looking bouncers working the door.

She strutted toward the man, with a deadpan gaze, and uttered, "Mookie, I see you're still groping muthafuckas at the door."

"Sunday, what the fuck you doin' back in New York?" the bouncer Mookie asked.

"I miss this hellhole, Mookie. I had to come back."

"I thought you were gone for good."

"Well, this is my home. And besides, I'm back here to take care of some business," said Sunday.

"You just be careful being back," Mookie warned her. "And how's Sheek?"

"Sheek is gonna be Sheek, a pain in my fuckin' ass sometimes."

Mookie chuckled. "That's what little brothers do."

Mookie stared at Nasir and frowned. Sunday took Nasir's hand in hers and pulled him closer and said, "This my boo, Nasir. He's good."

Mookie quickly sized Nasir up and replied, "Whatever! You ran into Squeeze yet? I know he wanna see you while you're in town."

"No, I haven't."

"You need to do that, Sunday. Smooth things over wit' the nigga. Look for him before he comes looking for you," said Mookie.

"Don't worry 'bout me, Mookie. I will."

Mookie nodded and waved them through. Sunday paid the twenty-dollar cover charge for both of them, and they entered the eleven-thousand-square-foot nightclub, which featured a long bar, a main dance area, a tiered area above the floor, and a reggae room to the side. Hip-hop music blared throughout the club, and the main dance floor was packed with well-dressed men and some sexy, scantily clad revelers.

"I wanna grab us a VIP section," said Sunday.

While Sunday strolled away to do her thing, Nasir looked around and took in the club, from the décor to the atmosphere. The Shadow was lively, but he couldn't help but notice several gay men voguing in the middle of the dance floor. And the ladies were beautiful. Going to nightclubs had never been Nasir's thing. He was more of a lounge, bar, and strip club guy. To him, nightclubs were a waste of time with wannabe fools. But this was what Sunday wanted to do.

Soon Sunday returned with a smile. She was clutching a five-hundred-dollar bottle of champagne.

"I got us a section," she declared proudly. Then she led Nasir to it.

They sat down in a spacious booth perched near the dance floor. Sunday was all smiles and was ready to have a good time tonight. She sat close to Nasir and popped open the bottle of champagne.

"Tonight is our night, baby," she proclaimed.

"Who the fuck is Squeeze?" asked Nasir out of the blue.

"He's nobody you need to worry about," Sunday replied nonchalantly.

"Well, Mookie acted like he was important to you."

"You jealous?"

"No. I'm concerned," Nasir countered.

"You don't need to be, baby. It's just some shit in my past and nothing for you to worry about. It was a long time ago," Sunday assured him. "Anyway, we came here to have a good time, right? I don't wanna think about anything else but you tonight. I wanna drink, dance, and fuck."

Nasir chuckled. "You're crazy. You know that, right?"

Sunday grinned. "And it's why you fuckin' love me."

It was actually nice to see Sunday smile. Seeing her in a black dress that accentuated her curves was astonishing to Nasir. Sunday became the center of attention in the middle of the dance floor. She and another gay reveler were competing against each other, doing a dance-off. The way Sunday moved to hip-hop, it seemed like at one time she probably had been a backup dancer to some pop star and thus knew every dance move known to humanity. She was born to dance. She did the pop, lock, and drop it. The shuffle. The Roger Rabbit, the butterfly, the running man, the Cabbage Patch, and the latest dances. Sunday was letting her hair down, becoming loose and fun, laughing and dancing. She was such a great dancer, it was hard to believe that she was killer.

Nasir became fixated as he watched his woman work magic on the dance floor. She was so attractive, and her moves were a turn-on for him. This was a different side to her, one that she kept hidden. It was a side Nasir wished he saw more of. And then, suddenly, Sunday became Denise. Denise became the one voguing with her hands and competing in the dance. Nasir was hallucinating. Denise had that smile that was alluring and fun to see.

"C'mon. I wanna go to the reggae room," Sunday said, taking Nasir by his hand and tearing him away from his sudden hallucination of his ex-girlfriend.

The reggae room was small and dim. It was a different atmosphere. It was where Nasir and Sunday became more intimate with each other. The young women were grinding against the men. Nasir and Sunday had their own personal corner, and there Sunday began gyrating and rolling her hips against her man, like she was slowly twirling a Hula-Hoop. Each slow, grinding rotation matched the beat. Nasir moved his hips in a more subdued fashion. They danced in this way for a few minutes before he pulled her closer and moved his hand up her leg and underneath her dress until he cupped her pussy. He began fingering and groping her while they danced. Sunday loved the subtleness of his probing and how his fingers slid into her.

"*Ooh*, you're being a bad boy, baby," Sunday chuckled.

Nasir grinned.

They continued to dance and grind against each other, and he continued to finger fuck her on the dance floor. Sunday wanted more. She was daring and horny. She wanted to fuck him right there and now. So, Sunday took Nasir by his hand, and they disappeared into the unisex bathroom and went into a stall. Quickly, Sunday pulled up her dress and curved her body over the toilet. Her phat pussy protruded. Nasir didn't waste any time thrusting himself inside her, salivating as he did so.

"Fuck me," Sunday cooed.

Nasir continued to enjoy her in the doggy-style position. It was a daring and risky act. While they fucked in the bathroom stall, they heard the comings and goings of other revelers. After entering the bathroom, a few ladies began to giggle, having figured out what was taking place in one of the stalls. Couples and strangers, either high on drugs, alcohol, or both, fucked in the bathroom on the regular. It was standard at the nightclub.

As Nasir was about to come, he squeezed her tits and pulled at her dreads. He came inside Sunday. The best sex was in public places, and Sunday was a freak like that. It turned her on. She felt driven to release sexual tension, and Nasir was her remedy. Afterward, the two collected themselves and coolly marched out of the bathroom stall like nothing had happened.

"And that's why you love me," Sunday joked.

Twelve

"I'm the one that's supposed to have your back," Sheek griped. "Why the fuck you bringing that nigga?"

"I know you do, Sheek. But Nasir and I got this. Y'all stay back, and we'll let you know," Sunday replied.

Sheek frowned. He didn't like it. They were about to meet with a dangerous man named Dodge, a Jamaican drug lord. Sheek didn't like seeing his sister's life entrusted in the hands of Nasir while they were meeting with a notorious figure. Furthermore, Sheek wanted to be the one to accompany his sister because he felt Nasir wasn't entirely down for their cause—to become rich and powerful by any means necessary. Yes, Nasir was from the streets, did dirt, and had a reputation. But Sheek felt there was something broken him. Something wasn't right with his sister's new boo. He knew they'd had a relationship long ago, before they'd moved to the Midwest. And she loved him, but things were different now.

Sunday assured Sheek that she had everything under control. This was business, and Dodge was a businessman. But there were stories about Dodge's sadistic and demonic behaviors. He was considered a demon in human skin. And a cannibal who devoured the flesh of his enemies and victims. Dodge was a dark being who believed that consuming the flesh of the departed was a way of forcing the souls of the dead into the bodies of the living, thereby endowing the living with some of the characteristics of the deceased.

Dodge was a peculiar and dangerous man with power and influence. And unfortunately, he was the only one willing to meet with Sunday to discuss business. Sunday and Nasir climbed into the Durango and headed to Brownsville, Brooklyn, to meet with Dodge that night. The thought of meeting with Dodge was frightening even to Sunday because he was known to become unhinged with paranoia sometimes and was extremely violent. To say that he was feared was an understatement.

Ironically, there was a full moon tonight, and the sky was clear. The moon was glowing yellowy white, loomed large, and was surrounded by an ethereal glow. And it was so clear you could nearly see every crater. However, Nasir and Sunday weren't interested in the beauty of the full moon or the night sky. Their minds were on something else, their survival and potential doom if this meeting with Dodge went wrong.

"How did you meet this nigga?" Nasir asked.

"He was referred to me," Sunday replied.

"Referred to you . . . by who?"

"A friend," Sunday told him. "Why are you having second thoughts about this?"

"Nah. I'm not. I'm just being cautious, that's all."

"I understand, but we got this, baby. I need your head fully in the game. If you're distracted by something, I need to fuckin' know, because we can't be caught slippin' out this bitch," said Sunday wholeheartedly.

"I'm fuckin' good," Nasir replied.

Nasir had heard the stories, and he was concerned. The last thing he wanted was to end up on a psychopath's dinner plate.

They arrived at the infamous Howard Houses in Brownsville. It was a quiet night in the hood. But when they climbed out of the vehicle on East New York Avenue, Nasir immediately noticed the men watching them from the towering rooftops and the young goons patrolling the projects like a pack of wolves. Dodge owned this neighborhood by utilizing fear, violence, and extreme intimidation. He was Nino Brown on steroids, and Howard Houses had become his personal Carter buildings.

Nasir and Sunday walked coolly through the projects and headed toward a thirteen-story project building. Before they could walk into the lobby, they encountered several goons loitering out front. Immediately all eyes were on Sunday; then they shifted to Nasir. Sunday seemed like a ray of sunshine that night in her tight blue jeans and high-heeled boots. She was a pretty girl, and this created unwanted attention for her.

"Yo, Ma, ya lost or sumthin'? That's ya nigga?" one of the men uttered.

"We're here to see Dodge," Sunday replied sternly, not one to beat around the bush.

"Dodge?" the goon questioned. "You sure you wanna do that? What business you got wit' him?"

"That's my fuckin' business, not yours," Sunday retorted.

Everyone was taken aback by Sunday's response. It was bold or stupid. Some men laughed at the reaction. But the one who was doing the talking frowned. He was tall and lanky, with big beady eyes, nappy hair, and black skin. The goons intimidatingly stepped closer to Nasir and Sunday. Nasir clenched his fists and continued to flank Sunday, who stood her ground. They were both armed, but if violence erupted, it would be a no-win situation for them. Nasir thought, *Is she trying to get us killed?*

"What the fuck you say, bitch? You know where the fuck you at?" the goon responded.

"I know where the fuck I'm at. I'm here for business wit' Dodge, not you! Anyway, Boomer referred me, nigga. I know y'all familiar wit' Boomer," said Sunday sternly.

Hearing that name changed the temperature in the room.

"Yo, Tater Tot, let her through, nigga," another goon ordered.

The goons in front of the lobby parted like the Red Sea, allowing Nasir and Sunday through. They entered the grungy lobby, and Nasir pressed a button on the wall for the elevator. Nasir's head was on a swivel while they waited for the elevator. However, Sunday remained calm and collected. She was confident that she and Dodge would come to an arrangement. She wanted to buy four kilos from him. Word around town was that Dodge had a direct connection with the Colombians. And Sunday had a plan, and it would catapult her into New York kingpin or queenpin status.

The two rode the elevator two flights before stepping off and finding themselves in a narrow hallway covered with graffiti and smelling of weed and fresh urine. The concrete floor was littered with empty beer and liquor bottles, cigarette butts, and crack vials, dumped by crack addicts. It was a dystopia but was home to many people.

They came to a door at the end of the hallway and heard rap music blaring from the project apartment. This was it; there was no turning back. Sunday and Nasir were committed to the cause of getting rich or dying while trying. Sunday glanced at Nasir, and his thoughts were etched on his face. *Do or die until the end.* Sunday knocked and waited. When the door opened, Sunday and Nasir were taken aback. A tall, butt-naked woman with a shaved head stood before them, clutching an assault rifle. She was pretty but threatening.

"Who yuh here for?" the woman uttered.

"We're here to see Dodge," Sunday replied.

"Wah business yuh got wid him?"

Sunday frowned. "Is he here or not? My business is not with you."

"Yuh nuh cum yah being disrespectful. Yuh hear? Mi will kill yuh yahso," she threatened.

Sunday wasn't frightened by her threats. She scowled at the naked woman and replied, "You think I give a fuck about you and your threats. Do it, bitch!"

Nasir was caught off guard by Sunday's reply. Was she crazy? Things were getting out of hand. There was a naked Jamaican Amazon woman with an assault rifle blocking their entry into the apartment. And in the hallway, he could smell the heavy weed smoke. It was becoming ugly. Already, they were in a no-win situation, and he wasn't there to die in some ghetto hallway. Sunday felt entitled to disrespect the woman on her own turf, and he knew that was stupid. Nevertheless, Sunday had no chill to her.

The naked woman prepared the assault rifle for action, and Nasir had no choice but to intervene.

"We didn't come here for any trouble," Nasir said, chiming in. "We came here to present Dodge with an opportunity and make him some money. He's expecting us."

The woman continued to frown. She was loyal *and* deadly, Dodge's personal attack dog. And they were going into the apartment only if Dodge approved it. Then, finally, they all heard someone say, "Amoy, let dem inside. Dem okay, mon."

Amoy scowled but then relented. She stepped to the side and allowed them into the apartment. Amoy glared at Sunday, and Sunday smirked at her. She did not like Sunday at all.

Nasir quickly took in the décor of the place, which was creepy. The apartment was dim. The walls were bright red. A large Jamaican flag was hanging in the living room, along with numerous religious artifacts and weird trinkets. Eerie dark artwork lined one side of a wall, giving the impression that Dodge was into voodoo or some dark spirits. Maybe he was a devil worshiper. Whatever Dodge was into made Nasir feel uncomfortable.

Amoy stood poised near the door, as if she didn't want them to leave. A second man who worked for Dodge was in the room too. He was tall, lean, and quiet. Dodge walked toward Sunday and Nasir and stood shirtless before them, his long, neat dreadlocks falling down to his shoulders. He was handsome and well built, but his dark, cold eyes seemed menacing.

"Mi hear yuh know Boomer. Him send yuh tuh mi . . . ?" Dodge asked.

"He did," Sunday answered.

"Him vouched fi yuh. How yuh know him?" Dodge asked.

"It's personal," Sunday replied.

Dodge laughed. "Personal, huh? Yuh fucked him?"

Sunday didn't want to answer the question. She wasn't about to expose her past or her private business to anyone. Nasir glanced her, his own concerns apparent in his expression, but she didn't budge.

"Mi hear 'bout yuh. Mi know who yuh are," Dodge added.

"Well, if you heard about me, you know that I'm a bitch about my business, and I don't fuck around," Sunday exclaimed. "And you don't need to know who I fucked or who I'm fuckin'. The only business you should be concerned about is how we gonna make some money together."

Dodge grinned. "Mi respect dat," he said. "Come sit, and we chat business, then."

Nasir remained skeptical and alert. He still wondered why Amoy was naked by the door, with an assault rifle. And there were the rumors of Dodge's cannibalism.

When Sunday sat across from Dodge, Nasir remained standing.

Dodge stared at Nasir and uttered, "Yuh nuh have to worry. Mi nah gon' harm yuh. Relax, mon. We talk business."

"If it's okay with you, I'm gonna remain standing," Nasir replied.

Dodge chuckled. "Yuh afraid! Let mi guess. Yuh hear rumors 'bout mi, huh? Yuh believe dem true?"

Nasir refused to answer. He didn't want to stay longer than they needed. And he didn't want to get comfortable in the apartment. His attention was on a subtle swivel.

"Listen, we're not here to talk about your personal shit. Your business is your business. I'm here for our business, Dodge," Sunday said, chiming in.

"Business, huh? Mi like yuh," Dodge said.

Just then, a noise came from one of the back bedrooms, and Nasir became even edgier. He was ready to reach for the pistol in his waistband and take no chances. Sunday seemed concerned too.

"What was that?" asked Nasir.

Dodge smiled and replied, "That's a slight issue dat mi dealing wit. Nuh yuh concern."

"I would feel better knowing what you have hiding back there. Just to be safe," said Sunday.

"Now yuh want to make it yuh concern, huh?" Dodge chuckled. "Fine."

Dodge nodded to his male henchman in the room, and the man retreated to the bedroom. Nasir and Sunday shared a concerned glance, but they kept calm. Moments later, Dodge's henchman dragged a hog-tied, gagged, and barely clothed hostage from the bedroom. He'd been beaten.

Nasir was taken aback. *What the fuck is this*? he thought.

"Yuh happy?" Dodge uttered with a grin.

Next, Dodge's attention shifted to the hostage. He stood up, brandished a knife suitable for a Rambo movie, and approached the man with vile intent.

"Yuh fucked up, nigga, and now yuh a' gon' pay. Yuh fuckin' hear mi?" Dodge exclaimed.

The hostage squirmed in his restraints, and his eyes grew wide with terror. Dodge crouched close to him with the blade and cut away at his ear. Nasir and Sunday were in utter shock. It was becoming a horror show.

"Mi a gon' cut yuh inna pieces. Yuh blood clot' steal from mi," Dodge shouted.

Dodge cut off his other ear and continued to berate him. The hostage was in extreme pain, and though his mouth was gagged with cloth and duct tape, his muffled screams seeped through.

"Take him back inna di room. Mi will finish wit' him when our company gon'," Dodge said to his henchman.

The man did what he was told and dragged the tortured and terrified hostage back into the back bedroom, leaving behind a trail of blood in the hallway. Dodge sat across from Sunday and wiped the blood from his hand. He then focused on his two guests and exclaimed, "Mi nuh like a thief or a liar, yuh hear?"

Nasir didn't know what to think. He glanced back at a naked Amoy, and she smirked his way. Owing to the naked bitch with the assault rifle, the shirtless, psychotic drug kingpin, and the hog-tied hostage being butchered, it felt like he was in a bad dream.

"Now we chat business," said Dodge.

Sunday and Dodge began to talk, but Nasir had second thoughts about jumping into bed with him. Was it a good idea? Especially after witnessing someone's ears being cut off? But Sunday wasn't deterred or intimidated. For her, it was another day in the park. It was the game.

"Yuh ready to ramp wild wid di big boys? Cuz dis grown men business, yuh hear?" said Dodge.

Sunday didn't flinch. "What, I need a big dick to make you some money?"

"It's fifteen a key. Is yuh dick big enuff tuh handle dat?" Dodge asked.

"Five keys, two on consignment," Sunday responded, negotiating.

"*Consignment*. Dat word contagious, yuh hear? Yuh crazy coming in mi home, chatting 'bout consignment. Mi want mi fuckin' money wen it's duh," said Dodge.

"I'm a businesswoman, and I'm not leaving here until we have some arrangement. I got plans, and right now, you saying no is impeding my plans," Sunday replied boldly.

Nasir was taken aback by her reaction. It was official; she had bumped her head and lost her mind. She wanted to get them killed.

"Sunday, we need to talk," Nasir mumbled.

"Not right now, Nasir. You see me talking. I'm fuckin' handling something. Can it wait?" she replied.

Her comment rubbed him the wrong way. He frowned and wanted to snatch her out of the chair, drag her into the hallway, and maybe smack some sense into her.

Dodge glared at them and chuckled. He uttered, "Yuh know wah? Mi like yuh. Yuh got balls. Mi tell yuh what. A fava fi a fava. Yuh understand?"

"What kind of favor do you need?" Sunday asked him.

"Mi want someone killed. Him name is Romeo, and him hard to get. Him trouble fo' mi, an' mi want him gon'," said Dodge. "Yuh kill him fo' mi, and mi will give yuh wah yuh need."

"Consider it done," Sunday replied wholeheartedly.

Dodge smiled. Their business was concluded. Sunday stood up, ready to depart, and Dodge did too. But Dodge had one more thing to say to them before they left. He stepped closer to both of them to ensure they heard him loud and clear.

"Mi want yuh to listen tuh mi clearly, yuh hear. Three things. Don't fail mi, nuh lie tuh mi, and mi want mi money when it's due, yuh understand, bredren? Or yuh become permanent guests in mi home," he proclaimed unequivocally.

"Yeah, we understand," Sunday replied.

With that, Sunday and Nasir both left the apartment. Nasir fumed. Sunday had placed them in debt with a psychopath, and he didn't want to be on that fool's radar. Nasir remained quiet until they both stepped into the elevator. When it began to descend, he heatedly pushed Sunday against the wall and gripped her by the arms.

He glared at Sunday and barked, "What the fuck did you just do? You fuckin' embarrassed me, and you're making promises without consulting me first!"

"Get your fuckin' hands off me, nigga!" Sunday shouted. "Are you fuckin' crazy? I don't need your permission to do shit! I'm doin' what the fuck I need to do to get paid! Do you fuckin' understand, Nasir?"

Nasir scowled. "How? By putting us in the crosshairs of Dodge?"

"Is my brother right about you? Are you switching up on me, nigga? Because the Nasir I knew from back in the day was always about his business and making money. We have come too far to get scared and turn the fuck back around, especially after the shit we did. I'm in it to win, and either you're with me or you're not," Sunday proclaimed sternly.

The elevator doors opened, and Sunday marched out of the elevator. Nasir sighed. He knew it was a bad idea to be in bed with a lunatic like Dodge, but Sunday was steadfast in her pursuit of money and power. Nasir was already knee-deep into shit with her, and it felt like he was sinking. She was running things, not him.

Thirteen

Zodiac stared out the vehicle's window like he was in some kind of trance. He watched the city come alive tonight. The yellow cabs flooded Eighth Avenue. A wall of pedestrians began crossing the street as he sat idling at a red light. Some places were closing for the day, and the nightlife was coming alive. Zodiac was on his way to meet with a man named Me-Time in Lower Manhattan. It was an odd name, but Me-Time was a strange individual with a particular set of skills that always proved helpful to Zodiac. He was a man of average height and wit. He was secretive. He was a clean-cut man in terms of his face, but his attire was a bit rugged.

Zodiac needed information, and he wanted it fast. He had a lot on his mind. The attempt on his life troubled him greatly. Knowing who was behind it was critical to his survival. He knew whoever was after him wouldn't stop because he was back in America.

Zodiac's driver, Buck, navigated the black SUV through the tight streets of Lower Manhattan and continued toward the West Side. Buck was a cool gentleman in his late forties, and he'd become one trusted figure in the organization. Wherever Zodiac went, Buck was driving or guarding his employer like he was in the Secret Service. Buck was the driver in Ghana who had quickly maneuvered the vehicle away from the heavy gunfire. He had saved their lives, and Zodiac was thankful.

Finally, they arrived at the pier. It was a little after 10:00 pm. This public area was a well-known tourist location, with museums, restaurants, shops, and a sports complex. Docked a few blocks north was the famous aircraft carrier USS *Intrepid*.

Zodiac felt comfortable meeting with Me-Time there. He and Buck left the SUV and headed toward the meeting location at the pier's edge. Buck coolly walked a few feet behind Zodiac, with his attention on a subtle swivel and a concealed Glock 17 on his hip. He was ready for anything. This time, no one was going to get the drop on them. He'd made that mistake in Africa.

The pier stretched into the welcoming Hudson River, with the dock and the river together like a kind of work of art and the New Jersey shoreline in the distance like a canvas. Zodiac spotted Me-Time. He had shown up early, as Zodiac predicted he would. He was a punctual man. CP time didn't exist in his book.

"Wait here. I wanna talk to him alone," Zodiac told Buck.

Buck nodded and remained where he was. His hand was close to his gun, and his eyes became sharp and focused. Anybody and everybody was an enemy in his eyes, including Me-Time, if he moved wrong. Buck didn't trust anybody.

Me-Time stood waiting for Zodiac. He was wearing a dingy black fedora hat, a Members Only jacket, and wire-rimmed glasses. His style was odd and unassuming. He puffed on a cigarette while gazing out at the river. Finally, he turned to see Zodiac approaching him. He was the man of the hour in Zodiac's book.

"What is it that you need from me?" Me-Time asked to avoid beating around the bush.

"There was an attack on me and my fiancée in Africa," said Zodiac.

"I've heard."

"What else did you hear?" asked Zodiac.

"There isn't much being said on any wire about the attempt on your life. Whoever's behind it is keeping quiet about it for now," said Me-Time.

"Well, I want you to *unquiet* the muthafucka and find out who's behind it. I'm willing to pay you double."

Me-Time nodded. "I'm on it."

"I'm curious. How did you hear about it so quickly?" asked Zodiac with a raised brow.

"Interpol has eyes on Joc, and you came across their radar," said Me-Time. "I found that out through my CIA connection."

"What? Are you serious?"

"Joc is a major international player, Zodiac, with probable ties to Boko Haram and Al-Qaeda. It's believed his men are seeking military training to kill foreign soldiers in Africa and rivals. He's highly insulated, and his money corrupted a lot of agents," Me-Time explained.

"I'm expecting my first shipment of two thousand kilos from him in a week. Can I trust it?" Zodiac asked.

Me-Time took a final pull from the cigarette and flicked it into the river. He stared deadpan at Zodiac and said, "Like I said, Joc is highly insulated. He's cunning and ruthless . . ."

"But he's on Interpol's radar," Zodiac uttered.

"He's been on Interpol's radar for the past three years, with no movement against him. Whatever case they have on him has become stagnant. I believe he's paying off someone on the top tier to always look the other way," Me-Time responded.

Zodiac sighed. He had a lot on his plate.

"Okay. Joc is my problem. I have to trust him for now. I want you to keep your ears to the streets and dig deep into your connections to find out who tried to kill me in Africa," said Zodiac.

Me-Time nodded. "I'll find out."

"Do that."

Zodiac held out a brown envelope filled with money, ten thousand dollars. Me-Time took the envelope with pleasure and grinned. "It's always good doing business with you, Zodiac."

Zodiac stared at him intently and uttered, "Me-Time, I'm not paying you for a service. I'm paying you for results."

"And you'll have the results. Give me a week," Me-Time replied.

Zodiac was content with the timeline. He pivoted and walked away from Me-Time and approached Buck.

"We okay?" asked Buck.

"Yeah. We okay," Zodiac replied unenthusiastically.

"Where to now?" asked Buck.

Zodiac thought about it. "Take me to Queens. I want to check on something."

The black SUV arrived in Springfield Gardens, Queens. It stopped before a modest single-family home in the residential neighborhood. Zodiac stared at the house with some nostalgia. It was quiet and dark. He knew this area well; it was where he'd grown up. And it was where his father and older brother still resided.

"I'll be back," Zodiac said to Buck.

Buck nodded. He was a man of few words. Zodiac climbed out from the back seat and approached the house. The house's exterior was in good shape, the front lawn was regularly cut, a rocking chair was on the porch, and a late nineties minivan was parked in the driveway.

Although Zodiac had a key to the place, he rang the bell. It was late, but he knew someone would answer the door. Finally, the front door opened, and his older brother, Markest, came into Zodiac's view. He was wearing a wifebeater.

"What do you want?" Markest asked with a steely glare.

"I was thinking about y'all. I wanted to come by and check up on him," Zodiac replied.

"At this time of the night?"

"I was in the area," Zodiac said.

"Sure you were," Markest replied incredulously.

"You gonna let your little brother in or have me stand out here all night?" asked Zodiac sardonically.

Markest sighed and opened the screen door to allow Zodiac into the house. Markest was a tall, bearded black man. He had a raspy voice due to chain smoking.

The house's décor was mediocre: it had secondhand furniture, childhood pictures decorating the walls and shelves, and religious artifacts everywhere. However, the sixty-inch television in the living room contrasted with the run-of-the-mill furnishings. Zodiac stood in the center of the living room, taking in his surroundings, reminiscing about his childhood. It wasn't the best childhood, but it could have been worse.

"How is he?" Zodiac asked his brother.

"He's sleeping right now," Markest replied.

"I wanna check up on him."

"Now? Tonight? It's been what? Nearly two years, Zodiac, and you decide to pick tonight to check up on him?" Markest griped.

"I'm not trying to argue with you," Zodiac replied.

"He's dying, Zodiac. That's how he's doing," Markest exclaimed.

Zodiac huffed. "That's why I'm here."

Markest relented. "Just make it quick and don't disturb him. He needs his rest."

Zodiac walked up the stairs and down the hall to the master bedroom. He slowly pushed open the door and stepped into the dark bedroom. He saw the silhouette of his father lying on the king-size bed. On the dresser near the bed were dozens of medications and an oxygen tank. Zodiac's father was dying from cancer. He was frail and bald and was wheezing in his sleep. Zodiac stepped farther into the bedroom and walked to the edge of the bed. There was an odd smell in the room, like something metallic mixed with chemicals.

Zodiac stared at his father silently in the dark. His imagination took over, and once again, Mr. Randle Ruffin was a healthy, God-fearing preacher and a loving father who tried to steer his two sons in the right direction. Unfortunately, at some point, both of his sons took a wrong turn somewhere and became products of the streets. However, Markest Ruffin changed his life and became a devoted Christian when he returned home from prison ten years ago.

Zodiac thought about how his father had always been tough on him and hadn't been shy in disciplining and whupping his sons whenever they did wrong. "Spare the rod spoil the child," Mr. Ruffin had always proclaimed. However, no matter how often he had disciplined his children, they had eventually turned to the streets and drug dealing.

"I love you, Pop," Zodiac whispered.

He turned and left the bedroom. Zodiac soon joined his brother at the kitchen table. "We need to talk," said Zodiac.

"What is it this time?" Markest replied in a low monotone.

"You should take Pop, leave town for a while, and stay in a nice hotel. The Marriott, Hilton, whatever. I'll pay for it," Zodiac suggested.

Right away, Markest was against this idea. He frowned and retorted, "I'm not doing that."

"Don't be stubborn on this, Markest. Just do this for me," Zodiac protested.

"No. It's not happening. Pop is sick, resting, and he's okay where he is right now, home. What trouble have you gotten yourself into, huh? Because I know that's the only reason you want us to leave here," Markest responded, reading his little brother like a book.

Zodiac had always been honest with his brother. "They tried to kill me and Trina in Africa."

Markest was taken aback by the news. "What? Do you know who?"

"No. And that's the problem. But I'm gonna find out. Until then, I want to make sure everyone is safe."

"You don't need to worry about me or Pop. We're good here, and we're always gonna be good here," Markest said unequivocally.

Zodiac sighed heavily. "Why do you always have to be so fuckin' stubborn?"

"That's not my world anymore, Zodiac. If you want it to continue to be yours, fine. But don't drag me and Pops into it."

Zodiac locked eyes with his brother. This was the same man who'd introduced him to the street life. When Zodiac was sixteen, Markest had put a gram of coke and a pistol in his hand and had molded him, Mob Allah, and Zulu into street hustlers and drug kingpins. The three of them used to look up to Markest, who ran the block and the hood with authority and an iron fist. Everyone feared him and respected him. In Zodiac's eyes, he was bigger than Nino Brown and Frank White combined. However, like every kingpin, Markest took a fall like Humpy Dumpty—and that fall was doing nearly fifteen years in a federal penitentiary.

"If you're not going to leave, then at least you need to protect yourself if something goes down," said Zodiac.

Zodiac removed a pistol from his person and placed it on the kitchen table. Markest stared at the gun like it was a foreign object or blasphemy.

"I have no need for that," said Markest.

"Take the gun, Markest. I'll feel better."

Markest chuckled. "*You'll* feel better. I haven't touched a gun in years, Zodiac. And I'm not about to start now."

Zodiac scoffed, "Oh, I forgot. God Almighty is going to protect you, huh?"

"I'm a changed man, Zodiac. You know that. I gave my life to the Lord a long time ago. I wish you would do the same. But I can't force you to do so," said Markest.

"And all I'm doing is looking out for and protecting the only family I have left," Zodiac countered.

Markest stared at his little brother with regret and despair. For a long time now, he'd wanted to have a meaningful conversation about his brother's lifestyle and choices.

"I hate that I brought the three of you into that world. Now you're the last one standing, Zodiac. That doesn't concern you. Mob Allah, Zulu, and Big Will, they're all dead. And now you tell me there was an attempt on your life in Africa." Markest groaned.

"I'm in it now, bro. And I'm in it to win. Not to lose," Zodiac protested.

"I'm sure those who have fallen before you said the same thing. And don't say you're different, because we all believe we're different and better. It's all a delusion. You're lifestyle, especially jumping into a relationship with some boy pretending to be a woman, is concerning."

"Listen, I came here to help and look out. I'm not looking forward to some church sermon," Zodiac griped.

Zodiac didn't want anyone preaching to him about Trina. She was the love of his life, and he didn't care what gender she was born as. What mattered now was Trina had become his ride-or-die bitch, and she was beautiful, intelligent, and devoted.

"You don't want to listen, nor do you want to change your ways. Far as I'm concerned, you and I are done here."

"So, just like that. You believe it's that easy, big bro. You may have changed, but guess what? You made a lot of enemies on those streets when you were running things, and niggas don't forget. So don't fuckin' judge me."

Markest stood from the table. He was a different man, and Zodiac refused to see it.

"Pop is in good hands, Zodiac. I pray for him, look after him, and I love him. He has all the protection he needs right now," Markest proclaimed passionately. "Good night, little brother."

Zodiac huffed. "Whatever!"

He stood too, pivoted, and marched out of his childhood home, defeated. He walked toward the idling SUV and climbed into the back seat. Buck didn't ask him any questions. However, what went on inside Zodiac's childhood home was his business. The only thing Buck asked was, "Where to next?"

"Take me home," Zodiac replied in exasperation.

Buck nodded. "Will do."

"Also, I want two men watching my father's house by tomorrow night. Make it happen," said Zodiac.

Buck nodded. "Consider it done."

If Markest didn't want to accept his help willingly, Zodiac would offer it indirectly and secretly.

Fourteen

"Do you miss him?" Detective Shelly Mack asked Emmerson, referring to his old partner, Acosta.

It was a foolish question. Of course Detective Emmerson missed his old partner. He thought about his friend every single day.

"Every single day," said Emmerson. "He was one of the best to do this job. He knew his shit."

"I've heard good things about him," Mack replied.

"He was a good man. And one helluva detective. The man had an eye for a crime scene. He could sift through mountains of irrelevant things to find the pertinent evidence. He had a methodical approach. His attention to detail and ability to see the big picture and zoom in on the little pieces that could lead to the resolution of a case was unparalleled. Acosta had the uncanny ability to view nine things at once and then determine which of those nine things had any relevance. There will never be anybody like him," Emmerson said, rambling on about Acosta.

"Why would he take his own life?" asked Mack.

It was a question that Chris Emmerson knew he would never get the answer to. Cops killed themselves every year because of many reasons. It was too bad that his partner had become part of the statistics. It should be considered a pandemic . . . cop suicide. The shit they saw and had to deal with on the regular was unimaginable. And sometimes, the mind did break. With Acosta's family gone, Emmerson knew there wasn't anything to prevent his partner from doing the unthinkable. Most times, coming home to a family, to someone who loved you and cared about you, could be the difference between life and death.

"I don't know why," Emmerson replied nonchalantly.

"The two of you were close, right?" she added.

"We were."

"And you didn't suspect anything?" Mack asked.

Shelly Mack was asking him twenty-one questions. She was a good cop, but she wanted to become a great detective. She wanted to make her mark in the NYPD, like Acosta did. Breaking a serial killer case six years ago was huge, and for his work, Acosta garnered the national spotlight. And it boggled her mind how a great detective like Acosta ended up eating his own gun.

Emmerson frowned slightly. He was done talking about his old partner. He changed the subject by uttering, "Who is this fool we're looking for again?"

"His name is Dante. He's a fence. Whatever's hot and stolen from wherever, especially jewelry and electronics, Dante's the man to see," Mack said.

"So, he's your CI," said Emmerson.

"A reliable one," Mack assured him.

Emmerson and Mack were working on the home invasion of the prominent business owner and family man. This case had made the front-page news, and now the spotlight was on them. Shelly Mack wanted to solve this case right away. She wanted that glory. She wanted to rise up in the ranks of the NYPD, become a sergeant, lieutenant, captain, and one day she wanted to become the first female commissioner of New York City. She was ambitious.

The two sat in the unmarked black Crown Vic parked across from a pawnshop on a busy boulevard. It was early in the morning, and the shop was closed. The traffic in the area was light. The morning sun poured through their windows. Mack and Emmerson sipped their morning coffee while waiting for Dante to open his pawnshop.

"How long has he been your snitch?" Emmerson asked.

"A year now. I busted him with some stolen items, nearly a hundred thousand dollars' worth of goods. It wasn't looking too good for him. It was prison or freedom. Of course, like they all do, he chose the latter. He agreed to help me out if I helped him out," said Mack. "They trust him. The crooks, thieves, lowlifes, dirtbags come to him if they want to unload stolen merchandise quickly and quietly."

Emmerson nodded. It was good to hear. They needed a break in their case. They had some time until the pawnshop opened. So it gave them a chance to sit and talk. Shelly Mack was an exciting person, with a colorful background.

"So, what's your story?" Emmerson asked her. "We've been partners for four months, and I still don't know anything about you."

Shelly Mack took a sip of her coffee and kept her eyes fixed on the pawnshop.

"There's nothing much to tell about myself. I grew up in foster care. I never knew my parents. I don't have any siblings, no cousins, or grandparents. My foster father used to sexually abuse me for years, so I ran away. When I tried to report him, they didn't believe me. I continued to run away until I was old enough to be left alone," Mack told him.

She went on. "I became a cop after my twenty-first birthday. I did well in the academy. I had to prove myself every day. After being on the force for a year, I made it my business to go after my foster father. I had a badge now, and they began believing me. I was able to have him investigated and eventually arrested. He's now serving life in prison for statutory rape, sexual abuse, and child endangerment, among other things. I hold grudges."

Mack looked over at him. "Do I look like I have the time for a boyfriend?"

"The one thing I've learned, being on this job for so many years and being a homicide detective, is always to make a life outside of this. You'll need something special to look forward to when you're not working a case and seeing the ugly side of humanity. I have my wife and kids, and they keep me grounded," Emmerson proclaimed wholeheartedly.

Mack nodded. "Duly noted."

Finally, some action began to happen. A white Benz parked in front of the pawnshop, and Dante climbed out.

"There he is," Shelly Mack announced.

"Mr. Dante, huh?" Emmerson uttered.

"A jack of many trades," said Mack.

Dante was a black man of average height, with a head as bald as a baby's bum. He wore a pair of faded blue jeans that covered his white Jordans and a stylish black shirt. He opened his pawnshop by unlocking the locks and lifting the rolling gate. Before entering his establishment, he checked his surroundings and felt everything was clear. He was ready to begin his day.

"We'll give him a minute to settle in," said Mack.

Emmerson was a patient man. This was her CI, or snitch. Finally, the two had waited long enough. They exited the Crown Vic simultaneously, coolly crossed the boulevard, and headed toward the pawnshop. Dante stood behind the counter, with the cash register open, when they entered the shop. When he saw the detectives entering, he closed the cash register and smiled.

"Dante, how you been?" Shelly Mack asked mockingly.

"Ms. Mack. It's been a while. What brings you to my place of business?" Dante said with an unnatural smile.

"I missed you, Dante. I wanted to come by and chat it up for a sec," Shelly Mack replied.

"And who's your new friend?"

"This is my partner, Chris Emmerson."

"A friend of yours is a friend of mine," Dante mocked.

"Well, since we're all friends in here, I need your help with something, Dante," said Shelly Mack.

"If I can help."

"Of course you can help. I wouldn't have it no other way," Shelly Mack replied. "You owe me, right?"

Dante's smile faded.

"And it looks like you've been doing quite well with this pawnshop since it opened two or three years ago. One of your many side hustles, huh? I hope everything in this place is legit," Shelly Mack added.

Dante's pawnshop was filled with many high-end items: laptops, cameras, cell phones, TVs, and jewelry. He sold some of the best jewelry in town. His pawnshop was one of his biggest moneymakers.

"What do you need from me?" asked Dante reluctantly.

"I know you've heard about the recent home invasion, a prominent family killed in their home a few miles from here. The father was murdered in his jewelry store in Jackson Heights," Shelly Mack said.

"I might have heard something about that."

"Well, I need your help on this one. The culprits stole a lot of nice and pricey things from the home and jewelry store. And I know you're the man of the hour when buying and selling nice things," said Shelly Mack.

"We can argue about that," Dante replied.

"Don't downplay your reputation to me, Dante. I know you. And I know you like to have nice things in your possession, including women. I also know everything in here isn't legit. If my partner and I begin digging, we can dig up a few grand larceny charges you wouldn't like," Shelly Mack told him.

Dante huffed.

Mack continued. "What do you know about that home invasion nearby? Have any questionable items come into your possession recently?"

"Not a damn thing, Ms. Mack."

"Are you sure about that? Because if you're lying to me . . ."

"Look, word on the street, there's a new crew out there. I never heard of them before, and I don't know where they're from. But they're ruthless," Dante mentioned.

"A new crew, huh? You have a name?" Mack asked him.

"No, I don't. The most I know about this crew is they ain't from here. And they might have a bitch running with them."

"And that's all you know?" Detective Emmerson asked, chiming in.

"That's all I know, real talk," Dante assured them.

Shelly Mack stared at Dante like she was a human lie detector. She was able to read people well. She deduced he wasn't lying to her. Besides, Dante knew the consequences of misleading and lying to Detective Mack. She played hardball, was a pit bull in a skirt, and was known to be a bitch if she had to be. Once someone was on her bad side, it was hell on earth.

"I'll take your word for now," Mack replied. "But if you find out anything or receive an unexpected visit from anyone, you better call me."

"I got you, Ms. Mack. I'm not trying to get on your bad side," said Dante.

"I know that's right. We've had a good relationship so far. So don't fuck it up," Mack replied.

"No doubt."

Shelly Mack gave Dante one final stern gaze, then pivoted, and she and Emmerson marched out.

"Well, that was a dead end," Emmerson uttered.

"They'll turn up, and it's only a matter of time before they come across Dante."

"What's up with him calling you Ms. Mack?" Detective Emmerson asked her.

"It makes him feel comfortable calling me 'Ms.' instead of 'Detective.' It gets him to trust me more," Mack replied.

Emmerson chuckled.

The two climbed back into the Crown Vic and continued to work the case.

"Are you hungry?" Detective Emmerson asked about two hours later.

"I can go for a bite," Mack replied.

"I know a great place you'll like. Mike and I used to go there all the time. It's close by," said Emmerson.

"Okay. I'm down."

Emmerson smiled. He was beginning to like Detective Mack. Of course, she could never replace Detective Acosta, but she was becoming a second-best partner. Shelly Mack was growing on Emmerson.

Fifteen

Ezekial stood at the pond in Central Park and took in the scenic area. It was a place where he could relax, enjoy his surroundings, and watch the wildlife. The local pond was beautiful, with its diverse vegetation; its various waterfowl, including large egrets, herons, ducks, and turtles; and an arched stone footbridge. It was a quick getaway from the hustle and bustle of the big city. Some people took to fishing at the pond to unwind. It was early spring, and everything was beginning to blossom. The sun had just risen, and it shone softly on the city streets, bringing a flurry of early morning activities.

Ezekial began feeding the ducks nearby. He tossed pieces of bread into the water and watched the ducks hurry toward their newfound feast. They excitedly dabbled at the slices of bread in the water. Some ducks tipped over and used their long necks to reach the food underwater. Ezekial smiled at their activity. He was alone but felt secure. No one was going to bother him here. He was an early bird, and he liked animals. Being around them and lingering in parks produced a certain calm and balance in his life.

As he continued feeding the ducks, Cashmere strutted toward him in her red bottoms and a tight red dress. She was not interested in feeding the wildlife or lingering in the city park. She stared at Ezekial and said, "It's time."

Ezekial nodded. "Look at this place, Cashmere, an oasis hidden inside a dystopian city. I loathe this city, but I love this park. I respect the wildlife here," he uttered.

Cashmere remained indifferent to his speech. The only thing she loved was money, sex, and power. She didn't give a fuck about feeding ducks and turtles, visiting parks, and sitting on the grass. She was the opposite of Ezekial. She hated parks. The grass made her skin itch. She was ready to return to the idling black Escalade on Fifth Avenue. Ezekial tossed the last of the bread into the pond and then turned to leave.

He and Cashmere strolled out of the park and climbed into the idling Escalade with Moses at the wheel.

"Are we good to go?" Moses asked.

"Yeah. Let's get this shit over with," Ezekial griped.

Moses put the SUV in drive and headed northbound, toward Harlem, a few blocks away. It was another pretty spring day, but Ezekial had things on his mind. The members of the Outfit, an organization he was part of, wanted to meet in Harlem in the early morning. Ezekial knew why they wanted to meet, but he tried not to worry about it.

"Are you okay?" Cashmere asked him.

"I'm fine," Ezekial huffed. "Why the fuck these fools want to meet at the crack of dawn is beyond me. I have better things to do with my time than be in Harlem this fuckin' early."

Cashmere leaned closer to him and placed her hand on his thigh. Looking at him with an expression of caring and confidence, she said, "They just want to meet. Besides, you're running things, not them. They need you more than you need them."

Ezekial heard her, but he remained silent. He shifted his eyes to the right and gazed out the window. The sight of penthouses and high-risers faded once they crossed 110th Street, where housing projects, bodegas, and drug fiends took over the landscape. They were officially in Harlem, a place considered the black metropolis. Since it was early morning, the area was still quiet and asleep. Nothing was open yet. Moses continued to navigate the Escalade north, toward 122nd Street. There he stopped in front of a luxury brownstone nestled in the middle of the block. Moses left the driver's seat and hurried to the vehicle's rear to open the door for Ezekial and Cashmere. The two climbed out and were immediately greeted by security standing out front, two men in black suits concealing holstered weapons. Ezekial and Cashmere were expected, so the men nodded respectfully and allowed them to pass. Cashmere followed behind Ezekial as they entered the three-story brownstone.

Once inside, they were met by another security guard, this one watching the door. He greeted the new arrivals and said to them, "Everyone's waiting in the back room."

The brownstone was sparsely furnished. But it was a spectacular-looking place. From the foyer they made their way to the great room, which was a kitchen, dominated by a vast black granite–topped island, and a living room combined. The living area had a fireplace, a huge television screen, and a dining room table with chairs. Ezekial preferred the basement, which was mainly one large playroom, with a home theater complete with a projector and a large screen, a pool table, and a bar. It also contained an office.

When Ezekial and Cashmere entered the great room, they discovered seven men with the Outfit sitting at the large dining room table, waiting for Ezekial's arrival. They were well-dressed, respected dons. Suddenly, all eyes were on Ezekial and Cashmere. The Outfit consisted of Ray Black from Harlem, Bruno from the Bronx, Kevin Charles from Newark, New Jersey, Baxter Johnson from Harlem, Antonio Francesco from Little Italy and Bensonhurst, Angelo Giuseppe from Philadelphia, Van Gray from Queens, Gregg Rice from Yonkers, and Monk

Dice from Brooklyn. Ezekial was from Jamaica, Queens, but he now operated in Miami. The Outfit had its hands in everything from drugs and extortion to sex trafficking. They settled disputes among the criminals and handled distribution and other drug trade–related issues. Like the Italian Mafia, they remained secretive, guarded, and powerful. Each man in the room had a substantial net worth and wielded influence nationwide and internationally. Collectively, the Outfit was worth nearly five billion dollars. Each member of the Outfit had three or more different passports with different identities.

Ezekial, Angelo, Gregg, and Baxter were in their late forties or early fifties and were the senior members of the Outfit. The other members were either in their late twenties or their thirties. Over two decades ago, the senior members had put the Outfit together to deal more efficiently with other gangsters in the Tristate area.

"It's about time. The man of the hour finally arrives," Ray Black commented. "Have a seat. Let's chat."

Ezekial sat at the table, while Cashmere sat in the background with secondaries in charge. She knew to remain seen and not heard.

"Let's get this started. We're not here for the pleasantries and to look at each other's ugly faces," Baxter said.

At fifty-six, Baxter Johnson was the eldest gangster in the room. When he was fourteen years old, in 1965, he became a numbers runner for the legendary Bumpy Johnson and learned a lot from Bumpy and his organization. Then he ran with Nicky Barnes and the Council in the 1970s. By the time Baxter was in his thirties, in the 1980s, he'd become one of the most feared and influential gangsters in New York.

"Yeah. Let's do this. I got places to be and money to make," said Ray Black impatiently. He was an eager hothead in his early thirties. Still, his pedigree was equivalent to that of men like Supreme, Stanley Tookie Williams, and Frank Larry Matthews.

He was a force to be reckoned with.

"I've called us all together because there seems to be a heated dispute between two members of this council, and we need to settle this," said Baxter Johnson.

Antonio Francesco stood up from his seat and griped, "My grievance is with Ezekial. Two of my men went missing while they were in Miami doing business for you, Ezekial. You needed help and information, and I entrusted it to you, Tony, and Mark. And now I'm hearing stories of how they were killed."

"I have no idea what you're talking about, Antonio. Someone gave you some bad information," Ezekial argued.

"You dare sit across from me and lie to my fuckin' face, Ezekial! You had my men killed . . . and for what? You think they failed you?" Antonio shouted.

"Are you calling me a liar?" Ezekial retorted.

"Yes. You damn cold-blooded coward! I did you a favor, and you stab me in the fucking back!" Antonio griped.

Cashmere quickly cut her eyes at Antonio and scowled. If looks could kill, Antonio would have been beheaded. She wanted to cut his neck from ear to ear. *How dare he mock and accuse Ezekial!* But she remained quiet while Ezekial continued to defend himself.

"What's been your beef with me, Antonio?" Ezekial grumbled.

"You sit there like the king of kings on this council when we're all supposed to be equal. You do what the fuck you wanna do, Ezekial, and belittle those you feel are underneath you," Antonio responded heatedly.

Ezekial scoffed. "You've sat at this table for how long now? Earn your keep, muthafucka."

Antonio slammed his fist on the table so hard, it shook violently. He then looked like he was ready to charge at Ezekial. But he didn't. He kept his composure and continued to rant. "Fuck you, Ezekial! You're gonna give me my fuckin' respect on this council. I may be younger than you, but I put in the fuckin' work and wealth to be here. I deserve your respect!"

"Well, I beg to differ," Ezekial scolded.

"Enough of this!" Baxter chided. "The two of you are going back and forth like fuckin' children. We're men, not boys. But this is one of the reasons why the Outfit was created, to settle our disputes like gentlemen in a room instead of like thugs on the streets."

"So, let's settle this, then. Because Mark and Tony were good men. You needed my help, and I gave you my hand, Ezekial. And in return, you spit in my fuckin' face! Mark and Tony were loyal and the best at what they did. And you put them in a pit for your dogs to kill," Antonio exclaimed.

"Do you have any proof of that?" Monk Dice asked.

"They never came back from Miami," Antonio hollered.

Everyone had heard the rumors about the two men's fate. But their bodies had gone missing. Antonio knew Mark's and Tony's bodies would never turn up.

"What was the reason for Antonio's help anyway?" Ray Black asked. "If you ask me, this shit could've been avoided if niggas get their own men to fix their own fuckin' problems."

"Tell them . . . He wants to wipe out Zulu, Zodiac, and anyone he believes was involved with his two sons' death. I gave him my prison connection to make it happen. Mark and Tony were on top of it. And I don't know what happened in Africa," Antonio revealed.

"You mean to tell me all this is over two little niggas you were estranged from, Ezekial?" Ray Black said.

Ezekial frowned and huffed. "They were my fuckin' sons, Ray . . . my fuckin' blood. And someone's gonna pay for their deaths."

"From what I've heard, Drip-Drip was a stupid, hot-headed knucklehead who was in over his head, and Rafe went crazy trying to revenge his brother's death. They got themselves killed," Kevin Charles commented.

"Why now, huh? That was six years ago, and now you all Rambo on this shit?" Bruno wanted to know.

"Rafe was killed three years ago in prison. And I've waited long enough. It's time," said Ezekial.

"You're emotional right now, and I understand. I've lost sons too," said Angelo Giuseppe. "But you need to start thinking rationally. What's done is done, Ezekial. It's the past. All of us together in this room are here to make our future better and become wealthier men."

"What good is having wealth and power if I can't punish those who killed my loved ones?" Ezekial protested. "I might as well be a fuckin' bum on the streets."

"Tell me you're not going through some midlife crises at your age," Ray Black joked.

The men went back and forth in the room. Antonio wasn't leaving the meeting without compensation or a reprisal against Ezekial. His pride was wounded. He felt the elders didn't give him the respect he deserved, because he was one of the youngest in the Outfit, thirty-two years old. Antonio Francesco came from a family of gangsters. His father was once a made man and a respected captain in the Genovese crime family, and so was his grandfather. However, Antonio fell short of becoming a made man in one of the five families, so he became the next best thing, a notorious drug kingpin.

"What is it that you want from the council?" Baxter asked Antonio.

"I want what is owed to me," Antonio answered.

"And what is that?" asked Baxter.

"An eye for an eye," Antonio responded.

Ezekial chuckled and scoffed at his request. "What, you want me dead? It's not happening."

"I'm with Ezekial," Van Gray stated. "No disrespect to you, Antonio, but are these two men worth going to war for? We have bigger problems than two missing goons."

"They were my lieutenants, and fuck you, Van! It's not about their rank but the principle. But, of course, you're going to side with him. Both of y'all fools are from Queens," Antonio griped.

Van frowned. "You definitely don't want any smoke with me."

"I want fuckin' justice!" Antonio hollered.

"For dead soldiers who can easily be replaced," said Bruno.

"And you're becoming emotional like Ezekial," Ray Black noted.

"Here's what I propose," Baxter Johnson said, intervening. "Since there's no proof, Ezekial must pay you a fine. And we're voting on it."

"How much?" Antonio asked. He expected the payout to be in the millions.

"A quarter of a million," Baxter replied.

Antonio was shocked and upset by the number. "What? That's it?"

"Don't be greedy, Antonio. Take the money," Ray Black suggested.

"Fuck the money! I want my respect, and I want his fuckin' balls!" Antonio angrily shouted at Ezekial.

Before a vote could be taken, Antonio and his second in charge stormed out of the room, upset. Antonio felt disrespected by the outcome.

Baxter huffed.

"I guess this meeting is adjourned," Ray Black said.

Most of the men of the Outfit departed. But Baxter remained behind.

"Ezekial. We need to talk," Baxter called.

Ezekial had just reached the door to the great room. He turned around and headed over to Baxter, and the two men stepped over to a corner of the room to talk privately.

"You need to fix this quarrel with Antonio. The last thing we need in the Outfit is bad blood between members," Baxter said.

"He's a young punk, Baxter."

"Yet you reached out to him for his help."

"He needed to earn his keep and become useful for something," said Ezekial.

"Still, his family goes way back, and they're respected and connected," Baxter said.

Ezekial scoffed. "Are you talking about the five families? They're done, Baxter. They don't control New York anymore. We do! We built this, you and me. And we never needed the Italians, Russians, Irish, anyone."

"Times have changed."

"Not for me. The last thing we need in their eyes is to become old men trying to keep up in a young man's game. And I'm not old. But I don't trust Antonio to be in the Outfit."

"What's done is done. And unless you're ready for a war with the Italians and whoever, make peace with Antonio," Baxter urged him.

Ezekial frowned. He respected Baxter. The man was three years older than him and harder than concrete, and some had pronounced him the new age Bumpy Johnson of New York. And although Ezekial was a powerful, dangerous, and wealthy man, he knew it would benefit him to remain on Baxter's good side. They were friends, and Ezekial had witnessed firsthand what the man did to his enemies. Ezekial had learned his cruelty and ruthlessness from Baxter.

"Out of respect for you, Baxter, I'll talk to him, and we'll figure this shit out," said Ezekial.

Baxter nodded, approving his reply. "Good. Make it happen. We started the Outfit not only to become wealthy men but also to become untouchable. You create a civil war within, then we become vulnerable."

Ezekial nodded.

Baxter was a man of few words. He said it once and didn't repeat himself. He pivoted and walked away from Ezekial, believing his friend would follow his advice. Ezekial stood there and watched his good friend leave the room. Then he sighed. Something was on his mind.

He and Cashmere headed back to the foyer, exited the brownstone, and climbed into the back seat of the Escalade. Moses got behind the wheel and drove off. Cashmere gazed at Ezekial, knowing something was on his mind. She knew him well.

"What are you thinking about?" she asked him.

"The future," he replied.

Sixteen

"The package somehow got lost or stolen," Row told Sincere as soon as he stepped into Sincere's cell.

"What the fuck you mean, lost or stolen, nigga?" Sincere griped.

"Catch had been sent to the hole to deliver something to our peoples back there, and the delivery was never made. Catch saying it was stolen."

"By who, nigga? He got fucked up?"

"He ain't really sayin', Sincere," said Row.

"What the fuck you mean, he ain't really sayin'? What the fuck! This is our money we're talkin' 'bout, Row. You think I got time for games and excuses and fuckin' losses? Nah, Catch gotta pay for that loss."

Row nodded, agreeing.

"Niggas is watchin' us, Row, and we can't look fuckin' weak right now. Either he stole it himself or he's in cahoots with someone. Catch gotta go, and I want it done in public. We need to make some noise, make a statement," Sincere proclaimed.

"Consider it done," Row replied.

Sincere huffed. He paced around his small cell and fumed. Power moves were being made inside the prison, and Sincere knew the new inmate, Rondell, was behind his sudden problems. A proxy war was happening between him and Rondell inside the state prison. Sincere had built an empire and a strong drug trade network and had gained absolute dominance in six years. However,

Rondell was now pulling the strings to unravel and eventually destroy everything Sincere had built. He was intent on taking control of the drug trade behind the walls of Elmira.

Row had more bad news for Sincere.

Row grumbled, "Finn, Mark, and Jacqueline were knocked during their visits."

"Are you fuckin' kidding me, nigga?"

"Nah."

"We had that situation sewed the fuck up!" Sincere griped.

"We did until a snitch," said Row.

Sincere continued to fume. Visitations were one of several ways in which Sincere and his organization could smuggle drugs into the state prison. Inmates' wives and girlfriends, as well as women desperate for cash, would secretly smuggle drugs into the prison, and inside the visiting room, they would pass the drugs on to the inmates. At the same time, specific guards were paid off to look the other way, and some of the others were utterly oblivious to the smuggling. When an inmate visited his other half in the visiting room, the couple was allowed to kiss twice: once when they greeted each other and once before the other half left. And it was during one of those two kisses that a balloon containing two grams of heroin smaller than a marble or something else would quickly be passed mouth to mouth. The inmate would swallow the balloon and later regurgitate it or shit it out. It was a profitable smuggle and had been happening for years. Everyone got paid, the inmate, the smuggler, and the corrupt guard. Those loving kisses between inmates and spouses formed part of a major entry port.

Sincere had it set up so sweetly that eight more prisoners would be in the visiting room, copping, on the same day. If one couple was caught, there would be several more who would make it through. And Sincere and his crew received a piece of everything. They flooded the prison.

Sincere and his crew would cut the heroin into quarter-gram pieces, then distribute the product via soldiers who sold them. The money was excellent. They made a fortune. They made thousands of dollars moving heroin and other drugs through an elaborate system of payoff, intimidation, and profit. It all helped to fund Sincere's activities and bolster his leadership.

Despite the rotten news Row had given him, he had some good news for Sincere.

"I did get some info on Rondell," Row announced.

Sincere's ears perked up. He was listening. "What's up with him?"

"He's connected, definitely a big deal. His uncle is part of some underground criminal organization called the Outfit. They ain't no joke. They national, shit, even international, with their reach. His uncle a crazy muthafucka with money longer than old train smoke," Row informed him.

"They close?" asked Sincere.

"Maybe so. But it ain't no coincidence that he was transferred to the same prison with you. Rondell got a personal beef with you," said Row.

"About what? The nigga don't know me, and I don't know him."

"But you knew his cousin."

"Who the fuck is his cousin?"

"Rafe," Row revealed.

Sincere frowned. "Fuck!"

"Yeah. We slaughter that fool back then. Didn't think the nigga had a father in the Outfit, some Mafia-type shit. I don't think they were close, though."

"It don't matter. We killed his son, and now he's planning on coming for us," Sincere replied.

"Let them fools come. I ain't scared of anyone of them. Fuck 'em!" Row growled with sureness.

Sincere's past had come back to haunt him with a vengeance. He remembered killing both brothers, because Drip-Drip was responsible for his little brother's death. Rafe had become drunken with revenge. Unfortunately, it'd cost him his life too. Sincere knew he needed to act rationally when confronting his sudden problem. Rondell's main agenda was getting revenge for the death of his cousin, and Sincere deduced that it had to be him and his uncle who had made an attempt on his life a few weeks ago. Since that attempt on his life had failed, Sincere knew his enemy's next move was disrupting his drug and cash flow and turning people against him.

"A'ight. We know who this nigga is. Let's prepare for what's to come. Because this shit here ain't gonna be the end of us," said Sincere with conceit.

"No doubt, my nigga. That's what I'm talkin' about," Row said and cheered.

"First thing, like I said before, Catch gotta go, and make it gruesome and public. We need to send out a message that you're either with us or against us. And if you're against us, then that's your life. We can't be weak on this," Sincere declared.

Row nodded. "A'ight."

"Also, we need to know what guard is still with us. If these fools wanna jump the fence to a different yard, then we make that shit personal. You and I got people on the outside that owe us, right? Then we go after their families for intimidation or worse," Sincere said.

"It's only a phone call away," Row said.

Row gave Sincere dap and a tight brotherly hug and exited his cell. Sincere took a seat on his cot to think things over. He was at war, and he planned on winning this war and surviving at any cost. It was time to clean house and remind everyone why he'd become a shot caller inside two state prisons. Sincere wanted to create something bigger and stronger, rivaling all the prison gangs in the country, the Black Guerilla Family, the Bloods, the Crips, the Latin Kings, the Aryan Brotherhood, and so on. He was a man with a vision, a lengthy prison sentence, and like many before him, he suffered from megalomania. This thing he was creating was going to be bigger than him. He wanted to have a stronghold on New York State prisons and beyond, where in return for membership and status in his organization, not a gang, those under him would enjoy power, prestige, influence, and protection. But first, he had to cut down the weeds, those who believed the grass was greener on the other side.

The attempt on his life—which involved surviving multiple stab wounds, killing an inmate, and seriously injuring two guards—had turned him into an icon and a legend. And so Sincere began to build something called KOS (Kings of Society). Because he believed himself to be a king. No matter where he was, he was meant to rule. Before, they'd turned him into a monster. Now he planned on becoming king.

Sincere decided to remain in his cell during the day's activities. He wanted to be alone. What he'd planned would generate some noise, fear, and chaos. It was time to react and implement payback. It was time to remind everyone why he was the boogeyman. The man had nothing left but his reputation and prison organization, which he was willing to protect and keep at any cost.

KOS had been born.

He'd told Row to make the call. Before his incarceration, Row had been a high-ranking gang member and had been considered one of the godfathers of one of the most notorious street gangs. He had controlled much of Brooklyn with drugs, intimidation, murders, and other violence. Row had had fifteen arrests for guns, possession, assault, and attempted murder before he turned twenty-one. He was the real deal, a boogeyman like Sincere. Now Row was serving a life sentence for shooting and killing two rival gangsters in public.

Sincere knew once that call was made, it would mark the point of no return. They were going after not only rival inmates and traitors but their families too. They made their move, and now Sincere would show everyone how the game of chess was played in real life.

"On the door!" the guard shouted.

Catch stepped out of his jail cell, joined the other inmates on the line for the morning head count, and prepared to leave his cell for mealtime. After the count, he headed toward the cafeteria for breakfast. It was early in the morning. Like every inmate, he followed a rigid daily schedule. Everyone had to be in specific locations at certain times. Catch was a handsome, smooth talker with a penchant for prison booty from flamboyant inmates. He'd become a booty bandit inside the prison, craving anal sex with the weaker inmates. He would forcibly rape other inmates, preferably scared new inmates. He was a fit, dotted-up, and intimidating man operating under the protection of Sincere and Row's organization. Therefore, Catch felt he could do whatever he wanted and get away with it.

Catch walked down the top tier with the other inmates. He moved with confidence. He was hungry for breakfast and ready to get his day started. While he moved, he already had his eyes on a specific inmate, a new fish or fresh booty that had come in with the fresh meat, a young man in his early twenties. Catch thought he was cute. He planned to make his move before they reached the cafeteria. It was the perfect time to assault the new fish and turn him into a prison punk, a weaker inmate forced to become a sex slave by another inmate in exchange for protection from other inmates. And it looked like this new fish would need a lot of protection. Standing alone in the yard, he was considered a lame duck, vulnerable to the harsh conditions.

Yeah, Catch wanted this one badly. He had an erection from just thinking about it.

Catch began skipping the line, bringing himself closer to the new fish. No one protested. He wanted to make his move before they reached the cafeteria since he knew about a blind spot, a hidden area, where he could grab the new fish from behind and make it quick. It was something he had done before. Catch had become a professional at quickly raping new fish and turning them into prison punks.

While he continued to skip the line, he fondled his crotch. The lust he had for this one was overpowering. He had light skin and curly hair and was slim. He was a pretty boy with no harsh pedigree who was in the wrong place at the wrong time. However, Catch was unaware that while he was stalking the new fish, someone was stalking him.

Catch was two inmates away from the new fish, and the blind spot from the cameras and prying eyes was just ahead. It was now or never. He couldn't wait to feel his hard dick slam into the new fish's booty hole and to have his way with him. This one was going to be special. Finally, Catch was one inmate behind the new fish. He grinned. This one was naïve and wasn't going to see it coming. Catch knew how to move like a thief in the night. However, two men surprised him from behind before Catch could skip the line again. Before Catch could react and defend himself, the men began butchering him with two large shanks. The attackers hacked away at Catch's neck with their shanks, trying to hit the major artery and take off his head. The assault was brutal, with the weapons pushing through to the other side of his body, the blades clanking against the stone floor. Once it was over, the men hurried away from the blood-soaked victim.

Catch lay dead, sprawled across the floor in a pool of blood, and the new fish stood there, wide-eyed from terror. He had no idea how lucky he was.

Mrs. Morrison had just arrived home from a long day at work. She pulled into the gravel driveway of her rural home in Elmira, New York, and climbed out of her old Ford SUV. Amy Morrison was a young, pretty white woman born and raised in a small upstate town. Her husband had just been hired as a correctional officer at the local state prison. They had been married for a year and wanted to raise a family at a low cost of living, which Elmira offered. In this small town with an aging population, farming, natural resources, and lots of nature abounded.

Amy Morrison gathered a few of her belongings from the SUV. She marched toward the single-family home with the wraparound porch on the open swath of land near the lake. Her nearest neighbor was a half mile down the road. She was a pretty woman, with long blond hair, green eyes, and a shapely figure. She was a dental assistant at one of the two dental offices in town and loved her job. She and her husband were well paid and happy about their occupations.

Amy and her husband loved their privacy, the lake, and their home, although it needed some renovations. Her husband, Martin Morrison, used to live in the city. He moved from Brooklyn to Elmira during his senior year in high school, and Amy quickly became his high school sweetheart. The couple loved their friends and the town.

However, unbeknownst to Amy, her husband had become a corrupt prison guard who could easily be bribed. Martin had fallen into debt to some dangerous men and had begun abusing his power at the prison, especially when it came to Sincere. Martin Morrison had become Rondell's duck in prison, and whatever Rondell needed, Martin and a few other guards provided. This had become a problem for Sincere. Now Sincere was ready to turn the tide. One necessity for to survival and supremacy was information. And now that Sincere knew Martin was a happily married man, he planned on benefitting from that information.

Amy climbed the steps to her porch and approached the front door. But out of the blue, she was unexpectedly blindsided by a punch to her face and fell backward. Three men clad in black appeared before she could run or holler for help.

"Grab that bitch!" one of the men exclaimed.

They began to attack her, and then they dragged her into the house, and she became a prisoner in her own home.

"You can blame your husband for this," the second man said.

When the front door closed, all three men continued to assault Amy, and her screams for help were futile, because the nearest neighbors were so far away. They tore open her shirt, exposing her breasts, punched and slapped her, and began taking pictures with a Polaroid camera of the assault.

"We got all day with you, bitch. This gonna be fun," said the man in charge.

Seventeen

"How are we gonna do this? I'm ready to get his money," Sheek exclaimed, eager to get the party started and be paid.

"We do this like we're robbing rich people in the suburbs," Sunday uttered. "We watch this fool's every movement, make our move, get in, kill him, and get out."

"And you think it's gonna be that easy?" Nasir replied.

"And why not? This is what we do, right?" Sunday argued.

"C'mon, Sunday, you can't be that stupid," said Sincere.

"Nigga, watch your fuckin' mouth about my sister," Sheek warned him.

"Whatever, nigga!"

"What you sayin', Nasir? This nigga can't be got?" Sunday uttered.

"Nah, I'm not saying that. Anyone can get got, but this nigga, Romeo, he's on a different fuckin' level. I mean, he's not stupid. He's cautious, he's protected, and he's ruthless and dangerous, like Dodge," Nasir proclaimed. "He controls much of Bed-Stuy. He owns real estate, clubs, businesses, whatever, and he's insulated. He always travels with a heavy and armed entourage, and believe me, these fools will shoot first and don't give a fuck about questions."

Sunday smiled. "I'm impressed. You did your homework on this nigga."

Nasir had learned from one of the best, Sincere, re-garding surveillance and reconnaissance. The man had come home from the military with skills, motivation, and knowledge. Unfortunately, Sincere was using his newfound skills and training to get revenge against those who had murdered his little brother.

"We can't go at this nigga blind and naïve," Nasir went on. "He's a force to be reckoned with Sunday. This isn't going in the back door of some rich suburban home and taking control. We fuck up, and we're dead."

"So, what do you suggest, then?" Sunday asked.

Nasir sighed heavily. What he wanted to do was not go through with killing a man like Romeo. He knew the backlash from it was going to be severe. Romeo was revered and feared in Brooklyn. He believed it was a suicide mission. They might as well be trying to kill the president. It was complicated and risky.

"We can't go in guns blazing," said Nasir.

"This needs to happen. We do this for Dodge, and we're set," Sunday reminded him.

"No doubt. No doubt," Sheek interjected.

Nasir groaned and said, "What is every man's kryp-tonite?"

Sunday immediately knew the answer. "Pussy." She grinned.

"No doubt. They call him Romeo for a reason," Nasir said. "He has a weakness for beautiful and exotic-looking women."

"Yo, what you sayin'? You tryin' to send my sister in to seduce and fuck this nigga?" Sheek asked Nasir.

"She can become our Trojan horse," Nasir replied.

"What the fuck is a Trojan horse?" Sheek questioned.

Nasir sighed and shook his head. "Read a book some-day," he mocked.

"Fuck you, Nasir!" Sheek shot back.

"Both of y'all shut the fuck up. We need to focus and plan this shit and make it happen soon. We ain't got all day," Sunday chided.

"Look. Our only way to get close to this nigga is a bitch," Nasir insisted.

"How about Diane?" Sheek suggested.

"She's cute, but do you think she has what it takes to reel in a nigga like Romeo?" Sunday uttered.

"Who then?" Sheek asked.

Sunday and Nasir locked eyes and had a silent conversation between them. They immediately established who their Trojan horse would be.

"I'm doing it," Sunday blurted.

"What? You crazy, sis?"

"My mind is already made up. It has to be me. Nothing can go wrong, and I know I can get this nigga to become vulnerable. It has to happen now. We need this," Sunday insisted wholeheartedly.

"He frequents a club on Utica Avenue called Pitch Black," Nasir said.

Sunday was ready to make her move. In her eyes, Romeo was already a dead man walking.

Sunday entered the popular club Pitch Black like she belonged on the cover of *Vogue* and *Playboy* magazine. Her look was sultry. She was wearing a formfitting, sensual minidress that featured a soft scoop neckline, which highlighted her cleavage. It was tight, eye-catching, and accentuated her deep curves. With her attire and her hazel eyes and her long, wavy dreadlocks flowing down her shoulders, she became the epitome of eye candy inside the place.

Pitch Black was packed on this Friday night. The line of club-goers waiting to get inside stretched down the block.

Cabs were dropping people off at the curb, and beefy bouncers in black were checking IDs and turning people away. Inside, it was dim, strobe lights were pulsing, loud music was coming from several large black speakers, and people were screaming in each other's ears to be heard.

Sunday looked like she had come alone, but she wasn't alone. Nasir and Sheek were inside the nightclub too, pretending not to know Sunday. She soon spotted Romeo in the VIP section of the club. He was the nucleus among his entourage, seated in the center of everyone and clad in a trendy Nike tracksuit and Air Jordans, with a platinum Cuban chain necklace around his neck. Romeo was flashy, and he enjoyed being the center of attention. Everyone had several bottles of champagne on ice, and the women flanking Romeo were beautiful. However, Sunday was sure she would be able to grab his attention. Besides, she knew she was one of the best-looking ladies inside the club.

Sunday grabbed a drink from the bar and pranced toward the VIP section. It was heavily guarded by Romeo's goons. No one was getting close to him if he didn't want you there or know who you were. Romeo was having the time of his life, and Sunday fixed her eyes on him. She figured all it would take was one glance her way and hook, line, and sinker. Yeah, she was that confident. And fortunately for her, Romeo had a clear view of her when she slowly walked by, staring his way.

Romeo's attention quickly shifted from the curvy, tight skirt–wearing hoochie on his lap to Sunday as she coolly strutted by, slightly smiling his way. Romeo was immediately captivated by Sunday's presence.

He mouthed, "*Damn!*"

Sunday had him, and now it was time to play somewhat hard to get. Romeo pushed the woman off his lap and began to pursue Sunday. He had to have her. The way her backside and tits looked in her dress was perfection. Sunday made her way through the crowd, pretending to be busy but knowing what would happen next. Sunday was acting like she was headed toward the restroom when Romeo approached her from behind and coolly grabbed her forearm to stop her.

"Excuse me, beautiful," said Romeo.

Sunday spun around and pretended to be annoyed. "Damn. Don't be grabbing on me like that."

Romeo smiled. "I wanted to get your attention. Don't you know it's unsafe to stare at me like that?"

"What? What makes you think I was staring at you?"

"So, you weren't? Because I know you were."

"Damn, aren't you arrogant and cocky," Sunday countered.

"When I like what I see, I'm not going to hesitate to go after it," he replied.

Sunday chuckled. "Oh, so you like what you see, huh?"

"Yes, I do," said Romeo, sizing her up from head to toe. It was evident from his lustful gaze what he wanted from her.

The two continued to converse, and Sunday was making some headway with him. She had Romeo's undivided attention. He invited her to accompany him to VIP, and Sunday accepted the offer. The moment she entered the VIP section with Romeo, the hate from the other ladies was obvious. They cut their eyes at Sunday and frowned at her like she was enemy number one. However, Sunday didn't feel threatened by them. She sat next to Romeo, and he prioritized her.

Meanwhile, Nasir and Sheek stood by the bar, sipping beers and other alcoholic drinks and swaying to the blaring hip-hop music. Sheek was becoming a little drunk, and Nasir had to check him. They didn't want a repeat of what had happened at the strip club. This lick was necessary, and it had to go down flawlessly.

Nasir removed the third drink from Sheek's hand and griped, "You need to chill with that, nigga, and focus."

Sheek scowled and snapped, "Nigga, don't be snatching shit out my muthafuckin' hands. What the fuck is wrong wit' you?"

"You wanna act up now? With your sister's life on the line?" Nasir countered.

Sheek huffed. "Fuck you!" But he knew Nasir was right. Besides, Sheek knew if he fucked things up tonight, there was no way his sister would forgive him. She was the most important thing to him besides making money.

Nasir observed the activity happening between Romeo and Sunday from afar. The two of them were hitting it off. They were laughing, flirting, and touching each other a little. A tinge of jealousy flowed through Nasir. Sunday was working Romeo, and he wondered how far she would take things. Would she fuck him? He didn't put it past her. Sunday would do what she had to, to make it happen in her favor. Right now, everyone needed to be calm and play their part. Nasir and Sheek were there to keep an eye on Sunday.

The night wore on, and the chemistry between Romeo and Sunday was solid and palpable. It looked like the real thing between them. Romeo was definitely smitten with her.

"I'm ready to get out of here," said Romeo. "You coming with me?"

Sunday grinned and nodded. "Of course."

Romeo and his entourage headed toward the club's exit. Sunday walked close to Romeo as they poured from the club. Then they made their way to a white Tahoe, and Sunday climbed into the back seat with Romeo. At the same time, Romeo's driver and bodyguard got in the front seat. Sunday was surprised that only three men, including Romeo, were inside the Tahoe and there was no car with Romeo's goons behind them. Inside the nightclub Romeo had been surrounded by at least eight goons, and it was known that he liked to travel with a large entourage for security reasons.

It was 3:00 a.m., and Brooklyn was becoming a ghost town. Nasir and Sheek hurried toward the car, got in, and followed behind the Tahoe. Although they knew Sunday could handle herself, Sheek and Nasir were anxious about her well-being. The faster they took out Romeo, the better.

Unbeknownst to Romeo, Sunday had turned on her cell phone inside her clutch bag and had secretly called Nasir. Nasir had taken her call and placed his phone on mute so as not to be heard. Fortunately, or unfortunately, he heard everything that was being said inside the Tahoe.

Romeo placed his arm around Sunday and got a bit frisky with her in the back seat of the vehicle. He began fondling her tits and then reached between her legs and tried to grab a piece of pussy. He made it clear to her what he wanted from her. He'd become an aggressive, horny hound dog. Sunday wasn't an angel, and she had had her fair share of dick, but this was different.

"I want you to suck my dick," he told her.

Sunday smiled and replied, "Damn. Why you gotta say it like that?"

"There ain't no other way to say it. You know what you came here for."

"No foreplay or nothing, huh?"

"Nah. It ain't no time for that. We gonna have some fun tonight. My goons might want some too. What y'all niggas think?"

Immediately, the bodyguard sitting in the passenger seat turned around and smirked at Sunday. He uttered, "Yeah, she's the best one tonight."

"No doubt," Romeo concurred. "It ain't no fun if my homies can't have none."

Romeo had *asshole* and *rapist* written all over him. Sunday knew things were about to go left quick. It was evident Romeo had done this before with his two goons, and Sunday was about to become his next victim. However, she kept calm, knowing Nasir and Sheek would have her back. And besides, she had concealed a small retractable box cutter inside her clutch.

Romeo unzipped his pants and pulled out his sudden erection. It was big and thick, and Romeo was ready to receive some oral action. Sunday stared at his manhood, both impressed and reluctant.

"You didn't think I had a small dick," Romeo smirked. "Yo, put that big dick in your mouth, shorty. Make me a happy man tonight."

The last thing Sunday wanted to do was suck his dick, but she had to remind herself it was part of the game, and it wasn't like she hadn't sucked dick before. But she knew Nasir and Sheek would flip out, because undoubtedly the two of them were hearing the entire ordeal via the cell phone in her clutch. In fact, she knew that they would be fired up, and that this would give them more of an incentive to kill Romeo. Sunday thought, *I'm gonna have some fun and give them a reason.* Besides, Romeo was cute, and she didn't want to let a big dick go to waste. Also, it was the perfect distraction.

Sunday leaned closer and took his erection into her fist. She started giving him a hand job. She used one hand to focus on his long shaft, slowly moving it up and down, while using her other hand to focus on his head. She kept her fingers loose and ran the tips over his head, back, and around the head in a circular motion. Then, with both hands, she made a twisting motion on his big dick while adding pressure to intensify the sensations.

"You like that?" asked Sunday.

Romeo groaned. "Ugh! Yeah!"

Sunday glanced out the back window and saw the Ford Explorer following Romeo's Tahoe.

"Yo, enough of the foreplay, bitch. Suck my dick already," Romeo demanded.

"Where we gonna fuck at, though?" Sunday asked, trying to throw her crew the 411.

"Don't worry about that. I gotta special place for that," Romeo replied. "We got all night."

He was done waiting for one particular service. He grabbed the back of Sunday's head and began pushing her face into his lap. Sunday resisted and griped, "Nigga, don't do that. Don't be forcing no fuckin' dick into my mouth. I got you! Wait!"

Romeo chuckled. "Damn, you a feisty bitch, huh?"

"I'm not your fuckin' puppet," she retorted.

"Bitch, I'm Romeo. You get into a car with me and my niggas, and you do what the fuck I tell you to do. I can make it bad for you tonight. Now, you gonna suck my dick, and you gonna suck my niggas' dicks."

Sunday frowned. It was about to get ugly. Now she didn't want to suck his dick. He'd pissed her off. She coolly picked up her clutch and calmly opened it. Then she reached in and grabbed the retractable box cutter, Romeo none the wiser. She had wanted to wait until they got to his place—wherever it was—but Sunday had said to herself, *Fuck it*. It was too risky to wait anyway. It was now or never.

The Tahoe stopped at a red light on an empty street. Sunday began jerking his dick again. "So, you want me to suck your dick, huh?" she said.

Angered by her remark, Romeo grabbed a fistful of her dreads, scowled, and cursed, "Bitch, you fuckin' deaf? Don't ask me that shit again!"

He was a known woman beater and a sexual predator, but this time he was preying on the wrong bitch. Sunday grimaced. He was hurting her, but she had a surprise for him. This had become personal. So, she opened wide and took him into her mouth. Romeo instantly moaned and became distracted from the oral pleasure. But it would be short-lived. Right away, he screamed in agony as his eyes opened wide from pain. Sunday had taken a hard bite of his genitals, and then she had sliced him with the box cutter.

"You fuckin' bitch!" Romeo cried out in extreme agony.

Both men in the front seat spun around and gawked at the blood gushing from Romeo's genitals. It looked like Sunday had cut off his dick and balls. The blood was everywhere.

"Kill that fuckin' bitch, man!" Romeo cried out.

Immediately, his bodyguard pulled out his gun and prepared to follow orders and kill Sunday. Sunday glared at him and was ready to lunge his way to defend herself. However, shots rang out, and glass exploded.

Boom! Boom! Boom! Boom!

Bak! Bak! Bak! Bak! Bak! Bak!

The bodyguard's head exploded, followed by that of the driver, who was hit several times. Both men slumped over and died in the front seat. Nasir and Sheek had ambushed them at the red light while they were distracted by the nightmare happening in the back seat. It was a bloodbath.

"Sunday, you all right?" Nasir hollered.

Nasir opened one of the Tahoe's back doors and saw the blood and Romeo tightly grasping his bleeding genitals, squirming around, and crying like a baby.

"You fuckin' bitch," he whimpered.

Sunday climbed out of the back seat, blood on her hands and dress. She was fuming. Now it was business.

She grabbed Nasir's gun. She wanted to have the honor of killing Romeo herself. She glared at him and uttered, "I hope it was fun and worth it, nigga."

"Fuck you, you bitch!" Romeo cried out and whimpered.

"C'mon, we need to go!" Sheek shouted.

Sunday had nothing else to say. She shot Romeo five times and ended his suffering. Nasir looked around, and fortunately, it was late, and the streets were empty.

"We need to go," said Nasir.

Sunday followed behind her brother and Nasir and got into the back seat of the Explorer. Sheek sped off, leaving behind a gruesome crime scene for the police to clean up. Romeo was dead, and Sunday was ready to collect her award.

Eighteen

Sunday stepped into the shower and let the hot water cascade down her body. She closed her eyes and let the water wash away her stress and pain, and the blood. She lingered underneath the cascading water and felt the its heat and the steam rising around her. She exhaled. Killing came easy to her, and sucking dick was nothing for her. Sunday's past was complicated. But she wasn't about to allow her past to predict her future. And she wasn't going to make the same mistakes again.

She despised men like Romeo, who beat women and wanted to control them. Years ago, before she and her brother had fled to the Midwest, Sunday had been in a relationship with a similar maniac named Squeeze. Squeeze was nothing to play with; he was a pimp and a drug dealer rolled into one man. She had met Squeeze when she was sixteen, and before her eighteenth birthday, Squeeze had had Sunday turning tricks for him on the streets and at underground spots. And to add insult to injury, he would beat her, and he forced her to have two abortions.

Fed up and yearning for something better, with the help of her little brother, she'd robbed Squeeze of fifteen thousand dollars and relocated to the Midwest to escape the repercussions. Five years later, she'd returned to New York, because Sunday had felt she had a crew to protect her and defeat any enemies trying to come for her. Sunday had had a goal, and that was to become a boss bitch in her hometown. Besides, she had missed New York.

Sunday stepped out of the shower and toweled off. She knotted the towel around her, wiped away the fog on the mirror, and stared at her image. Sunday was still glistening from her shower. She was so pretty that it was hard to believe she was a stone-cold killer. Her hazel eyes were deceiving, and she moved like a demon. She was considered a femme fatale—using her feminine beauty and sexual allure to trap victims like a Venus flytrap did flies. She was a free-spirited, ambitious, self-aware, and sexually empowered bitch unafraid to express and explore her sexuality. Sometimes her attitude toward sex was apathetic. Men were either completely afraid of her or mesmerized by her—but for many men, it was hard to keep up with her. Sunday was like the black widow spider.

However, Nasir was different. Sunday entered into a relationship with Nasir when they were teenagers. She was fifteen at the time and in foster care. And Nasir was sixteen. It was right before Squeeze came into her life. Nasir and Sunday became an item and were inseparable when they were teenagers. Sunday wished she'd lost her virginity to Nasir, but that honor had gone to her foster father when she was fourteen. However, nothing good stayed too long in Sunday's life. Nasir became heavily involved in street life, and Sunday met Squeeze. But unbeknownst to Nasir, there was a pregnancy, followed by an abortion and no regret. Sunday didn't want to become anyone's mother. She knew she wasn't built for motherhood.

Sunday walked into the bedroom. Nasir was seated at the foot of the bed, in a pair of basketball shorts and a T-shirt, brooding over something.

"You okay?" she asked him.

"I'm fine," he responded casually.

"What are you thinking about?"

"I'm just lost in thought, bae, that's all."

Sunday scoffed. "About what? What happened tonight or about her?"

"I'm not thinking about her," Nasir replied, referring to Denise.

"I hope not. I came before her, and I'll come after her," Sunday noted charmingly. She then grinned and said, "We did it! We actually pulled it off and bodied that nigga for Dodge. We're in, Nasir. Oh my God! It's gonna happen for us. My pussy is wet just thinking about it."

She unknotted the towel around her and let it drop to the floor. She was stark naked in front of Nasir, hinting at what she wanted next from him. Sunday straddled Nasir at the foot of the bed, and they passionately kissed.

"I want you to fuck me right now," Sunday stated.

Sunday became aggressive. She peeled off his T-shirt, helped him remove his shorts, and pressed her breasts against his chest while straddling him again at the foot of the bed. She always knew how to make him so hard, his dick would look unnatural. Sunday ran her hand over his crotch, carefully aimed, and guided the hard dick inside her. She moaned in reaction to the quick penetration.

"*Ooh*, fuck me, Nasir," Sunday cooed.

Cupping her full breasts with his hands, Nasir took her hardened brown peaks into his mouth and began to lick them softly. He went back and forth between both tits while fucking Sunday and sending delightful sensations throughout her body. They repositioned themselves, moving from the foot of the single bed to the center, and there Nasir pushed her legs back and continued to thrust himself inside her. The sex became intense, and Nasir became intoxicated with Sunday's scent. She couldn't get enough of him and vice versa. No one was able to fuck her like Nasir. And no man could hold her interest as long as Nasir did.

Sunday knew the ways of the heart. Men were afraid to enter into a relationship with her, afraid she would chew them up and spit them out, which she occasionally did. And the men who tried to tame, control, or own her made the biggest mistake of their lives.

"*Oh shit*, Nasir . . . Fuck me!"

She climbed on top and began to ride his dick. It was time for her to have control. She grabbed his wrists to pin him down, so he couldn't do anything but lie there and enjoy the view. It felt incredible to her to have this control during sex. She loved letting Nasir see her tits bouncing when she rode him. It always turned him on, made him harder, and he always moaned louder. Sunday took it up a notch and dug her nails into his chest, giving him some pain and pleasure. She tilted her head back and gazed at the ceiling, cupped her breasts, and played with her nipples while bouncing on his dick.

"Shit. I'm gonna come!" Nasir announced.

Grinding was a pretty good way to guarantee an orgasm for them both. Sunday used her hips and not her legs; then she leaned in and kissed Nasir lovingly. While she did so, her cell phone began to ring.

"Fuck!" she cursed.

Whoever was calling her had chosen the wrong time to call.

"Don't answer it," said Nasir.

But she figured it might be important, so she answered her cell phone anyway. She leaned toward the ringing phone on the nightstand and snatched it. She flipped it open and immediately exclaimed, "Who the fuck is this?"

"Waah gwaan, gyal. Yuh surprise mi," said Dodge.

"Dodge?" Sunday replied, taken aback by his sudden call. "You already know."

"Mi should've neva doubt yuh. Mi hear yuh cut off fi him dick and balls." Dodge laughed, finding humor in the gruesome act.

"I wanted to send a message."

"And dat yuh did."

"So, this means we're in business, right?"

"Mi keep mi word. Yuh will have everythin' tomorrow night," said Dodge.

Sunday smiled. "Good to know."

"Yuh a dangerous gyal, Sunday. Mi like yuh," Dodge told her. "Respect."

"It's good doin' business with you," Sunday replied.

Dodge said, "We'll see," and hung up.

Sunday was all smiles while Nasir was still inside her. She beamed like a shining star. The fact that Dodge was impressed with her work made her want to come immediately. She stared at Nasir and excitedly hollered, "We're about to become fuckin' rich, baby! We takin' over shit! Ooh, fuck me, bae. Finish fuckin' me right now!"

Sunday began to ride the dick like she was aiming for first place at the finish line on a racetrack, using the power of her back legs, hips, and ass cheeks with freakiness and skills. Everything was about to change for her and her crew. She had a drug connection and killers who would do her bidding to ensure she achieved her goals.

"We got the connect. Now how are we gonna distribute it?" Nasir asked Sunday. "You think we're gonna just walk into some drug dealer's territory and take over?"

Sunday looked at Nasir, grinned, and nodded. "That's exactly what I'm gonna do. And I know where."

Nasir looked at Sunday with bewilderment. She was scary, and he believed she suffered from a touch of psychosis. Sunday did whatever she wanted without fear. That was what made her so dangerous—and effective.

"No more home invasions. No more being looked down on by everybody, muthafuckas thinking they're better than me cuz they got a dick. No more being broke. No more looking for our next come-up. This is our final one. This is gonna be the takeover. You, me, Sheek, Recut, Havoc, Diane, we're gonna become a fuckin' dynasty," Sunday declared enthusiastically.

Nasir stared intently at her and noted a familiar die-hard attitude. Sunday had that same look on her face that said they were getting their way by any means necessary. He had seen that same expression on Sincere's face years ago, when he carried out revenge for his little brother. Once they got started, there was no stopping them.

The two were parked outside an abandoned warehouse in an industrial part of Brooklyn, waiting for one of Dodge's men to make the delivery. It was a quiet and warm night. Sunday took a pull from a cigarette while she sat and waited in the passenger seat of the Ford Explorer. While she conversed with Nasir, her attention was on a swivel, and a Glock 19 sat on her lap. Soon bright headlights rounded the corner and approached their parked vehicle.

Sunday knew it was them. She smiled and said, "Here we go. Our bricks to building this dynasty."

She stuffed the gun into her waistband; then she and Nasir climbed out of the Explorer to greet two of Dodge's men, who'd arrived in a nondescript burgundy Camry. The passenger went to the trunk of the Camry and re-moved a midsize black duffel bag from it. Clad in black, with bald heads, looking like two characters from *Tales from the Hood*, they approached Nasir and Sunday with grim-looking expressions.

The passenger handed Sunday the duffel bag and said, "Ten keys, like you asked for."

Nasir was shocked to hear it was ten kilos instead of five. *What the fuck?* he thought.

"You fuck this up, Dodge will definitely fuck you up . . . nice and slow at first, and then the fun will begin," said the passenger.

"Y'all ain't gotta worry about me. I got this," Sunday responded with confidence.

Both men turned and went back to the Camry. Sunday and Nasir were officially in business. However, Nasir needed to speak his mind.

He cut his eyes at Sunday. "So, you just double the product without consulting with me first?" he barked.

"Consult . . . ?" Sunday chuckled. "I consulted with myself for our best interest. Fuck five keys. Ten will get the ball rolling. I got Dodge's attention. Now it's time to benefit. There's no award without risk, Nasir. You know that."

Nasir huffed. "How we gonna do this?"

"I know where we're gonna hit and hit them fast," Sunday replied.

"And what you think gonna happen if we fuck this up?"

"We're not gonna fuck this up, Nasir. Trust me. Don't even think like that. We're about to be fuckin' rich and respected on such a high note. We gonna run this city soon."

"What location we're looking at?" asked Nasir.

"Baisley Park Gardens. My old stomping grounds," Sunday told him. "I owe Squeeze a visit anyway."

Nineteen

Sincere got *KOS* tattooed across his chest. While he was getting buzzed by a skilled inmate named Flip Side, Sincere and Row sipped on some hooch, an alcoholic drink made from sugar, fruits, and yeast that was fermented in a plastic bag. While the men were enjoying some hooch, getting buzzed, and talking business inside the jail cell, they had one of their soldiers stand guard outside the cell, on the tier, with his head on a swivel. It was a show of strength and dominance.

It was back to business for everyone, and KOS was on the rise. It was a new day. Word of Catch's brutal death, and that of two other inmates, and the assault and rape of the prison guard's wife had spread like wildfire throughout the prison system and on the streets. The fact that they had gone after a prison guard's wife could open a can of worms and create problems for Sincere and everyone else. But Sincere didn't give a fuck. They'd started it; he was going to finish it.

Sincere sat on his bunk, looking like a don. He was shirtless while Flip Side used the improvised tools to get it done—a pen spring, some homemade ink, and a toothbrush battery. The tattoo showed his affiliation and rank. Kings of Society represented wealth, ethnic strength, and racial solidarity. Like with his kids' names, Sincere had *KOS* tattooed on his chest, close to his heart.

Row nodded. "It looks good, my nigga."

"Where are we at with next week?" Sincere asked him.

"We got it set up. We got a bundle comin' in through two guards. It should hold us down for a moment," said Row.

"And what about Rondell?"

"Since we took out Catch and some others, he's been quiet. Maybe too quiet, if you ask me. Maybe he got the hint and knows to back the fuck off and not fuck wit' us," Row answered.

"Nah. Something's up," Sincere replied.

"Whatever that fool got planned, we gon' be ready for him," Row assured him. "Anyway, I heard ya boy is back in town."

"Who?"

"Nasir," Row said.

"What the fuck brings him back to New York?" Sincere asked.

"Unfinished business, I guess. But word on the street is he's with a crew and a bitch. And rumors are they took out this nigga named Romeo for a major player," said Row.

Sincere was listening and was intrigued by the news. What was his old friend Nasir up to? Sincere still held a grudge against the man, and things would never return to the way they were. His sister was dead, and there was no coming back from that. However, Sincere couldn't help but think if things hadn't gone wrong with their friendship, Nasir would be such a great ally on the streets. He had always been resourceful, loyal, and deadly when he needed to be. Row had taken Nasir's place, becoming Sincere's right-hand man.

But Sincere had bigger things to worry about. This beef with Rondell was ongoing, and Sincere knew it would worsen before it became better. But what was *better*? It was when he defeated his enemy and continued to be a shot caller inside the prison, he decided. He was going to remain a prisoner. There was no get-out-of-jail-free card for beating the opposition. Sincere probably would never see the light of day. He would never have a relationship with his kids. There would be no career, no a lovely house, and no peace. There would never be anything normal in his life again. There would always be a Rondell in the game, some foreseen threat going by a different name, wanting that top spot and the notoriety. And the greed made every day a challenge. Sincere remembered an old saying he had heard when he was in the military: *There is no calamity greater than lavish desires. There is no greater guilt than discontentment And no greater disaster than greed.*

Sincere remained quiet while Flip Side continued decorating his chest with a symbol representing power and unity. Suddenly, something was happening. The inmate posted outside the jail cell whistled loudly, indicating someone was coming, a prison guard or guards, and most likely a foe more than a friend to them.

"We got company," said the inmate.

Flip Side immediately stopped tattooing Sincere's chest, and he began breaking the tattoo gun apart. Sincere and Row looked at each other, knowing what was most likely happening. They'd let off the nuclear bomb, and its repercussions were about to follow. But they were prepared for the aftermath.

The correctional guard named Morrison came into the inmates' view and scowled at Sincere. Sincere stood up from his bunk and glared back at the man.

"Everyone, leave now!" Morrison barked.

But no one listened to him. They stayed put, remaining defiant. Officer Morrison began to fume. He was the authority, yet Row and everyone else glared at him like he was their equal or, worse, a June bug, someone subpar.

"You think I'm playing with y'all niggas?" Morrison shouted. He stepped into the jail cell, exuding hostility.

"Y'all niggas, go. I'll be all right," said Sincere.

"You sure?" Row asked.

"What the fuck do you think this is?" Morrison shouted heatedly.

He and Row locked eyes. Row wanted to knock his head off, not caring that he was a correctional officer. In Row's mind, they ran the prison, and Morrison was a guest in their home. Row, Flip Side, and the third inmate relented and walked away from Sincere's jail cell, leaving him alone with the guard. Everyone knew Sincere was capable of handling himself and holding it down.

With everyone gone, Morrison glared at Sincere and shouted, "You attack my fuckin' wife!"

"I don't know what you're talking about. I didn't even know you were a married man, CO," Sincere coolly replied.

"I'm not playing any more games with you, mutha-fucka!" Morrison shouted. "Your fuckin' goons went to my fuckin' home and put my fuckin' wife in the hospital. I should fuckin' kill you right now!"

He angrily approached Sincere and got in his face, with his fists clenched. Sincere was undaunted and unflinching. He matched Morrison's angry gaze and replied, "If I were you, I would think about your next move."

"Fuck you!" Morrison screamed.

"I understand you're upset. But it will behoove you not to do anything stupid. You're able to see and speak to your wife right now. Be grateful for that. Hypothetically, what if that was to change because of some additional unforeseen circumstances?" said Sincere, smirking.

"How the fuck did you find her?" Morrison growled.

"Like I said, CO, I had no idea you were married."

"Bullshit! I swear to God, I'm gonna make it hell for you and everyone connected to you if you don't tell me who attacked and raped my wife!" Morrison angrily threatened.

Sincere stood his ground. Morrison didn't intimidate or scare him. Sincere knew he had the upper hand in this tug-of-war. He knew having information was always a powerful and critical advantage; it was checkmate on the chessboard. And it wasn't about just having information but what you could do with that material. Sincere had acquired some powerful allies from his time in the military, on the streets, and by becoming a feared shot caller inside the prison. But he also had made a lot of enemies.

"How about your wife doesn't make it home, CO? Or, better yet, how about the rest of your family's well-being? Your mother, your older brother, and your nephew, Tommy. Think about their well-being, CO," Sincere uttered.

Morrison was taken aback. How did this inmate know about his family?

"Yeah, I know everything about you, CO," Sincere said when Morrison remained quiet. "I did my homework, and you owe some powerful and dangerous people a lot of money because of your gambling debts. Is that why you decided to align yourself with one of my rivals? Now I understand why you became his bitch. I don't blame you. The money can be good. But guess what now, nigga . . . ? You fuckin' work for me. Fuck Rondell!"

Morrison frowned. Now he felt backed into a corner, with no way out.

"You don't understand. He'll kill me. He'll kill you, your family, and my family too. If you know about his uncle, you will kill yourself before it gets worse for you and your family," Morrison warned.

"Nigga, did you forget about what happened to your wife? And who the fuck I am . . . ?"

"It doesn't matter, Sincere. These people are connected and powerful in ways you can't imagine."

Sincere huffed. "That's why I got you now, nigga. And if you love your wife and your family, you're gonna help me out and help kill Rondell. I know he is the one that tried to have me killed. I'll give you twenty-four hours to think about it," Sincere told him.

Morrison looked like he believed the devil himself would come for him if he began to help Sincere. Morrison stood there quietly and looked defeated. Though he was tall, muscular, and intimidating, suddenly, the guard looked like he was made out of marshmallows. He didn't challenge or argue with Sincere. He simply pivoted and walked out of the jail cell, giving Sincere the impression that he now had one over on Rondell.

"You finally got that bitch-ass guard in the pocket, huh?" said Row.

"Checkmate." Sincere laughed.

Row sighed heavily.

"What's on your mind, Row?" asked Sincere.

The two men walked the yard on a cloudy day. The yard was the epicenter for many social activities and for exchanging information. It was the social gathering spot, for better or worse. Unfortunately for the two of them, things were becoming worse. Sincere and Row conversed about business while they circled the yard, passing inmates working out and engaging in prison recreation programs. Row was concerned about a few things.

"We're taking hits from a few fuckin' guards, Sincere," said Row.

Rogue prison guards were planting weapons and drugs in inmates' cells, particularly at the behest of Rondell. Some guards were spreading false rumors and relaying private information from inmates' files to other inmates, violating department policy. Also, one KOS member, Julius, had been found dead and handcuffed to a chair. He'd been tortured. The violence inside the prison was escalating and spilling outside, into the streets.

"This bitch, Morrison, I don't give a fuck what we got on him. I don't trust him," Row mentioned.

"He knows what's best for him. I trust his fear," said Sincere.

Suddenly, the alarms began blaring throughout the yard, indicating something terrible had happened. The prison guards went on high alert throughout the yard and demanded that everyone hit the ground face-first. Guards began running to where an incident had taken place. Sincere and Row looked at each other with bewilderment while lying face down on the ground, their arms outstretched, trying not to get shot.

"What the fuck is this?" Row mumbled.

Sincere had no idea what had happened, but he would soon find out. Radios crackled loudly. The entire prison was about to go into lockdown.

Unbeknownst to Sincere and Row, Officer Morrison had been found dead in one of the jail cells, hanging from one of the vertical pipes. He'd successfully hung himself with a bedsheet. Morrison had chosen death over having any more harm come to his wife and family.

Twenty

On a night with a full moon, Zodiac and two of his men, one of them Buck, arrived at a run-of-the-mill import-export warehouse in Newark, New Jersey, near Port Newark. The black Yukon maneuvered toward the entrance to the warehouse. An armed guard allowed them through the gates into the sprawling structure, where Zodiac was expected to pick up his prize. As Joc had promised, two thousand kilos had been shipped or smuggled from Africa, then had gone through the Caribbean, and now it had arrived in America. An 18-wheeler tugging a large shipping container slowly backed into one of the loading docks. Zodiac, Buck, and the third man climbed out of the SUV and began to wait for everything to be unloaded from the shipping container.

It was a process.

The rear doors to the shipping container opened, and several men on forklifts began removing items from it. Zodiac wanted to be on hand for the first shipment; Buck would oversee future deliveries. The men in the warehouse began removing dozens of large bales with concealed narcotics and stacking them neatly for Zodiac to view them.

One of Joc's men, Lale, smiled at Zodiac and said, "We in business now, eh?"

Zodiac didn't respond to him. He continued watching them unload the bales from the shipping container and then decided to make a phone call. Someone answered on the other end, and Zodiac uttered, "Send them in. We're good."

Zodiac ended the call, looked at Buck, and said, "Make sure nothing goes wrong."

Buck nodded and replied, "I got this, boss."

Zodiac eyed Buck, silently saying, *I know you do*. He then pivoted, and he and the third man climbed back into the Yukon and began exiting the warehouse. While Zodiac was leaving, two box trucks with a grocery store logo on the sides entered the warehouse. Zodiac stared at them on his way out. The box trucks belonged to him. They were part of his chain of grocery stores called Queens Shop Cuisines. It was one of the many businesses Zodiac owned and laundered his illicit wealth through. The kilos would be concealed in complex secret compartments outfitted in the box trucks and then would be distributed to Zodiac's processing locations throughout Queens and Long Island.

He was in business with one of the most feared and skilled traffickers in the world and was ready to continue building his empire. The shipment was worth sixty million dollars. Joc would be a solid connection for Zodiac, a different direction, and a giant step toward utter supremacy in the streets of New York. Joc had a sophisticated trafficking network that circled the globe, utilizing international cruise ships, submarines, cargo ships, and planes. Whether by air, sea, or land, Joc's product was destined to enter the country illegally or legally for profit and wealth. Zodiac had an endless supply of imports to choose from.

Zodiac sat back and gazed out the passenger window. He glanced at the time on his Rolex, with a price tag of seventeen thousand dollars, and sighed. Despite the Rolex, Zodiac chose to keep things simple, dressing in casual corporate attire. He didn't want to attract any attention to himself. Although he was a very wealthy and powerful man, he was stressed. The more money, the more problems.

Someone was out to kill him.

Zodiac had become the wholesaler to many dealers in the Tristate area and had expanded his distribution through other criminal organizations. He was becoming Queens's top crime lord. He'd opened many legitimate businesses and wanted to maintain a low profile. But he was stepping on the toes of powerful people and rival organizations, one being the Outfit. Zodiac had befriended celebrities, athletes, and politicians. He rubbed shoulders with tyrants, dictators, and the entertainment world's elite. Zodiac owned properties in Miami, the Dominican Republic, Atlanta, California, Chicago, and Arizona. He had millions of dollars in offshore accounts, from Switzerland to the Cayman Islands. He owned a sprawling ranch of several thousand acres in New Mexico, where he'd placed some livestock to increase its value.

Zodiac had become more successful, influential, and business minded than his brother, Markest, had ever been. And he had surpassed Mob Allah and Zulu in terms of wealth, status, and insulation. But he thought about his brother and his father, and Markest's prediction, his words of doom, began to ring in his head. *How long will it last?* Because in his line of work, someone would always be gunning for him.

"Where to, boss?" the driver asked him.

Zodiac turned his attention from the industrial streets of Newark to his driver and said, "The pier with the view of the George Washington Bridge."

A few seconds later he received a phone call from Me-Time. It was the call he'd been waiting for. He hoped it was good news and immediately answered.

"I hope you have some good news for me," said Zodiac.

"I might. If you want to call it good news. Can you meet me in an hour?" Me-Time responded.

"I can. Where?"

"I'm in the city right now. Uptown," said Me-Time.

"Come to the pier near One Hundred Twenty-Fifth Street."

"Okay."

Zodiac ended the call and became pensive in the passenger seat of the Yukon. He knew whatever Me-Time had to tell him wouldn't be good news. The only thing he anticipated was finding out the name of the man or men who had a contract on his head.

They headed toward Manhattan via the Lincoln Tunnel. Once they arrived in Midtown Manhattan, they took the Westside Highway toward Harlem and exited near an antiquated café on 125th Street. Zodiac climbed out of the Yukon and walked toward the pier on the Hudson River with a view of an illuminated George Washington Bridge in the distance. Me-Time had a thing about meeting clients near the water. He was already standing by the railing, waiting for Zodiac's arrival.

When Zodiac was face-to-face with his source, Me-Time handed him a file.

"Good news. I found out who placed a contract on your head. The bad news is that I found out who put a contract on your head," said Me-Time.

Zodiac clutched the file and locked eyes with Me-Time. "Who . . . ?"

"Ezekial. Are you familiar with him?"

Zodiac nodded. Who wasn't?

"You mean to tell me the Outfit wants me dead?"

"It's not the Outfit that wants you dead. Only Ezekial," Me-Time replied.

Zodiac was taken aback and confused. "Why? Is this about business?"

"No. It's personal," said Me-Time.

"Personal?" Zodiac was surprised.

Zodiac knew the man only vaguely. They'd never met. But he was familiar with the man's brutal reputation. The last he'd heard, Ezekial was in Miami. He'd been in Miami for the past ten years. He was a feared and powerful individual and one of the founding members of the Outfit. Mob Allah and Zulu had spoken of the Outfit as if they were boogiemen who wanted to be like one of the five mafia families of New York City. But the truth was that Ezekial was growing old. He was in his early fifties now, and Zodiac couldn't remember when the last time was that Ezekial had set foot in New York.

"I thought he retired from this life," Zodiac stated.

"He never retired. He stayed quiet and insulated," said Me-Time. "But this beef with him is about his two sons."

"Two sons?" Zodiac was baffled.

"Rafe and Drip-Drip."

Of course Zodiac knew who they were. Mob Allah had gone to war with them under false pretenses. Sincere was the mastermind of everyone's downfall. And now here it was, six years later, and once again, the actions of Sincere and everyone else had come back to bite him in the ass and become a problem.

"I didn't know he had two sons . . . especially them two idiots," said Zodiac.

"He kept it a secret. They were estranged."

"And he's coming after me because he believes I had a hand in their demise. Sincere is the culprit behind his sons' deaths. And why now? This shit takes on a whole new meaning now. It's now a case of 'revenge is a dish best served cold,'" said Zodiac.

"From the information I've gathered, he's a compli-cated man," Me-Time said.

"And what about the Outfit? Are they backing him on this revenge nonsense?"

"From my understanding, they're against it, and some internal conflict might be happening inside the organization."

Zodiac had stayed out of the Outfit's crosshairs for a long time, but he had known it would be only a matter of time before their paths crossed. He'd become an influential figure in the Tristate area. His business with Joc had made him a distributor and catapulted him into their hemisphere. *Money, Power, and respect.* That was what it was all about. New York was a big city, with enough money for everyone—but the criminal underworld was small, ruthless, selfish, and devious. Powerful men like Zodiac were determined to be in someone's crosshairs at all times, since there were always those who wanted the throne or those who wanted to continue to sit on the throne.

"Look at the file I gave you. It might explain a lot," Me-Time uttered.

Zodiac opened the file. It contained several pages of information, complete with medical jargon, and a few pictures of a boy.

"Who is this I'm looking at?" asked Zodiac.

"He has lung cancer, stage two," Me-Time informed him.

"Shit!"

How the fuck did he get the boy's medical records? Zodiac thought.

Me-Time was good at his job. He was resourceful, stealthy, and persistent. His contacts in the CIA and other covert agencies benefited Zodiac. Me-Time was expensive, but he was worth it.

"There's a tumor larger than in stage one, but the cancer hasn't started to spread into the surrounding tissues. It will. And he might have a survival rate between fifty-three to sixty percent . . . a five-year survival rate," Me-Time explained.

"Who's the kid?"

"Ezekial's. He has a third son, sixteen years old, living in California," Me-Time said.

Zodiac stared at the photo and saw the likeness between father and son. It boggled his mind. *Why now? And why keep his third son a secret?* Zodiac had decided not to have any children or a family. Trina was the closest thing to a wife, and she understood the risk of being with him. His father and older brother were his past. But Zodiac understood that having a family in this life made you vulnerable. Because if your enemies couldn't get you directly, he knew your family was possibly put on the hit list to hurt you intentionally—and send a message.

"My guess is Ezekial is becoming an unhinged man, is wanting to burn down and destroy everyone he believes is against him or did him and his family wrong. He's making amends, you might say, for his two sons," Me-Time said.

"And I'm in his path, huh? I had nothing to do with his two sons' deaths. It's an excuse to come after me, especially after my deal with Joc in Africa."

"You're a powerful man, Zodiac. You're becoming a threat to him and the Outfit. And he's a dying man, becoming a man with nothing to lose."

Zodiac huffed.

"You have all the information needed. Do with it as you please," said Me-Time.

Zodiac nodded. He was grateful. "You'll have the remainder of your fee wired tomorrow morning."

"Thanks." Me-Time turned and disappeared from Zodiac's sight.

Zodiac turned and marched back to the Yukon. He climbed into the passenger seat and frowned.

If it was a war Ezekial wanted, then Zodiac would give him one. He'd come too far to back down from anyone. The future was his to predict and protect. He was the last man standing, and he wasn't going out like some bitch. What Zodiac had built with the help of Mob Allah and Zulu wouldn't crumble because of some aging gangster with a chip on his shoulder and most likely going through a midlife crisis. And like Ezekial, he was a powerful man himself.

Twenty-one

"Ah, Ah, fuck me!" Cashmere cried out.

She was riding Ezekial's big dick on the king-size bed, about to have a sensual explosion inside her glorious insides. Cashmere's body lit up with pleasure as he pistoned in and out of her while he tightly squeezed her ass and tits. It felt like every single cell in her body was screaming in joy. It was an unearthly pleasure. As Ezekial continued to hammer in and out of her like a madman, Cashmere increased the tempo, riding him faster and faster, working her hips up and down the entire length of his thick, hard dick. He was one helluva man, and she loved everything about him. She began to moan as her body bounced up and down.

"Ooh! Ooh! Yes! Yes! Ooh!" Cashmere yelled.

Abruptly, Ezekial decided to flip Cashmere over onto her back. He was now in charge of the sexual performance. He rolled her tits in the palms of his hands and massaged the bouncy flesh. Cashmere moaned softly and arched her back and lifted her pussy to him. Quickly, he buried his face in her shaved snatch. Her eyes began to roll back in her head as Ezekial lifted her ass high off the bed and thrust his face deep into her pussy.

"*Oh, fuck!*" Cashmere cried out.

Her legs dangled in the air, and she squealed like a piglet as Ezekial licked, lapped, and tongued her pussy, tasting her juices, pinched her nipples, and cupped and squeezed her ass, driving her over the edge.

Ezekial didn't give Cashmere a chance to regain her breath. He released her legs, sank between her thighs, thrust his erection into her, and began bombarding her with his big dick as if conducting missile strikes. She stared at him wide-eyed as he stretched the muscles in her cervix and prodded her with hard, rocking jabs, hammering at her pussy and building an orgasm. Cashmere howled, screeched, shrieked, and lovingly threw her arms around Ezekial. He kissed her deep, forcing his mouth tightly down on hers, and Cashmere's cries of ecstasy died in his throat.

Cashmere groaned and cried out, "I'm gonna fuckin' come, baby!"

She emitted a sharp cry, followed by a shriek, and clawed at the bedsheets while Ezekial pounded into her like a battling ram. Soon they both orgasmed at the precise instant. Cashmere cried out like a hurt animal when she came, her mind spiraling into absolute bliss as the orgasm rocked her world.

Ezekial collapsed beside her for a moment, winded. He lay there, his mind blank, while Cashmere lingered on cloud nine. He'd needed that sexual encounter. Ezekial had a lot on his mind. And Cashmere was one of the few things that acted as a stress reliever for him. She was loyal to the bone. Ezekial removed himself from the bed without saying a word to Cashmere. Still naked, he entered the bathroom and closed the door behind him.

Cashmere remained lying on the bed, trying to collect herself. The dick still had her pussy throbbing, and she wouldn't mind going for round two with the man she was in love with. While she lingered on the bed, she thought about her future with Ezekial. She knew they would never get married or have kids. Cashmere couldn't have any children. She had structural problems in her reproductive system— blocked or scarred fallopian tubes, which hindered sperm from reaching her eggs and an embryo from attaching to the uterine wall. It wasn't meant to be, and Cashmere had accepted her fate. Children would get in the way, anyway, she believed.

Cashmere's upbringing had made her the bitch she was today, and she wouldn't change a thing about it. She removed herself from the luxurious king-size bed and walked toward the floor-to-ceiling windows. She stood naked in front of the windows, where, because of the darkness and outdoor lights, she could see parts of her reflection. From her towering perch, she had a spectacular view of the glistening city, a city of enchantment and richness—but it was a *Gotham City*, filled with its own villains, kingpins, and antiheroes. New York City could be breathtaking to behold, but it wasn't entirely about what you saw. It was also a heartbeat of opportunity, chaos, and destruction. Its atmosphere was one of beauty and pain. They called this place "the city that never sleeps" and this state "the Empire State" for a reason. New York City was always alive, working, and living; this place was an ominous machine. And for you to grow here, you had to become a monster.

Cashmere opened the sliding door to the furnished terrace and stepped outside, where lights were blazing from every skyscraper and every office block. The moon cast a ghostly glow across the sky, making the night seem somewhat sinister. She took in everything and grinned. This was peace. This was living. This was power.

Meanwhile, Ezekial stared at his reflection in the bathroom mirror. He was brooding about something, and his expression as somber. He opened his medicine cabinet, removed two bottles of pills, opened them, and swallowed several pills, huffing and frowning. Although he was in his early fifties, he was still an imposing man with a strapping physique. But he was ill with cancer.

And ever since his doctors had diagnosed him with the unfortunate disease, Ezekial had been in denial to some degree. He was supposed to be a god, but gods didn't get sick and die. Ezekial had a lot to live for and a lot to do. He wasn't done conquering, building a kingdom, and seeking revenge on everyone he believed had wronged him or betrayed him. Ezekial thought forces were trying to take away and destroy everything he'd built. And it was in his power to prevent that from happening.

He thought about his two deceased sons, Rafe and Drip-Drip. Their names at birth were Monroe (Rafe) and Jeffery (Drip-Drip). Ezekial had had a thing with their mother, Gloria, a beautiful stripper turned hustler and crack dealer back in the day. Before there was Cashmere, Gloria was his ride-or-die bitch. She was tough, innovative, and a dime piece. It was easy for any man to fall in love with Gloria; she was like a temptress. And it was easy for Ezekial to get her pregnant twice. She gave birth to Ezekial's two sons four years apart.

After Drip-Drip was born, things began to fall apart between them. Gloria became confrontational about Ezekial's womanizing ways. She was in love with him and wanted to be the only woman in his life. But Ezekial refused to change, and tension grew in their relationship. Unfortunately, when his sons were just one and five, the cops and a task force knocked down Ezekial's door, and prosecutors hit him with an eight-year sentence. When he came home, Gloria was gone with his two sons. She didn't want anything to do with him. Rafe and Drip-Drip didn't know their father; he barely existed for them. However, Ezekial continued to create a powerful empire, while his son tried to do the same.

Ezekial exited the bathroom and joined Cashmere on the terrace. He embraced her from behind, compacting her petite, curvy body in his strong arms. They both were still naked as they gazed at the bright lights and towering skyscrapers from their million-dollar perch.

"Beautiful, isn't it?" said Ezekial.

"Every time I see it, especially with you," Cashmere replied. "But I miss Miami."

"We'll be back there soon after I burn this all down."

"Why?"

"There won't be a future for us in Miami or anywhere else until those who think I'm weak and getting old are dealt with. At that meeting with the other members of the Outfit, I saw how they were looking at me, perceiving me . . . like an aging man hugging the throne, someone who doesn't need or deserve what I've built. And I'm hearing rumors," Ezekial explained.

"What rumors are being said about you?"

"Ones that can get me killed by my own people," said Ezekial. "It's why I have to strike first. I need to spill as much blood as possible to keep power. You understand, Cashmere?"

"I do. But you can't go against the Outfit alone," Cashmere told him.

"I know. And I have allies I can trust."

"Are you sure you can trust them?"

"If going against the Outfit will benefit them, I can. If not, then I can't. And I can be very persuasive, letting them know going against me will be fatal," Ezekial said.

"And how will you know who is with you and against you? If words get out—"

"It's already done, reluctantly starting with the head. There are too many muthafuckas' hands in the pot, and it's time to diminish the dividends around the round table. The smaller the number, the better," Ezekial proclaimed.

Cashmere turned around to stare Ezekial directly in his eyes. "When you mean, the head . . . ?"

Ezekial locked eyes with her. His look said it all. She immediately understood from his despondent look alone. This would hurt him, but in his mind, it needed doing. This wasn't just about money and revenge; it was also about self-preservation.

Cashmere listened, and she wasn't against his plan. Whatever road Ezekial would take, she would be along for the ride.

"'Whoever is first in the field and awaits the coming of the enemy will be fresh for the fight; whoever is second in the field and has to hasten to battle will arrive exhausted.' A quote from Sun Tzu's *The Art of War*," said Ezekial.

"'The quality of decision is like the well-timed swoop of a falcon which enables it to strike and destroy its victim,'" Cashmere proclaimed, knowing *The Art of War* herself.

"It's why I love you," Ezekial said wholeheartedly.

The two kissed passionately, still naked, with the blaring city lights behind them. Ezekial cupped Cashmere's ample ass cheeks and grew another erection. For a man in his early fifties, his sexual stamina was astonishing. He had the energy of a man in his twenties, and Cashmere loved every minute of it. Before long, Cashmere was bent over the railing to the terrace, with her legs in a downward V. Ezekial once again was deep inside her from behind, enjoying the sweet feel of her glorious insides.

In the Brooklyn parking garage, Ezekial sat in the back seat of the Lincoln Navigator with the blacked-out windows. It was nearing midnight when he glanced at the time on his watch. He sighed heavily but continued to wait patiently. The level of the garage he was parked on was empty. And Ezekial and his driver had a direct view of vehicles coming and going. He was dressed immaculately in a Thom Browne suit, wing-tip shoes, and a retro black wool-felt top hat. Ezekial looked like he was the true and only don.

He told his driver, "If they don't arrive in five more minutes, then I know my answer and where they stand."

His driver nodded.

Two minutes later a black Range Rover with the same blacked-out windows and black rims arrived on the level where Ezekial was parked. Behind the Range Rover came a black luxury Benz. They parked opposite the Lincoln Navigator, and doors began to open.

"It's about fuckin' time," Ezekial griped.

It was time. This was the beginning of what they called "the changing of the guards." Ezekial and his driver climbed out of the vehicle to meet with Ray Black, Van Gray, and Monk Dice, who were there to meet with Ezekial covertly.

"This some clandestine shit, Ezekial. Why are we here?" Monk Dice said.

Ezekial looked at Ray Black. "You didn't fill them in?"

"I figure you can tell them yourself," said Ray Black.

Ezekial gave all three men a steely glare and stepped closer to them. And without sugarcoating it, he revealed, "I'm going after the Outfit."

"What?" Monk replied.

"What you mean, going after the Outfit? It's something you helped build," said Van Gray.

"Are you trying to start a fuckin' civil war, Ezekial?" Monk uttered.

"There's already a civil war happening with us. You think I'm stupid? I know what's been happening. There's unrest between the old and the new . . . the old, including myself. Your generation is ambitious, vulgar, smart, but fuckin' naïve and savages! And I know Antonio and Kevin have been slowly planting thoughts about revolutionizing. Men like Baxter, Angelo, and myself are a dying breed, right?" Ezekial said, eyeing Van Gray and Monk Dice.

Both men averted their eyes from his stern gaze. He was reading their thoughts and knew what they were planning. Ezekial was great at reading the room and reading people. He hadn't got where he was by being naïve and reckless.

"Some of us feel we're only getting the crumbs and leftovers from a multibillion-dollar operation. Me and my men are doing all the hard work, while your generation gets to live extravagantly in Miami," Ray Black responded.

"Brooklyn alone generates nearly a billion dollars in revenue, Ezekial," Monk said, chiming in.

"First off, I've earned that fuckin' respect and way of life, Ray," Ezekial growled. "And second, I understand y'all grievances with the Outfit. The room has become too crowded. Too many hands in the pot, along with opinions. Especially with the Outfit worth north of five billion dollars."

"There's no disrespect to you, Ezekial. We all know your pedigree. It's why we all agreed to meet with you this way. We want to hear you out," said Van Gray.

"I'm not here to waste anyone's time. It's time to destroy and rebuild. And you're either with me or against me with this. Whoever is not with me is against me, and whoever does not gather with me will forever perish. I'm ready to put any old beef and grievances to bed and let us arise anew and united stronger than before," Ezekial declared emphatically, eyeing all three men.

Ray Black, Van Gray, and Monk Dice looked at each other awkwardly. These were full-fledged gangsters, dangerous men who committed unspeakable acts of violence. But there was something about Ezekial's presence that had become daunting to them. His soulless dark eyes would stare at and almost through you, as if you were transparent. It felt nearly like he knew what you were thinking. Ezekial was a gangster who embraced Machiavellianism. He could quote Sun Tzu, George Orwell, Shakespeare, generals, and others at the drop of a dime. He could be sly, deceptive, and manipulative.

Ezekial had their undivided attention. He knew each man's strengths and weaknesses. That was a reason why he somewhat trusted Ray, Monk, and Van during this clandestine gathering. Their strengths were their viciousness, their youth, their eagerness to expand, and their unsatiable desire to rule. Like many other men, their weaknesses were their greed, impatience, stubbornness, a certain lack of organization within their crew, and their flesh. Yes, the flesh was always weak, something Ezekial understood far too well from his past experiences. Women had been men's downfall for centuries.

However, the main reason Ezekial trusted they would make the right decision was that he had dirt and incorruptible information on these men that could destroy their livelihood, get them imprisoned for life, and tarnish their celebrated reputations. Monk Dice was a closet homosexual with a desire for underage boys. Van Gray was stealing from everyone, including the Outfit, an action that warranted death. And Ray Black was a male whore. He was fucking the wives, girlfriends, and daughters of his lieutenants and some members of the Outfit. Ezekial had come to this meeting prepared. He would force their hand if they didn't join him willingly. These men pretended to be kings on the chessboard when they were merely becoming pawns for Ezekial.

"Victorious warriors win first and then go to war, while defeated warriors go to war first and then seek to win. You see, fellows, with the four of us together right now, we've already won," said Ezekial.

Ezekial fell silent and stared at them intently. His sudden silence was menacing and intimidating. He knew what to say, but he had also learned to say less than was necessary.

"If this goes wrong, Ezekial, we're all fucked," Ray Black uttered.

"It won't go wrong. It has already begun," Ezekial coolly replied.

Ray, Van, and Monk shared concerned and awkward glances. Whatever Ezekial was plotting, they had no choice but to acquiesce to his diabolical plan. And the first target on his hit list would result in heartbreak, but it needed doing for him to progress.

Twenty-two

Killing season . . .

Baxter Johnson had become a creature of habit. He woke up early every morning, around 6:00 a.m., drank his coffee, read the morning paper, walked a few miles on the treadmill, and checked some of his business investments via his laptop. He kept up with current events by viewing news programs. Baxter lived his life more like he was a complacent CEO of a Fortune 500 company than a notorious crime boss. He had a wife of forty years, a girlfriend of five years, five adult kids, and eight grandkids, and he was like the Energizer Bunny; he could keep going and going. During over thirty years in organized crime, he had served only four years in prison, for a tax evasion charge and a minor gun charge when he was thirty-six.

Baxter had become a straightforward, content aging man with an infamous past. He liked his tailored suits, expensive shoes, pinkie rings, glazed doughnuts, and aesthetic gold chain and cross. Though he was extremely wealthy, Baxter lived a frugal life. He hated to stand out and be flashy. One look at Baxter Johnson, and he could easily be confused for an aging man who had an office job. He owned a printing company, a scrapyard, laundromats, nightclubs, real estate, and a development company. He invested millions of dollars in start-up companies. There were yachts and memberships in private country clubs. Baxter loved to golf. Golfing and spending time with his family were the loves of his life. And there was the girlfriend, Adriana.

Adriana was a petite and curvy twenty-three-year-old European beauty who worked as a receptionist at his real estate firm. Though he was forty years her senior, it didn't stop Baxter from having a passionate and steamy affair with her. She'd become pregnant twice by Baxter, and two miscarriages had followed. Although Baxter was in his midfifties, women flocked to him like he was a magnet. With his wealth, power, influence, he was the quintessential strong, handsome, and self-contained gangster.

Baxter finished his morning coffee, folded his newspaper in two, and left it on the kitchen table. He stood up, fastened his suit jacket, pivoted toward his wife, Elana, and kissed her goodbye for the morning. It was their morning routine. Elana was content in being the trophy wife and housewife. She was forty-eight but looked thirty-eight, aging gracefully after bearing five children. She had womanly curves and long, luscious hair, and she needed no make-up to make her look flawless.

Elana smiled. "Have a nice day, hon. And don't forget to pick up something nice for your grandson's birthday this weekend. He's turning eight, so nothing babyish."

Baxter chuckled lightly. "I won't. They grow up fast, don't they?" he said.

"Yes, they do," Elana replied.

"Don't expect me home until late tonight," said Baxter.

"As long as you make it home, I'm okay."

Baxter smiled. "Forty years later, I always make it home to you."

They kissed again, and then he grabbed his things and headed for the door. Elane stood there watching him with her customary endless gaze.

He had a busy day ahead of him. But Baxter planned to see his mistress before anything else. Waiting outside his home was his security guard and chauffeur, Darius. Darius, who was in his late thirties, had been Baxter's chauffeur and personal bodyguard for nearly a decade. The two had a tight bond, akin to that of a father and son.

Darius sat in the idling black Escalade, clad in a dark suit and tie, waiting patiently for his boss and mentor to exit the luxurious five-bedroom home in New Jersey. Baxter inspired his people to dress the part and be the part. Darius had once been a violent young goon who'd been in and out of prison, until Baxter stepped in to mentor him and mold him into the perfect gangster with a gun and class.

Baxter exited his suburban home, wearing a charcoal three-piece suit, carrying a leather briefcase and sunglasses, and looking like he was the businessman of the year. Darius stepped out of the SUV to open the passenger door for his mentor and boss. He didn't mind the minimal duties assigned him. He was learning a lot from the crime boss and was hoping to fill his shoes one day.

"Good morning, sir," Darius greeted formally, his chin up and posture erect.

"Good morning, Darius," Baxter responded cordially before sliding into the passenger seat of the Escalade.

Before Darius climbed back into the driver's seat, he noticed Mrs. Johnson lingering on the threshold of the front door. She was wearing a purple silk robe, and though she was a grandmother, she didn't look a day over thirty-five. She had a certain charm about her, and Darius knew his boss was lucky to have married her. He also knew Baxter had the best of both worlds.

"Where to first?" Darius asked Baxter.

"Take me to Adriana's place. I need my morning fix before I start my day," said Baxter.

Darius smiled and nodded. He didn't judge his boss for his infidelities with his wife. And although Elana was one helluva woman, a man would be a man, no matter how old. Also, Adriana was one hot piece of ass.

Darius put the vehicle in reverse and backed out of the driveway.

The suburbs were a haven for a crime boss like Baxter. He had kept a low profile over the years, built an empire, and raised a wonderful family, with his offspring succeeding in medicine, politics, entrepreneurship, and music. Baxter had beaten the odds so far, defying death and life imprisonment. He was respected—feared too. In fact, he was one of the most feared criminals in New York. Though Darius was his muscle, even without him, Baxter thought his life would never be threatened. No one would ever kill him; they wouldn't dare.

The Escalade arrived at the towering building in Irvington, New Jersey, and stopped near the front entrance. Before Baxter exited the vehicle, he told Darius, "I'll be here no less than an hour. I do have a busy day. Go get us a cup of coffee."

Darius nodded. "Will do."

Baxter stepped out of the SUV. Unbeknownst to him, his movement was being monitored. Before he could take two steps away from the vehicle, two men in ski masks and armed with semiautomatic pistols, calmly walked toward him and opened fire.

Bak! Bak! Bak!

Boom! Boom! Boom! Boom!

Baxter was immediately hit in the chest several times, which threw him back against the SUV. Darius hurriedly grabbed his gun to return gunfire, but before he could do so, a third masked gunman, armed with a shotgun, approached from his blind side and fired into the driver's side window, shattering glass and striking Darius in the back of the head. He was immediately killed. It was a horror show. The masked men then sprinted away from the bloodshed, leaving Baxter Johnson dead on the ground and Darius a bloody, gruesome mess in the front seat of the Escalade.

Someone had done the unthinkable; they'd publicly killed Baxter Johnson, a notorious crime boss from Harlem. He was the equivalent of Bumpy Johnson, Carlo Gambino, and Lucky Luciano.

Ezekial knew that to be proficient and successful, every target on his kill list needed to be taken care of before the news of Baxter Johnson's death could spread. Ezekial knew it was about timing. Once the word got out that a significant kingpin had been gunned down in public, everyone would be on guard, and he would lose the element of surprise. No. Ezekial wanted to strike while the iron was hot. And although it was nearly impossible to go after dangerous, respected, and feared kingpins with armed men and killers, some of whom weren't predictable in terms of their routine, every target needed to be killed by noon that day. Therefore, he'd sent out Doc and Cashmere to help him get things done.

Bruno stared at the playing cards in his hand and remained stoic. He was playing in an underground game of high-stakes poker, a high-status game held twice a week in different discreet locations. Some of the wealthiest and most influential people took part in the game. The players, ranging from doctors, lawyers, politicians, rappers, and gangsters to kingpins, athletes, and celebrities, had deep pockets and were passionate gamblers. No matter their background or occupation, everyone in the room had a common interest: playing poker and winning. The game was hosted by a beautiful woman named Oliva. She was from Germany and had migrated to the States twenty years ago to build a business in shipping and receiving. And now she rented hotel penthouses, businesses, lounges, and lavish homes to host her high-status poker game.

This time the game was being played in the basement of a popular bar in Westchester, and there was a ten-thousand-dollar buy-in, and the blinds were fifty and one hundred. Eight men, including Bruno, were playing at the oval card table. He was a compulsive gambler but a good poker player. Oliva treated her players with the best amenities, from top-shelf liquor and snacks to girls, if they so desired after a loss. She took in 5 percent of the pot from each poker hand.

It was a night of chips flying, drinks being put down, cards being flipped, and players jumping up in victory or angrily pounding their fists against the table in defeat. Some players angrily threw their cards at the dealer when they lost, and Oliva would have to check them. If they couldn't play nice, they would have to leave the game and would probably never be invited back again. Oliva's sponsors were Armenian gangsters, and they were nothing nice.

During the game's high point, the pot had reached eighty-five thousand dollars, and Bruno was holding a four of a kind, four straight aces. It was a great hand, the third highest in poker.

"I'll call," Bruno uttered, matching another player's bet.

There was a raise, and two players chose to fold, turning their cards in to the dealer face down. Only two remained to win the huge pot, Bruno and a rapper named Cho-Cho.

This was the moment of truth. Bruno knew he would win the jackpot—a hundred thirty thousand dollars was nothing to him, pennies on the dollar. He wanted to win, but poker wasn't about the money. It was the intensity of the game that helped to feed his ego. Playing poker was about reading people, analyzing risk versus reward, and persuading people to do what you wanted them to—often in subtle ways. It was about understanding your motives and your competitors.

Bruno was confident. He'd been playing poker for a long time, and he knew he had this pot.

"Full house, muthafucka!" Cho-Cho exclaimed, displaying two jacks and three kings.

It was a great hand, and Cho-Cho was ready to celebrate and collect his winnings . . . until Bruno displayed his cards on the table.

"A straight flush," Bruno boasted, smirking.

Cho-Cho was so shocked, his jaw nearly hit the floor. "What the fuck!"

"I don't play the odds. I play the man," said Bruno.

Cho-Cho frowned and accepted his defeat. There wasn't anything he could do about it but mope. Bruno was a criminal kingpin, and his reputation in the Bronx was diabolical. Everyone knew Bruno was not only a compulsive gambler but also a dangerous figure. With the snap of his fingers, he could make anyone disappear.

"Good play," said Cho-Cho.

Bruno reached forward to collect his winnings, but then something happened. Sudden chaos erupted. Before Bruno could collect his chips, the doors to the basement flew open, and two armed men wearing masks burst into the room, wielding Glock 19s. Everyone assumed it was a robbery—but how? There was armed security for the game provided by the Armenians. It was a high-stakes card game with hundreds of thousands of dollars in play, which needed to be protected, and so the location was guarded.

Everyone froze where they sat or stood; no one dared to move or even flinch. Even Bruno kept still, glaring at the masked men, who he assumed were there to rob him of his winnings. He remained undaunted, believing his reputation and pedigree would scare them off.

"Y'all fools know who the fuck I am?" Bruno growled.

One of the men smirked and replied, "Yeah, we do."

And with that said, both men aimed their guns directly at Bruno and opened fire.

Boom! Boom! Boom! Boom!
Boom! Boom! Boom!

The basement room lit up with gunfire, and bullets tore through Bruno like he was paper thin. The force of the gunshots propelled him out of his chair, and his bullet-riddled body spilled to the floor. He lay dead in a thick pool of blood. One of the gunmen coldly walked over to the body and fired two more rounds into his head. It was overkill.

"Shit!" someone shrieked.

The other patrons at the card table were left unharmed.

One of the gunmen addressed the room's occupants, saying, "Y'all have a nice day." Then the two killers turned and coolly marched out the back door. Everyone was stunned. Did that just happen? they thought. But it did. Bruno's bullet-riddled body sprawled across the basement floor was proof of that.

Cho-Cho sat there, terrified. He was going to be sick. Before he knew it, he was hunched over and hurling chunks of the day's leftovers onto the floor.

Angelo Giuseppe, the fifty-two-year-old don, was killed when Doc and his men opened fire with a submachine gun on him and his associates early in the morning, while they were visiting a courthouse where an ally of Angelo's was on trial. It was a brazen murder in public—messy too. Doc and his goons didn't give a fuck. The gunfire sent a wave of panic through the area, and when the cops finally came, Doc and his men were long gone. Angelo's body was left sprawled across the courthouse steps, leaking blood like a broken faucet.

Doc removed his mask while he was in the back seat of the Ford SUV, grinning and laughing at the bloodshed they'd caused. Killing and the ensuing chaos gave him a rush. Doc was a psychopath, a social predator with some mental illness. He was effective at killing, torturing, and intimidating.

Doc made a phone call and stated, "Yeah. It's done. We're on our way back to New York right now."

The morning sun poured through the quiet Brooklyn neighborhood, indicating it would be another bright day, with new hopes and aspirations. There was a pearly glow in the sky. Multiple businesses and shops were beginning to open up for the day. The morning traffic was starting to fill the streets. Alarm clocks had gone off, eyes had popped open, and immediately everyone was off to the races, readying for to work, school, or the myriad tasks for the day. Bensonhurst was a residential neighborhood in southwest Brooklyn. It was filled with the best bake-shops, grocery stores, and restaurants, as well as with immaculately kept homes, some with Victorian-style or Italian-style architecture, and it featured the breathtaking Verrazano-Narrows Bridge promenade. Bensonhurst used to be the Little Italy of Brooklyn, but now it was diverse.

One particular business in Bensonhurst was a pizzeria owned by Antonio Francesco. Antonio owned several successful pizzerias throughout Brooklyn. And although these places were less profitable than his other business, pizzerias were Antonio's pride and joy. Antonio's pizzerias were renowned for their coal-oven pizzas. The pies were always fresh, hot, and delicious. The crust was nicely charred, and the pies boasted the perfect ratio of sauce to toppings.

Antonio's pizzeria was the heart of Bensonhurst. It sat on the corner of the block. On this particular morning, two men arrived to open the pizzeria. They unlocked the rolling steel gate and raised it. Then they entered the pizzeria and began to prepare for another busy day. An hour before noon, a dark blue Lexus ES 330 arrived at the pizzeria. Antonio, wearing a burgundy Adidas tracksuit; a beautiful, leggy, blond-haired woman wearing a track dress and strappy heels; and two of Antonio's henchmen climbed out of the car and walked into the pizzeria. Antonio liked to be hands-on at this this particular pizzeria because it was his first. He enjoyed making pies. His uncles had taught him the business while he was growing up. It was a family tradition, along with a life of crime.

"*Ciao. Buongiorno,*" Antoinio called, greeting his employees in Italian.

"*Buongiorno*, Mr. Francesco," they replied in unison.

The ovens were being turned on, and the employees were beginning their daily preparations for making pizza pies and other menu items.

"I'll be in the back if anyone needs me," said Antonio.

Antonio and the beautiful woman he'd come with disappeared into the nearby back office to engage in something more friendly and fun. Antonio's two henchmen knew it would be a while, so they sat at one of the tables, ordered coffee, then sipped and waited.

The moment Antonio closed the door behind him, the blond woman lifted her tight dress to her waist, displaying her petite figure, shaved pussy, and lovely curves. This was routine. Antonio quickly dropped his pants and thrust himself into her from behind, with her bent over his desk. Immediately, Antonio's cell phone began to ring atop the desk, but distracted by the blonde's gloriousness, he decided a piece of pussy was more critical at the moment than his ringing phone. Unbeknownst to him, an associate was calling to inform him about the deaths of Baxter Johnson and other Outfit members early that morning. The caller wanted to warn Antonio of possible pending danger, but Antonio didn't want to be interrupted.

Meanwhile, four men sat parked across the street from the pizzeria. They had witnessed Antonio's arrival.

"This is y'all's window. Go in and take care of it," said the driver.

Everyone nodded. Three goons masked up. Two of them armed themselves with semiautomatic pistols, and one goon gripped a shotgun. They coolly exited the Chevy and boldly crossed the street to assassinate one of the most dangerous men in the city.

Right away, all three men charged into the pizzeria with their guns blazing. First, they opened fire on Antonio's two hoodlums, who were caught off guard and blinded by the quick attack. One got hit with a powerful shotgun blast that lifted him off his feet and sent him crashing into the wall like a bug. And before the second could react and return fire, he was hit with a barrage of bullets, which mangled his body. He collapsed face down across the table. The employees were dumbfounded and frightened, fearing they were next to be killed. But the gunmen weren't there for them; they were looking for Antonio.

"Where is he?" one of the men yelled.

One of the employees pointed in the direction of the back office.

All three men hurried to the back office to finish the job. One of the men kicked open the office door and rushed into the room, only to be met with a volley of gunfire from Antonio.

"You niggers come for me! I'll kill you all!" Antonio screamed.

Gunfire erupted between Antonio and the two gunmen left standing. The blond woman crouched behind a desk, screaming at the top of her lungs. Bullets ricocheted everywhere. It was chaos.

"Fuck you, niggers!" Antonio shouted heatedly.

A standoff ensued.

The killer with the shotgun swiveled sharply with the deadly tool, pointed, and let it explode like a cannon into the room.

Chk-chk boom!

Pieces of the desk went flying everywhere, and the blond-haired woman was caught in the cross fire. She lay sprawled in a pool of blood behind the mangled desk, her body contorted from the shotgun blasts. Antonio's eyes grew wide with rage at seeing the woman's body.

"Muthafuckas!" he screamed.

He emptied the clip at his assailants and quickly knew he was fucked. It was the only pistol he had on him to defend himself. But promptly, luck was on Antonio's side. Blaring police sirens could be heard in the distance. And though Antonio despised the police, the sound of them coming was music to his ears.

"We need to go!" one of the gunmen shouted.

They were reluctant to leave before killing Antonio. But they didn't have a choice. If they didn't flee the scene now, they would have to deal with an entire police precinct. Having no choice, both men retreated, leaving behind their dead friend.

When the smoke cleared, Antonio stood there, angry and dumbfounded, with his emptied pistol down by his side. Someone had tried to have him killed, and he had an idea who it was.

Twenty-three

Detective Shelly Mack poured herself a cup of coffee, walked to the kitchen window, and stared into her backyard. It was another warm and sunny day. Although it was her day off, Detective Mack still had cases on her mind, especially the one concerning the Rockford family. She couldn't forget what'd happened to that family. It troubled her that whoever or whatever monsters were responsible for killing those kids and raping that teenage girl were still out there, roaming free. She wanted justice for that family and was determined to get it.

However, the DNA they had taken off the mother's and the daughter's bodies didn't match anything in their system. There had been no eyewitnesses to the crime, no cameras, and no snitches or informants to point fingers at anyone. And it had been nearly two weeks, and still no word from her informant, Dante.

Shelly Mack knew cases like this one could grow cold quickly. But she also knew that whoever was behind the family members' murders wouldn't stop, and it wasn't the killer's or killers' first rodeo. She had a hunch that these might have been their first murders in New York, but the monster or monsters behind such appalling acts weren't new at this. The way everything had been planned and executed, the killer or killers had to have been watching the family for a while, especially the father.

The Rockford family was well known and well liked, and so there was extreme pressure from the community, the victims' extended family and friends, fellow officers, and the media to solve these murders. And this responsibility had been placed on her shoulders. This was the "big one" for Shelly Mack, the case that would pave the way for her. All eyes were on her and her partner, Detective Emmerson.

Shelly Mack was a determined and capable police detective in the New York Police Department. She wanted to outshine her superiors, the naysayers, and make rank someday. But what drove her to excel was the feeling that she was speaking up for the dead, her victims, and she didn't want to fail them. This was why she was trying to micromanage this entire case, making all the decisions. There couldn't be any fuckups anywhere. When the culprits were identified, apprehended, and indicted, there couldn't be any loopholes or ambiguities to allow for their release or, worse, their acquittal. The horrendous acts done to the Rockford family were unforgivable. They should be punishable by death or life imprisonment. No fuckin' parole!

Mack got on her laptop and logged into a particular database, and then she began scrolling through various websites. She searched for crimes like the one she was investigating, those involving wealthy or well-to-do families being murdered in their homes and the girls being raped. It was a long shot, but it was something. These monsters had to have left a trail somewhere, in some state.

Mack spent nearly all morning on her laptop, searching for something to link her crime with another crime somewhere. She and the Queens precinct also communicated with the Queens district attorney. The captain always strived to get someone from the Queens County District Attorney's Office on board immediately after a major criminal event. The DA's office encouraged the police to notify them of any significant crimes and investigations right away, and the Rockford investigation was a major criminal event. Personnel with the Queens DA were available to the detectives 24-7, to guide them through the cases as they evolved.

There was an open murder case in Arizona that struck a chord with Shelly Mack. It involved a jewelry store heist and a family found duct-taped and killed. The family's home had been ransacked and robbed of all its valuables. Mack perked up and read on. The murders had happened some months back in a small town a few miles south of Phoenix. Five people were killed, including the father. The case had too many similarities to hers: for instance, the nineteen-year-old daughter was raped and murdered and the father was killed at a jewelry store. A cop, the victim's brother, was also killed.

Mack decided to make a phone call to Arizona. She got in contact with the lead detective on the case there, a man named Michael Jesseph. Their conversation was brief. Mack informed him of her similar case, and she told him she believed the similarities between the cases weren't a coincidence. Detective Jesseph thought so too. But there had been no leads in his case, and unfortunately, his investigation had ended badly. He was a small-town detective with few resources. And although the case had garnered some national attention, it hadn't been enough to involve outside agencies. The federal government and state agencies didn't believe that, one, the murders were the work of a criminal enterprise, such as organized crime and drug trafficking; that, two, they were hate crimes; and that, three, they were perpetrated by a serial killer. For these reasons and others, they refused to get involved.

Mack ended the call, disappointed, but she wasn't discouraged.

She finished her second cup of coffee and decided to go into her backyard to attend to her sprawling garden. She put on gardening gloves, grabbed her shears, and stepped into her small but neat backyard. Mack took pride in her gardening and landscaping. She had the best of both worlds: a flower garden and a vegetable garden. Both were beautiful and productive. Surprisingly, she had a green thumb for growing tomatoes, cucumbers, and squash. Her soil was nourished with organic matter, such as compost, manure, and leaf mold. The compost she had easily learned to make at home, for free.

Her flower garden had been planted parallel to her vegetable garden. It contained a multitude of green plants and white, pink, and purple perennials, and the effect was energizing. Her roses were beginning to bloom, and she enjoyed their silky petals and perfume as she passed under the arbor. Shelly Mack loved the wonderful way her roses looked and how the blossoms seemed to change color when the sun shone on the petals. Her vegetable and flower gardens had become her private oasis away from the wicked, sinful, foul, and vile doings of humanity. It improved her mood and provided hope and inspiration. Seeing plants and flowers grow helped with any depression or anxiety; it also helped her think clearer.

She planted her knees in the dirt and began tending her garden. She watered, weeded, trimmed, pruned, and mulched, adding a protective layer of organic material to prevent soil erosion and conserve moisture. The tending was a lengthy process, but she loved it and took her time.

It was mid-afternoon. The sun bathed the backyard in its warm light, while the blue sky was dotted with fluffy white clouds that drifted lazily above the gentle breeze. Shelly Mack's mood harmonized with the nice weather. Her day was perfect . . . until her cell phone rang and the ringing echoed from the kitchen into the yard.

She sighed, knowing it was work calling. She always remained on standby in case her partner or others had some urgent news. It was the job. It was her life. It was the world. Her interlude in her garden paradise was about to come to an end.

She got off her knees, brushed off the dirt, and walked toward the back door of her home, pulling off her gardening gloves as she went. Her phone stopped ringing before she entered the kitchen, but she knew it would ring again.

And it did.

Her cell phone chimed a second time, and it was her partner calling. "You know it's my day off, right?" said Mack.

"Have you seen the news?" Chris Emmerson asked her right away.

"No, I haven't. Why?"

"Turn it on right now," said Emmerson.

Shelly Mack made a beeline for the living room, the cell phone to her ear. She searched for the remote control, located it, and turned on the television. She changed the channel to the news and watched the report on Baxter Johnson's violent death in New Jersey.

"Crime boss Baxter Johnson was gunned down early this morning in Irvington, New Jersey, while visiting an unknown female," the reporter announced. "He had just exited his SUV in front of a residential building when three gunmen ran up and shot him several times, killing him, and his driver was also . . ."

"Fuck me!" Mack muttered.

"There were several coordinated hits early this morning. One in Philadelphia . . . Angelo Giuseppe. Bruno was killed in Westchester, and there was an attempted hit on Antonio Francesco in Brooklyn," Chris Emmerson said.

"What is going on?"

"Something big. A gang war, some kind of takeover," Emmerson answered.

"Do we know who's behind it?"

"All I know is the victims were part of an organization called the Outfit. These men were prominent figures in the underworld. Whatever is happening, it's happening fast, and it's violent. My guess is it's coming from the inside," Emmerson told her.

"By who?" she asked.

"The list is long," said Emmerson. "But I assure you it's gonna get ugly out there. Captain wants us to come in for a special briefing today. A kingpin like Baxter Johnson gets killed in public, and the city becomes topsy-turvy."

Shelly Mack sighed heavily. *Of course.*

She knew the escalating gang violence would put a hold on her investigation of the Rockford family murders. If it wasn't one thing, it was another.

New York City was on fire. Members of the Outfit were at war with each other, and no one was safe. The deaths of Baxter, Bruno, and Angelo Giuseppe had ignited a shitstorm in all five boroughs and beyond. Antonio Francesco was on the warpath. They had come for him and missed, and now he was ready to burn it all down. A nightclub was shot up in Harlem, leaving three dead. A drive-by happened at a local bodega in Brooklyn, killing two. A robbery at a Bronx apartment left four dead, and six kilos were taken. A couple at a Queens café were gunned down. A house fire in Queens wounded two. A worker was stabbed in the head on a Bronx street. The streets of New York were filled with blood and chaos, and everyone was on high alert. Pandora's box had been opened, releasing carnage, violence, and mayhem, and there was no way to close the lid.

Kevin Charles, from Newark, and Gregg Rice, from Yonkers, had aligned themselves with Antonio. The death of Baxter Johnson and their peers had angered them. Everything had been going good, moving smoothly, until an aging bad apple had decided to disrupt the status quo. They knew the only one capable and bold enough to execute this kind of violent takeover was Ezekial. His greed, jealousy, and paranoia were toxic, and his rampage for revenge was spreading like a virus. Kevin Charles and Gregg Rice had deduced that Ezekial wasn't acting alone. Therefore, Ray, Monk, and Van Gray became enemies of the Outfit. They'd foolishly transitioned from kings of a dynasty to idiotic lieutenants because of Ezekial.

Ezekial's presence had become a curse, tearing everything apart, unleashing a civil war.

Emmerson and Mack arrived at another crime scene in Queens. It was already a circus, with police bustling about and lots of lookie-loos stopping by to catch of glimpse of the dead and the reporters arriving to get footage of the carnage. It was a real block party. The gathering crowd was behind yellow police tape, looking straight ahead, craning their necks, squinting, and gossiping, and some were even laughing. Sadly, death and violence were common occurrences to the residents.

Both detectives pushed through the crowd and ducked underneath the crime-scene tape to join their fellow officers and detectives already on the scene. There were two bodies underneath bloody white sheets. The smell of death lingered in the air like a thick fog. This was the second shooting in four days. Both detectives slipped on rubber gloves and moved closer to inspect the bodies. Detective Emmerson squatted near one of the bloody white sheets and slid it back to reveal the deceased.

Detective Mack stood over him. The victim was young and had been shot to shit at least seven times. A bullet had pierced his right eye, his chest, and his throat. He was dead before he hit the ground.

"You know him?" Mack asked.

Detective Emmerson nodded. "His name is Gizmo. He is eighteen and was a worker for Van Gray."

Emmerson went to inspect the second victim. He was familiar with the second dead man too. "This is Darryl James, one of Van Gray's lieutenants." Detective Emmerson stood up, ripped off the rubber gloves, and huffed.

A uniformed cop walked up to them and said, "A witness said it happened fast. Two gunmen in black came up to them while they were leaving the store and opened fire. Then they took off in a gray van or something."

"They know who?" Emmerson asked.

"C'mon, Detective. In this neighborhood, where mum's the word? We're lucky we got that much from someone," the cop replied.

Detective Emmerson sighed heavily and uttered, "Thanks," to the cop.

The good news was that they were able to identify the victims. The bad news was there were going to be a lot more victims.

Detective Emmerson looked at his partner and said, "It's gonna be a long summer."

Twenty-four

It was perfect, Sunday thought. *Home sweet home.*
She stared at Baisley Park Gardens, a low-income and
low-rise housing project in Jamaica, Queens, rife with
drugs, gangs, and violence. Being back home stirred
some mixed emotions inside her. She'd left years ago, but
now she was back to pay her good ole friend Squeeze a
visit and become something she'd always dreamed about.

"I say fuck this place," Sheek growled as he stood right
behind her. "It ain't nothin' but bad news and fucked-up
memories in the first place."

"For us to move forward, we need to confront our past,"
said Sunday.

"Fuck the past, and fuck that nigga Squeeze. You really
tryin' to see that nigga right now?"

Sunday grinned. "He's the only fool in our way."

"And I'm gonna make him move out our fuckin' way,"
said Sheek. "Believe that shit."

"Just chill out, Sheek. I got this. I have a plan," said
Sunday.

"I know you do, sis. But I don't like that nigga. I never
did." Sheek huffed and puffed.

It was a beautiful spring day. Across the street in
Baisley Pond Park, kids were playing on the community
playground, a cricket game was happening in an open
field nearby, and park goers were enjoying a sunny spring
day by mingling, barbecuing, playing sports, fishing in
the pond, and relaxing on the park benches. The sprawl-

ing park was a direct contrast to the poverty-stricken low-risers across the street.

Sunday stood at the entrance to the low-risers, clad in a pair of coochie-cutting shorts that displayed her ample ass cheeks, a tight cropped top that accentuated her tits, and Nikes as bright white as snow. Sunday's ebony skin shined as if she had recently oiled it or had sweated after a long, hard workout, and her sultry wavy locks looked healthy and stylish on top of her head. She was the epitome of eye candy, and one could easily confuse her for a young around-the-way girl searching for some thug loving.

Sheek followed his sister into the housing project, a 9mm tucked snugly in his waistband. He wasn't about to take any chances. His job was to protect his big sister at any cost. His head was on a swivel and his hand was near his tucked pistol while they walked toward the courtyard. As usual, the bright spring day had enticed a crowd of people to the area. On the hot asphalt, young teens were playing a game of skelly, a children's street game played with bottle caps in New York City and other urban areas.

Rap blared from an SUV in the parking lot. A few locals sat outside their apartment doors, chatting and trying to keep themselves cool on the hot spring day. And there were the hustlers and drug fiends scattered around the housing projects; drug transactions were done quickly and subtly.

Sunday stepped into the dilapidated courtyard, where Squeeze was hanging out. He sat perched on a bench, flanked by a few of his goons, and was wearing black cargo shorts and a wifebeater that hugged his strapping physique. Squeeze was a physically imposing man. He sported a large Cuban link gold chain with a diamond cross at the end of it. His bald head gleamed in the sunlight, and his arms were covered with tattoos. There was a presence to him: his deep-set dark eyes seemed to cut into you like a sharp blade.

A girl lazily swaggered across the courtyard, moving in Squeeze's direction. With her hair in disarray, her sunken eyes, and her run-down attire, she screamed *dope fiend*. Sunday watched as the girl picked up her pace and hurried toward Squeeze, eager to get his attention. And she did. It was clear what she wanted, her daily fix, but she was short of funds. Squeeze stared at her like she was dirt, but she gazed at Squeeze like he was the Almighty himself. He had something she desperately desired. Some words were exchanged, and the girl began to scrounge around in her pockets, looking as if her life depended on it—and maybe it did. *Squeeze* found humor in her anguish and suffering.

He smirked and uttered, "You gonna bless my nigga for that high?"

She would do anything for it. Whatever it took.

"I got him, Squeeze. I got him. Whatever you need from me . . . ," she replied rashly.

"Do that first, come back, and then we'll talk," he said.

A lad who looked to be no older than fifteen grinned. It was evident to everyone in the area what she was expected to do. She was no stranger to trading sexual pleasures for her needed fix. There was still a nice shape to her skinniness, and a pretty girl hid behind her drug addiction. She hurriedly vanished with the boy into the hollow of the project building nearby to do what was needed.

"Fiend-ass bitch," Squeeze muttered with antipathy.

Sunday frowned at what she'd witnessed. His action was a harsh reminder of her past. He was still the same—an egotistical, sadist, and demented monster.

Sunday boldly began marching his way to get his attention. The moment Squeeze saw her approaching, he scowled. He kept his eyes on her like a lion watching his prey, crouched threateningly in the distance, ready to pounce. Sheek was right behind her, his own scowl aimed at Squeeze.

"I heard you were back in town," Squeeze said when Sunday reached him.

"I am."

"You got my money, bitch?" he growled through his clenched teeth, not one to beat around the bush.

"No, I don't, Squeeze," Sunday coolly replied.

Squeeze chuckled at her insane reply. "Let me get this straight. You steal fifteen grand, fuckin' leave town for a few years, and now you got the fuckin' nerve to come back here without my money, plus interest. You and your brother are either stupid or fuckin' suicidal. Either way, I'm gonna get my damn payback."

"I came here to talk," Sunday responded.

"Ain't nothin' to talk about. You either pay me what you stole, plus fuckin' interest, or how 'bout you don't walk out here alive?" he threatened. "Fuck that. How 'bout it be like old times? I'ma take you upstairs and fuck you in all three holes like there's no tomorrow and paralyze you, bitch."

Sheek pouted heatedly like someone had shoved a sour lemon in his mouth. He clenched his fists and kept his hand near his tucked pistol. He was itching to put a bullet in Squeeze's head. But it would lead to his own death and his sister's. Sheek and Sunday were flanked by several men, who were glaring at them like they were the Antichrist. The courtyard was an adequate size. It hosted a few long-standing benches, and these marked the boundaries of an antiquated playground for the kids, but no children occupied the area on this warm spring day or any other. The courtyard had become the de facto hangout spot for drug transactions. The drug dealers and drug fiends frequented the area day and night and had lookouts perched above on rooftops.

"I owe you, so let me make it up to you," said Sunday.

Squeeze became upset. He removed himself from the bench and stood threateningly over Sunday. His deep-set dark eyes looked ominous as he stared at Sunday. His goons circled them, and it looked like things were about to become ugly for them. Yet Sunday remained undaunted and levelheaded, although she and her brother found themselves in the lion's den, with the lion's sharp teeth ready to tear them apart.

"Bitch, you fuckin' steal from me and come back here like we cool like that? You done fuckin' lost your damn mind, Sunday," Squeeze exclaimed.

Sheek was ready to yank out his pistol and begin blasting. If they were going to kill him, then at least two or three were dying with him. He knew coming back to the projects and meeting with Squeeze was stupid. The man was a lunatic.

However, before things became physical and violent, Sunday uttered, "I have access to five kilos. It's yours, Squeeze."

Sheek was taken aback. He cut his eyes at his big sister and exclaimed, "Are you crazy, sis!"

Squeeze didn't believe her. He was offended. "You lying to live, bitch," he muttered venomously.

"No. I'm not," Sunday replied casually.

She whipped out her flip phone and went to a picture of her with several kilos of cocaine. She handed the phone to Squeeze. He stared at it and knew she wasn't lying. The date on the picture was recent.

Squeeze glared at her incredulously and said, "How the fuck did you get access to that many kilos?"

"Does it matter? It's yours," said Sunday.

Squeeze chuckled suspiciously. "Mines, huh? And what do you want in exchange for it?"

"I just want to come back home and not fear for my life anymore, my brother's too. I miss Queens. I want to make amends with you. I fucked up. I know. But this should make up for it, right? It's way more than what I took from you," Sunday proclaimed wholeheartedly while locking eyes with him.

Squeeze looked at his right-hand man, Tater, and they agreed silently. To both men, it was a win-win for them. He turned his attention back to Sunday and said, "A'ight. We can work something out. You got some breath again, bitch."

Sunday smiled. "I'm glad we could work something out."

"No doubt. Come by tomorrow night with everything, and we'll be squared," said Squeeze. "I got you."

Sunday nodded, okaying everything. "Same place?"

"Bitch, it's been five years . . . What the fuck you think? I'll send you the new location where to meet. And we'll take care of business."

"Okay."

Sunday and Squeeze locked eyes again, and it was apparent there was an uneasy truce between them. Of course, there was something devious behind Squeeze's eyes, and he struggled to hide his greed. His wolves backed away from Sunday and Sheek, and they were allowed to walk away.

The moment they were out of the lion's den, Sheek became irate. He was confused. "I know you ain't 'bout to give that fool no five kilos, Sunday. You lost ya fuckin' mind?"

"Don't worry about it, Sheek. I'm on top of things," she replied.

"You better be, sis. Cuz you know that nigga ain't to be trusted. The moment you give him those five kilos, he's gonna kill you anyway," said Sheek.

"I know," Sunday answered.

Before they climbed into the car, Sunday observed the girl from earlier emerging from the projects. Her appearance remained disheveled, and her eyes were sunken from her drug dependence and obsession. A minute later, she hurriedly trekked away from the courtyard, clutching her fix. It was apparent she had given up her soul for it. Sunday could only imagine what the teenager had done to her in some stairwell or hallway.

She knew because she'd been there herself. She'd sucked dick in building stairwells and hallways many times. She'd been fucked by so many different men that sex became dull and meaningless, a job to make her pimp, Squeeze, richer. There had been the threesomes in various apartments and underground locations, the constant disrespect she'd endured, and the drug use. Squeeze had made sure he had a hold on Sunday that so solid and secure, she believed what he was doing to her was natural and to her benefit.

It was a miracle that she'd escaped with her life and his money. But she had. And now Sunday was back, stronger and better than ever. She was hyper-focused. She knew what she wanted, what men who had tried to control and abuse her had—money, power, and respect. She repeated aloud to herself daily, "It's my time to shine."

Sunday watched the girl walk briskly in the opposite direction. Then she disappeared up the street to find a place to get high for the day, only to return the next day and repeat the same process.

"Sis, what the fuck? Let's go," Sheek exclaimed, snapping her out of her daydream.

Sunday climbed into the Jeep, and they left the area.

***

Sunday got out of the Jeep, clad in a short denim skirt that showed off her long, defined legs, her high heels, and a revealing halter top that drew attention to her thick cleavage. She could easily be mistaken for a club goer, but Sunday had a different reason to be dressed like some club hoochie. She was a bad bitch, for sure. But she wasn't about fun and leisure tonight. Business and appeal were on the agenda.

It was late, and she was alone. Sunday had concealed a .380 and a kilo of coke in her small handbag. Now she stared at the odd, big house on the ghetto block and knew it was a risk to be here and to have come alone. But this was something she had to do, meet with a shot caller who went by the name of Bray. They had something of a history.

Surprisingly, the block was quiet. It was late, three hours from the dawning of a new day. The house Sunday stood in front of was the biggest one on the block. It bore a slight resemblance to a Victorian home and had a wrap-around porch, while most of the places on the boulevard were rowhouses or single-story homes.

She approached the porch steps and then climbed up them, clutching her small handbag tightly. The front door opened when she reached the porch, and two men exited the house. They didn't look friendly at all. One gripped a .45 and scowled at Sunday.

"You in the right place, shorty?" this man asked. "Especially lookin' like that?"

"I know I am. I'm here to see Bray," said Sunday.

"Bray . . . ?"

"Tell him Sunday's here to see him," she responded.

"Sunday?" the second man uttered, somewhat familiar with the name. "You Sunday?"

Sunday stared at both men intently. "What the fuck you think?" she replied gruffly.

She was done explaining herself. They stared at her, and something about her oozed trouble, but her confidence and bravery were attractive.

"A'ight, c'mon," said the first man.

She was allowed into the house. Sunday knew she was in the right place when she stepped foot into what appeared to be a trap house. There were so many niggas inside the living room that it looked like the processing center at Rikers Island. The smell of weed permeated the entire house. Rap music blared, and a few pretty girls kept the goons company. Several men were playing *Call of Duty* on a PS2. A small arsenal of guns was in plain sight. The house had seen some better days: the paint was peeling off the walls, the shutters were crooked, and the place was sparsely furnished with run-down furniture.

There was confusion at first when Sunday entered the house. Everyone thought she was another well-dressed hoochie joining the party, ready to give up some pussy. Jealousy immediately stirred among a few girls when they saw Sunday. She was pretty and sassy, and her wardrobe wasn't cheap. They knew that from a distance. Sunday noticed the look on the girls' faces, the rolling eyes, the side looks, and the envious mocking under their breaths. But the fellows gave her a different look, one of wonder.

Sunday guarded her handbag and remained nonchalant while the wolves were circling. It had been a long day, and she wasn't in the mood to tolerate anyone's bullshit.

"Damn, shorty. You came to see me?" one of the men in the room joked.

"Where the fuck is Bray?" she demanded to know.

"Oh, you saving that pussy for the big boss, huh? How 'bout I sample some of that before you fuck him? See if it's worth his time," said the same man. He laughed.

The disrespect made her frown. Sunday glared at the fool as if she wanted to cut his head off with a samurai sword and kick it somewhere far.

Out of nowhere, over the rap music and the chatter, Sunday heard someone say, "I heard you were lookin' for me."

Sunday quickly pivoted and placed her eyes on Bray. It seemed like he had appeared out of nowhere. Although she expected to see him, a part of her was surprised to see him again. Bray was a handsome man in his midthirties, with a beard so thick that it could conceal a pistol. He moved with a confidence that bordered on arrogance. He was tall, with features that seemed to have been chipped from rock.

"I'm surprised you came back into town. I thought you were gone for good," said Bray.

"I'm back for a reason," said Sunday.

"It gotta be a good reason for you to risk your life comin' back here."

"I already saw Squeeze earlier," she said.

Bray was taken aback. "Oh, really? And he left you breathing?"

"He's the reason why I'm here," Sunday confessed.

Bray chuckled. "I'm listening."

"Is there somewhere we can talk privately?" she asked.

Bray began to walk off, and Sunday followed him into another room, a den or a small office. Bray closed the door behind them and turned his undivided attention to Sunday.

"Why are you here?" he asked.

Sunday opened her small handbag and removed the kilo of cocaine from it. She placed it on an old writing desk he had in the room. Bray was utterly dumbfounded.

"What the fuck you doin' with a kilo, Sunday?" asked Bray.

"I need your help," said Sunday. "And if you say yes, that kilo is yours."

"I'm listening," Bray told her.

"I wanna take out Squeeze and take over Baisley Park Gardens," Sunday revealed.

Bray chuckled, but he knew she was serious. "And how do you plan on doing that?"

"With your help," she uttered seriously. "I have a connect now and came to you with a gift. I can supply you with the product. I just need the muscle."

"You need me to become your patsy and go to war with Squeeze now that you're back in town," said Bray. "I used to fuck you, get you high. Now you want me to work for you?"

"I want us to become rich, Bray. And I liked you. I still do. You always treated me fair and nice when I was just some young ho sucking dick, not knowin' any better," she stated.

Bray stared at her deadpan and uttered, "Yeah, you did change."

"I'm not that bitch you used to know. That was a long time ago," Sunday replied.

"Not too long ago," Bray quipped.

"I'm here on business, with a proposal. You control the Blood Mafia Boys, one of the most feared gangs in New York. But I know there's trouble on the horizon. Crews are splintering into several smaller factions and warring with you. Fuckin' with your business, testing your leadership," said Sunday.

"You did your homework, I see. And you're here to help me with that, huh?"

"Of course. You need money, influence, guns, power, whatever it takes to shut down your rivals and keep you in power," Sunday declared. "You help me take down Squeeze, and I'll help you stay in good health with your gang. I owe you that."

It was an enticing proposition. Bray was a career criminal who delighted in violence and was known to personally dish out a beating to his enemies and betrayers. The Blood Mafia Boys, called BMB for short, was a street gang with its own rules and organizational structure. Members reportedly had quotas to fill every week. But their hierarchy was becoming unstable.

Bray gazed at Sunday and noted that she was dressed appealingly. Yes, she *was* different. And tempting. And nostalgia for their sexual rendezvous crept into his thoughts.

"One question," he uttered gently. "You came dressed the way you did for what reason? To entice me into saying yes to your proposal?"

Sunday grinned. "I wanted to look nice tonight. But if it helps with your answer . . ."

Bray stepped closer to Sunday, invading her personal space. He towered over her and looked down at her with a rich gleam in his eyes. It was obvious what he wanted from her.

"So, you wanna fuck me for you to say yes?" Sunday asked facetiously.

"You knew the answer to that when you decided to come here," Bray replied. "Besides, I miss it."

"I'm with someone," she uttered barely above a whisper.

"And yet you still came here, knowing what I would want from you."

"Y'all niggas are all alike," she stated.

Bray leaned down and passionately kissed her. Sunday didn't fight him off. His kiss was deliberate and thorough. His hands lifted her denim skirt, massaged her hips, ass, and thighs as they kissed. Sunday pulled herself closer to him. Bray maneuvered her toward the writing desk, and then he hoisted her onto it. He undid his belt, pulled down his pants, and released his huge, thick dick.

Before she knew it, Bray was between her legs and inside her. Sunday's pussy became a pool of wetness, which overflowed and ran down the inside of her legs.

"*Oh, fuck.* Fuck, yes," Sunday moaned. "Fuck me!"

Sunday pulled her legs up and wrapped them around Bray. She wanted him deep. He pulled her to the edge of the desk and thrust hard and fast, filling her pussy with one strenuous movement.

"Oh fuck!" she cried out.

Bray grabbed her tits, squeezed her ass, and continued to ram his hard dick inside her, edging her second by second closer to an orgasm. She moaned and gasped with pleasure, his bare chest pressed against her breasts, and his hard, big dick opening her insides like a doorway.

"I'm gon' come!" Sunday announced breathlessly.

Bray increased the pressure of his rhythm and strokes. Next, Sunday's hips lifted from the desk, and she came with a shuddering gasp. He continued to thrust into her hard and deep. Then, with a loud groan of release, Bray came too. His hard dick began jerking inside her gushing wet pussy, and he delivered squirt after squirt of thick cum.

What began as business had turned into something pleasurable.

"So I guess that's a yes to my proposal," said Sunday, collecting herself by pulling down her skirt and fixing her halter top.

"Let's make us some money," Bray replied. "Fuck Squeeze!"

Sunday grinned. She was excited, but there was one problem now: an old flame had been sparked by fucking Bray, and a part of her wanted to rekindle their fling. The dick was good—really fuckin' good.

But what about Nasir?

Twenty-five

Sheek and Nasir were surprised that Sunday had gotten Bray to agree to their terms. She was known to be convincing and influential when she needed to be. She had a knack for what Vito Corleone in *The Godfather* would call "making them an offer they can't refuse." However, they hated that she had gone alone to meet with him, but Sunday had insisted on doing so.

Aloof, Sunday sat in silence in the back seat of the Ford Explorer. Her mind was elsewhere as they headed toward the low-rise project buildings. Beside her was a small duffel bag containing the five kilos for Squeeze. Sheek and Nasir were in the front seat, and following behind them in a Dodge were Havoc, Recut, and Diane. She thought about last night's sexual rendezvous with Bray. It had stayed in her mind like a magnet on a fridge. She had enjoyed it a little too much. And she felt a little guilty about having cheated on Nasir. He remained clueless and believed it was only business between them. He'd been good to her. But Sunday thought of fucking Bray as bringing her a step closer to doing what she needed to do. Tonight was the night everything was going to change. Once Squeeze was killed, the area would be annexed by Bray and his gang. It was a gold mine, and Squeeze's dominance over it was about to expire. Sunday was going to make sure of that.

She was nervous but fearless at the same time. She didn't want anything to go wrong.

"You know, once you give him those five keys, you ain't
leaving that apartment alive, sis," said Sheek.

"You think I don't know that," Sunday replied.

Bray and his gang were her contingency plan.

They arrived at the low-rise projects around 10:00 p.m.
Squeeze had texted her the location. It was an apartment
on the third floor. Sunday, Nasir, and Sheek climbed
out of the Jeep and headed into the projects. Squeeze
had his men everywhere, on the rooftops, loitering in
the lobbies, the courtyards, and the stairwells, and on
the streets. If there was a supposed police raid or a rival
attack, Squeeze would know ahead of time. Things were
coordinated to give him and his crew ample time to
escape or to eliminate anything incriminating inside the
apartment. It was a fortress.

Sunday was dressed in cargo pants, a black shirt, and
Timberland boots. She was fitted for combat, and her
mentality was urban warfare. She clutched the duffel bag
tightly, wanting to get everything over with. The main entrance to the lobby was cluttered with a few of Squeeze's
goons, who were drinking, gambling, and frolicking.
Only some were on guard. When they noticed Sunday,
the chatter, drinking, and gambling stopped, and she had
their undivided attention. She was expected.

One of Squeeze's goons said, "Nah. Only two of y'all
are going up."

Before Sheek could protest, Nasir decided it would
be him. He and Sunday proceeded into the main lobby,
while Sheek stayed behind with their rivals. Sunday and
Nasir felt like they were lost in a thick fog, with no guiding light. The warm night and the full moon had brought
out the dope fiends, the crazies with gone minds and lost
souls. Addicted crack whores were sucking young dope
boys' dicks in the dim stairwells; dealers were floating
around every inch of the projects, peddling dope or coke;

and residents remained trapped in their apartments for the night, feeling like prisoners of war in their own community.

The tension was heavy to Sunday and Nasir. It felt like they were journeying into the pits of hell, ready to confront the devil. However, Sunday was determined to escape hell unscathed and alive. They arrived on the third floor. The narrow hallway was covered in gang graffiti, and the smell of weed permeated the entire floor. Nasir followed behind Sunday, searching for the apartment. It was the last apartment at the end of the hallway. It stood out because the door had been changed. It was painted black and made of steel, making it harder for cops or anyone else to force their way inside. A slot was also embedded in the door to facilitate drug transactions and to identify visitors.

Sunday knocked and waited coolly for someone to answer. It didn't take long for someone to open the door. One of Squeeze's men glared at Sunday and Nasir. He stepped to the side and allowed them into the apartment. Before they walked from the foyer, the man said, "Nah, y'all need to be searched."

He quickly patted Nasir up and down first, confirming he was unarmed. But he took his time searching Sunday for any weapons. He frisked her nice and slow, squeezing her ample ass and cupping her tits. Sunday frowned and cringed, disgusted that she was being fondled by this creep.

"You done?" Sunday muttered with contempt.

He smirked. "Yeah, you good."

Sunday cut her eyes at him with disdain. She felt disrespected and violated but stomached it and kept it moving. When she and Nasir entered the living room, Squeeze was waiting for them. He was sitting on the couch, smoking a blunt, wearing a wifebeater and a do-rag. His Timberland boots were untied, and his thick Cuban link gold chain with the diamond cross gleamed. Sunday counted four men in the room, not including Squeeze, and three naked women sat at a worktable in the kitchen, their faces veiled by surgical masks. They were cutting heroin with lactose and quinine in precise quantities to ensure the purity of the product.

Squeeze stared at the small duffel bag Sunday was carrying and grinned. "Damn, you actually fuckin' came. You really want ya life, huh?"

"I'm here to do business," Sunday replied coolly.

"Let's do some business, then," said Squeeze. "You got those five keys in that bag for me, right?"

"I do," said Sunday.

Squeeze's smile remained on his face.

Nasir stood solemnly by Sunday's side. His concentration was like a hawk's. He paid attention to every detail—two of Squeeze's men sat, and two stood, on guard, no doubt ready to strike if needed or when ordered to. He and Sunday were outnumbered and unarmed, and Nasir felt it was a mistake to have shown up when the odds were entirely against them. There were no draperies on the windows or pictures on the walls.

Squeeze's black eyes screamed hatred and betrayal. As he smiled, he bared his large white teeth at them, and he stared at Sunday like she was food to him, his elbows against his knees and his fingers clasped. He always seemed ready to pounce from a sitting position.

"Show me what you got," said Squeeze.

Sunday stepped toward the glass coffee table, where a pistol was displayed. She slowly placed the duffel bag near the gun and unzipped it with a certain sureness. Squeeze watched her every movement. The gun on the table was taunting her. The room was still, like she was about to perform some magic act and the audience was mesmerized. Nasir remained on edge. It was all about the timing.

Before Sunday could show him the goodies, there was sudden knocking on the apartment door. Squeeze and his goons went on high alert. One reached into his pants for the butt of a gun. Nasir and Sunday stood frozen.

"Who the fuck is that?" Squeeze cursed, becoming agitated. "Check it out."

A man went to the door to inspect the sudden visitor. He gazed through the slot and replied, "It's Megan, Squeeze."

Megan was the girl from the courtyard yesterday afternoon, the one who'd disappeared somewhere to give the fifteen-year-old dealer some head. She had on a skirt today and a dingy T-shirt. Her black hair was matted, and her lips were dry as the desert.

"Squeeze, c'mon. Open the door for me. I need to see you," Megan hollered from the hallway. "I'll fuck you or whoever right now. I just need to see you."

Megan was making a scene. They didn't need that kind of attention while Sunday was about to hand over five kilos of cocaine.

Squeeze frowned and said, "Fuckin' dope fiend bitch. Yo, get rid of her right now."

The man at the door nodded.

Unbeknownst to Squeeze and everyone else, Bray and his men were inside the project building. They had been hiding out in two different apartments since early morning. It was in keeping with the plan. They'd snuck into enemy territory using the Trojan horse technique. With the help of some inside sources and cooperating residents, they would remain hidden inside the apartments until the time to act came.

And the time was now. Before Sunday had knocked on Squeeze's door, she'd sent a text to Bray that read Come now. In the text she'd also given him the apartment number.

The Blood Mafia Boys were armed and ready. Nearly a dozen soldiers withdrew from the two apartments they'd been waiting inside and posted themselves at various places throughout the building for a premeditated strategic attack.

Squeeze's goon swung open the steel door to confront Megan. However, he was in for a rude awakening. Right away, he was met with violence and force. The barrel of a hand cannon, a Desert Eagle, was thrust in his face. Bray and his men had been hiding out of sight of the door slot while they allowed Megan to do her thing: to have that door open and draw out the guard. When he took a step out of the apartment, the attack happened. The butt of the .50 cal was slammed into the guard's face, and he crumpled to the floor, howling in pain.

Seven of Bray's armed goons rushed into the apartment like a swarm of bees, ready to sting everyone inside it. Being all bark and all bite, Bray's brutes drilled several bullets into three of Squeeze's men, killing them instantly, while the fourth ran into the kitchen. Squeeze reached for the gun on the coffee table, but Sunday got to it first. With his only line of defense in the hands of Sunday, Squeeze broke into a run and raced toward one of the bedrooms while Sunday let loose with the gun.

Bak! Bak! Bak! Bak!

All four shots barely missed Squeeze as he took cover inside the main bedroom and slammed the door behind him. He locked it, hoping that would give him some time. Sunday and Nasir chased after him, while Bray and his men took care of the fourth and final goon. The goon tried to use one of the naked workers as a shield, but it was useless. Bray shot the girl and the aggressor. He was heartless.

Meanwhile, Squeeze was panicking. He opened the closet door and desperately searched for his assault rifle. However, Sunday and Nasir burst into the room before he could find the weapon.

Squeeze pivoted and scowled. "You fuckin' bitch! You set me up!"

"You was gonna kill me anyway, nigga! So fuck you!" Sunday yelled.

Squeeze glowered at Sunday. Raw anger shot through him. He wanted to tear her apart with his bare hands, but now she had the advantage. It was too late; he knew this was his end. Nasir aimed his pistol at him, but it wasn't right for him to kill Squeeze. This duty was left to Sunday.

Sunday glared at Squeeze, and everything he did to her when she was young raced through her mind like an electric shock. Her resentment of him had grown inside her like a tumor, and rage gripped her now. She replaced her gun with a stainless-steel ice pick with a wooden handle, which she'd kept concealed on her person until now. She held the tool in her fist.

"Fuck you gon' do with that, bitch?" Squeeze taunted her, though he was defenseless and had nowhere else to run. "C'mon, bitch. Let me break your fuckin' neck." He scoffed and chuckled.

Sunday didn't respond to his taunt. She wanted to see this muthafucka suffer, and a quick bullet to the head wouldn't suffice. But a loud gunshot suddenly reverberated in the room before she could charge him and take her revenge with the ice pick. Squeeze had been shot in the head, and he collapsed face down on the floor. Sunday and Nasir turned to see that Bray had fired the fatal shot.

"What the fuck you playin' with this nigga for? We gotta go," Bray exclaimed.

Nasir chuckled.

Sunday suddenly felt cheated.

Bray didn't give a fuck what she felt.

Sunday retrieved her duffel bag, and everyone fled from the apartment, leaving behind a bloody massacre—and seizing a lucrative opportunity of a lifetime. The area, near JFK Airport and two major highways, was prime real estate for drug trafficking and transactions.

Sunday felt sour at first that she wasn't the one to kill Squeeze. But the feeling was short-lived. She'd done it. This was the come-up she had always dreamed of. Baisley Park Gardens belonged to her now that Squeeze was dead. Through Dodge, she would supply Bray and his gang with the kilos needed to maintain the territory. But first, they had to allow the heat to die down with the authorities and take care of some loose ends. Squeeze was feared and respected, and Sunday expected some backlash and retaliation for his death.

Twenty-six

Sincere's King was in a difficult situation. Gent was a comfortable position against Sincere's isolated king. Sincere placed his rook on c2, as usual, and waited for Gent to move his knight or bishop. But he began to wonder whether he'd made the right move. Gent thought for a moment, and he continued his attack. He realized checkmate wasn't going to be as easy as he'd thought. Sincere was now playing defense, and his only motive was to protect his king from being in check. He needed to either block, evade, or capture the attacking piece to get out of check. But when push came to shove, Sincere knew winning this match against Gent was nearly impossible. The best he could do was probably have the match end in a draw.

Sincere felt at peace when he played chess with Gent, especially after the entire prison had been locked down for nearly two weeks. It had been hell for all the inmates. Prison lockdowns were more challenging than any other aspect of an inmate's stay in prison. Everyone was locked in a cell for nearly twenty-four hours a day, with one cellmate, and the inmates had to endure it until the problem was contained. There was limited access to food and the bathroom. There was no access to education, recreation, or any communication with family.

No one existed outside their cells. The prison system would forget to treat them as humans. And the wear and tear on these men's souls created aggression, resentment, and depression. Lockdown gripped these men savagely, like a cold winter night. Long periods of lockdown were mentally and emotionally taxing. If a man was weak and depraved from drug use, he could lose his mind on lockdown in a matter of hours. The silence and the cell restriction could shake anyone to the utmost degree and cause an inmate to fight for his sanity.

Officer Morrison's death or suicide had had a domino effect inside Elmira Correctional Facility. At first, the warden and prison officials had believed he was murdered by another prisoner. Fortunately, the medical examiner had deduced that it was a suicide. But the damage had already been done.

Sincere had done his best to endure the lockdown. He had constantly worked out, doing push-ups, sit-ups, and dips at the edge of his bunk. He would stare longingly at the pictures of his kids on his walls, would talk to them or talk to himself. Sincere had had to use the sink in his cell to clean himself; unfortunately, it had had to substitute for a shower. And though he had tried to keep himself active and focused, being stuck all day long in a jail cell without any real movement had worked against him. And he'd struggled to stay sociable.

Sincere continued to be on defense against Gent's queen, knight, and rook. It was an intense game. Of the dozens of times they had played together, Sincere had racked up only a handful of wins against him.

"You're slacking, Sincere. I see it coming," said Gent.

"Listen, old man, I spent damn near two weeks in my own head. I got this," Sincere replied, chuckling.

"Rise up, then king, and make the move," said Gent.

He saw his chance, but it was risky. But just as he was about to move, the tension inside the dayroom rose, like a storm was coming. Rondell had entered the dayroom, and his presence was nothing nice. Sincere kept cool but aware.

Rondell came Sincere and Gent's way. Sincere watched his every movement closely. Every inmate in the dayroom watched these two men like it was the Cold War. Rondell stood over Sincere and Gent's chess game. Sincere remained seated, undaunted by his presence. They'd just come out of lockdown, so Sincere figured Rondell wasn't there to create a problem, not yet anyway.

"Hey, old man, can I have a private chat with my friend here?" Rondell asked Gent coolly.

Gent looked at Sincere, not budging, because he was told to. If Sincere was cool with it, then he was cool with it.

Sincere nodded and said, "It's cool, Gent. I'm good."

"You sure, Sincere?"

"Yeah, we good," Sincere replied.

Gent stood up from the table reluctantly, and before he walked away, he cursed, "Goddamned knuckleheads interrupting my damn game. No fuckin' respect."

Once Gent was gone, Rondell sat opposite Sincere. Sincere glared at Rondell with contempt and suspicion, not knowing what he was up to. Everyone on both sides stood on guard. Although the lockdown had been lifted, all it took was one wrong movement from either party for the tension to escalate into violence.

"Sincere, right?" said Rondell.

"You know my name," Sincere responded.

Rondell chuckled. Of course he did. He looked down at the chessboard. "I'm more of a physical kind of guy. I like contact sports, football, boxing, where you can break something in another player. Now, those are manly sports."

"This game isn't for everyone," said Sincere. "It's a thinking man's game, requires planning and strategy. Others may not have the time or interest to learn and practice the game."

"I guess not. But you can be smart and bad at chess at the same time. Just because a person is not skilled at chess does not mean they are not intelligent," Rondell replied.

"The one thing I've learned about playing chess is when you see a good move, look for a better one," Sincere observed.

Rondell chuckled at Sincere's statement. He was somewhat impressed by it.

"I underestimated you, especially with Morrison. Man took his own life because of you," he said. "You're a survivor, charismatic and shit. You survived a hit by inmates and guards. And went to war with two drug kingpins. And here you are, running things inside here with the KOS. Muthafuckas believe you're Superman in this bitch. "

"I'm no Superman," Sincere replied casually.

"Of course not. But I wonder, what's your Kryptonite? What drives and scares you?"

"Keep coming after me or my people, and I'll show you personally what drives me and what will scare *you*," said Sincere.

"You know my uncle wants you dead, right?"

"I know."

"You see, my uncle, once he has this grudge against you, it's like you're marked for death. And that, my friend, is like all hell coming after you. There's no escaping the inevitable. He blames you for my cousin's demise. His two sons and he will have his vengeance."

"I don't give a fuck about your uncle or you. Just know this. You're coming for me, and I'll be coming for you. Like I did with your cousins Rafe and Drip-Drip. Fuck 'em both! I hope they both burn in hell. And I guarantee you'll be joining them soon."

Rondell frowned. "The balls on you, nigga. You put my cousins in the ground and disrespect their names now."

Sincere glared at his enemy so hard, it seemed like fire and brimstone shot forth from his gaze. He exclaimed, "Fuck you! And fuck your uncle!"

Despite Sincere's disrespect, Rondell kept his cool. Everyone was watching them talk in the dayroom. It was like the heads of two states or countries discussing terms, business, or solutions. But there would be no solution or peace. This was personal to Rondell. And Sincere didn't scare easily.

"I heard you once wanted to be a cop. Is that true?" asked Rondell.

"Sacrifices needed to be made," Sincere uttered vaguely.

"There are two types of sacrifices, the correct ones and mine," Rondell replied. "This is my world, my prison. You'll be gone soon."

With that said, Rondell knocked over both kings on the chessboard and walked coolly away from him. Sincere sat there quietly for a moment. He looked undeterred by Rondell's words. But he knew the storm was about to become much worse.

Sincere sat alone in his cell and stared at the pictures of his kids lining the bleak gray walls. He had one weakness, and it was his family. He missed his kids and their mother. He would do anything to see them in the flesh again. His worst fear was something happening to them because of his actions. If any harm came to them, he would never forgive himself. He still grieved Denise's death. Nasir had introduced his sister to a life of crime, but Sincere blamed himself because he hadn't been there to protect her and guide her. How could he?

He missed his family. But he accepted that he most likely would never see them again. Photographs would be all he had of them. He would never become the available and active father that children needed. He didn't know anything about his son. What was his favorite sport to play? If it was basketball, Sincere wouldn't be that cheering father in the bleachers or on the sidelines. He wouldn't be there to play catch with Tyriq in the backyard if it was baseball. There would be no talk with his sons about the birds and the bees. He wouldn't be the guiding compass his sons needed in life, for he, too, was lost in violence, revenge, and anger. Another man would become that guiding light or torch in his sons' life. A man he knew nothing about. A man who was now laid up with his ex, Monica, every night.

His daughter Ashley, who was now five years old, wouldn't become Daddy's little girl. As a father, he wouldn't be there to protect her from those monsters underneath her bed. He wouldn't be there to tuck her in every night, read her bedtime stories, and kiss her good night daily. He would never be able to hold his daughter the way a father should, with profound love and assurance, and would never become a protective shield around his daughter—a warrior for her. There would be no walking her down the aisle on her wedding day, no vetting and scaring off any boyfriends. The things that a daughter needed, Sincere would not be able to provide. Over time, he would become a stranger to her and vice versa. But worst of all, Ashley would be calling another man Daddy.

His other daughter, Akar, had been foreign to him for so long now, it felt like a lifetime since he had last seen her. His tears and his memories of her remained frozen in time. He sometimes needed to remember what she looked like. She was thousands of miles away, in a small town in Japan, being raised in a different culture, under a different government, and in another language. He had only one picture of her. It had been taken so long ago, around her first birthday, that it didn't seem real to him—maybe she was a faint dream. And he tried his best not to wake from it, for dreams were quickly forgotten once you awakened and opened your eyes. But she wasn't a dream. She was a young girl growing up in Japan. Akar might as well have been light-years away, in a different universe, one impossible to travel to.

This was his fate—regret, imprisonment, perpetual grief, and loneliness—when Sincere chose vengeance over family and forgiveness. His mental health had been imperiled by years of violence and bloodshed. The death of his little brother, Marcus, had consumed him with rage and hatred, and he'd been like some bloodthirsty creature in the night. Yes, he had adapted to the harsh environment in prison like a chameleon, become a monster, and started a prison gang called KOS.

Though he was feared, respected, and influential, and was becoming a force to be reckoned with, Sincere missed his old life. He wanted his family. He wanted to see them every day, to grow and laugh with them. If he could do it all over again, he wouldn't make the same mistake of continuing to be a soldier on the warpath, instead of a brother, a son, a father, and a husband. He missed holding Monica at night. He wished that once again, he could keep her close in his arms or be held in hers, their heartbeats in rhythm and their laughter echoing. He would do anything to make love to Monica again, to feel her glorious insides one final time.

The heartbreak, pain, and anger Sincere felt daily, he bottled up like lightning and brought it down on his enemies like an atomic weapon. There was a heavy weight pressing down on his chest. Sincere felt like he'd fallen on a cactus, and tiny needles had punctured his heart a million times over. He'd spent most of his time in a place full of violence and destruction, and so his aggression was a protection method.

Now he felt numb.

It had been quiet for two weeks now. Business in the prison had returned to normal. Inmates were receiving their drugs and other illicit services. The guards had fallen back with their aggression toward the inmates, and some programs were back in service. Sincere knew this was the calm before the storm. A man like Rondell was always plotting and planning. He had enough influence to launch a surprise attack. Sincere tried to ready himself for any attack or payback, but it was nearly impossible to know when and where it might happen. His influence on the guards was weakening. Since Morrison's death and the attack on his wife, many guards had begun to resent Sincere and the KOS. This gave Rondell the advantage he needed. It was time for him to yell out, "Checkmate."

Something rotten was in the air, and it was about to funk up the place. KOS was in what inmates called a heat wave, getting much-unwanted attention from the guards and other gangs.

Row and his cellmate, Trek, were about to enjoy some homemade hooch inside their cell. It had been fermenting in a plastic bag and was now ready for consumption. It was a quiet afternoon. Suddenly, four guards appeared at the entrance to their cell, and Row stood up, on alert. They were there to conduct a cell search on the cellblock.

"What the fuck is this?" Row exclaimed.

"We're here to search your cell," said one of the guards.

Row frowned. "Y'all muthafuckas really doin' this?"

"Step out of the cell, Row, and you too, Trek."

Row remained adamant about being left alone and resisted. "Fuck y'all!" he cursed. "Y'all can't be doin' this shit!"

"We can do this the easy way or the hard way. Either way, we're coming in there to search your cell," said the guard with authority.

Quickly, Trek picked up a small object, placed it in his mouth, and swallowed it. The guards immediately charged into the cell, but Row charged the guards and punched the first one in the left eye and struck the second guard with an elbow blow. Trek became aggressive too, and chaos ensued. Punches were thrown, and though outnumbered, Row and Trek were relentless and foul with rage. A guard tackled Trek to the floor like a linebacker drilling a quarterback from the blind side. Row's eyes dropped to check on his cellmate, and then they darted back to the guards, and he charged them with an equal measure of fury and terror. They were going to kill him. A guard heatedly administered OC spray to Row, grabbed him in a body hold, and forced him to the floor. They quickly handcuffed Row and Trek while they were face down and cursing.

Both inmates were brought to their feet and escorted from their jail cell. But something came over the guards, and the atmosphere turned ominous. Shockingly, one of the guards decided to remove Row's handcuffs while they were on the top tier.

"Fuck you and your cunt mother," one of the guards spewed.

Row immediately struck the guard in the face, and he was tackled and beaten. He struggled and fought relentlessly. But he was overpowered. Then he was thrown from the top tier. . . .

Trek screamed in agony and anger. "Y'all muthafucka gon' pay for that! Fuck y'all. Fuck y'all!"

Row was dead.

Twenty-seven

What IS the difference between a psychopath and a sociopath? Psychopaths have emotional deficits, lack remorse, believe their actions are justified, and take pleasure in inflicting pain on others. Sociopaths are antisocial and violate the rules. Sociopaths can have a weak conscience, and they will often justify their violent and appalling actions. Who is more dangerous? A psychopath or a sociopath? When it comes to war, they both are valuable and vital.

Doc lacked empathy and took pleasure in inflicting pain like a psychopath. His actions were often deadly, and his personality was volatile, like that of a sociopath. His mental state was disturbed and fragile. His troubled past, which had created his scars, had molded him to have poor impulse control and had sharpened his urge to kill. He'd become the perfect assassin for Ezekial. One who was loyal, deadly, and eager to get the job done—and fearless about any consequences. He despised law enforcement and disloyalty to the Outfit.

Doc sat in the passenger seat of the moving black GMC truck and loaded lethal rounds into the Heckler & Koch G36C like a soldier on his way toward the battlefield. In a way, he was. He gripped the fierce weapon and admired it, ready to put it into action soon. Yes, the thrill of conflict and bloodshed. Nothing excited him more, not even sex. He was weird like that. Chaos was what Doc lived for, especially creating bloody crime scenes that would make the headlines.

His backup was the Steyr SPP and the SIG Sauer P226. This man was a maniac who planned to leave nothing alive and moving. Their target was one of Antonio's establishments in Red Hook, Brooklyn, a scrapyard he owned underneath the BQE. It was a thriving business where old vehicles and machines were collected and either sold or prepared for being used again. Doc planned on putting an end to that this afternoon.

The look in Doc's eyes was that of a soulless man with a desire to take center stage through violence and bloodshed. There was no warmth, no humanity, just narcissistic tendencies with a dose of grandiosity.

"Anything moving in there goes down. Y'all hear me?" said Doc. "Fuck it up!"

The men nodded.

Doc and his gang of four armed men arrived at the scrapyard during peak hours. The sun was at its highest point in the sky. The air was hot and moist, and the day was bright. Because vehicles and machinery were loaded and unloaded constantly, the yard had a lot of space for storing cars, machines, materials, and equipment. When they arrived, men were busy operating forklifts and crane magnets, and dump trucks were moving in and out of the yard. Antonio's scrapyard was located near the ports and was parallel to a narrow river. This location meant that materials could be transported by ship as well as by truck and train.

The sleek black GMC truck stood out like a sore thumb when it pulled into the scrapyard. It caught the attention of a few workers, but none of them thought anything of it. For all they knew, it could be a businessman scheduled to meet with the yard's manager. However, the vehicle sat idling near the main entrance, and it became difficult for the dump trucks to come and go.

"What the fuck is this?" the manager muttered aloud to himself. His name was Chris, and he was a tall, thin man with failing hair and dark eyes. "What the fuck is their problem?"

Bewildered by the idling GMC truck near the entrance, he decided to investigate. Flanked by one of Antonio's henchmen, he marched over to the vehicle, then stepped up to the passenger window to scope it out. Antonio may have owned the scrapyard on paper for money laundering, but this had been Chris's domain for years. The occupants of the GMC were holding up the traffic.

Chris coolly patted the passenger window to get the occupants' attention. The goon behind him stood alert and quiet, aware of the civil conflict between his boss and Ezekial. He holstered a Glock 17 underneath his suit jacket. His hard, intense stare was not visible thanks to a pair of dark sunglasses. He was cool but watchful.

"Hey, you need to move this thing right now. You're blocking my trucks," Chris hollered.

Suddenly, the front passenger door opened, and Doc stepped out, clutching the Heckler & Koch. His piercing black eyes shot daggers at the manager.

Chris saw the weapon and uttered, "Jesus! What the fuck?"

It would be the last thing he said. Doc opened fire with the automatic.

Bratatat. Bratatat.

The manager danced violently from the bullets shredding his flesh, and then he flew off his feet and hit the ground. Immediately, the henchmen reached for his Glock 17 to retaliate, but a spray of bullets coming from multiple gunmen tore through him before he had a chance to fire back.

Chaos ensued right away inside the scrapyard. All five gunmen opened fire on anything moving with sharp, precise three-round bursts. A spray of bullets tore through the windows and walls of the office trailer, shattering everything, and a woman shrieked in terror from the inside. Workers dove to the ground and scrambled for cover. What the fuck was happening! A day of work had transitioned into a mass shooting.

While his men were executing anyone moving the outside, Doc made his way into the office trailer to finish off anyone trying to hide from his madness. He came across a young female receptionist cowering and crying behind a desk. Suddenly, when she saw Doc, a strange, thin man bearing scars, wearing round bifocals, and towering over her with the smoking automatic weapon, her eyes grew wide with fear, as if the Devil was standing before her.

"Please, don't kill me," she begged, trembling. "I just started this job yesterday."

Doc stared at her with apathy; he felt nothing for her. Anything connected to Antonio Francesco had to be taken care of. So, he removed the pistol from his waistband and leveled it at her chest.

"*No! No! No!* Please," she cried, begging for mercy.

He fired repeatedly. The bullets punched through her chest and neck, causing a gaping hole in their wake, which quickly filled with blood. The blood gushed out, and a pool quickly formed around her and soaked into her clothes. Doc stared at his victim indifferently, pivoted, and marched out of the trailer. The dead were scattered everywhere. His men were merciless and relentless; they'd created a whirlwind of carnage.

It was done—a powerful message had been sent.

They hurried toward the idling GMC and climbed in, and the vehicle sped away from what Doc considered a masterpiece of carnage. Doc laughed and grinned.

The police were a minute or two away.

***

The city was becoming a powder keg. It was ready to implode on itself. The murders at the Brooklyn scrapyard had made national and international news. They'd left a bad taste in everyone's mouths. The negative spotlight, the gang war, and the brutal bloodshed were like poison to New York City. The Big Apple was becoming the Rotten Apple, stinking like a decaying corpse, the putrid smell churning so many stomachs. The violence mirrored that during the crack epidemic in the eighties and nineties, and bodies were piling up like the dead during the Vietnam War.

The bold public massacre at the Brooklyn scrapyard had the mayor, the governor, and many other politicians in an uproar. How did a tragedy like that happen? many wondered. The residents of the city were afraid and angry. Something needed to be done.

"We're pissed off. This is senseless violence," said Mayor Anthony Key at a public press conference. "We're working hard to find and apprehend the culprits responsible for yesterday's massacre. And we're working extra hard every day to make this city safe. These monsters, when they are apprehended—and believe me, we will find them—they will be prosecuted to the fullest extent of the law and will be jailed for the remainder of their natural lives. The gang violence happening in this city ends today!"

There were tons of questions from the press. However, the mayor pivoted sharply and marched away from the podium, refusing to answer a single one.

The feds were in the city to investigate the scrapyard massacre. The criminal underworld was up in arms about this unwanted attention, and many believed Ezekial had gone too far. Trouble from the federal government, among other law enforcement agencies, was on the horizon.

Zodiac frowned at the day's headlines about the Brooklyn massacre. "This is gonna be bad for everyone," he muttered.

"You had nothing to do with it," said Trina.

"It doesn't matter. This is gonna bring down the heat from the feds and politicians looking to make a name for themselves. What the fuck were they thinking!"

"Maybe we should leave town for a few weeks, until all of this is over," Trina suggested.

"We can't right now. I have another shipment from Joc arriving next week, and I have a few affairs to take care of."

"And you think it's wise for you to oversee nearly two thousand kilos while all this is happening? And you said Ezekial wants you dead, for some reason. I don't know why. You can try to separate yourself from this, but I can't see how."

"We'll be all right," said Zodiac hesitantly.

"You don't sound too sure, Zodiac."

"I'm sure, Trina."

Zodiac went to his bar and poured himself a quick drink. He downed the shot of vodka and sighed heavily. He had a lot on his mind. Every move he made and every breath he took could be his last. There was a cost to being the boss, the one on top. *Heavy's the head that wears the crown.* And Zodiac's head began leaning to the side slightly. He couldn't remember the last time he had had a good night's sleep. Nightmares, his demons, the past, the present, the future, and his enemies kept him awake at night.

Then his cell phone rang. It was his brother, Markest, calling. Seeing that his older brother was calling him this late meant it was troublesome news. He didn't want to answer the call. The last thing he needed was more bad news. However, Zodiac answered the phone and uttered, "What's up, bro?"

"Pop is dead," Markest uttered nonchalantly.

"When?" Zodiac replied in the same tone.

"An hour ago."

"I'll be there soon," said Zodiac.

"Nah. I got this. I don't need your help."

"He's my father too."

"Yet I cared for him until his last breath," Markest countered.

Zodiac frowned. It wasn't a shock to him that his father had passed. He had been a sick man. They had had an estranged relationship, yet it saddened Zodiac that he hadn't had the chance to say goodbye.

"I'll pay for his funeral," said Zodiac.

"Nothing fancy. You know how Pop was."

"Yeah. I know."

The call ended. Trina stared at him, knowing what had happened by listening to his conversation. She uttered, "I'm so sorry."

"He was old. It was bound to happen soon," Zodiac replied.

Zodiac poured himself another shot and downed it. Trina watched with some concern. She wished she could remove his burdens and give him a clean slate. But it was impossible. The only thing she could do was comfort him and be there for him.

"From ashes to ashes, from dust to dust. You'll rise again. In this, I'll trust," the pastor said over the Lincoln Spruce Blue casket about to be lowered into the ground. "You're in our hearts till the end. We will meet again, my departed friend. You may be gone, but I know you're near."

Zodiac, his brother, Markest, Trina, and several others stood around the casket. The mood was highly somber and subdued. And although his father's service and burial had been dignified so far, few mourners had shared positive stories about the deceased. It felt like a place of disposal for Zodiac—a place enclosed by mounded earth. Eventually, this was how it would be for everyone, some sooner than later.

Several armed men in black suits vigilantly guarded the burial site. They were at war, and Zodiac didn't want to take any chances. He'd heard about the massacre in Brooklyn, six people dead, the innocent and the culpable boldly gunned down in public. He didn't want any part of this conflict, but it was at his door. Ezekial had a grudge against him and damn near the entire underworld, and he was out for blood like a hungry vampire.

Zodiac stood tall and stoic near his father's casket. He was clad in an all-black three-piece suit with notched lapels. Dark shades covered his eyes, a holstered 9mm was concealed inside his suit jacket, and his wing tips were like mirrors. He stood there with his hands clasped, almost aloof from the pain or grief he felt. He'd become a man of wealth, substance, class, power, and enemies. Yet today he felt vulnerable and weak. No one was invincible to death. He thought about the incident in Ghana when several hitmen had nearly killed him. In his line of work, death was always around the corner, karma too. Zodiac thought about how many men and women he'd sent to an early grave, whether by his hands alone or by an order he'd given.

His father had died peacefully in his sleep, but Zodiac knew his own ending most likely wouldn't be peaceful. Instead, it probably would be abrupt and violent. He wouldn't see it coming at all.

Markest had protested having armed guards at their father's funeral. He saw it as a sign of disrespect. Their father was a peaceful and God-fearing man. It was blasphemy that his younger brother had brought his troubles and worries to their father's final resting place. However, Zodiac had insisted and hadn't taken no for an answer. So, they'd quarreled. Markest had finally relented. Markest disapproved of many things concerning his brother, including his sexual preference. Markest despised the fact that his brother had decided to become involved with someone who was transgender.

Trina looked to be every bit a beautiful woman, with curves, tits, ass, and long black hair, but she wasn't one to Markest. How could his little brother fall so deep into sin? How could Zodiac go against everything their father stood for? Markest cut his eyes at Trina, who stood silently by his brother. She wore a tight black dress, something appealing and eye-catching. He frowned.

"My only hope is that in peace, you'll rest," the pastor continued. "I still miss you. I bet you guessed. I'll see you soon. It's a must."

While the pastor was giving the eulogy, the sudden arrival of a luxury Lincoln Continental put everyone on edge and alert. The guards were poised to react. Zodiac kept his hand near his weapon. Markest scowled. *What now?*

The doors to the Lincoln opened, and when Antonio Francesco and his goons climbed out, it seemed like all hell was about to break loose. Immediately, Antonio lifted his arms into the air like wings and uttered, "I come in peace."

It was the cliché greeting.

Zodiac wasn't buying it. He walked over to Antonio and growled, "What the fuck are you doing at my father's burial?"

"I take it you know who I am. I came to talk, Zodiac. We both have a common threat right now," said Antonio. "But first, I give my condolences to you and your family. Whatever you need from me, let me know."

"I don't need anything from you but for you to leave," Zodiac barked.

Antonio scoffed. "He's going to keep coming for you, no matter what," he said. "You and I stand a better chance if we work together rather than apart."

Zodiac grumbled something that no one could make out. He was skeptical. Antonio was bad news, and everyone knew it. He was a borderline racist. But Zodiac decided to hear him out. He didn't want any conflict at his father's final resting place.

"Let's go for a walk, then," said Zodiac. "And let's make it quick."

However, Markest was against it. He glared at his brother and uttered, "Zodiac, what are you doing?"

"I'll be a moment," Zodiac told him.

Zodiac and Antonio went for a walk to have a talk. Markest couldn't believe it. How dare his little brother conduct business during their father's burial? Markest was a changed man, but Zodiac's actions made him ready to return to his old ways. Markest gritted his teeth and clenched his fists, but he would do nothing. Not today, and probably not ever. Violence wasn't part of his way of life anymore. In memory of his father, he wouldn't lose control and embarrass himself on this day.

"I appreciate you taking a moment to hear me out," Antonio said politely.

Zodiac listened while Antonio did most of the talking. He tried to pitch him the idea that they needed to work together. But first, Antonio came clean to him, saying, "Let me clear the air and say this. It was me who attacked you in Ghana."

Hearing that, Zodiac wanted to snap the other man's neck right there. His blood boiled; however, he swallowed down his violent impulses and anger. Instead, he decided to hear him out.

"It wasn't personal with me. It was just business. Ezekial wanted to outsource the hit using my men. It didn't work out how he had expected. And when they failed, he had them killed," said Antonio.

"I was with my woman when it happened," Zodiac revealed.

"Like I said, it wasn't personal. This life we live sometimes comes with more risk than reward. I lost my father and grandfather to this thing of ours. Women too."

"And you expect sympathy from me?"

"No. I want your ears and understanding. Ezekial will continue to come for you and for me. I know him. The man is *pazzo*! He has this God complex and is willing to burn it all down. This civil war with the Outfit must end before we lose everything."

"From my understanding, you're on the losing end of this thing. Now that you're desperate, you come seeking my help, *after* you tell me you tried to have me killed," said Zodiac.

"Men stumble on stones, not mountains," said Antonio.

"What the fuck does that mean?"

"Recognize the threat now, in time, so you can adjust to it early," said Antonio. "To Ezekial, I'm the bigger threat now, and you're the stone. But that won't last."

Zodiac was curious to know if it was wise to share what he knew about Ezekial or what? How would it help him? Though Antonio had come to him for help, he was still an enemy. But now that he was in conflict with one of the most powerful crime lords in the nation—and therefore was the enemy of Zodiac's enemy—he had to be a friend. But in this business, there were no such things as friends.

"He's sick. He's been diagnosed with cancer," said Zodiac.

This was a surprise to Antonio. "And you know this how?"

"I had my guy look into it after the attack in Africa. He was able to retrieve his medical records."

"So, he's a dying man with nothing to lose. Which makes him even more dangerous."

"Use it how you feel fit," said Zodiac gruffly.

The men stopped walking and stood next to a towering headstone belonging to a man and a woman who died half a century ago, in 1955 and 1957. The granite headstone was a final commemoration of this couple's meager existence on this earth. Zodiac glanced at the engraving and had the sudden realization that they were surrounded by death while discussing war.

"I can offer you a seat on the Outfit when all this is over," said Antonio. "You'll have an alliance so strong, you'll be untouchable. You'll have international connections and an unlimited supply of product and protection. I know you're an influential and dangerous figure, Zodiac. And you're smart. But you're alone out here. Alone, you can do so little. Together, we can do so much."

Zodiac wasn't buying it. He knew Antonio was a desperate man. He was trying to survive this civil war between the Outfit members. Ezekial had him on the run and nearly wiped out. But Antonio was right: with Mob Allah and Zulu dead, Zodiac had no alliances with anyone. It felt like he was becoming a man without a country.

"I know you don't trust me. No disrespect, but do you have a choice. To fight the raven you may have to make an alliance with the serpent until the battle is done," said Antonio.

Zodiac understood that an alliance with a powerful person was never that safe, and the battle or war was never that easy to win. Also, there were no permanent alliances, only permanent interests.

"When this is done, I don't wanna see you again. You go your way, and I'll go mines," said Zodiac.

Antonio smiled. "Agreed."

If an enemy has alliances, the problem is grave and the enemy's position strong. If an enemy has no alliances, the problem is minor and the enemy's position weak, Zodiac thought as he walked away.

Twenty-eight

Dr. Midian was a respected professional in the medical field. Not only was he a great doctor who possessed the personality traits of conscientiousness, openness, extroversion, and agreeableness, but he was also was a great listener and was empathetic toward his patients. No matter their diagnosis, he made his patients feel comfortable and relaxed, understood their concerns, and explained complex medical concepts in a way that was easy for them to understand. He was someone who validated his patients' pain and treated everyone with professional courtesy. Dr. Thomas Midian was a fifty-two-year-old white man who loved his career and was one of the best oncologists in the country. He was expensive but worth it. And that was why Ezekial had turned to him for treatment. That and the fact that what was diagnosed in his office stayed in his office.

Although he was a highly respected doctor, Dr. Midian was still a man with needs and weaknesses. So one evening, after the office had closed, Dr. Midian and his young receptionist decided to partake of some extracurricular activities before they went their separate ways. Their affair had become routine, though the good doctor had been married for over twenty years and had four kids. He couldn't get enough of his receptionist, Mary, and Mary had fallen in love with him.

Fuck, she is tight, Dr. Midian thought. Her gripping pussy was like a cock ring around this thick dick.

Grasping her hips, he thrust into her hard as she lay curved over his work desk. He happily buried every inch of his erection inside her eager, wet pussy.

"Oh, yes, fuck me," Mary pleaded, pushing her pussy back against him, desperate to come with him inside her as he impaled her from behind, with her skirt hiked up, her blouse open, and his pants twisted around his ankles.

She gasped at the size of him as he filled her so completely. The feel of his hard, thick dick stretching her open and filling her completely was driving her wild, and she was reaching for an orgasm. Excited and growing wetter by the second, Mary pushed back while Dr. Midian squeezed her ass and tits. Overcome by lust, he rammed himself between her legs, driving into her as deep and hard as he could.

"I wanna fuckin' come, Dr. Midian. Make me fucking come!" Mary hollered.

The two were engrossed in some mind-blowing, hot sex, and unbeknownst to them, they were about to have some unwanted company. Quietly, the office door opened, and three armed men entered the doctor's office. Dr. Midian had his back turned to them and continued thrusting and enjoying the glorious insides of his receptionist, oblivious to the malefactors' presence. For the three men, it was a sight to see. They thought he would be alone, working late in his office, but this looked like more fun. They smiled.

"Oh God! Fuck!" Mary cried out. "I'm gonna come."

"Can I go next?" one of the men hollered.

The sudden unwanted interruption coming from behind them made Dr. Midian pull out from the pussy so hard that he nearly sprained himself. Mary spun around and shrieked at the presence of three scary-looking black men. She snatched her blouse shut before pulling down her skirt and leaped off the desk. Dr. Midian hurriedly pulled up his pants to make himself decent, but both he and Mary looked disheveled in the strangers' ominous presence.

"What the heck are y'all doing in my damn office?" Dr. Midian hollered.

"Relax, nigga. We're here to talk. All we want is some information from you, and you can go back to fuckin' white bread there," said one of the thugs. "She is cute."

"Get the fuck out!" Dr, Midian roared.

The remark caused the thug to thrust a 9mm in his face. "Shut the fuck up and chill. Don't make it worse for yourself, nigga."

From the look on the man's face, Dr. Midian knew they were serious. Mary cowered by the desk, trying to keep her blouse closed and her private parts covered the best she could. She was terrified. The armed men stared at her like she was fresh meat.

"What do you all want?" Dr. Midian asked.

"We are just here for info on one patient of yours. Ezekial Montoya," replied the thug who was doing the talking.

"I—I can't give that out. There's doctor-patient privilege. I could lose my medical license."

The thug aimed his pistol at the doctor's head and barked, "How 'bout you lose your life first? Or, better yet, how 'bout I shoot this bitch first in front of you?"

The thug then aimed his weapon at Mary's head, and she trembled and sobbed. Dr. Midian knew he didn't have a choice. They were going to kill them both. His steely gaze lingered on the men, and he knew there was no escaping this predicament.

"Ezekial Montoya. I want every piece of information you have on him right now."

Fearing for his life and Mary's, Dr. Midian reluctantly logged into his laptop and retrieved Ezekial's medical information and some personal files. He huffed as he printed out the information and handed it over. The gunmen were pleased. This was what they needed to hunt down Ezekial and kill him.

Dr. Midian scowled, and Mary was cried and trembled by the desk as the men coolly left the office, leaving their two victims traumatized and filled with dread.

Cashmere sat in silence in the back seat of the luxury Range Rover. She had a lot on her mind. She was surrounded by chaos, and her life had become topsy-turvy. The civil war going on with the Outfit affected her too. It affected her practice and personal life. Cashmere had had to change up her routine, but she refused to go into hiding. The power struggle between Ezekial and Antonio and what was left of the Outfit was raging out of control. She hadn't seen Ezekial in nearly three weeks. He'd gone into hiding, and she missed him. Cashmere had no idea where he was. It was how Ezekial wanted it, her not knowing his whereabouts, because he believed it was safer for her. However, it was driving Cashmere crazy. The man she had known nearly all her life and loved unconditionally was in hiding, and it felt like she would never see him again.

How could she go back to a normal life without Ezekial around? Cashmere had considered returning to Miami, but Ezekial had warned her before his sudden departure that Miami probably wasn't safe for her. Therefore, Cashmere was taking up residence in a rural upstate home an hour outside the city and seven miles from the nearest town. It was owned by Ezekial, but his name was nowhere on the property. He felt that if he or she ever had to go into hiding, the property there wouldn't be linked to him.

The black Range Rover arrived at the property, ten acres of land near a beautiful lake and towering mountains. The place was divine. The house, which looked just like it belonged on the rolling landscape, was surrounded by lush greenery: large trees, shrubbery, and fields of grass. The lake was glimmering like it was made of diamonds, and the atmosphere was convent quiet. The blue sky seemed to have been engraved on the still, clear lake. The magic of the lake, the sprawling acreage, the fresh mountain air, and the privacy could cause an "aha" moment.

Soon after Cashmere and her two-man security arrived on the property, dusk began to settle on the land, the green replaced by blue shadows and then the blue fading to gray. By then the two guards, as efficient as the Secret Service, had checked and secured the property and the perimeter. This was for her protection. If anything were to happen to Cashmere, both men knew they were as good as dead. When Cashmere was finally allowed to enter the house, she was stunned by its beauty. Though it was too dark out now to see, she knew it had incredible views through the floor-to-ceiling windows.

Exhausted from the day's events and the drive, Cashmere began to unwind for the night. In the privacy of the main bedroom, she undressed and took a shower. She played with herself under the cascading water for a moment. Cashmere closed her eyes and thought about Ezekial. She wished they were together now, because not having him around was a nightmare. But now that she was ensconced in his house, she felt certain she would see him again. In her eyes, Ezekial was a man who was too big to fail and too big to go down. She'd seen him overcome many difficult and trying situations over the years. He'd helped take down government regimes and dismantle rival drug empires. He could become unstoppable, as he had no fear and was a calculated thinker. And he was a psychopath. Cashmere was confident Ezekial would always come out on top, no matter the odds.

Cashmere finished showering and masturbating, left the shower, and toweled off. She knotted the towel around her and stepped into the adjacent room. She peeked out the bedroom window and took in the vast nothingness for miles. It was dark and quiet. The darkness surrounding the house felt heavy, oppressive, and almost supernatural. Cashmere hated the country. She was a city girl. Still, Ezekial had insisted she stay hidden and protected until the danger had passed.

Cashmere decided to don a pair of sweatpants and a T-shirt. Before going to bed, she wanted to do some reading. However, she quickly abandoned that idea when she heard a slight commotion outside the bedroom. It might be nothing, or it might be a problem. No matter what, Cashmere wasn't taking any chances. Immediately she removed her Glock 26 pistol from her handbag, held it firmly at her side, and began investigating the disturbance she thought she heard.

The entire house was dark, too dark for her comfort. Cashmere called out to the guards but received no answer. She moved carefully, with the pistol in both hands now, and became swallowed up in silence and darkness. Something was off. She had the nightmarish thought of her enemies finding her in such a remote location. *And if so, how?* she wondered.

Cashmere carefully moved throughout the house with the Glock 26 stretched out in front of her. If anything moved wrong, she was going to blast first. *Fuck asking any questions.* It was kill or be killed. She continued, slowly moving throughout the house, inspecting rooms and specific areas. It was too quiet and eerie. She'd stopped calling out for the guards, because she knew somehow that they were dead. Her intuition screamed that she wasn't alone, that unwanted company was lurking in her presence.

Her heart pounded like a hummingbird's wings with each breath she took. The booming was furious and incessant. She'd become a character in a horror movie. Cashmere cautiously entered the kitchen. The moment she did so, she felt an ominous presence nearby. It was lurking on her left side, hidden in darkness. Cashmere pivoted suddenly to fire her gun at this unwanted company. Still, he was quicker on the draw, ready to react with harsh violence. The butt of a sawed-off shotgun slammed into the side of her face, and she went down like a boxer who'd been knocked out. Her face was on fire.

As her eyes adjusted to the dark, Cashmere determined that the man who had struck her was wearing all black and had a hoodie pulled over his head, concealing his identity. He was tall and muscular, a beast of a man. He aimed the sawed-off shotgun at Cashmere, and she didn't move. She couldn't move. She lay frozen. The pistol she carried had spilled from her hands when he struck her and had slid across the kitchen floor.

"Where the fuck is he?" the assailant growled.

Cashmere chose to remain silent rather than give up the man she loved. But in reality, she had no idea where Ezekial was hiding. Even if she did know, she wouldn't relay his whereabouts. She was loyal.

He leveled the shotgun at her head and growled, "Bitch, I will shoot you in the fuckin' face if you don't start talking."

Cashmere remained undaunted by his threat. Deep in the pit of her stomach, she knew she was already dead. So she refused to give up Ezekial.

"Are you really ready to die for that fool?"

"I'm already a dead woman," Cashmere shot back defiantly. "Fuck you!"

The assailant chuckled. "You really wanna do this?"

"Fuck you!" Cashmere vehemently repeated.

The assailant sighed heavily. His orders were to retrieve information first and kill her last. So he placed the shotgun on the kitchen counter and removed a sharp blade from his person. Cashmere watched him loom closer to her, knowing what would happen to her. He could have quickly fired the weapon and taken her life. But no, the assailant had decided to make this personal.

He punched her repeatedly while she was on the floor, and Cashmere blacked out momentarily. The salty taste of the blood in her mouth woke her up. When she opened her eyes, the assailant was towering over her, smirking.

"Fuckin' hurts, don't it?" he taunted.

Although she had never felt more hopeless in her life, Cashmere matched his smirk and uttered, "Fuck you!"

Yeah. It was going to be a long night. This man was no stranger to doing this. He struck her again, this time in the stomach. The blow was so hard, the air was sucked out of her lungs. Cashmere raised herself up on her hands and knees, whimpering. She remained on all fours, gasping for air that just wasn't there. Without a doubt, he was going to torture her before she died. This man was determined to make her last night on this earth a living hell.

"Can't fuckin' breathe, bitch. Get used to it," he exclaimed.

He pulled out a pack of Newports and lit a cigarette. He took a long, deep drag and glared at Cashmere, who was still on all fours, still trying to catch her breath.

"Where the fuck is Ezekial?" he growled.

Once again, she flashed a stubborn smirk his way while showing him her middle finger. Her defiance was becoming intolerable to him. It was time to make things much more unbearable. The assailant roughly grabbed Cashmere, the burning cigarette still in his hand. She fought, knowing what he wanted to do to her, but his strength was massive. He cruelly put out his lit cigarette on the side of her face, and Cashmere hollered. Then he picked her up and violently threw her into a corner of the room. Her head slammed into the wall, and she dropped, wincing in pain. He marched her way as she braced herself against the wall.

"It doesn't have to be this way," he said. "You gotta lot of heart. You're tough bitch. I'll give you that. I see why Ezekial likes you. You think he would go this hard for you?"

He got no reply.

"You're making this too much fun for me," he said.

Once again, she shouted, "Fuck you!"

Angered by her stubborn remark, he kicked her in the face with his right boot, and Cashmere screamed. Blood poured from her mouth now. Her face was black and blue, and she was beaten up badly.

Cashmere crawled on the floor to escape him, but he was right behind her. He used the knife this time and cut across her back and neck. Then he shouted, "Where the fuck is he, bitch!"

He kicked her in the ribs, and she folded like a chair on the floor; agony and pain gripped her like a lion's jaws.

"This is becoming old, Cashmere. I can make the pain go away. Just tell me something."

Cashmere chose to remain quiet. The damage had already been done. He would kill her anyway, and at least Ezekial would be safe. She owed him his life, and now it was time for her to pay up and allow death to collect her soul. But Cashmere also knew that once word of her brutal death had hit Ezekial's ears, there would be hell to pay. The assailant who would take her life would receive a lot worse. She counted on it.

This would be the final time Cashmere locked eyes with her attacker. She glared at him bitterly and defiantly, panting and wheezing from the beating but knowing what his fate would be—worse than hers.

He giggled. "Nothing, huh? You're that fuckin' stubborn? Fuck it, then. I guess this is the end of the road for you."

The assailant retrieved the sawed-off shotgun and stood over a defeated and battered Cashmere. She refused to turn away from her fate. The assailant aimed the sawed-off shotgun at her while she hugged the floor.

It was time.

He shook his head, uttered, "What a fuckin' waste," and fired.

Boom!

Twenty-nine

The streets of New York smelled like gunpowder, blood, and death, a malodor that hung over the city. It filled the mouths of those who lived in areas plagued by gang violence and disaster. Screams and cries of terror also filled the air, and they were so harrowing, one would have thought they were made by beasts, not humans. The bodies were piling up in borough after borough. The skies began to glow red from fire as the tug-a-war for power, control, and dominance continued between the Outfit, rival drug crews, and vicious drug empires.

Communities were haunted by the discovery of decaying bodies as the violence sucked the life out of everything. But the communities' nightmare was Sunday's bliss. She didn't scare easily, and nothing would stop her from becoming the queen kingpin of this city. Every murder she and her crew committed, every gun that blasted, every soul that departed, and every ounce of cocaine and heroin that was sold on the streets was a step toward her domination. The city was on fire, and Sunday wanted to douse it with more gasoline. If the violence continued, she was sure to become a rich woman and a dominant and influential figure in the city.

Sunday, Nasir, and Sheek rode quietly toward the pickup location. She expected to receive twenty kilos from Dodge. The last shipment had moved fast, like drinking water in the desert. Business was good. Her arrangement with Bray was paying off. But there had been a few hiccups since they killed Squeeze in order to annex Baisley Park Gardens. Although Squeeze was dead, a few loyal minions had been fighting against her tooth and nail. When they killed Squeeze, it had created an opportunity for one of his lieutenants to take over. Now the Blood Mafia Boys were warring with Squeeze's legacy. The low-riser projects had become a battleground for drug trade control and dominance.

Sunday was fine with the trouble in her newfound territory. It was expected. Muthafuckas were upset, and a few niggas were adamant about not allowing some bitch to suddenly take over what they'd built with Squeeze over the years. This was their home—and their domain to rule. Sunday had to get her hands dirty and kill a few niggas herself to prove a point: she was the real deal, and she could be just as ruthless as the men or worse. And Bray was a monster she knew would help her further her dominance. He had the cruelty necessary to convince any doubters that Sunday was nothing nice to play with—and to keep the money moving.

For once, everything for Sunday was going as planned. But Nasir had begun to throw some resistance her way.

"Twenty kilos, Sunday? You trying to get us killed?" he'd griped the day before, when they'd discussed the pickup. "You're pushing the boundaries right now."

"Scared money don't make no fuckin' money, nigga," she'd countered. "We own the fuckin' projects now. We did it, nigga. Fuck, Nasir, enjoy it. We're becoming bosses, and I ain't tryin' to look back."

Nasir had been watching the news and reading the papers. He was well aware of the extent to which the the city was under siege and on fire with gang violence and trouble. Murders had tripled in the past few months. It seemed like every other day the headlines carried news about a ghastly murder or murders committed in one borough or the other. The mayor had declared war on the crime and violence plaguing his city and had sworn to crack down on the drug kingpins and the drugs. But worse, the FBI had gotten involved. And they were an entity that Nasir didn't want to mess with.

Nasir felt it was time to scale things back, not magnify the risk. But Sunday was her own woman and was in charge of things. And she wasn't shy about letting it be known.

"I fuckin' built this!" she'd snapped at him. "And I'm not having anyone or anything tear it down and take it from me."

It was clear to Nasir who was in charge. And it was also clear that Sunday was becoming power-hungry. Her need and compulsion to control people and things clouded her thinking and tarnished her judgment of people. All the influence she wielded was making her feel as if she was invincible and untouchable. She had Dodge as her connect, Bray as her street distributor, and Sheek, Havoc, and Recut as her muscle. Who was going to tell her no?

But worse, Sheek followed right behind her and was behaving as a sadist in the community. Recently, two girls had been brutally attacked, raped, and murdered. Their bodies had been found naked in vacant apartments in the projects. As far as Nasir was concerned, Sheek's sickness was written all over the crimes. Nasir was familiar with Sheek's sickening behavior. When they'd robbed wealthy homes, kidnapped the fathers, and terrorized families, Sheek had made it a habit to viciously beat and rape the daughters and strangle them afterward. Sunday had despised it at first, but then she had turned a blind eye to her brother's vile ways. The come-up had become more critical.

"You know your brother killed and raped them girls, Sunday. He's becoming bad for business," Nasir had warned her. "He can't control himself, and they'll come for him, and he's gonna be our downfall."

"No one is gonna fuckin' touch my little brother," Sunday had angrily replied. "Ain't no proof he did shit."

Nasir had huffed in response. He used to be able to talk some sense into her, but now Sunday refused to see what was staring her in the face. How could she not see that Sheek was becoming their weakest link? he'd wondered. It would be only a matter of time before detectives or the feds connected these vicious rapes and murders to her little brother, especially now that there was DNA testing.

Sheek needed to go, and Nasir knew Sunday wouldn't kill her brother.

They soon arrived at the designated location for their re-up. Sheek steered the dark green Tahoe into a Brooklyn parking garage. They drove up the ramp to the fourth level and were soon met by two of Dodge's men, who were sitting inside a blue 1970s Chevy Chevelle SS 454. It was a remarkable vehicle. The Tahoe stopped next to the Chevelle, and everyone began climbing out of their cars.

Sheek was impressed by the Chevelle. "Damn, that's a nice fuckin' car. I need me one of those."

The driver of the car, Dodge's vicious henchman named Point, grinned and replied, "Yuh like dat, huh . . . ?"

"Yeah. I do."

"Yuh keep bringin' us wi' money an' yuh'll have one soon, bredren," said Point.

Sheek nodded. *For sure!*

Sunday wasn't there to talk about nice cars; she was there for business. She interrupted their conversation with, "You got that for us, right?"

She tossed a duffel bag containing nearly half a million dollars at their feet. Point smiled. "Business is gud, mi see."

"No doubt, really fuckin' good right now," said Sunday. "So, we ain't got all fuckin' day."

Point chuckled. "Respek, love. Yuh ah bad bitch, mi see. Mi see why Dodge likes yuh," said Point.

Point went to the trunk of the Chevelle, opened it, and removed a duffel bag similar to Sunday's. He handed Nasir the bag.

"Twenty kilos. Yuh gud fa dat?" Point asked Sunday.

"What you think? I'm running things now, and Dodge knows it."

Point grinned. "He do. Keep up de gud work."

"We just need to keep each other happy, right?" said Nasir.

"Yuh smart, an' yeah, yuh right," Point said.

Their transaction was quick. Nasir placed the duffel bag containing twenty kilos into the back of the Tahoe, and everyone got back inside their vehicles. The Jamaicans departed the scene first. The engine of the Chevy Chevelle roared like thunder inside the tight parking level, and the vehicle sped away.

"Damn!" Sheek uttered, impressed.

Following behind the Chevy, they exited the parking garage under the evening sun, which cast long shadows on the ground. The setting sun set the sky ablaze. Sunday was happy. Sheek was happy. But Nasir was concerned. Besides the issue with Sheek and the matter of taking chances with more kilos, Nasir had noticed something different about Sunday. Ever since Bray had come into their lives, Sunday had been more volatile and somewhat indifferent to his needs and concerns.

"Fuck, yes, fuck!" Sunday cried out, thrusting and gyrating her hips and fucking Bray's dick desperately, on the edge of coming.

Bray slammed into her with his dick throbbing, needing to come. They were in the back room of one of his trap houses, with the door closed. It was time to celebrate, since business was booming, and they were doing it in style, fucking their brains out.

"Fuck," she gasped. "Oh, fuck!"

Excited by the sight of her, Bray pushed his dick deeper inside her. He forcefully cupped her ass cheeks and squeezed her tits and continued to fuck her like she was a porn star.

"Oh God," Sunday cried out, still on the edge of having an orgasm.

Fuck, her pussy is good, Bray thought. Frantically, he thrust into her. His balls began tightening, and his dick was ready to explode. Their breathing became shallow. Sunday hadn't thought about Nasir once while Bray was dismantling and rearranging her insides. She'd become selfish about her needs and pleasure. She liked Nasir, and he was a good lover, but she had a mind-blowing history with Bray. He was on her level, didn't doubt her, and took what he wanted, like Sunday.

"Oh fuck!" she screamed, and then she gasped and came, jerking on his dick, her legs shaking from the orgasm. "*Ooh, fuck*. Yes!"

She continued to scream, and her body began jerking uncontrollably on his dick as another intense orgasm took her by storm. She didn't think she was going to cum that hard. Bray followed up by coming himself. His hard dick burst and jerked inside her, each ejaculation making him spasm against her.

Nearly breathless, he uttered, "Damn. Fuck," while pulling out of her.

Sunday climbed off his lap and had to regain her composure. Her legs continued to quiver a bit. She grinned at Bray and said, "Damn, I needed that."

Bray matched her grin and replied, "What, your boy ain't fuckin' you like that?"

"He do me well. But you, Bray, you know we got history, and that dick is crazy."

Bray continued to grin. His ego was in the clouds or higher. He loved this version of Sunday. She came with the works, giving him some good pussy and making him money. He was glad she came home.

"Your boy, he ain't gonna become a problem, right? Because I'll kill the nigga if he comes at me because of you," Bray said.

"You ain't gotta worry about Nasir. He good. Besides, I'm good at what I do. And I'm the boss bitch. I run the show," Sunday proclaimed wholeheartedly.

Bray nodded and smiled.

Sunday began dressing. She put her panties back on and pulled up her jeans. Bray started to do the same. She had come here to deliver ten kilos to him personally, and the sex was what she had wanted to happen next.

"My niggas probably heard us in the next room," said Bray.

Sunday laughed. "And . . . ? Now they know my pussy is good to you."

Bray laughed. Then he uttered, "But, yo, on some serious shit, I might need your help with something."

"What you need from me?"

"You know I'm warring wit' my own niggas, and that ain't right. But I got a lock on one troublemaker. Punk-bitch nigga named Yaz," said Bray. "I had love for the nigga once. But now he out there talkin' that shit 'bout me and tryin' to come at ya boy. He want the crown, always did. But I think he a snitch, and I need him gone. I know ya brother is crazy enough to go after him."

"Say less, bae. I got you," said Sunday.

Bray nodded and smiled. "That's why you my bitch, Sunday. You 'bout that life fo' real. Ain't no play-play wit' you. Shit, I might off that nigga Nasir just to be with you."

Sunday snickered at the thought of it. She then replied, "Nah. I like him. He's useful, and he got my back."

"But I got your back more," Bray insisted.

"I know."

Before she departed, they shared a deep and passionate kiss, with Bray squeezing on her booty one last time for fun. Sunday giggled, blushed, and said, "You better stop, before we fuck again."

Bray grinned at the thought of it. Finally, Sunday walked out of the back room, leaving Bray utterly satisfied with their business arrangement. But then he had a second thought about their conversation about Nasir. He hated to admit it, but he'd become jealous of him, and he knew eventually that nigga would become a problem.

Sheek was a wicked and reckless muthafucka. Everyone who knew him felt he was born to get into trouble and raise hell. His sister was on top of the world right now, building an empire whose might would not be challenged. But Sheek had become tired of being in her shadow. He wanted his own thing. He wanted to grow his own crew and create a name for himself. They feared him because he was a violent monster. He didn't give a fuck about anyone besides Sunday.

He and Havoc had recently got together with two of Bray's thugs, and they had begun robbing homes in Queens, primarily in affluent areas, and terrorizing families again. Sheek had missed this. The money was good, but the adrenaline rush was much better. Sheek got off on seeing the fear on these people's faces, and it was a sadistic pleasure to rape and beat their daughters. It made him feel like a god, since he had the power to make the victims feel helpless. At the same time, he robbed the families of their valuables, brutally defiled their daughters right before their very eyes, and ultimately took their lives. This behavior wasn't going to stop. It was an intrinsic part of him; it gave him both pleasure and a purpose. The two girls he had raped and murdered in the projects had barely appeased his hunger, since they were promiscuous young whores Sheek had merely taken advantage of. And their deaths barely made the news: they were nobodies, and few people would miss them. Sheek needed something more stimulating, something that involved greater risk-taking to feed his ego and satisfy his cravings.

He liked abusing and raping young white girls because of their entitlement and sheltered lives. He and his sister had come from nothing. They'd been mocked, beaten, and abused while growing up in Queens. It'd gotten so bad that they had had to flee the city. They had returned years later to get revenge and had succeeded. Squeeze was dead, the streets were theirs, and now it was time for Sheek to pick up where Sunday had left off.

Sheek, Havoc, and Bray's thugs would cruise through the suburbs of Queens and put their scheme to work in one of two ways. One, they'd adhere to Sunday's method, stalking the father of a successful business or company and holding his family hostage. And two, Sheek would stalk a young snowflake or privileged black girl or woman as she left school or work. When her guard was down, he would swoop in and kidnap her right there. He then would threaten her and force her to divulge her address. She and the others would go there with the girl and shock the family with a blatant home invasion. His crew would ransack the home in their search for money, jewelry, and other valuables and would terrorize the family, while

Sheek would rape the girl in a different room or right there for her parents to see.

He got off on that, creating pain and agony for these families.

Sheek kept his vile activities from his sister, knowing she would disapprove of this. It would get in the way of what she was building.

Sheek was breathing heavily as he pulled up his pants and began buttoning them. His face was sweaty, like he'd just run a marathon. But he'd just finished raping and strangling another girl in her bedroom. She was seventeen, and her contorted body was now sprawled across her bedroom floor. This one had fought hard but had eventually fallen victim to his vile desires. Sheek stared down at his atrocious work, stoic and unmoved. He didn't care that she was the captain of her cheerleading squad and an A student on the honor roll, and that she had planned to attend Columbia University next fall. The only thing that mattered to him was satisfying his twisted needs and becoming rich from the stuff he stole from homes.

Within a month, they'd hit four homes in different areas. First, they had struck in Far Rockaway, and then they'd moved on to Ozone Park, Jamaica Estates, and Valley Stream. And as they all had begun to amass a small fortune, Sheek had become a serial killer in the community.

Havoc stepped inside the bedroom and saw the girl's naked body and remained deadpan.

"What y'all got?" Squeeze asked him.

"We got enough. They have some good shit. But we need to go," said Havoc.

Sheek left the room and went to finish what they'd started. The girls' parents were bound and gagged in the living room. They were in absolute grief and pain, knowing what this monster had done to their daughter. The mother's eyes were flooded with tears and unbearable pain. She wanted to scream but couldn't, because of the tape covering her mouth. However, her muffled cries pierced the duct tape. The father was beside himself with agony too. Sheek stood over them with the gun in his hand and executed them like it was a regular day in the neighborhood.

The men hurriedly exited the mansion-style home and retreated to the work van, which was disguised as a delivery vehicle, parked in the driveway. The three men climbed inside and sped away from another one of their horrific crime scenes. Sheek was elated. They'd come up with some good shit, and Sheek wanted to hock it immediately for the right price.

One of Bray's goons, Web, announced, "I know someone we can go to. He'll give us a good price for all this shit."

"Yeah? Who?" Sheek asked.

"My boy Dante. He owns a pawnshop," Web replied.

"Let's do this, then," said Sheek.

Later that evening, they arrived at Dante's pawnshop to hock the stolen items for a reasonable price. Web introduced Sheek to Dante. Dante was willing to give them the amount they were seeking for the stolen valuables. In addition, he was able to take down Sheek's information, and unbeknownst to Sheek and everyone else, Dante secretly recorded the entire transaction.

When the three men left his pawnshop, Dante immediately picked up the phone to make an urgent call.

The phone on the other end rang several times before Detective Mack answered.

"What's up, Dante?" she said.

"I might have something for you. What y'all been looking for," Dante answered.

Thirty

Danielle was a beautiful, tall woman. She was aesthetically appealing and seductive in nature, and notorious gangster and crime boss Monk Dice felt like he was the luckiest man to have her in his life. The doting couple lived in a brownstone in Brooklyn Heights, which had been a wealthy and prominent area of Brooklyn since 1834. The neighborhood was high class, quiet, and noted for its low-rise architecture and numerous brownstones and rowhouses built before the Civil War.

Danielle and Monk were an "it" couple, considered to be at the top of the food chain. They had become something like Jay-Z and Beyoncé. They were highly respected, loved, and even feared. Monk Dice's reputation had traveled through Brooklyn and the other four boroughs like a savage winter storm. And Danelle took full advantage of being the girlfriend of a feared gangster who was part of the Outfit. There were the shopping sprees at high-end retail stores, the limelight and VIP treatment at every nightclub they attended, the jealousy of her friends and family, the best clothes, the expensive jewelry and, best of all, her brand-new Lexus RX 350, fully loaded, which Monk had purchased for her. Also, the sex was great with him. Danielle had been into bad boys and thugs ever since she was young. She felt she'd struck gold when she met and began fucking with Monk Dice.

Danielle was living on cloud nine with Monk. Her man had Brooklyn on lockdown.

She arrived home, parked, and climbed out of her Lexus, a few shopping bags in her hand. She looked cute and casual in a high-tied button dress and a pair of wedges. It was a beautiful sunny evening. Danielle was excited to show her man the things she'd bought, and they planned to have dinner tonight at an exclusive Manhattan restaurant. Tonight would be their night of dinner, laughter, and romance. One of the things Danielle had purchased was lingerie for much later. She planned to entice her man with lingering sweet kisses, a seductive show, and some foreplay, and she'd suck his dick so good, he would begin to suck his thumb.

She entered the brownstone, excited. "Monk? Baby, you home?" she called out.

She didn't receive a reply back. Danielle placed her bags on the foyer table and called out to her man again. She knew he was home, because she had noticed his Benz parked outside.

"I got something special for us . . . maybe you." She chuckled.

She crossed the living room and continued looking for her man, and when she entered the bedroom, she received the shock of her life. Monk Dice was dead. In his boxers and shirtless, he lay slumped against the headboard. He'd been shot multiple times, including in the head. Blood was everywhere.

Danielle couldn't believe what she was seeing. She immediately shrieked so loud, she damn near shattered the windows. Suddenly, she learned she wasn't alone with her dead boyfriend. Monk had just been killed. The killer emerged from the bathroom, carrying the Glock with a silencer. He was dressed in black and unmasked. Danielle stood in his presence, frozen and terrified. The killer locked eyes with a wide-eyed Danielle. He remained calm, though he hadn't expected her.

"Please, I—I won't say anything. I—I swear . . . ," Danielle pleaded, her voice shaking.

"I know you won't," the killer replied.

He raised the Glock and fired twice at Danielle. She dropped before his feet like a sack of potatoes. He fired another shot into the back of her head. Her blood began to pool on the hardwood floor. The killer racked the bolt, checked the chamber, unscrewed the silencer, and stowed both parts in his jacket. He pivoted and calmly left the bedroom. Another member of the Outfit was dead. They were dropping like flies.

Ezekial rode quietly in the back seat of the luxury Cadillac. The man had so much on his mind that it had become hard for him to sleep at night. Having Baxter Johnson and a few other Outfit members killed was becoming costly, and all this death was haunting him. No one was making any money. Knowing his men had missed the chance to kill Antonio was upsetting. His rival was out for revenge, and he had help from fellow crime bosses Kevin Charles and Gregg Rice. Ezekial had also heard that Zodiac was in an alliance with Antonio. The pressure was intensifying. Antonio had placed a five-million-dollar bounty on his head, and Ezekial had done the same and more, amping up his bounty by placing ten million dollars on Antonio's head.

Everything was becoming ugly, and Ezekial knew it would get worse before it got better. Until then, every move he made was cautious, calculated, and done quickly and quietly.

Ezekial was on his way to a private airport in New Jersey. He'd contacted his pilots hours earlier to inform them he was leaving the country. When he arrived at the small airport, he wanted his Learjet gassed and ready for takeoff. New York City had become dicey and un-predictable. He'd started something, and he planned on finishing it. But first, he wanted to regroup and rethink his next move, and he planned to do that outside the country. He had the manpower, money, and influence to finish it, but it would take longer than expected.

No family was left for his enemies to come after, except for Cashmere and his nephew, Rondell. And they both were ruthless and dangerous, just like him. Ezekial felt there was no need to worry too much about them. But he wanted to ensure their safety. He wanted Cashmere to stay hidden and safe on his upstate property until further notice from him. No one knew about it, he believed. However, Ezekial was worried about Cashmere, and he wondered if the men he had provided for her security would suffice.

He arrived at the local airport in a remote part of New Jersey. The driver navigated the Cadilac onto the tarmac, toward the Learjet, which was prepared to leave once Ezekial boarded. His pilots were standing near the boarding stairs, ready to greet Ezekial. But before Ezekial could climb out of the vehicle, his phone rang. It was Doc.

Ezekial answered with some uneasiness. "What is it, Doc?"

"It's Cashmere. She's dead," said Doc.

The news hit Ezekial like a sledgehammer to his chest, and then it felt like he was hit and run over by a semitruck. Word of her death damn near knocked the wind out of him. Ezekial remained quiet for a moment, seething. Then he began repeatedly punching the back of the headrest.

"She was found tortured and beaten at your house upstate," Doc added. "What do you need me to do?"

Molten anger surged through Ezekial, and rage gripped him in what felt like a headlock. Yet the news also saddened him, and he had a heavy heart. He blamed himself for Cashmere's death. He was stupid to leave her alone when a war was happening. He should have made her leave the country instead of telling her to hide upstate.

"Turn around," Ezekial told his driver, Moses. "We're going back."

Moses nodded and then steered the Escalade away from the Learjet, leaving the pilots shrugging their shoulders, confused.

Ezekial never allowed his emotions to get the better of him, but the news that Cashmere was dead had shattered his heart into pieces. His eyes began to water, but he didn't shed a tear. She was everything to him, and now someone had brutally murdered her. He vowed to revenge her death at any cost. He owed her that. Whoever had killed her, Ezekial was gonna make them wish they were dead.

He stared aimlessly out the back window, overcome by grief. He stared until his phone rang again. Ezekial was hesitant to answer when he saw it was Ray Black calling, but he took the call anyway.

"What?" Ezekial answered gruffly.

"What the fuck you mean, what? Monk is dead, that's what!" Ray Black griped. "They killed him and a bitch in the brownstone."

More bad news.

Ezekial groaned. *Fuck!*

"We need to fuckin' meet, Ezekial," said Ray Black.

"I'm kind of busy, Ray."

"Nah, fuck that. Whatever the fuck you got going on, this shit is more important. I'm losing money, men, and we got the fuckin' feds, the DEA, task forces, and the state fuckin' police up our ass, nigga . . . all because of some God complex you got, muthafucka!" Ray Black was heated and frustrated.

"I understand you're upset, Ray, but watch your mouth. Remember who the fuck you're talking to," Ezekial warned him.

"Nigga, fuck that! I'm not one of your fuckin' subordinates. I'm your fuckin' equal in this shit, Ezekial. And somehow, you fuckin' forgot that shit! I'm Ray Black, nigga, and we need to fuckin' meet up. Van agrees, too," Ray exclaimed.

Equals? Ezekial had no *equals* in this world. In his mind, he was a god. He huffed. Ray was becoming a pain in his ass.

"Listen—" Ezekial started.

"No, you listen, nigga!" Ray Black chided, interrupting him. "We're bleeding out here, Ezekial. Antonio's pissed off, and he's coming for us with an army I can't even fuckin' fathom. We fucked up by siding with you. Now I'm lookin' like a fuckin' naked asshole holding a big dick, with no pussy to fuck."

"'The two most powerful warriors are patience and time,'" Ezekial responding, quoting from *War and Peace*, Tolstoy's very long novel. "I guarantee this storm will pass over us."

"Muthafucka, you think we got time or patience? Fuck your ideological *The Art of War* quotes, nigga. We need to meet now and discuss this shit!"

Ezekial sighed and didn't both to correct Ray Black. There was no talking or calming him down, either, so Ezekial relented and said, "Fine. Give me the time and place. I'll be there."

"I'll do that. Look for my call within the hour," said Ray Black with finality.

When the call ended, Ezekial was seething. He'd just gotten the news about Cashmere, and now Ray Black was trying to boss him around. It wasn't about to fly like that, Ezekial thought. He was the king of kings out here. He'd been killing people since men like Ray Black and Antonio were in diapers. Now he needed to remind these streets and his rivals why he was the most feared muthafucka in the first place.

"Moses, take me upstate to Elmira Correctional Facility. I need to see my nephew," he said.

Moses nodded. "No problem."

Ezekial's arrival at Elmira Correctional Facility created an uproar among the guards, the staff, and the inmates. Word of him being at the facility spread quickly. The moment he stepped inside the state prison, everyone was on edge. Although it was a state prison, Ezekial moved throughout the facility like he owned it. He went through the routine security checks with ease, and the guards treated him with respect, knowing the type of man he was. He could ruin their lives and end them with the snap of his fingers. They were guards, but they were human beings with families first.

Mr. Montoya was how they addressed him at Elmira.

After going through the routine security procedures, the guards escorted Ezekial to a private room reserved for lawyers and their inmate clientele. He received no quarrel from the warden or superiors about his sudden special treatment. The last thing anyone wanted was backlash from Mr. Montoya, either from the streets or from his high-end connections.

Ezekial took a seat at the table, choosing the one that faced the doorway. He was alone momentarily, waiting patiently for the guards to bring him his nephew. The room was grim, relatively small, and dingy, with no windows. The door was steel and equipped with locks and bolts. The air tasted like stale bread and shit. The room seemed devoid of oxygen, and a chill permeated it.

Finally, there was some activity. The steel door opened, and the guards escorted his nephew inside the room. He was handcuffed and shackled. The guards unlocked his restraints, and one of the guards said to Ezekial, "You have ten minutes with him, Mr. Montoya."

Ezekial nodded, grateful.

The guards left the room and closed the door behind them. Rondell stared at his uncle and grinned.

"It's been a while, Uncle E," Rondell said.

Ezekial stood to hug his nephew. They embraced, and then Ezekial asked him, "How are they treating you in here?"

"As expected. Your name means a lot inside here," said Rondell.

Ezekial didn't respond to the remark. He sat back down at the table, and Rondell lowered himself into the chair across from him. Rondell was excited to see his uncle again. He uttered, "It's been a while, Uncle E. What brings you?"

Ezekial stared intently at his nephew. There were no cameras or listening devices inside the room, so Ezekial felt free and comfortable to share what was on his mind.

"I didn't have a close relationship with my sons. They barely knew me. But I loved them," he began. Rondell was listening. "But with you, you became a son to me, Rondell. When my sister fell ill and eventually passed, I took you under my wing and taught you everything I wanted to teach my sons, and you learned quickly. Now, the fear and respect you have, I carry that."

Rondell nodded, agreeing with his uncle. "No doubt."

"I had you transferred here for a reason, and that *reason* still exists today," said Ezekial.

"I've been on it, Uncle E. But this muthafucka is like a fuckin' cockroach, hard to fuckin' get rid of," said Rondell. "And he's smart and respected too."

"He killed my sons and your cousins and needs to go. The longer he breathes, the more agitated I become. But I see I've been going about this the wrong way," said Ezekial.

Rondell was listening. "What do you need me to do?"

"Just wait," Ezekial replied.

"Wait . . . ?" Rondell was confused.

"To really destroy a man and distract him with emotions and heartache, you need to take away the thing he loves the most," Ezekial proclaimed. "And I've already set that in motion. He took something from me. Now I'll take something from him. Then he'll become so overwhelmed with grief that he'll come after you for revenge. He will want to kill you to get to me. He'll become sloppy from anger and rage. And when he does, you fuckin' destroy that bastard."

Rondell nodded. "I will."

Ezekial started to cough heavily out of the blue. The cough was so heavy, it took him a while to catch his breath.

Rondell became worried and asked, "Uncle E, you okay?"

Finally, Ezekial stopped coughing and was able to breathe again. He replied, "I'm fine, Rondell. I'll be even better when Sincere is dead."

Some of the greatest battles will be fought within the silent chambers of your soul. It was a saying Sincere had heard from his sergeant when he was in the army. Sincere had heard about Row being killed by the guards, and he was fuming. Sincere wanted to kill every last guard who'd been involved in his friend's death, but he couldn't make that move, not right away, at least. He didn't want KOS to look weak. But Sincere was also beginning to deal with internal struggles that he had to face. The depths of his mind had become unrestrained and infected with madness. He was suffering from psychosis and was disconnected from his reality. He'd built something inside a state prison and had become an icon to many inmates. But he was haunted by what-ifs. What if he had listened to Monica and his sister and hadn't sought revenge for Marcus's death? Where would he be today? Denise would still be alive. Or what if he had never left for the military? What if he and Nasir had never killed that man on Long Island while committing a robbery? What if he had become a cop instead of a gang leader?

What if! What if? What the fuck if? Sincere knew he had created this monster he'd become during his moments of self-examination and remembering. It felt like he hadn't had a choice. The chaos, violence, killings, and war had made him truly discover who he was and what he was capable of. He'd faced some of the most challenging battles on the streets and in combat zone and had survived them all. He was born to become a warrior. Yet now Sincere felt weak and vulnerable. Confused too.

While he sat in his cell, reflecting, Trek came to him with some news.

"Ezekial Montoya is here vising Rondell," said Trek. "What you want us to do?"

Sincere frowned upon hearing the news. But he responded, "Nothing."

Trek was taken aback. "What . . . ?"

"Do you think we'll get close to him right now?" said Sincere.

Sincere knew Ezekial and Rondell were planning his demise.

Thirty-one

Detective Mack knew this was the big break in her homicide case. Given what Dante had shown her, she knew there was sufficient evidence to get an arrest warrant and an indictment for Sheek. The surveillance footage Dante had shown her had clear images of Sheek and two other men pawning stolen items from a crime scene at his pawnshop. Everything Sheek pawned at Dante's shop had to be identified, searched for fingerprints, tagged, and bagged. Dante had been upset, since he would lose nearly sixty thousand dollars in merchandise, but Detective Mack hadn't taken no for an answer. She'd also warned him that he could be charged with receiving stolen merchandise and hindering an investigation if he didn't want to cooperate.

"Y'all some muthafuckas, for real," Dante had griped. "I'm trying to do you a favor, and I'm getting fucked with no Vaseline. I don't know why I even called you."

"Because you live that life, Dante. You associate with criminals and profit from them. And I'm looking out for you too. But look at it this way, Dante. You're helping to get a monster off these streets. If these items are connected to a home invasion and multiple murders, you'll be considered a hero."

Dante huffed. "Man, you gonna make me go out of business."

"You're too smart to go out of business, Dante," said Mack.

"Whatever, Detective. I've done my civic duty for the year. I'm retired," he groaned.

Shelly Mack laughed. She was grateful he had called.

Detective Mack had got some decent fingerprints off a few things, and when she'd run the prints, one of them matched that of a Clifford Daily, also known as Sheek. He had been off their radar for a while, but now he had popped back into their system with a vengeance.

"I know his sister," said Detective Emmerson as he and Mack discussed the case at her desk the very next day. "She used to turn tricks for this asshole named Squeeze a few years back. He was one nasty and mean son of a bitch. Word on the streets back then was the siblings fled town because of some trouble."

"Oh, really? What kind of trouble?" she asked him.

"Don't know."

"Do you know where?" she asked.

"I didn't look into it. They were small fries back then. Nothing to worry about."

"Well, the brother graduated to home invasions, maybe rape, murders, and assault," said Mack. "His prints connect him to several more crimes, and I guarantee when we collect his DNA, we'll get him for every rape at those locations."

"We'll get him. The captain's about to put out a BOLO for him in the streets. We'll find him and fry his ass," said Detective Emmerson.

Shelly Mack beamed with pride and a sense of accomplishment. It had been a long and tiresome case, and now she was ready to see her suspect arrested, booked, and doing life in jail. After Emmerson headed out to grab lunch, she sat at her desk and replayed Dante's surveillance footage of Sheek. He was a scary-looking guy. She could only imagine the horrors these families had endured when Sheek got his hands on them. His recent victim was only seventeen years old. The photo of her contorted naked body on the bedroom floor was disturbing. The sight of something like that would stay with Shelly Mack forever. She was so disgusted by his crimes that she had the urge to vomit. What he deserved was the death penalty.

It was time to launch a manhunt for this monster and take him down.

Shelly Mack wanted to punch and spit in the face of this monster. She wanted to castrate him and make him suffer. She wanted to make him feel excruciating pain and ensure he would never harm, rape, or murder another girl again.

You can find me in the club, bottle full of bub'
Look, mami, I got the X if you into takin' drugs
I'm into havin' sex. I ain't into makin' love . . .

50 Cent's "In da Club" blared throughout the club, and everyone went crazy. Club Skylight was a popular nightclub near Hillside Avenue in Queens. A line of club-goers was waiting to get inside, and beefy bouncers were checking IDs and turning people away at the entrance. A girl stamped hands with the club logo and collected the cover charge. Inside was one heck of a party. The dance floor was packed with revelers partying like it would be their last night on earth. No one could see the dance floor; it was wall-to-wall people dancing to the club music. The strobe lights pulsed throughout the club, and the bartenders rushed to keep up with orders.

Sunday and her crew were tucked away in their private VIP section, away from the chaos of the cramped dance floor and the sweaty partygoers, who were moving to the music like they were puppets on strings. This was their night to celebrate, and they were doing it in style and ratchetness. The men were wearing Timberlands, Jordans, jeans, gold chains, Yankees caps, hoodies, and swag. But Sunday stood out as the sexy bitch in charge with her pink minidress featuring a V-neck. The dress hugged her young curves and accentuated her ample bosom. Her entourage was popping expensive bottles of champagne as skimpily dressed bottle girls carrying glowing trays of drinks or empty bottles went back and forth to the bar.

Everyone else stood out too. They were loud, raunchy, and impatient. Tonight was their night to party and have a good time. They felt and *were* on top of the world. There was so much money flowing in from the streets that spending a hundred thousand dollars inside the club felt like pennies on the dollar to them. Sunday had done it. She'd become a boss bitch, and she wanted to treat her family and crew to a good time tonight. With the bottles of champagne came the pretty ladies who were willing to show the men more of a good time and some party favors.

Sunday stood up from the cushioned settee and raised her champagne bottle in the air to grab everyone's attention. She grinned proudly and said, "Look at us tonight. We fuckin' did it, my niggas. We here, on top of the fuckin' world, and ain't shit stopping us. We fuckin' run this shit, right?"

Everyone applauded and hollered, "No doubt! No doubt!"

Sunday nodded and grinned some more. Everything she'd worked hard for had led her to this moment and had given her the respect she'd longed for.

Bray joined her and shared his own words of celebration. "BMB and MSK united, and we out here gettin' it, and fuck everything else. We shuttin' shit down, muthafuckas!"

The goons, killers, hustlers, and wolves hollered. They were becoming so loud in the VIP area that they caught the attention of the club revelers over the blaring rap music. Sheek, Havoc, Recut, and Diane stood up with everyone else and hollered the loudest. But Nasir remained seated. He wasn't moved by everything that was going on. He sat there looking pensive. From the noise they were making on the streets, the killings going on over territory, and the reckless behavior Sheek was demonstrating, he knew this bubble of money and lifestyle would soon pop.

But what bothered Nasir more was the fact that Sunday and Bray were fucking behind his back. He couldn't prove it; it was his intuition telling him. Bray had gotten too close and comfortable with Sunday for his comfort. There was something about him Nasir didn't like. He was cocky and arrogant. And Sunday had begun moving differently with him. They weren't fucking like they used to. Nasir knew Sunday was a freak and was always dick hungry. And she was becoming power hungry too. She had let it be known to everyone that the takeover of Baisley Park Gardens was only the beginning, that there were bigger things to come. Sunday had eyes on annexing other projects and territory throughout Queens. She had developed a megalomaniacal attitude and an obsession with exercising her power and dominating others.

She had become a real bitch.

The night went on. A row of shot glasses was filled by one of the bottle girls. Nasir picked up a shot glass and downed its contents in a hurry. He then looked over at Bray and Sunday, who were sitting together, discussing something privately. He frowned. The alcohol fueled his negative emotions, and he was overcome by anger, insecurity, and jealousy.

Bray noticed the foul looks coming from Nasir. He cut his eyes at Nasir and griped, "Yo, Nasir, why the fuck you keep lookin' at me like that? You gotta fuckin' problem with me, nigga?"

"Yeah, I got a fuckin' problem with you, nigga! Why you up on my bitch like that?" Nasir snarled.

"Nigga, what?"

"You fuckin' heard me, nigga!" Nasir exclaimed.

The tension between these two men became thick as molasses. Bray wasn't about to be disrespected by anyone, and especially Nasir. He countered, "How you know she was ya bitch in the first fuckin' place? I was fuckin' her before ya ass came along, nigga. Don't fuckin' disrespect me, nigga!"

"Fuck you, nigga!" Nasir hollered.

Bray leaped up, ready to put his hands on Nasir, and Nasir did the same. Members of both gangs began to look uneasy. Was this really happening?

Sunday immediately came between them and shouted, "What the fuck are y'all doing? We're not doin' this shit here. We family. Y'all niggas fuckin' hear me!"

Nasir and Bray glared at each other with utter contempt. Sunday could barely keep them apart. Bray was a bigger beast, though, with more muscles and greater violent tendencies. She loved his aggressive nature but didn't want any conflict between her people. It was bad for business.

"Y'all niggas chill, you hear me?" Sunday shouted.

"You fuckin' this nigga?" Nasir asked gruffly.

Sunday stood there, looking a bit dumbfounded. Nasir had openly put her on blast, and she didn't like it at all.

"You really tryin' to do this here, Nasir?" Sunday groused. "I think you're drunk."

"I ain't fuckin' drunk, Sunday. And I ain't stupid either!" he snapped.

Bray clenched his fists, Nasir continued scowling, deep in his feelings, and Sunday needed to exhale. But before things escalated between the two men, security de-escalated things. Sunday wasn't in the partying mood anymore, and it was time to leave. Everyone gathered up their troops, and they began exiting the nightclub.

Nasir walked behind the entourage, still seething. But nothing was going to happen tonight. He knew he needed to calm down and think rationally. He liked Sunday, but she wasn't Denise. And everyone was making too much money for him to rock the boat.

Sunday, Bray, and MSK and BMB members were lingering outside the nightclub. There was still a line outside to enter Skylight. All eyes were on Sunday and her crew. They stood out as they were tipsy, they were laughing, and they were looking fly and rough. The hiccup with Nasir and Bray had clearly been forgotten.

Nasir noticed it first, the black Toyota Sequoia SUV parked at the end of the block. For some strange reason, he felt something didn't seem right about it. He could see the silhouettes of three men sitting inside the vehicle, and it appeared that they were waiting on something or someone. Sunday and everyone else began walking toward their cars. That was when the headlights of the Toyota came on, and it began approaching the group. The Toyota started moving slowly toward Sunday and her crowd, then quickly accelerated as the windows rolled down. Nasir knew right away what this was.

Fuck!

"Sunday, it's a fuckin' hit!" Nasir screamed. "Get the fuck down!"

Before Sunday and her company could react, automatic gunfire erupted from the Toyota.

Bang! Bang! Bang! Bang! Bang!

Pandemonium ensued. Startled pedestrians began to run or hit the ground, and everyone desperately tried to scramble out of the way, screaming as they went. The line outside of Skylight evaporated immediately. Sunday ducked and quickly took cover. But Bray, Sheek, Nasir, and a few others snatched their pistols, raised their weapons at the speeding Toyota, and opened fire.

Nasir held his weapon low, followed behind the Toyota, and made a mental note of the license plate number before he opened fire too. But the vehicle was too far away. It sped down the block and made a sharp left turn, disappearing from Nasir's view.

He heard Sunday scream, "Shit! Fuck. Havoc!"

Nasir pivoted and saw that Havoc had been hit twice in the chest and stomach. Nasir ran toward him, shoving running bystanders out of his way as he went. Sunday was clutching Havoc in her arms, cradling his body, fuming. Nasir knew he was dead.

"Sunday, we need to go!" Bray hollered.

"These muthafuckas!" Sunday shouted.

Bray snatched her away from Havoc's lifeless body, and they hurried toward the vehicles. Nasir and Sunday fled in separate cars. They both were upset and devastated about Havoc. He'd become family, and now he was gone. Nasir and Sunday knew one thing for sure: someone would pay for their friend's death.

The death of Havoc had become the most minor of everyone's problems. Word had gotten back to Sunday that there was an arrest warrant out for her brother and Havoc—and that there was no doubt that indictments would be sought for the two men—for the alleged commission of multiple murders, home invasions, rape, and other egregious crimes. The prosecutors were coming for Sheek with the force of Thor's hammer, thunder and lightning right behind it.

Sunday became so upset about this that she attacked her brother with fury and screamed, "What the fuck did you do?"

"I wanted my own thing, sis," Sheek shouted.

"Your own thing . . . ? What the fuck are you talkin' 'bout? You had your own thing. You were a part of this, an empire," Sunday retorted. "Something you helped me build."

"Nah. This is ya shit. You run the show with Nasir and Bray. I'm a muthafucka in the background, waiting for your orders. I don't like to idle, sis. I wanna keep busy," Sheek told her. "I liked what we were doing in the Midwest and when we came here—getting money, raiding their homes, creating terror for these white muthafuckas thinkin' they better than us. And I liked fuckin' their daughters. I like the fear in their eyes when I take everything from them—their dignity and security, including their life. I'm a fuckin' monster, Sunday, but you already knew that. You saw it wit' ya own eyes, and then you turned a blind eye to it."

"You fucked up," Sunday muttered.

"Fuck that! I did me." Sheek pivoted and left his sister standing there, fuming.

Sunday was irritated. She had had no idea Sheek and Havoc were still committing violent home invasions and her brother was raping girls. This was serious. What her brother had done was unforgettable and grotesque. The government would crucify her little brother and everything he was associated with. Sunday knew this was something she could not fix.

"They're coming for him," said Nasir, breaking his silence. "He fucked up. And he needs to eat that."

Sunday cut her eyes at Nasir, her anger showing. "What the fuck are you sayin', Nasir?"

"You already know what I'm saying," he replied. "He's done. They will eventually find him and fuck him up for what he did. It's all over the news, national too. He's a liability to all of us, Sunday."

"My brother ain't a fuckin' snitch!" she snapped.

"Do you know that for sure? Sheek can destroy all of us right now. And you worked hard to get here."

Tears began to trickle from her eyes. She was hurt and devastated. First, Havoc, and now she had to decide about her brother.

"If you can't do it, I can," Nasir said.

Sunday stared at Nasir, pain, anger, and confusion etched on her face. Knowing what needed to happen to Sheek was devastating. Not wanting to look weak, she quickly wiped the tears from her face and took a deep breath. That look of pain, anger, and confusion suddenly turned into one of determination. She locked eyes with Nasir and reluctantly said, "He made his bed. Fuck it! Now he can lie in it."

She gave the order, but it was a hard pill to swallow. Nasir nodded. Sunday spun and walked away so fast, she was gone in the blink of an eye. Nasir lingered in the room, knowing what needed to be done. He was cool with Sheek, but he'd become reckless. Now it was time to take out the trash.

Unbeknownst to Sunday and everyone else, Nasir was the mastermind behind the drive-by that had taken Havoc's life. He had wanted to take out Bray, but Havoc had got hit. He knew the drive-by was sloppy, but no one would suspect him of being behind it, because of his heroic movements that night. Nasir had secretly linked up with Yaz, one of Bray's enemies, and the two had decided it was their time to shine. First, they would take out Bray, and then Sunday if she became a problem. However, this thing with Sheek had become an issue, and it needed to be resolved right away.

Nasir knew it would just be a matter of time before it all crumbled and he would be back to square one.

Sheek wasn't worried while riding in the car with Nasir and Recut. He sat quietly in the back seat, staring out the window. He believed his sister was looking out for him. He knew Sunday would do something to help him out and would not allow him to drown or go down for his crimes. He didn't want to spend the rest of his life inside a prison. And although Sunday was upset with him, Sheek knew his big sister would forgive him and make some kind of arrangement for him to go off the grid.

"You're hot right now, nigga. Sunday wants you out of town until shit cools down," Nasir said.

"I'm cool wit' that," Sheek replied. "Where y'all taking me?"

"We on a need-to-know basis, Sheek. You'll see," Nasir told him. "Sunday made all the necessary arrangements for you."

Recut was driving. Nasir nonchalantly sat in the passenger seat. Sheek sighed and continued to gaze out the window. They turned down a dark urban street in the ghetto, and Sheek noticed a car ahead of them, a black Yukon.

"What's up? Why we here?" Sheek asked.

"We need to change cars," Nasir informed him.

"Change cars? For what?"

"Nigga, you're hot right now, and Sunday is taking the necessary precautions to keep you safe," Nasir replied.

Sheek believed him. He knew Sunday loved him, and she wouldn't harm him. So, he climbed out of the gray Pontiac Grand Am GT with Nasir and proceeded toward the black Yukon. But before he could get close to the SUV, Nasir quickly removed a gun from his waistband, aimed it at the back of Sheek's head, and fired without any hesitation. Sheek dropped dead, and Nasir put three more holes into him.

"Sick muthafucka," Nasir exclaimed.

He and Recut threw Sheek's body into the trunk of the Pontiac, wiped the car down entirely, jumped into the Yukon, and left the scene.

Thirty-two

Antonio Francesco felt like celebrating. The tide had turned in his favor in the war with Ezekial. Zodiac was a better ally than he thought he'd be. Cashmere and Monk Dice were dead. They were able to disrupt Ray Black and Van Gray's pipeline and business throughout the city. Everyone was losing money and men, and the government and the mayor had implemented task forces out the ass to bring down every criminal organization in the Tristate area and stop the violence happening in the city. The feds were probing and yearning to hit the kingpins with RICO charges. The DEA was coming for the drugs, the ATF wanted to hammer everyone for the guns, and the NYPD was trying to annihilate them for the murders.

But Antonio wanted to celebrate like they'd won something special. Zodiac felt the man was a fool. He knew there was nothing to celebrate about. It was all falling apart. Antonio and Ezekial had become addicted to violence and bloodshed. Ezekial was a dying man with nothing to lose. Antonio had such a massive ego that it was a shock to Zodiac he wasn't tipping over.

"I underestimated you, Zodiac," said Antonio. "Working with you is the best decision I've made. Who would have known? We're soon gonna have that mulanyan Ezekial by the balls. And I'm gonna cut 'em off my fuckin' self. I don't want cancer to kill him, because I wanna do it myself."

Antonio was full of life. He said to one of his men, "Questo è un negro intelligente . . ."

They looked at Zodiac and laughed. Zodiac had no idea what Antonio had said to his men, but he understood the word *negro* in the sentence. The man was praising and insulting him all under one breath.

"We make a good team," said Antonio. Antonio then looked at his men and said, "Questo è un negro con cui posso lavorare. Beh, allenati, eh?"

Everyone laughed besides Zodiac. There was that word again, *negro*. Zodiac kept his cool. But Antonio's ego trip was becoming a journey to nowhere.

Zodiac knew it was time for him to leave Antonio's restaurant. The air was becoming too thick for him. He finished off his scotch and said to Antonio, "It's getting late. I'm leaving."

"So soon?" said Antonio.

"It's been a long day."

"It has. But for us, victory is on the horizon," said Antonio.

Zodiac nodded.

Antonio raised his glass toward Zodiac and uttered, "*Salute.*"

"*Salute*," Zodiac responded, not knowing what the fuck it really meant. He stood up, turned, and marched toward the front door.

Antonio's eyes lingered on him.

When Zodiac left the restaurant, Buck opened the passenger door for his boss, and Zodiac slid into the passenger seat. Buck got behind the wheel and waited for Zodiac to tell him where to go.

"Take me the fuck home, Buck. I'm tired," said Zodiac.

Buck nodded. "I got you, boss."

***

The weather was gradually changing, and another season would soon be upon them. The season wasn't the only thing that needed to change, Zodiac thought.

The night was still young, and Zodiac sat outside on the balcony. He was slumped in his chair, a glass of brandy in his hand. Trina soon joined him, clad in a long silk robe. She sat on Zodiac's lap and wrapped her arms around him.

"What is on your mind?" she asked him.

Zodiac groaned a little; there was a lot on his mind.

"Are you worried about going into business with Antonio?" asked Trina.

Zodiac sighed as he stared off at nothing in particular. "He's a fuckin' fool, and he doesn't see me as an equal. And he never will. Even called me a nigger in Italian. I can see why Ezekial wants him dead."

"And what about you?"

"I don't know. This war is costing me a lot. If it continues, it won't end well for nobody."

"So, end it," Trina said point-blank.

Zodiac gave her a look that said, *You think it's that easy!*

"Only two men are creating the problems," she mused. "When one goes, most likely, this war ends. So, who goes? Or better yet, who are you close with?"

Zodiac thought about it and realized that Trina was onto something. Between Antonio and Ezekial, whose death would benefit him the most? Antonio was an egotistical racist, and Ezekial was a dying man with a God complex. Who was the lesser of the two evils?

It was time to end things, and thanks to Trina, Zodiac figured he was the key.

***

"It was pride that changed angels into devils. It is humility that makes men angels," Markest said to Zodiac.

"What . . . ?" Zodiac replied.

"There are two kinds of pride, good pride and bad pride. 'Good pride' represents our dignity and self-respect. 'Bad pride' is the deadly sin of superiority, which reeks of conceit and arrogance," said Markest.

The brothers stood on Zodiac's balcony at his penthouse palace and were having a drink. It was a lovely night, with a bright full moon and clear skies. Zodiac was surprised his brother had come to visit him. Markest never took the time to go to his place, so Zodiac wondered what had changed.

Both men took in the magnificent sweeping view of Central Park and the unparalleled skyline view of the city. Markest was taken aback and uttered, "This is a nice view. I admit, I am amazed."

"It's why I come out here to think," said Zodiac.

Markest nodded. He understood. "You like to come out here and think, huh?"

"Enjoy a drink or two and collect my thoughts."

"So, let me ask you something. How long do you think it will last, little brother?" said Markest. "I watch the news. I know what's happening, and it's only a matter of time before they come for you, either the law or judgment day."

"You can't come to my place and not judge me, can you, Markest?" Zodiac griped.

"I came here to help you."

"*Help* me? You think I need help . . . ?"

"Yes. Pop's gone, and Mob Allah and Zulu. I'm the only family you have left, Zodiac."

"I still have Trina," Zodiac countered.

Markest chuckled. He had his own thoughts about Trina, Zodiac's trans girlfriend, but he decided to keep his opinions to himself for now. Tonight it was about the violence and bloodshed his brother was mixed up in.

"Everything you have comes with a cost. Your soul, little bro. And sooner or later, there will be a price to pay. I know. I've been there myself."

"You can't let me live, huh, Markest?" Zodiac argued.

"If I didn't love you, I would let you be. If Pop didn't love us, he would have kept quiet about our wrongdoings and allowed us to destroy ourselves. But he always preached to us because he cared. Now I'm caring about you, knowing I don't want to get that call one night about you," Markest proclaimed wholeheartedly.

Zodiac sighed heavily.

"Listen, it's your life. I know. You're a grown man, and you'll do whatever you want. I'm just that beacon of light to guide you when that change comes," said Markest. "An arrogant man forever thinks he can do much more than he can. An ego always looks at his face in the mirror and never in his eyes."

Zodiac scoffed. "I see myself every day."

"I know. You're the last one, Zodiac. You have a choice."

Markest downed the rest of his drink and was ready to leave. He placed the glass on the small table, grabbed his jacket, and threw it on.

"Thanks for the drink and the talk," said Markest. He stared at his little brother and added, "Some rise by sin, and some by virtue fall."

After sharing his words of wisdom, Markest turned and left the balcony, then made his way to front door of the penthouse, passing Trina without uttering a goodbye. She knew how he felt about her, and she didn't care much for him either. After Markest left the apartment, Trina went to join her man on the terrace.

"Everything okay with you?" she asked him.

Zodiac sighed heavily. His brother had gotten into his head.

"What did he say to you?"

"Nothing I haven't heard before," said Zodiac.

The luxury black Cadillac arrived at the top level of the parking garage and stopped near an idling dark green Tahoe. Ezekial, Moses, Doc, and another mean killer were inside the Cadillac. Ezekial wasn't taking any chances tonight. He didn't trust Zodiac and his men but was willing to hear them out. The moment the Cadillac arrived, the occupants of the green Tahoe slowly exited the vehicle. Everyone in the Cadillac got out, and Ezekial glared at Zodiac and his henchmen.

The groups met between the two vehicles under the black sky. Everyone was on edge. Weapons remained concealed, and trust was a thin line. Zodiac and Ezekial stared intently at each other. This would be a moment when an alliance was forged or a conflict intensified.

"I didn't think you would come," said Zodiac. "But I'm glad you did."

"I'm here because you have an interesting proposition for me."

"I do. I was never your enemy, Ezekial. I had nothing to do with your two sons' deaths. That was in the past, and the men responsible still live, from my understanding."

"And they'll be dead soon. I've made arrangements for it. And from what I know, you have to. You're in cahoots with Antonio. Because of you, he isn't rotting in the ground yet. You're helping him win."

"You left me no choice. You came for me in Africa."

"I was led by emotions then," said Ezekial.

"And now . . . ?"

"Now I'm more rational with my thoughts. I know you know about my cancer diagnosis."

"I do."

Ezekial chuckled. "Funny thing, when a man has been diagnosed with death, every decision he's made and every regret he's had becomes clear as day. I can't afford to die. I'd lose too much money."

Zodiac wasn't laughing.

"Death is inevitable—some might even say it is a terminal inconvenience or a reason to suddenly stop my transgressions. But I'm a stubborn man, and before I die, I will burn it all down," Ezekial declared.

"Just leave me out of your chaos. It's all I ask from you, Ezekial."

"In exchange for what . . . ?"

"I'll serve Antonio to you on a silver platter. It is what you want, right?"

"It is. But I also want something else," said Ezekial.

Zodiac moaned. "And what is that?"

"Someone dear to me was tortured and killed a few weeks back. Her name is Cashmere. I want the name and location of the individual behind it."

"I wasn't a part of that," Zodiac uttered.

"I don't give a fuck if you were a part of it or not. I want a name."

Zodiac huffed. "I've heard Antonio brag about a man named Salvatore. He's one of Antonio's top hit men."

"I know him."

"Well, that's between you and him," Zodiac said. "My only concern about tonight is where you and I stand once we depart from here."

Ezekial stared at Zodiac with intent, anger, and some respect. They could kill each other right now and be done with it. Or he could consider Zodiac an ally for now and use him to finally kill Antonio and everyone associated

with him, including Kevin Charles and Gregg Rice. And
then he had something special planned for Salvatore.

"Death is one of the few *sure things* in life, and it's also
something we all have in common. But tonight it won't
be."

"I'll set it up. Get the muthafucka to come out from his
hole, and then you whack-a-mole his ass," said Zodiac.

Ezekial nodded. "Get it done, and we're good."

Zodiac nodded too.

Both groups pivoted and went back to their idling
vehicles. Alliances had changed. But Zodiac knew that
unions didn't mean love any more than war meant hate.
It was about survival and his best interests.

Ezekial was the lesser evil in his eyes.

When Antonio received the call from Zodiac informing
him that he had the whereabouts of Ezekial, Antonio
became so elated he damn near had an orgasm. Zodiac
promised to meet them there. Antonio was having dinner
with his goons in the back of the restaurant he owned,
but the sudden phone call disrupted everything. Right
away, he ordered everyone to get their guns and be ready
in five minutes to head to the location given to them by
Zodiac. It was about timing.

Two cars were idling outside Antonio's place of business. The Brooklyn street was quiet and calm—maybe too
peaceful. Antonio and his men poured out of the restaurant and piled into the two waiting cars. Antonio climbed
into the front seat of one of the two Benzs, cocked back
his SIG Sauer P226, and uttered, "I want four bullets
in this mulanyan's head. And we kill everyone moving.
Nothing is left standing. Y'all fuckin' hear me!"

Everyone nodded, acquiescing to his demands.

But before they could drive off, two dark SUVs suddenly stopped parallel to the Benzs at the curb. Antonio was dumbfounded. *What the fuck is going on?* He immediately figured it out.

"Fuck! Drive off now! Drive, muthafucka!" he yelled. "Get me the fuck out of here!"

But it was too late. Multiple AR15s protruded from the SUVs, and those who held them opened fire on the Benzs. A fusillade of shots pelted both cars in less than a second. Glass shattered, and blood spattered everywhere. The volley of gunfire, which sounded like fireworks popping, made the men dance violently in their seats. The entire scene was loud and intimidating.

The front passenger door of one of the Benzs opened suddenly, and Antonio stumbled from the passenger side, screaming, and was shot multiple times. Still gripping his pistol, he yelled, "You muthafuckas!" and attempted to return fire. But his efforts were futile. The AR15s viciously tore his midsection to shreds, and he collapsed on the ground.

But it wasn't over yet. One of the shooters exited the SUV, marched toward Antonio's body, and shot him twice in the head at close range. Then he kicked him in the head and shouted, "Fuck you, bitch!"

The assassins fled before the police came.

It was game over!

Thirty-three

And so it begins . . . the end . . .

Detective Emmerson and Mack arrived at another crime scene in Queens. Death and destruction seemed to reign supreme in the city. The NYPD had their hands full because of this war between different crime factions. But when news spread about Antonio Francesco and several of his men being gunned down in front of his place of business, everyone went crazy. The streets felt like Chicago in the 1920s and early 1930s, when Al Capone was running things and was at war with George "Bugs" Moran and the North Side Gang. Of course, the Thompson submachine gun, organized crime's weapon of choice in the twenties, had been replaced with high-power assault rifles, and they were becoming common on the streets.

Law enforcement had already begun cracking down on crime, and several task forces were intent on taking down every criminal organization by any means necessary— snitches, intelligence, surveillance, undercover agents, and more. The government intended to bring down the hammer of justice on the bad guys.

Things had become worse for the streets because of Sheek. His reckless activities had made national news and had pointed the spotlight on Queens and Long Island. One of the families he had targeted had ties to the mayor of New York and a Queens police captain. When word had spread about their brutal demise, the gloves were off, and shit was about to hit the fan for everyone and anyone involved.

"I swear to everyone that while I'm in office, every criminal, from the petty thief to the iniquitous drug dealer, criminal syndicate, drug crew, and homicidal lunatic, will feel the ubiquitous wrath of my office, the NYPD, the state, and the federal government. Injustice and crimes like this will not carry the day in my city. Do you understand me! We will find you and everything you're associated with, and you will all be prosecuted to the fullest extent of the law. And that I promise!" the mayor had proclaimed wholeheartedly.

He'd received thunderous applause for his speech.

The streets were nervous.

The federal government was ready to pounce.

When the detectives arrived at the crime scene, two uniformed cops were standing near a gray Pontiac Grand Am GT. The car seemed to be abandoned, and a strange smell came it. People in the area had become curious and were standing nearby, wondering what was happening. Mack and Emmerson climbed out of the car and approached the officers and the Pontiac. Detective Mack was on her high horse today. The mayor was serious about cracking down on crime, and whatever resources the NYPD needed, they had it, no questions asked. So, there was a statewide manhunt for Sheek and several other culprits they'd connected to these appalling crimes. Unfortunately, they had one suspect in the morgue, Havoc.

And he wasn't talking.

Shelly Mack knew it was only a matter of time before they found and arrested Sheek.

Detectives Mack and Emmerson stood by the Pontiac, knowing they wouldn't be introduced to anything pretty once they opened that trunk.

"We had complaints about the car being here for a few days, and there's a smell coming from it," one of the cops said. "We wanted to contact y'all before we opened it."

Detective Mack sighed heavily. "Open it," she said.

Both detectives readied themselves for the worst. One of the cops took a crowbar and jimmied open the trunk. Right away, they were hit with a foul smell.

"Fuck! Whoever it is, is fuckin' ripe!" the cop uttered.

When Detective Mack looked inside the trunk, she was shocked and angry at the same time. It was Sheek's body. He'd been shot multiple times, including in the back of his head.

"Is that . . . ?" Emmerson asked her.

"It is. Fuck!" Mack cursed.

Emmerson shook his head. "Damn."

"She had him killed, Emmerson. She knew we were coming for him, and she had her own brother killed. She executed him to save her own ass."

They had had him and Havoc dead to rights for the crimes. Sheek's and Havoc's fingertips had been found at two crime scenes, along with another set of prints. Unbeknownst to the Sheek and his crew, surveillance cameras at the pawnshop and at one of the homes had captured them coming and going. They'd been sloppy, and Detective Mack had been ready, until a moment ago, to place Sheek in handcuffs.

"This isn't a dead end for us, though," said Emmerson. "We still got his sister and her crew for other crimes."

"I know. But I wanted him, Emmerson. I wanted him to pay for what he did. This is the easy fuckin' way out," Mack griped.

She stood there and gawked at the dead body of a vicious and vile serial killer and rapist with so much contempt that it almost seemed as if steam was coming out of her ears. She wanted to spit on him, but she controlled herself. What he'd done to many families and girls was unforgivable and unthinkable.

"I hope you're burning in fuckin' hell right now, you goddamn monster," she exclaimed.

She pivoted and marched away from the horror. This wasn't the end of things. Sunday, Bray, and their entire operation was going to collapse. The detectives had snitches ready to testify, and an undercover was inside Sunday and Bray's organization.

It was only a matter of time before they were all in handcuffs.

Sunday sat alone in the dark room. Her emotions were all over the place. A deep gloom had overcome her, and she suffered everything from sadness, frustration, anger, and delusions. Her brother was dead, and her world was beginning to crumble. She began to wonder if she'd made the right choice. Could she have fixed it, instead of allowing Nasir to kill her little brother? There was no doubt that her brother was a liability and a monster. But he was the only one whom she loved unconditionally. Her face became contorted, and she shook her head and wept.

Not only was her brother dead, but also her business had begun to suffer. Any association with Sheek was a stigma to everyone. The fact that the mayor had decided to get tough on crime and then had called Sheek out was a sign of the end. Dodge wanted to disassociate himself from Sunday because of the bad press and her brother's actions. Bray was becoming increasingly wary too. Sunday was hitting a wall due to her problems and the uncertainty.

Unfortunately, her problems didn't end when she had her brother killed. They were only beginning.

They were coming for her and her organization. The one she'd built from the ground up from blood, sweat, and tears was crumbling. An NYPD detail and multiple task forces had implemented a series of citywide raids, and arrests had been made to fulfill the mayor's desires for "a reduction in crime and revenge." No one was safe. No criminal organization was impervious to the reach of the law. Task forces had raided multiple locations in Queens, including Baisley Park Gardens, seized nearly thirty kilos of cocaine and heroin, taken roughly half a million dollars in cash, and got almost two dozen illegal guns off the streets.

What was worse was that snitches were coming out of the woodwork, telling everything to save their ass. Diane and Recut had been arrested during the raids. They'd been caught red-handed with several ounces of dope and guns on the tables. One had had a body on it. Diane had decided to cooperate with the authorities and had told them everything they needed to know. She had even gone as far back as their crimes in the Midwest. Worse than that, Bray and his crew had been selling narcotics to several undercover officers, and it had all been captured on the wire and surveillance.

Everyone was falling like dominoes.

A sudden knock at the door made Sunday snap out of her sadness and tears. She wiped her face and called, "What?"

"It's me, Nasir. We need to go."

Sunday huffed. She stood up and collected herself. She and Nasir planned to flee New York City for a while and hide somewhere down South. They'd made arrangements in North Carolina. A warrant was out for her arrest, and Sunday didn't want to see a jail cell anytime soon, or ever, for that matter. They were taking everything from her, but she was determined to prevent them from taking her freedom. Nasir was still by her side, and she was grateful for him.

Sunday opened the door and allowed Nasir inside the room. They stared at each other with matching concern. What was next for them? How long could they outrun the authorities? This was the first time Nasir had seen Sunday looking weak and vulnerable. She was no longer that vicious, power-hungry, violent bitch trying to dominate the streets. She'd become this scared and naïve little girl suddenly. Her eyes said it all, telegraphing her despair and hopelessness. Her brother was dead, her crew was turning on her, her enemies wanted her dead, and every cop in the city was searching for her.

"We gonna be good, Sunday. I got your back," said Nasir.

Sunday nodded. "I know. Thanks."

"We need to leave right now."

Sunday put on her jacket, zipped it up, and tucked a 9mm into her waistband. She followed Nasir out the door, through the building she was hiding in, and then they exited through the back door into an alleyway. An idling Jeep was waiting, along with two goons watching the area. The weather had changed, and the temperature had dropped.

Sunday walked toward the rear door of the Jeep. But as she was about to climb into the vehicle, Nasir raised a .45 to the back of her head and fired.

Bang!

Sunday's body dropped to the ground in front of the Jeep door. The two goons didn't react, because they knew it was coming. Nasir stood over Sunday's body and sulked. It had to be done. She was wanted by too many people, cops and enemies alike. And unbeknownst to

Sunday, Nasir had gone behind her back to construct a different deal with Dodge. And sealing their transaction and new business relationship had to be in Sunday's blood. Dodge liked her, but like her brother, she'd become a liability to everyone.

Nasir would become the new face in Queens—and soon, king of kings. It was his time to shine, like he had always dreamed of, to finally wear the crown. And when the chaos eventually died down and the heat from law enforcement diminished, the streets would go back to doing business as usual. Yaz would become Nasir's distributor throughout Queens, and Dodge would supply him with all the needed kilos. Nasir and Yaz had formed a working relationship, and now, with Bray and Sunday gone, they were the ones on top calling the shots and pulling the strings.

"What you want us to do wit' her body?" one of the goons asked.

"Leave it. Let the cops find it and end their investigation," said Nasir.

Nasir climbed into the Jeep with the two goons, and they sped area from the area, leaving Sunday's body to rot in the cold.

Thirty-four

A new day . . .

Sincere sat in the chaplain's office, a familiar place for him to receive bad news. And it was bad news he got. What the chaplain told him was devastating, and Sincere couldn't believe it. The chaplain watched Sincere's eyes widen and rim with tears when he heard that Monica, her husband, Concord, and his son Tyriq were all dead. The only fortunate thing was his five-year-old daughter Ashley was still alive. The family was riding in Concord's Benz truck and was on their way home when they fell victim to a sudden drive-by. The Benz was pelted with bullets and everyone but Ashley was killed.

There was no word on the shooters.

"Where's my daughter now?" Sincere asked with sadness in his voice.

"She's in temporary foster care," the chaplain replied.

Sincere's eyes continued to mist over. There were tear tracks on his face.

"I'm sorry, Sincere," said the chaplain.

Sincere's face contorted as he struggled not to cry, but it was a losing battle. His heart raced, and he felt like he was being crushed. Grief and agony filled his chest, and a choked wheeze escaped his throat. His stomach felt like it was being twisted, and nausea overtook him. When Sincere tried to stand, he fell to his knees, weak and overwhelmed by absolute terror and agony.

"*Nooo!*" he screamed.

He shuddered violently and made noises like those of a strangled animal. The chaplain did his best to console him, but in reality, he could do nothing at all. Sincere's family had nearly been wiped out by something evil, and the chaplain could only allow Sincere to grieve privately. He remembered that not too long ago, he had had to give Sincere the news about his sister. Now his son and his son's mother were dead.

Sincere knew who was behind his family's death, and he was determined to make them pay. Revenge became the only thing he could think about. He stood up, dried his tears, didn't say a word to the chaplain, and angrily marched out of his office. Sincere didn't want to hear anything about mercy, forgiveness, or God. The only thing he wanted was vengeance and bloodshed.

He was seething when he connected with Trek. When Trek and other KOS members had heard what happened to his family, there was no denying that Rondell and everything related to him would be dead.

"We got you, Sincere. Believe me, it's gon' be hell on earth for every muthafucka involved, especially in here," said Trek.

Any humanity left inside Sincere was gone entirely. They had taken nearly everything from him. Nothing was left but his two daughters: one was in foster care, and the other was being raised in Japan. There was no way for him to see them again. His hope was gone.

This cold-hearted and merciless world had created an inhuman monster. Now it was time for Sincere to show his enemies how vicious he had become and what he was capable of.

The following day, an officer who was monitoring inmates in the mess hall corridor witnessed several inmates arguing. Suddenly, two inmates attacked another inmate, and they proceeded to viciously assault him. The guard hurried toward the scene and ordered the inmates to stop fighting, but they ignored him. He radioed it in, and OC spray was utilized on the inmates and was effective. The inmates were removed from the corridor. However, a second incident occurred inside the mess hall. Four KOS members began brutally assaulting another inmate. Punches were thrown, and chaos quickly ensued.

Rondell saw what was happening, quickly rose to his feet, and removed his homemade shank. It was happening. Sincere would come for him, and he and his goons would be ready for him. Rondell's men stood behind him in the rear of the mess hall and waited for anyone to charge their way.

More fights broke out inside the mess hall, and the violence soon escalated to a full-blown riot. An inmate smashed his elbow into the side of another inmate's skull, hitting the soft spot high on the temple, and knocked out his teeth. Two inmates were repeatedly stabbed. Another KOS goon snapped a man's neck like it was a tree branch.

The guards were outnumbered and overwhelmed. The alarm sounded.

Sincere became unstoppable. Whoever got in his way was immediately dealt with, like a boot to a bug. One rival took a shank in the eye, and a second was repeatedly hit so hard that Sincere nearly beat him to death. Sincere swung a chair, and it broke upside his second rival's head.

The chaos began to spread from the mess hall into the corridors and other areas of the prison. Guards were being brutally attacked and overwhelmed. KOS members began heatedly shouting, "KOS! KOS! KOS!"

In a rage, Sincere was unstoppable. He and a few KOS members charged Rondell, who was waiting for their attack.

"Fuck you and your fuckin' family!" Rondell screamed. "You come any closer, and I'll gut you like a fuckin' pig!"

This sent Sincere over the edge, and armed with a weapon, he took another step forward, crowding Rondell and his men. Sincere's men attacked the others, while Sincere went for Rondell. Sincere charged and tackled him like a linebacker drilling a quarterback from the blind side. The shank clattered from Rondell's hand and skittered across the floor, leaving him defenseless. Both men fought and struggled on the floor. Rondell was bigger and stronger, but Sincere was utterly consumed by rage and hatred, and this gave him enormous strength.

Sincere swung and slammed his fists into Rondell's face. Rondell struck back twice, but Sincere was unfazed by the blows. They fought fiercely—exchanging kicks to the gut, punches to the face, elbows in the side—and then Sincere headbutted Rondell so hard, his skull vibrated painfully. Sincere headbutted him again, and there was a loud crunching sound, and then Rondell's nose began to spew blood.

"I'm gonna fuckin' kill you!" Sincere screamed heatedly.

Sincere grabbed his weapon and didn't hesitate to use it. Rondell lay there helplessly, his demise growing closer.

"You come after my family, I'm gonna kill you . . . kill you all!" Sincere snarled.

Rage flowed through Sincere like lava and pounded in him like a drumbeat. He angrily plunged the blade into Rondell's face. With this stab, he could taste blood. His anger felt good. Sincere continued to strike Rondell's face, feeling a sick anger. He went from stabbing Rondell in the face until he was utterly unrecognizable to repetitively punching him, because the blade had broken off in Rondell's flesh.

Rondell's face looked like bloody ground beef. He'd been dead for minutes already, but Sincere didn't care.

He continued to brutalize the man's body. His foot came up, and he kicked Rondell in the face. Sweat and blood trickled down Sincere's face.

A few inmates stared in horror at what Sincere had done to Rondell. It was a scene out of a horror movie. If they weren't afraid of him before, they definitely were now. Now he'd become a different kind of monster.

Exhaustion suddenly overwhelmed Sincere, and he collapsed on the floor. He took a deep breath and exhaled, then inhaled again. He inched his arms underneath him and pushed himself up onto his hands and knees. His breathing was ragged. His head swam. Everything was blurry for a minute, then came back into focus again. He inhaled some more and felt a bit more stable.

The alarm continued to go off, and the sound echoed through the prison. Inmates began running through the facility, attacking guards and staff that got in their way and damaging anything that wasn't nailed to the floor. A riot was happening. The inmates were taking over the prison, and panic ensued.

Sincere remained on his hands and knees and was protected by his gang, KOS. The respect and fear he enjoyed went through the roof. He was undoubtedly the supreme leader of KOS, Kings of Society, and his band of ruthless, hard-core killers and inmates were becoming a force to be reckoned with. They would follow Sincere into the depths of hell. He had earned their respect. He was a charismatic leader who had brought a gang together and was now shaping its reputation.

As pandemonium engulfed the facility, Sincere remained on his hands and knees, his face coated in blood. He seemed dazed and oblivious to what was happening around him. The only thing he could think about was his family. His mind was on a loop of pain, agony, and anger. While he remained in a dazed state, inmates throughout the prison began to roar and chant, "KOS! KOS! KOS! KOS! KOS!"

This would forever be Sincere's world, his destiny. KOS had become his family now.

Kings of Society.

Epilogue

Six Months Later . . .

Ezekial's cough was becoming worse. It took him longer to catch his breath and regain his composure. He was dying slowly, but business had to continue. The death of his nephew, Rondell, was heartbreaking. When he'd heard how his nephew was killed, Ezekial had placed a two-million-dollar bounty on Sincere's head. He and Sincere had two things in common: no family left and unending tenacity.

Although Ezekial received from a medical specialist the best treatment and medication money could buy, his condition had barely improved. He was weak and tired most of the time and didn't have much of an appetite. He was back in Miami now, trying to handle a few of his affairs and his business. And besides, the weather was better in Miami. The only thing missing was Cashmere. He missed her a lot. But Ezekial took pleasure in knowing her killer had suffered greatly. Ezekial and Doc had beaten and tortured Salvatore for four days, and six months later, the police were still finding pieces of him in different boroughs.

Ezekial threw on his Armani suit jacket, checked his image in the mirror, and left the doctor's office. He was feeling much better today. His doctor had him on some new medicine, which was doing its job at the moment, giving him some energy. Ezekial wanted to get something to eat at his favorite restaurant in South Beach.

When he left his doctor's office, two goons were waiting patiently for him outside the room. Flanked by his men, Ezekial coolly moved through the lobby of the medical facility with an air of power about him. There was a presence to him that caught everyone's attention. He seemed more like a prime minister than a cold-blooded aging gangster.

When they exited the building, Ezekial told one of his men, "Get the car. I'll wait here."

Despite his condition, Ezekial lit a cigar in public and waited for his man to bring the car around. He took a few puffs and took in the beautiful view of South Beach, with its splendid beaches, palm trees, blue sky, and exquisite women.

Since Ezekial was distracted by his expensive cigar and the view as he waited for the car to come around, he was unaware of the trouble brewing nearby. A young thug clad in a black hoodie and shorts eagerly marched toward Ezekial. His attention was focused on the aging gangster. The closer he got to Ezekial, the more he scowled. Then he removed a Glock 17 from the pocket of his hoodie. The moment Ezekial saw him coming, it was too late. The young thug already had his arm outstretched, the pistol at the end of it. He screamed, "KOS, muthafucka!" and he fired rapidly.

Boom! Boom! Boom! Boom!

All four shots struck Ezekial in the chest, and he flew back against the wall and then sagged to the ground, the cigar still clenched between his teeth. His bodyguard tried to return fire, but he was too slow on the draw and was shot dead immediately.

"KOS, nigga! That's for Sincere's family!" the thug shouted.

He began to retreat from the scene.
Ezekial was dead.

Zodiac stood on the cliff and gazed at the sliver of white sand, the gash of zephyr-haunted cliffs, and the wide slash of bay. It was a watery wonderland, and the beach was drenched in a lightning-gold dawn haze. The horizon was a thin silver seam where the canopy of sky met land and sea. It was as if they had been welded together perfectly. In the distant sky, rays of light splayed out and filtered through cracks in the clouds.

He was back in Ghana with Trina. He was beginning to love the country. He had developed a close relationship with Joc and had even thought about Ghana becoming his permanent residence. Trina was all for it. Business had resumed in New York, but his brother's words plagued him and filled him with guilt.

Ghana was perfect. Zodiac felt New York had become a death trap for him. Although Antonio was dead, plenty of rivals would still love to see him dead and to take over everything he'd built over the years. Men like Ezekial, Ray Black, Van Gray, Gregg Rice, and Kevin Charles were still alive, in power, and hungry, and the competition was still fierce. But another name was now ringing out in the streets: Nasir. He was a growing force too.

Zodiac sighed and stood on the cliff like he was a statue. He had a choice to make. While he stood there, observing the beauty of Mother Nature, one of his men approached Trina and said something to her. He then left her side, and Trina went to inform Zodiac about what she'd been told.

He looked at Trina and said, "What is it?"

"Ezekial's dead. He was gunned down in Miami yesterday afternoon," said Trina.

Zodiac wasn't surprised.

"Do you want to return to the States?" she asked him.

Zodiac had to think about it. He'd made enough money to last him for three lifetimes. He and Trina were living like a king and queen in Ghana. If he returned to New York, there was the possibility he'd suffered the same fate as Mob Allah and Zulu. Right now, he was winning. He was alive and free.

Markest had told him to reflect on his inner conflicts and find the strength to overcome them. Personal growth required him to face his fears, doubts, and insecurities head-on. By acknowledging and addressing these internal battles, he could emerge stronger, wiser, and more resilient.

It took every ounce of strength in Nasir's body and his soul not to come so quickly. But Brenda was putting it on him. She was riding him so good, his eyes had damn near shifted to the back of his head. He decided to flip it on her and change position. He tossed the thick and curvy beauty onto her back and pushed her legs to her chest and drove his dick inside her until his cream coated her insides.

Needing a breather, Nasir fell on the bed beside Brenda and pulled her close. He needed a minute to calm down. She didn't. Brenda climbed on top of Nasir. She kissed him passionately and slammed her pussy down on his stiff shaft.

"You gon' kill me with all that good pussy, girl," Nasir laughed.

Brenda grinned and laughed. She was the saddest bitch in town, and Nasir couldn't get enough of her. She'd become this trophy bitch. She was thick and leggy, with a body that would make Jennifer Lopez and Beyoncé jealous. Something about Brenda made him want to keep her close and around. He'd met her on the humble when he climbed out of his luxury Audi one day and saw her coming out of the bodega near his operations. He went over to greet her, and they exchanged conversation and numbers. The rest was history.

Nasir had become something he always wanted to be: a drug kingpin. He moved twenty to thirty kilos every two weeks and had the block on lock. He, Dodge, and Yaz had become a powerhouse throughout the streets of Queens and Brooklyn. Still, it hadn't happened without any hiccups. Murders, hate, and cops were standard in his world.

Brenda was a woman on a mission. She placed her feet on the bed, her hands on his chest, and rode him like a champion. She made eye contact with Nasir and used her muscle to milk him again.

"Oh, fuck, baby. Damn!" Nasir groaned.

He reached up to play with her nipples, and her juices coated him. When he came a second time, he was finally done. He hated and loved the way she made him lose control.

As if on cue, Nasir's phone rang. He answered it immediately. It was business. Brenda kissed him, removed herself from the bed, donned a long robe, and left the bedroom, knowing he didn't want her to know about his affairs.

"We're still on schedule, right?" Nasir asked.

The reply made him nod and smile. Business was good.

Nasir donned a pair of pants and a shirt and walked from the bedroom to the living area of the apartment. There were several half-naked women, one smoking a cigarette, at a worktable covered with drug-cutting apparatuses and two kilos of cocaine ready to be processed.

Nasir left the apartment and took the elevator to the rooftop of the eight-story building. It was a beautiful spring night, with a glowing moon, and Queens was illuminated for miles. Nasir lit a cigarette, took a few drags, and took it all in with pride. He then screamed, "The world is yours, muthafucka."

Sincere ran the state prisons.

Nasir controlled the streets.

To be continued in . . .

Kings of Society